LATHAM'S LANDING II

RETURN TO CAIRN ISLE

TARA FOX HALL

LATHAM'S LANDING II: RETURN TO CAIRN ISLE
Copyright © 2024 by Tara Fox Hall

ISBN: 979-8-88653-295-1

Melange Books, LLC
White Bear Lake, MN 55110
www.melange-books.com

Published in the United States of America.

Cover Design by Caroline Andrus

To Jennifer, who narrated the first Latham's Landing Anthology and asked for years for a sequel. And to John, a good friend who kept me on course to get this done. This one's for you.

CHAPTER ONE

THERE'S NO THRILL LIKE THE THRILL OF WAITING TO SEE A DEAD woman's pictures. Oh yes, there is...doing it twice in three years.

Police Chief Robert "Bob" Stahl leaned over his paper-stacked desk, and tried to look capable, and firmly in control. Snatches of whispering from his staff of five outside the office intensified, scraping at the raw wounds of earlier that morning.

"Damn, the chief looks *pissed*..."

"Didn't you hear? The island got another couple this morning."

"No, it's more than a couple this time. There's even some kind of helicopter that blew up."

"That's bullshit. People have been dying out there for years. They wouldn't have decided to finally send the Army in now, especially in the middle of winter!"

"I didn't say the guy was Army, just that he had a helicopter out there."

"Maybe it was drugs? They're saying that three cops got killed out there, too."

"First time any of us were killed there. I'm glad the dog lived at least. Too bad he can't tell us what he saw."

"Everyone shut up out there and get back to work!" Bob thundered. "Right God-damn now!"

There were mutterings, then creaks and typing, as his officers and secretary returned to their desks.

Bob rubbed his eyes, his finger bumping against his reading glasses. *Getting too God-damn old for this.* He picked up the phone and dialed. "Jerry, do you have anything on that film for me yet? I told you this was top priority."

"Which film?" Jerry sniped back irritably. "I told you right off that water-resistant isn't the same as waterproof. Both these cameras you brought me have been submerged completely and left underwater for at least a while. Both of them took heavy impacts, the 35MM more than one. The 35MM is worse off, but the digital camera has a dead battery, and I don't have the new one in yet. I'm going to have to wait anyway until the digital one dries out before replacing the battery, if I see any moisture inside it. What the hell happened out there? Do you even know?"

Always the same: accusation and anger that he wasn't doing enough to stop the deaths. Fear always mushroomed after the island claimed another life. It didn't matter that the lives lost at Cairn Isle were almost always from outsiders. The people of Schuyler County—his people—knew better than to go within sight of the island.

"Bob!"

"No, we don't know what happened," Bob said acidly. "Because while we have a reported explosion, there's no smoke or flame visible on the island. Yes, we have two adults, one female and one male, who were found in a boat near the shore. The boat was locked in ice about ten feet out, half submerged. You understand what that means?"

"Yes," Jerry said, subdued. "Cairn Isle did its freeze-thaw routine. The two were trying to escape and didn't make it. Do you know who they are?"

"One of them is Barb Usher. The dog we found was hers. She reported a vehicle on the shore hooked to a trailer and a floating gas can in the water two days ago."

"And you were just getting around to going to check it out?"

"I hoped someone was burning the damn house out there down," Bob growled. "And the vehicle was registered to a woman that is wealthy who has no police record and isn't reported missing.

2

So no, I didn't send anyone out there. But when I saw this woman's file was flagged in connection with a double murder a few months ago, I did place a call to some detective in her hometown who acted like he couldn't be bothered." He paused. "What Barb didn't tell me was that she was planning a visit out there herself; the cameras you're working on are hers. I need to know what's on them."

Jerry was quiet. "You know it's not going to matter," he said finally. "But okay. Let me get back to it."

Bob replaced the phone, the buzzing of the dial tone exacerbating his headache.

"Chief Stahl?"

Bob looked up to two men who were in his doorway. *Feds, just what I need.* "Are you with Homeland Security?"

"No, OVC, Human Trafficking Division," one of the men said, flashing a badge. "Officer J.C. and this is Officer Victor. We need to talk to you."

"You've got the wrong person and probably the wrong county," Bob commented. "This is all rural around here. There's no massage parlors or anything."

"We're looking for a witness who went missing," J.C. continued. "Her name is Chung Lai." He flashed a picture of a pretty Asian woman. "We think she was kidnapped by a man who goes by the name of Mac Ready. He's a former military pilot who works for Charter Collins, one of the people that Lai implicated with her testimony. She never made it to the safehouse. Mac's currently missing. So's his helicopter."

"What the hell are you telling me?"

"Look," Victor said abruptly, whipping out his phone. "This video was uploaded last night from some kids camping on the shore onto YouTube." He hit play.

One teen was telling another teen some joke, when suddenly behind them there was an intense light. Amid swearing and exclamations from the teens, the camera got dropped then picked up as several louder booms sounded. Finally, the camera righted and zoomed in on a barely visible island, just in time for a loud whoomph and a glowing fireball to appear. The boys filmed it for a few seconds, then there was an animal howling noise quickly supplanted by a growing wind. The camera was dropped again, then cut off.

"Did you talk to the boys?" Bob said.

"You don't seem surprised to see that one of your constituent's houses blew up."

"That house doesn't belong to any of my people," Bob said coolly. "Did you talk to the boys?"

"Not yet, that's why we're here. Mac Ready is a pilot, like I said."

"Chief Stahl?" his secretary said, walking up with another couple. "These officers want to see you, also."

"Detectives Watkins and Loggins," the man said, flashing a badge. "She's Loggins. We're here to talk to you about two missing detectives, Drake and Bowman."

Bowman, fuck, he's the detective I talked to about the car Barb reported. "All of you come in and shut the door," Bob said tiredly. "What missing detectives?"

"Three, actually: Lease, Drake, and Bowman," Victor added, glancing at the two detectives. "Good that you arrived when you did. We won't have to go back over anything. Lease is suspected to be working with Collins in trafficking women; Lai implicated him."

Three dead cops and one of them dirty. And I thought it couldn't get any worse. Bob sighed inwardly. "How do you know the missing detectives are here?"

"I'm betting the boat you found is the one rented out to Lease; his brother runs a boat rental shop at the other end of the lake. He reported Detective Lease missing today. We moved fast because we suspected that Lease might have rented the boat to escape to the island. He and Mac were planning to dispose of Lai there, then they could fly to another state."

"They didn't fly anywhere, though; they blew up," J.C. said darkly. "Either a falling out between the two, or Lai decided to fight back. She was formidable and wouldn't have gone down without a fight."

The island probably enjoyed her best of all. "What is it you want?"

"We want to know everything you know, then we want to go out to that island," Victor stressed. "We have to know if our star witness is alive or dead."

She's dead. They're all dead. "Let's go then gentlemen," Bob said, grabbing his coat. "You can ride with me or follow behind. If you ride with me, I'll fill you in on the ride."

―――――

"So, you're saying that you think that the explosion we saw on the YouTube video wasn't caused by the helicopter crashing?" J.C. said finally.

I can't believe they all wanted to ride with me. "Hard to say, until we get there," Bob said, pushing down the shiver of fear. "But there's a possibility that the missing woman, Carolyn Stone, attempted to burn down the house on Latham's Landing in revenge for the death of her boyfriend. He was killed out on the lake in a boating accident some time ago."

"You have a lot of boating accidents here, don't you?" Loggins quipped.

"The lake is shallow, and storms can come up suddenly," Bob said defensively. "Fishermen usually can read the signs and get off the lake in time. But we get a lot of college and high school kids on Leighton Beach, which is down at the other end of the lake. They used to rent boats to waterski, now it's mostly jet skis. They're told to stay in sight of the beach, but every year at least a couple come down to see the whole lake. They don't know where its shallow and likely hit rocks."

"They die?" Loggins pressed.

They disappear. "I wouldn't know; that's another county, not Schuyler," Bob said evasively.

"Can you tell from the video which location on the lakeshore the kids were shooting the video from?" Watkins asked.

"I'm guessing it was from Carl's Point. The real name of the island was originally Carl's Island, after Latham's eldest son. Carl's Point is a popular spot because it sticks out onto the lake. You can get a fairly good view of the lake house without going out on the water."

"Can you take us there?"

"Yes. But first we're going to talk to Lease's brother. I want to know if your two detectives were with Lease when he rented that boat."

———

"Waste of time. I've never seen someone so evasive," Watkins griped, flashing a dagger look back at the shabby boat rental building.

"At least he rented us a boat," J.C. said, as he and Victor hooked a medium-sized boat trailer up to Bob's SUV. "Though the motorboat doesn't look big enough for all of us."

"It's big enough," Victor assured him.

"Lease's brother might have known Hawk was dirty. Or he might not have," Bob said, sliding behind the wheel.

"But he thinks his brother Hawk is dead. It's obvious. Why would he think that?" Loggins mused.

"Because people who rent boats to go to the island at night usually don't come back," Bob answered. *Or during the day, either.*

The fivesome arrived at Carl's Point, but there was nothing there except the remains of a fire that still held smoking embers.

"I think you've got to be right," Loggins said, looking out at the island. "A helicopter can't have crashed there. We'd see wreckage and the wreck would still be burning, like this fire. There's no sign of any wreckage. The house looks intact if a little run down."

Bob looked out at the island, his lips tightening. *Oh, it's intact all right, but even this far off I can see that some of the new work I've been hearing about in town is still there, even if most of it is missing. Old Randy even came in one night raving about a belltower and how he heard it peal at the stroke of midnight.* "The one side of the house is sunken sometimes."

"What do you mean, sometimes?" Loggins asked.

"When the water level rises," Bob said vaguely, then turned. "We're not going to find anything else here. If we're going to the island today, we need to go now."

"Can we launch from here?" Loggins asked, looking into the murky water. "There's no rocks?"

"Shouldn't be," Bob said, then winced at his choice of words.

They launched the boat, then used the motor to reach the island in a half hour, tying up to a pinkish granite dock at the side of the island.

The five walked up the bleached granite stairs, then spread out over the lawn on their way to the main house.

"Someone had a fire here on the front lawn," Watkins said, kicking at a large ash pile. "It's still warm."

"What I find odd is that there's not much snow here on the island," Victor said slowly. "Yet there's a good foot on the mainland shore all around the lake. Why is that Chief?"

"I'm not sure," Bob said. "Maybe whatever burned here last night melted it all? We had record high temperatures measured here on the lake in the last few days. But it's supposed to go back down into subzero by later tonight."

"Hey, isn't anyone else going to say how none of this fits together?" J.C. said loudly. "We have video of an explosion, and yet the house is not only here but it is also undamaged. There's a spot where there's been a fire on the lawn, but no other sign anyone has been here. There's no sign of the missing girl Carolyn, the three detectives, or of Chung Lai! No sign at all they were ever here!"

That's curious. What is that smell? Bob crouched down near the fire, then took a deep breath, trying to place the odd scents. He reached down and picked up a small twig. *This isn't wood, it's some kind of herb.* He stuck it into his pocket fast, inside a pocket pack of tissues. *That's why this is here, but nothing else is. Whatever Carolyn came here to do, she came prepared. She hurt the island somehow, left a scar it couldn't heal over. I have to find out what this herb is.* "Let's walk around, see if we see any more signs."

The five people walked around the side of the house, finding nothing out of the ordinary.

"What's that out there?" Loggins asked suddenly, pointing.

"The Sea Room," Bob said, glancing up. "A small house made of glass, connected to the island by a stone bridge."

Four pairs of eyes stared at him, incredulous. "This house has been here for decades and got weathered to a near wreck but there's a house of glass the same age nearby at water level still intact?"

"Latham was a shipping magnate – he built ocean vessels. The glass isn't window glass, it is heavy-duty marine glass made to line underwater windows in ships," Bob said patiently. "And as far as I know, yes, it's still intact."

"I'll bet that's where he killed her, if he did it here," Loggins said, taking a step forward. "We should check it out."

Bob looked up to answer and stopped, mouth opening as he took a sharp intake of breath. At the top of the house, on one of the side balconies, a cloaked figure was watching him from the heavy shadow on the house, pinprick red eyes glowing.

I know a warning when I see it. "Chung Lai wouldn't have been taken to the Sea Room," Bob said loudly, staring hard at the figure. "Why bother walking her out there two miles each way? You know what the easiest scenario is? Carolyn came here to burn the house, and she drove over here across the ice in a snowmobile, then couldn't get back in the sudden thaw. She did her best, but it didn't work for some reason, so she sat down to stay the night. But Mac made arrangements to meet Lease here and flew in Chung Lai. Lease arrived by boat, maybe he even wrecked on the rocks, and never got to land. But Mac probably killed Chung Lai and Carolyn, then flew away in the helicopter. Or maybe the helicopter did blow up here, and its wreckage is in the lake."

"Hey," Victor called. "The main door here is open. We should go in and check it out."

"You go ahead," Bob said, still staring at the figure. It suddenly stepped back into the shadows, disappearing. "I'll check around the side of the house."

The four cops went into the house. Bob already knew they wouldn't find anything. "You're not stupid, are you?" Bob said softly. "You're hiding now because it's one thing to take people who won't be missed. It's another to take cops who are here searching for the missing."

There was a sudden splash at the shoreline, as if a huge fish had jumped. Bob drew his gun and moved closer.

With a small ripple, a head broke the surface of the water. "I mean you no harm," the woman said, pushing back her long red hair. "Lower your gun. I'm no ghost."

"Yeah, you're a fucking mermaid here to sing me a love song," Bob said, unflinching. "Where the hell is Bowman?"

"Dead and eaten," the woman said, flashing a smile of long, pointed fish teeth.

Bob fired, the shot tagging the woman's shoulder in a spray of red blood. The woman hissed and disappeared beneath the waves. Bob stared at the water and blinked, but the red blood on the rocks stayed there, already drying as it spread over the stones.

Bob moved around the side of the house, picking his way through waist-high old weeds. He'd only taken two steps before something grabbed his supporting leg, dragging him down mid-step. He moved to get up and something landed on him, pushing his face into the ground. He tried to move but the heavy weight pinned him like a squirming and helpless bug.

"Turn back. Take them to the sunken side," a hoarse voice growled in his ear.

Bob shifted, kicking hard, and pushed over on his side, lunging for the gun. He grabbed it and thrust it out, looking in all directions. But whatever had landed on him was nowhere in view.

Bob struggled out of the weeds and back the way he'd come, his desperate looks behind showing him only shoreline. He hurried to the front door, where the four detectives were coming out of the house. Victor and J.C. looked untroubled as they talked, but Loggins seemed distracted, and Watkins was sweating heavily, his expression pale. *I don't need to ask them if they heard my shot. It's obvious they didn't. I need to corner Watkins alone before they leave.*

"Let's go around the sunken side," Bob said, moving fast. "I heard something."

The other officers drew their guns, then hurried after him. They moved as a group as they rounded the house, then stopped, staring.

"I guess we found the copter," J.C. said, then whistled. "Christ, what a mess."

The broken off tail of the helicopter rested in the shallow water; a piece of rudder just visible above the surface. Other pieces of the 'copter lay strewn in the water and on the thin stretch of shore, some resting on top of a blown apart snowmobile half in, half out of the water.

"There's a body!" Victor ran to the edge of the water, then began pulling the body up onto the shore. "It's Chung Lai."

"And that's what's left of Mac, still in the 'copter cockpit," J.C. said heavily, pointing into the water.

"The snowmobile must be Carolyn's. She's likely dead, too." Bob gazed into the water, his eyes darting, sure he'd seen a large shape moving away from the sunken wreckage. *You didn't see a mermaid. You did not.*

"I'm calling it in," Loggins said. She came over to Bob. "We'll need to close off this area."

"It's already closed off," Bob murmured, looking again towards the house, where the cloaked figure was again watching him. He rubbed his eyes and looked again. The figure was gone.

———

"So, it's being ruled death by misadventure?" Bob said into the phone.

"Yeah," J.C. replied. "They looked at Chung Lai's body. She'd been shot twice, but not lethally. Mac had been shot dead. We're guessing she got loose in the cockpit as he was about to land, and they struggled. The helicopter went down, and crashed into Carolyn's snowmobile, igniting the gas tank, which exploded, and blew the helicopter's gas tank too."

"But we didn't find her body," Bob commented. "Carolyn's body is missing."

"Not yet, but it will probably wash ashore," J.C. replied. "Some of the divers who recovered Mac's body did find some of Carolyn's bags in the water, plus her coat, and her driver's license. They found gas cans, too, blown apart. It's not surprising that the fireball on the video was as large as it was."

They didn't all die in an explosion. And who heard of a woman getting loose and not only grabbing a man's gun while he's flying a helicopter, but shooting him in the heart just before they crash? "Glad we can close this up. I heard that the cops are still missing?"

"No, we found Lease. He was separate from the others. His jacket was caught on the wreckage of some old dock near the back of the house. But we did find blood on his jacket and pants, a lot of blood. DNA match to both Drake and Bowman, I'm afraid."

"So he killed them."

"We assume so, though we haven't found the bodies. But we've been over every inch of the house and in the sunken parts of it, too. Nothing's there. Plus, his gun was out of bullets, and equipped with a silencer. It's likely he rented the boat with Bowman and Drake, got them out onto the water, shot them both, and then dumped them over the side. He tried to go home, but instead got caught in a sudden storm."

"And shot himself out of guilt or desperation?"

"Yes. But how did you know he was shot and not drowned?"

Bob closed his eyes. *Because that's always how it is. Those that die on the island are found on the island if they are found. Those that die in the water around the island...those people aren't usually found, and if they are, just their bones. And now I finally know why...they're eaten.*

"Bob?"

"I'm just glad it's over," Bob said. He hung up the phone before J.C. could answer.

———

"It's nice that you come every day," the nurse said, as she adjusted the pillow of the prone figure on the bed. "But there's no change."

"In either of them?" Bob asked, his eyes flicking from Barb's unconscious figure to the other inert person, the unknown male who'd been found in the boat with Barb.

"No, I'm sad to say. But it's surprising they both lived, Chief. The doctor said it was because it was so cold, that it slowed them from bleeding out from their wounds." She smiled and left the room.

The male had a serious chest wound from a compound bow arrow, and two gunshots, neither serious. Yet he'd almost bled to death. Barb also had been shot, but her more serious wound was from some kind of huge knife with a serrated blade. It had nicked her liver and speared her gallbladder. The only thing that had saved her life was that she hadn't pulled it out, but left it in. It was sitting in evidence now, though only tagged with the date and Barb's name.

The man, whomever he was, had carried her wounded to the boat, where he'd been shot twice as they left, possibly by two different people. He'd saved her life.

What was also in evidence was the man's clothes. They had blood on them too, from the man himself and Barb. But there were spots of another four kinds of blood there also, said the lab. Most of the blood was Chung Lai's, but some did belong to Lease and to Mac. The fourth small bloodstain didn't belong to anyone tested connected with the incident, but Bob thought it likely who it belonged to. "Carolyn," he said aloud. "You went there to end things and met your end, but not before tangling with Lease and Mac, maybe trying to get between them and Chung Lai. But who was this guy to you? Did you hire him to help you burn it down? He wouldn't have left you there to die, so you had to have been dead when these two fled. But we never found your body. What happened out there?"

The chief's cell rang. "Yeah?"

"I have those pictures ready, Chief. Come over and get them. Bring some scotch."

———

"Here's your scotch, Jerry," Bob said grudgingly, setting the full bottle down on the counter with a clink. "Now what's so unsettling?"

Jerry took a breath, held it, then let it out, reaching for the bottle. He twisted off the top and took a gulp.

"What the hell's gotten into you? There must have been almost no usable film, yet you tell me you've already got all the pictures from both sets of film developed."

"No, I got all of them," Jerry said nervously, breathing hard.

Stahl laughed. "There's no way—"

"I know that!" Jerry shouted, his eyes flicking to Bob and then away. "Don't you think I know that? The digital battery read dead this morning, but I hooked it up to the computer, and a few seconds later it was beeping fully charged. The batteries in the other unit were shot, water had gotten into the camera, but the film itself was dry. That one had only ten pictures on it, though."

"And the other?"

"Three short recordings, and another five pictures."

Barb had gotten out there planning to document the paranormal. Probably in the lake somewhere was another bag of unused film and extra batteries. "What's on them?"

"Look for yourself," Jerry said, handing him a short stack of eight by tens.

"Why did you make them so goddamn big?" Bob turned the first picture around, righting it. It was a view of Latham's main house as the boat was pulling up to it. "Holy shit on a shingle."

The house in the picture wasn't the house he'd visited this afternoon. This house was much, much bigger, with outbuildings aplenty, and a huge three-story mansion behind the much smaller turn of the century house with pillars. And the stairs: a huge, long stairway that went up from the shore all the way to the front door.

"You ain't seen shit yet. Keep fucking going."

Bob kept going down the stack. The pictures were all of the house, as Barb must have gotten closer and closer to the island. One had her dog Cooper in the way, blocking the view. "These are the same."

"Look closer on the shore."

Bob peered close, his eyes widening. Two figures stood on the shore, too blurry to make out any details. Both were dressed in winter clothes and boots. There was camping equipment near where they stood, and a fire burned near an erected tent, a snowmobile nearby with a sled hooked to it. Mounds of melting snow and ice surrounded them. "That's got to be the guy we found in the boat, and the missing woman, Carolyn."

"Fuck them, look at the last photo!"

Bob flipped to the last photo. In this one, it was night, the moon was shining down. *Fuck, that's not the moon. It's the Sea Room, bright as a sun. What the hell had Carolyn stirred up? The island had gone into some kind of defense mode...something it hadn't ever done before. Visible to the side of the Sea Room was a tall black spire, blotting out the stars, the light from the Sea Room showing the spire to be brickwork or stonework of some kind.*

"You see that? You fucking see that! That's the fucking belltower that asshole Garvey said he was seeing, which no one believed! Now you tell me how that wasn't there in the day, and it was there at night!"

"You know the island changes," Bob said, studying the day and night photos. "But you're right: it's there at night or at least it was the night Barb was there. I thought old Garvey was full of it. I was out there today, Jerry. More than the tower is gone: the three-story mansion, those stairs, and the outbuildings on either side in the photos are gone, too. Only the original house is left." *But are more remnants of these structures visible in the day? Is that why I was stopped from going further inland? That figure in the black robe knew what the cops represented, and he gave them enough to satisfy them and get them gone. He sent whatever grabbed me in the grass to direct me to the wreckage, and he watched us until we left. Although Watkins saw something, and possibly Loggins, too, that cloaked figure purposely made sure that no one got hurt. Logic says that whatever was going on out there with these new buildings, Carolyn managed to hurt Latham's Landing in some significant way, and it wants time now to regroup.*

"What's it all mean?" Jerry shouted, interrupting his thoughts.

"Drink up and calm down," Bob said curtly, still examining the photos. "And play me the recordings."

The first recording was just Barb's opening statement taken from the shore near her car, where she stated what she planned to do: photograph Latham's Landing from the island, with views from the water both leaving and arriving. She sounded professional and prepared about both her goal and the house's history, with a clear plan to leave at 2:00 p.m., well before dark. She'd referenced extra motor gas, oars, boat patch, extra food, even a waterproof camera system and cellphone. She'd brought her dog as a warning system, with plans to leave the moment he seemed uneasy. What was strange to Bob was that Barb wasn't there to study the evil ghosts of the house, but rather something she thought had come there from outside the island: some kind of water spirit called a Husterman.

"We'll skip the rest of that one. It's about twenty minutes too long, and it's obvious she's not sure if what she's looking for is something bad or good." Jerry hit a few buttons.

Bob's eyes widened as he watched Barb come into focus. This was a very different Barb, eyes wide, hair bedraggled, clothes dirty and stained. Cooper was near her, whining and cowering.

"It's night and I'm still here," she said in a cracking voice, then cleared her throat. "I would've been dead before noon, if Carolyn hadn't saved me." The camera panned past Cooper to a sleeping woman, then back to Barb. "She was smart: she brought not only a gun, but Christian-blessed tokens and bullets plus Wiccan magic."

"What. The. Fuck." Bob's mouth fell open.

"Helter's just over there," Barb said, gesturing to a figure just out of focus in the darkness beyond the fire. "I get the feeling he doesn't want to be photographed, so I've only got a few minutes."

The mystery man. "Helter," Bob said aloud.

"No one's saying anything negative, but we might die here," Barb said, biting her lip. "And I wanted to leave a record if that's how this is going to end." The camera panned up again, to the house. "We saw a helicopter come in low. Helter shot at it. Whoever was flying it flew off, but we saw it land on the back of the island. Then...then the tower went...went up."

"What the hell does she mean "the tower went up"?" Bob demanded.

"The belltower," Jerry said, taking another drink. "Watch. She pans up to it."

On the screen, the camera was reversed, and the house came into view, a tall belltower looming above them. A bell pealed low and menacing in the still air.

"Helter's coming back." The recording stopped abruptly.

Mac's helicopter. He had to park it somewhere if he took girls to the island. So the island gave him cover. Jesus.

The third recording started as abruptly as the last one had ended. Carolyn, Barb, and another injured woman were sitting near a smoky fire.

"Why are you here?" Barb asked, as Carolyn cleaned up the woman's wound.

"Mac brought me here," the woman answered with loathing. "He hates women. He disposes of used up girls at the brothel." She spat on the ground. "He brought me and Delilah here in his helicopter." She snorted. "I'm too much trouble. All for trying to get out of that life."

She must be Chung Lai.

"What did you do?" Barb asked.

15

"I turned in a cop," Chung Lai said bitterly. "He helped the brothel stay in business by alerting my boss to raids and took a weekly payoff." She spat again. "His name is Hawk Lease."

A howl sounded. Cooper growled. The three women turned, horrified.

Shapes were just beyond the light, moving low and fast. They circled the fire.

"What's keeping them back?" Chung Lai asked, her wide eyes afraid.

"There's twice as many as before," Barb murmured.

The recording abruptly stopped.

"Now you tell me how there were wolves there last night," Jerry said, shaking a bit. "That's a wolf howl, not a coyote. There's been no attacks on sheep here for a decade, not even by coyotes."

"You didn't see any wolves," Bob told Jerry. "Give me the recordings. The official story is that the film was too ruined for you to make anything of it."

"What about that crooked cop?" Jerry complained, as he popped out the recording and handed it to Bob.

"You know as well as I do that his is one of the missing bodies we didn't find. That means it's not going to be found. He's dead."

"I know," Jerry said, swallowing hard. "But what are you going to do? It's obvious that Latham's Landing is out of control. Wolves? Belltowers forming and...fuck, I don't even know what to call it, disappearing?"

"Exactly what do you think I can do?" Bob raised his voice. "What haven't I tried, over the years? Putting rope boundaries on the water doesn't work. They just tear loose in the first storm, which is usually the night after we get them installed. People have tried to burn the house, and it can't be burned! The place is already off limits, has been for years! Yet people tend to show up there anyway, not a lot, but just enough to keep it fed..." Bob trailed off, as his cell phone rang. "What is it?"

"Chief, the two people who survived in the boat...they're awake."

CHAPTER TWO

B<small>OB BURST THROUGH THE DOORS OF THE</small> I<small>NTENSIVE</small> C<small>ARE UNIT</small>, livid, and strode up to the main desk, addressing the head nurse. "Where's the deputy I left here?

"He got called away to a domestic disturbance," she replied, her icy demeaner a perfect copy of Nurse Rachet. "You are shorthanded tonight, he said."

Tonight, and every night. Keeping deputies is harder and harder with each passing year. "Did you see the man leave?"

The head nurse turned to the cringing woman next to her. "Hallie here was on duty. She's the one who reported he'd awakened."

"Hallie, come with me." Bob led her into a room with a sleeping elderly man with a bandaged head. "Tell me everything. Start from the beginning."

"I went in like I always do, at the beginning of my shift, to empty the fluids and put in a new bag. I saw the man blink after he groaned."

"When was this?"

"I started at six."

"What did you do?"

"I didn't do anything. I had my hands full with the woman's colostomy bag. By the time I'd washed up and got over to him, his eyes were closed again. I nudged him, asked him if he was okay, then told him he was safe here at Nunda Memorial. I didn't get a response. His vitals were normal. His heart rate was low, like he'd slipped under again. I checked his IV, then went back to the woman and finished up with her. The man didn't stir again, not even when I was changing his bags. So I thought maybe I'd imagined it. When his heartbeat flatlined a little while later, we rushed in and found him gone."

"This was when?"

"About nine p.m. He'd pulled out everything, even his catheter and done it so quietly that no one noticed until he removed the heartbeat monitor. He tried to put it on the woman but that's not like in the movies. The alarm sounds immediately when the device doesn't sense a heartbeat, even if it registers a heartbeat a few seconds later."

Helter may or may not have known that but he's smart to have left that for last. "How did he get out of here? His personal clothes aren't here, or his shoes. They're down at the police station."

"He took some of the woman's spare clothes. Her mother brought them."

"He take her shoes, too?" Bob said sarcastically.

"Her slippers."

Bob let out a breath in annoyance. "Is there anything else I need to know?"

"Yeah, I'm glad that I didn't walk in on that guy. He ripped open all of his stitched wounds getting free and left the blood behind to prove it. But no one heard a sound."

Helter's a hard case. But I knew that already. He survived getting injuries that would have killed another man. "And the woman?"

"She woke up, but she's in and out. We called her mother, and she should be here any moment. Follow me."

Bob followed Hallie irritably, wanting to push past her and hurry to the room. They arrived to see an elderly woman sitting near Barb, clutching her hand happily. Barb's eyes were open, but she looked exhausted.

"Barb, I'm Chief Bob Stahl." He stood at the foot of her bed.

"I'm sorry, but I need to ask you a few questions if you are able to answer."

"She needs to rest," Barb's mother protested, clutching her daughter's hand tighter. "I'll get the doctor." She hurried out the door. Hallie turned and left after her.

"There was a man found with you in a boat, Barb. Can you tell me his name?"

"Where's Cooper?" Barb asked weakly. "Did you find him? We saw him close to the far shore, where we left the vehicles. Did he make it?"

"Cooper's fine. I've been keeping him. Tell me about the man, Barb. He survived with you though he was injured."

"Thank God," Barb said, beginning to cry. "Where's Carolyn?"

"Carolyn is missing," Bob admitted. "We haven't found her body."

"No," Barb wailed. "No, no, no! She can't have died on Latham's Landing! She was the strongest of us, the most prepared!"

"Barb, we have every reason to think Carolyn made it off the island. I found Cooper locked in Carolyn's vehicle. Someone also pushed the emergency button in that car, to request help. But there was no trace of her on shore."

Barb blinked, stared up wildly at Bob, and screeched. "They got her! They got her!"

Hallie pushed past Bob, a doctor on her heels trailing Barb's mother. "This patient needs to rest. Get out, both of you!"

"They got her!"

"Who got her?" Bob urged, as the doctor slid a needle into Barb's IV. "Who, Barb?"

Barb's mouth worked, but nothing came out. Her eyelids fluttered, and she collapsed back against the bed.

"She's going into arrest!" Hallie cried, sounding an alarm.

"Get out right now!" the doctor ordered.

Biting back his retort, Bob grasped Barb's mother by the arm, and steered her out of the room quickly filling with techs. He helped her to a chair near the main desk. "I'm sorry about your daughter."

"No, you aren't," she said tiredly, rubbing her eyes. "Why aren't you asking me what she meant by 'they'?"

"Look, I—"

"Because you already know, don't you?" she interrupted. "Go away, please. Just go away and let us heal."

———

Later that night, Bob was sitting on his porch with Cooper, the dog chewing on a large bone treat. He let out a yawn, the weariness in his bones at odds with his anxious restlessness.

She thinks that the Hustermen got Carolyn. She's likely right. People go missing and people die on the island. But the handful who have made it off the water in storms in the past all lived. Until now.

Bob took a long swig of his beer. *Damn it, we didn't need more fucking evil here on the mainland. Worrying how many the island was going to take every summer was bad enough. Now there's something stalking the shore, too!* Bob finished his beer, then set it down. *That's it. It's time to retire.*

The sound of tires crunching on his long gravel drive whispered on the night air. The dim light in the blackness, accompanied by a click, as someone got out. More crunching, as someone walked in the blackness toward him.

"Hi. What do you want?" Bob called, slipping his hand down to his gun at his side.

"Not here for a fight, Chief," came a growly voice, as a huge shadow of a man stopped just out of the porch light. "Just came to give you this, as I was asked to."

"What is it?"

A padded envelope was thrown onto the stones just below the porch steps. Cooper whined, then got up and went to the front door, scratching to go in.

Bob thought of just sitting there, asking whomever it was to bring him the envelope. But there was a rank animal smell on the night air now, making his nerves suddenly on edge. Bob rose, then let Cooper inside. Resisting his urge to go inside after the dog, he turned and descended the stairs, picking up the envelope. Opening it revealed ten thick packs of hundred-dollar bills. "What's this?"

"We heard there were two survivors, a woman and a man."

"We" who? "I can't talk about that."

"There was footage found. What was on there?"

"Nothing," Bob lied. "The film was damaged. Couldn't be processed."

"Good," the man said with approval. "The man will say nothing. Keep the woman silent, Chief."

"She's going to be out of it for a while," Bob admitted, shifting. "Who are you? Come into the light."

"I'm here for an... for interested parties. I'm unimportant. Take the money, Chief. And buy the island."

"What the hell is this?"

"Ban any visitors. Starve it."

Whoever he is, he knows. The unnerving feeling was stronger now, the urge to run making him shake slightly. "You know that won't work. There are always more kids, people in boats, thrill seekers—"

"No," the figure said with simple finality.

"There's fishermen, if nothing else," Bob persisted, wincing at the slightly shrill tone in his words.

"Exclusive rights to the water for fishing and boating have been purchased for the livestock fields and farmland surrounding the lake. The two remaining boat rental businesses have already been purchased. They will not reopen this spring. The bed and breakfast and all other lakeshore businesses had already closed, years ago. There will be nowhere for anyone to legally access the water, not even the shoreline. An arrangement with the livestock owners is being reached—"

"People will still come! They always do!"

"That's why we need you, Chief. We need someone to keep watch for us, to live here and enforce the lake stays empty of people. Once you buy the island, the rights I spoke of will attach to your deed with no action from you. You'll have complete authority."

"What if the owners won't sell?"

"They will. They insured the house for a few thousand and hoped to use Helter to collect. They are waiting for your call with a price in mind."

"How do you know all this? Who ARE you?"

"There's enough extra there to pay for your time," the man said, ignoring him. "But this may be a full-time job at the beginning. Take early retirement. There's also a list of instructions inside the envelope, simple and easy to follow. Follow them to the letter."

"Why should I?"

"Because we're on the same side, Chief. You tried to stop the deaths for years. Together, we can, if you work with us."

"What if I say no?"

"Then we'll have to ask one of your deputies," the voice said with an audible shrug. "But that means clearing a path for them to be the chief of police, and the power that comes with it. Don't think you want that."

He's saying they'll kill me. Bob drew his gun. "Show yourself or I'm blowing a hole in your car."

"Fuck with the car and you're dead," the voice growled, this time the sound so animalistic that the words were hard to understand.

Bob forced his hand to keep steady. "Come into the light."

There was a flare of a match being lit, the glow of a cigarette, then a soft voice with a lisp said, "Let him think it over. Let's go."

Two of them. There's fucking two of them. Damn it, he said we, and I thought he meant his boss.

The gravel crunching came again, this time retreating. The dome light went on weakly, showing THREE men getting into the car. It backed up and drove off, the noise fading again to silence.

———

Barb,

Sorry I didn't stay long enough to say goodbye. I'm glad you made it off, and angry that I did when Carolyn didn't. She deserved better.

You won't see me again in this part of the world, I don't ever want to see that island again. Don't go there. ~~even if you think you have to.~~

H.

Barb put the letter down. *You don't have to worry, Helter. I'm done with paranormal investigations.*

"Who is that from?" her friend Kim demanded. "I found it on your bedside table one morning, back when you were still in the hospital."

"The guy who was found with me on the island, the one in the coma," Barb replied, folding the letter, and slipping it into a drawer, grimacing at the dust on her still-cluttered desk. "It was good for you to check on me, Kim. But you've got your own life. You don't need to stay with me anymore."

Kim nodded. "I do have to get back. Michelle's been out of control, staying out late with her friends. She's leaving for college in a couple weeks, thank goodness; Luke's been too busy at work to keep tabs on her. But you call me if you need anything, ok? And take it easy, okay?"

Barb stood. "There is something I need, actually, if you'll come with me?"

"What?"

"Cooper."

———

Bob was smoking his second cigarette when the two women rolled up in Barb's new SUV.

"Nice car," he said, as Barb stepped out. "You must have traded in the old one."

"This one has a panic button, something I decided I needed," Barb said, fixing him with her stare. "I've come for my dog, Cooper. Cooper!"

There was sudden scrabbling of claws from inside the house.

Bob opened the door, as the large golden dog hurtled through and launched off the porch toward Barb. She hugged him fiercely, then looked back at Bob. "I also want my cameras."

"Both of them were recovered, but I don't think either still works. In any case, they aren't here. They're in the police evidence room. Carolyn is still missing, you know."

"She isn't missing," Barb said levelly. "She's dead."

"She's missing," Bob stated, visibly surprised she was able to maintain composure after her previous outburst. "She made it off the island, Barb."

"If she was alive, she'd be here," Barb said right back. "Something pulled her back into the water is my guess. But I'm not here to discuss that. Thank you for taking care of my dog while I was in the hospital. I want my cameras back when you're done with them, including all the footage you developed."

"We couldn't develop any of it. It was in the water too long."

"You need to learn to lie better," Barb retorted, snapping a leash onto Cooper's collar. She helped him into the backseat. "Drop off the pictures to me by the end of the week, or you'll hear from my lawyer."

"Aren't you afraid to talk to him like that?" Kim asked when they had driven away.

"I left all my fears on that island," Barb said in reply. "It's time to make a new life, one far away from here."

"What about your friend? You really think she's dead?"

"Yes," Barb said, after a moment. "But he's right that if she made it off the island then there's a chance she isn't. The police searched the shore, all of it, and nothing was found, though. If she wanted to leave, she could have left with Cooper. But she didn't."

"She probably stayed to make sure you both got help," Kim said, resting her hand on Barb's shoulder. "She thought there was a chance you could be saved."

"Then she stayed and died because of us," Barb said, wiping away a tear. "Thanks a lot for saying it out loud."

"I'm sorry. I didn't say it to make you feel guilty."

"But I am guilty all the same, aren't I?" Barb gritted her teeth, then focused on the road ahead. "I need to know if she's dead, Kim. The key will be learning that truth without leaving the shoreline."

"How are you going to do that?"

"I don't know. But I'm going to find a way."

CHAPTER THREE

Two Years Later

"Damn it!"

Carly reached down again into the cool murky water, trying to grip the slippery stone. The ones near shore were always coated with seaweed, and the ones out in deeper water had zebra mussels, sharp as barnacles. *Thank God for heavy gloves.*

She reached down again, then brought back up another rock, tossing it up on shore. Almost time to quit; she had enough for her garden. *If decorative stones weren't so damn expensive, I wouldn't have to risk getting arrested for stealing fucking rocks.*

Carly tossed up another rock, this one landing near the posted sign on the neon painted metal pole, the bright fluorescent "No Trespassing" sign almost glowing in the thin gloom. She stared at it, noting the glow in the dark raised lettering. Word was the retired Chief Stahl had gone batshit after that big fire on the island years ago and become obsessed with Latham's Landing. He'd spent his entire retirement bonus buying the damned place. That next week the signs went up all around the lake: no trespassing. Everyone had remarked how it was crazy, him putting them up on land fifty feet from the shore, that he didn't have the right. That even if he owned the island and the shore, he didn't own the lake itself. But no one had laughed later that month when the sky opened up, and it rained ten inches in forty-eight hours. The lake had already been high. The added water had driven up the water to record levels, flash flooding streams which all emptied into the lake. And the Chief, through some strings he pulled, got them to keep the water in the lake high for a week. The old main house on Latham's Landing, which had always been dry in the wettest years, had finally been fully submerged.

That whole summer was a washout, with inches upon inches of rain, and long periods of the lake being flooded. By the end of that summer the house, which so many had feared for so long, had succumbed to the water, its foundations rotting enough that it began listing to one side.

Carly looked out onto the water, looking for the telltale sign of the rooftop, which had begun falling in a few weeks ago. She focused on the second story, still rising above the water, but at a slant. She found it reassuring, like so many others did. The house, after so many years of dominating the landscape, was finally subdued.

Not that you'd think old Stahl noticed. Old geezer still patrolled the lake's perimeter in his SUV at least once a week, checking his posted signs were up and clear of weeds, and that there were no footprints anywhere near the water. He'd run off a lot of kids that first year, pressing charges on anyone that'd come within a foot of the signs. The police force had backed him up, too. Pissed a lot of people off in those first six months, when the air grew hot, and the Leighton Beach couldn't be used. The sandy cove was so far at the other end of the lake that it wasn't even visible from here. No one swimming there had ever died, not ever. A petition to designate a section of shore as public land was started by some kids he'd tossed out, linked to YouTube. The video of him warning them off went viral through the town, and it looked like Leighton Beach was going to revert back to the town. Then in August, the Chief had taken out a whole page in the newspaper. It was a simple ad, all black with white letters. It listed out each year since 1900, and the corresponding number of missing people or deaths on the lake. Some were in the high forties, but most were in the teens and twenties. The current year was the only one that listed zero people dead or missing.

After that the petition fell apart, and Chief was allowed to keep the lake to himself with no interference. No more deaths. Not so much as a peep from the island.

Carly wouldn't ever have come here in the old days, no way. *But it was safe now.*

There was a high-pitched humming sound, then the daylight intensified ten-fold. Carly shut her eyes, covering her face with her arms, and letting out a yell. There was a clap of thunder. The very air seemed to shake, then it subsided.

Carly opened her eyes, then scrambled to the shore, scanning the sky for thunderheads and finding only heavy clouds. She looked back at the water in fear, just waiting for something to happen, to reach out and make a grab for her. But the water just lay flat, not a ripple breaking its surface.

She looked over at the remains of the house, needing reassurance there was no threat. Her mouth fell open. "What the hell? Where is it?"

———

"Tom, come on! I'd like to actually see the overlook today," Andre griped, looking at the map. "We have another mile to go just to get there."

"Fenton's got a garter snake. We're taking turns holding it," Tom called back from the cluster of pre-teens fifty paces back on the wood path.

"He was just slithering there, at the base of the tree," Fenton said, passing the frantic snake off to another of the boys. "Careful, you'll drop him."

Andre took a breath to tell them they were losers for getting excited over a garter snake, then kept silent. He turned, putting his binoculars up to his eyes again, trying to catch sight of the hill they were supposed to be heading to on today's hike. *Mountain my butt, it's probably a pile of rocks...* He panned right, then stopped. "Tom! Come look at this!"

Tom came running up, the others in tow except for Fenton, who was putting the snake down near the edge of the trail. "What?"

"There's an old house there. Look."

Andre took the binoculars. "There's not supposed to be anything there."

"Houses don't just appear," Tom sniped. "We'll have to go have a look."

"I don't know," Fenton said slowly. "There's something wrong about it."

"Wrong about it how?" Andre said, passing the binoculars to Fenton. "It's just an old house."

"Hey, those are my binoculars. Use your own," Tom said, grabbing them from Fenton. "You were bragging all last night about the expensive ones your dad got you."

"He wants me to make Eagle Scout, like him," Fenton said, flashing a winning smile. "The best requires the best, after all."

"You say that one more time and I'm going to punch you in the face," Karl said, pushing past the group. "Let's go investigate, unless you're all too scared." The bigger boy headed off through the trees.

Reluctantly, Tom, Andre, Fenton and the other ten boys followed him.

The house was a good mile distant, but they made excellent time through the tall weeds and thorn trees, with a little blood to show for their efforts. The group pushed out of the brambles, standing right before the main steps of the house.

"Do you think it was some frontiersman that built this? It's old enough."

"Don't be stupid. This isn't a log cabin. It's a mansion of some kind. Must have been a tycoon's summer home."

"Maybe a hundred years ago. It's not close to any road. We aren't even close to any ghost towns, Andre."

"That's what's wrong about this, guys," Tom said, as he walked to the edge of the stairs, peering around the side of the house. "We're supposed to be on state land. There shouldn't be any dwellings here. Not so much as a shed. So how'd they get all this up here? There's no road, just the dirt trail we're on that's shoulder wide."

Karl glared at Tom. "Stop yammering about state land. I've seen plenty of old hunting cabins and things on state land, and some of them were pretty fancy. People build them thinking no one will notice, and they usually get away with it for a while, before someone does and turns them in. But it's rare that the structure gets knocked down and carted away. It just gets posted off limits and eventually falls to ruin. This land probably wasn't state land back when this was built, anyways. Look at the tongue in groove wood: this house is old. Or maybe we're closer to the edge of state land than we thought we were."

"Look, are we going in or not?" Fenton looked at his watch. "We're already off the trail, and we're falling behind schedule. We've got another four miles at least, maybe more, because I'm not going back through those thorn trees to get back on the main trail."

"I'm going in," Bruce piped up, pushing through the crowd, and walking up the steps. "There might be something worth some good money on Ebay."

"You think you're going to haul a few antiques through the woods?" Tom called after him. "You're crazy."

"Crazy or not, I would like to at least see if there's furniture in there, maybe some old maps or something," James said, heading after Bruce.

Tom, Andre, and Fenton watched the rest of the troop go in. "Aren't you going?" Andre said to Fenton.

"Hell, no." Fenton grinned widely. "Part of being an Eagle Scout is being smart. We are miles from help, even if I do have my personal locator."

Always boasting about his family's money and shit. Andre shifted his feet, looking again at the house.

Tom started next to him, with a swift intake of breath.

"What?"

"Thought I saw someone in the window," Tom said, with relief. "But it's just the light on the old glass."

"Let's go around the side," Fenton said, moving off. "I think I hear a spring. Maybe we can fill our canteens."

Andre followed him. "Come on, Tom. We'll give them fifteen minutes to look around the house."

The three boys went around the right side of the house. "Damn, but this is bigger than I thought," Andre remarked, as they trudged past a long row of windows. "Maybe it was a hotel, not a private home."

Tom walked closer, reaching out to touch the clapboard near the base of the house. It was soaking wet to the touch, almost like water was oozing out of the wood from within. "It's stained weird, guys. Almost like it flooded before." *But where would that much water come from?*

"It's probably from it being so damp because of climate change. There's a lot more rain and snow now here in Michigan than there used to be."

The boys finally reached the end of the house and looked around to the back. There was a spring there, a stream of good size. It just skirted the house's base, coming out from the trees. There was a small waterfall running down the hill, collecting in a pool at the bottom. It had been lined with some kind of red stone that had sparkles in it, shimmering thought the running water.

"Pretty fancy, with all that red stone," Fenton said, as he took off his backpack and got out his canteen. "That might be granite. I think you're right, Andre, this was some kind of hotel." He leaned over the pool, dipping in his canteen.

"Hey, aren't you going to test it?" Andre asked.

"I have water purification tablets," Fenton snorted. "That's why I brought them so I wouldn't have to be testing water when I'm thirsty enough to be trying to suck the water out of mud."

"Here, fill mine, too, please," Andre said, getting it out of his pack.

Tom went around Fenton, looking again at the stream and water-fall. There was something odd about it. *That rock must be granite. It almost looks like mini ledges...maybe old stairs?* He got out his phone and took several pictures.

"Hey, you're not supposed to have that," Fenton called, looking over his shoulder.

"You brought a personal locator. I can bring my phone to take pictures."

"That's not..." Fenton's words were cut off, as he was dragged into the water, disappearing headfirst with a splash

"Fuck!" Andre and Tom said, throwing themselves backward.

The pool water muddied, becoming bright, blood red.

Tom reached forward, and grabbed the strap of Fenton's pack, dragging it back. The boys ran back the way they had come, only to stumble on a dark-skinned woman in a turban picking leaves at the front of the house.

"I was low on witch hazel," she said, turning to face them as she tucked some leaves in a leather bag. "This is a good spot, in more ways than one." She smiled, dark eyes glittering.

"Who are you?" Andre stammered.

"What am I is a better question," she said, putting down her basket. Her mouth split open, revealing pointed teeth. "But you won't like the answer." She lunged at Andre, who screamed and threw his pack at her.

The boys ran back the way they had come, to the still bloody pool of water. Both boys kept their distance, going beyond it and following the stream. They stopped to catch their breath when there was no noise of pursuit.

"What was she?" Andre panted.

"Something not good," Tom said, rummaging in Fenton's pack. He found the personal locator and triggered it, sending an SOS. "What the hell? That can't be."

"What?"

"The SOS I sent is time and date stamped. We've lost five hours."

"That's crap. That can't be right!"

"Look at my phone," Tom said, tossing it to Andre. "We're supposed to be at the rendezvous point in fifteen minutes."

"That's not important! What is important is that we get help. Fenton's...injured."

"He's dead," Tom said coolly. "And if we don't get out of here, we're going to be dead, too."

"What about the rest of the troop? We can't just leave them."

"It's been five hours. I think they would have come out by now if they were going to. Do you hear anything? Have you heard anything since they left us and went in there? If they were alive, they'd be shouting or making some noise. There's been no sounds, nothing."

"Maybe they just lost time like us."

Tom stood. "Look, I'm getting out of here. I've seen enough horror movies to know when I'm in one, Andre. You want to go back to the house, go ahead."

Andre looked back in the direction of the house, then shook his head. "No, you're right. It's going to be dark in a few hours. We need to get help. Let's hike as fast as we can, try to make the meeting."

"They'll send people back from that point when we don't get there in a few hours," Tom said reassuringly, as the pair walked off.

————

They had gone only a few miles when they heard the first howl.

"Wolves?"

"Can't be. Must be coyotes. Besides, even if it was wolves, they don't attack people. That's a myth."

Another howl sounded much nearer, then another. Andre and Tom looked at one another, then sprinted to the nearest pine tree. But the branches broke as they tried to climb.

Too much weight. Tom hurried to another, dropping Fenton's pack and his own, grabbing his canteen and pulling himself up. This time the branches held.

Andre stopped, then hurried to Fenton's pack and grabbed it for himself.

"Don't bother, it's too heavy!" Tom called, still climbing.

Andre hurried to a rock outcropping, boosting himself up. He kept climbing to a ledge, then took off his pack and tossed that and Fenton's up to the top. With effort, he climbed the rest of the way, then sat there, panting.

The howls were louder now, all around them. But there was nothing visible making the sound.

Tom kept climbing until just below the top of the tree, where the slight wind was enough to sway him back and forth. He looked down hungrily on Andre, sitting enjoying Fenton's stash of food.

A gigantic black dog loped up, followed by another, then another. They glared with red eyes at Andre, far above them, then let out a group howl.

"Too bad you can't fly," Andre jeered down at them. He stood up on the rock.

There was the crack of a rifle. Blood blossomed at Andre's throat. He staggered and fell backward off the rock, landing with a sick thud at the base. The dogs were instantly on him, ripping flesh from bone.

Tom looked away, swallowing hard, trying not to vomit.

A horse neighed below.

Excited, Tom looked down. Below him was a male rider with long dark hair in a ponytail, dressed in a red hunting outfit. His bay horse's English saddle was shining with fresh oil, its braided mane gleaming.

"Alas, no wolves," he said, as he loaded his single shot rifle. "But my hounds have found some sport." Then he looked up, straight at Tom. "Come down from there, boy."

"No way."

"I can knock you out of that tree easily enough, and there'll be nothing left of you like your friend. I'd rather not have that."

"What do you want?"

"You, of course."

"For what?"

The man smiled. "Just come down, and we can handle this like the gentlemen we are."

"No. You'll have to shoot me." Tom pressed himself close to the tree, trying to make the smallest target possible.

"I think not," the man said, striking a match. He leaned over from the saddle and lit a few pinecones, which burst into flame, igniting the lower branches.

"Help! Someone, help me!" Tom screamed, trying to climb down.

"Too late for that," the man said, nudging his horse. They rode a short way away, then stopped, watching. The dogs had finished with Andre's remains and gathered in a loose group near the horseman, most of them lying down, chewing meaty bones in their bloodied jaws.

The flames licked closer and closer, the heat and smoke suffocating.

"Help!" Tom began coughing, frantically trying to climb out onto a thick branch which touched a neighboring tree. He slipped and fell, landing on his back with a crunch of bone. He writhed turtle-like, as the horseman rode up to him, then dismounted, tossing him over the saddle.

Tom sobbed, struggling weakly. The man mounted again, and rode off through the woods, the pack following at his horse's heels.

———

"Houses don't just disappear," Bob Stahl said patiently, frowning at the middle-aged angry man standing at his door. "Yeah, I heard Carly's tale of wonder down at the Country Kitchen. She's been telling everyone. But it's all crap. The house is still there under the water, the whole thing. You can see the second story just fine from the shore. And I'm not decreasing the water level, so don't ask."

"I'm not here for that."

Bob rubbed his eyes. "Who are you again?"

"Dakota Mann. I'm here because I've been losing sheep on and off these last couple years, ever since you flooded the lake."

The mermaid found another food source. I worried initially that she would draw people into the water, but the signs I put up worked. But sheep can't read signs. "Take it up with the current police. I'm retired."

"Yeah, and you own the rights to the shore for the entire lake now. I want permission to go into the shallows and look for remains. The bodies aren't on my land, so they have to be there in the water."

"If they drowned in the lake then they won't be found. You're a local; you know that. You sold the rights to the lakeshore, Mr. Mann. Besides, scavengers likely made off with the mutton. What will finding bones do to help you?"

Dakota's eyes were like chips of ice, in spite of the bright sunshine streaming down. "My father sold the rights, not me. He said he didn't have a lot of choice in the matter, as I recall."

None of us had any choice in this, and you'd have thought the same if you'd been there with those three men that night...if they were men. But whatever they were, they were right. Flooding the lake stopped the deaths. So it has to stay flooded. "What's done is done."

"I said that I *wanted* permission, as in past tense. Now I need permission. One of my field hands is missing. I think he went after a sheep that got near the water and possibly drowned."

Bob's stomach fluttered. *If he went in the water...* "Can't he read English?"

"I'm done with this, Stahl. I've been to the cops, and they'll be here presently with a warrant to search the water's edge. Maybe they'll get you to lower that damn water." Mann turned on his heel and left.

"Damn it." Bob grabbed a cigarette out of his jacket pocket, put it in his mouth, and then stepped to his phone, dialing fast. He let out a breath of relief when the line was picked up.

"What is it?"

"We have a problem."

CHAPTER FOUR

DAKOTA STOOD AT THE SHORELINE A FEW FEET AWAY, GLARING AT Bob as he spoke to the current chief of police, Bob's former deputy Sal Upner. "You can't be serious."

"I'm sorry, Bob," Upner said, his cocky smile at odds with his words. "But I have a court order here signed by the state supreme court. There's no way around this."

Not that you want to help me anyway, but then you always were a shit for brains. "We used divers for years anytime we had anyone go missing, Sal. What do you think you're going to find by draining the goddamn water out?"

"We aren't draining the lake dry," Sal reiterated for the second time. "Otherwise, we'd have problems with the DEC and the EPA. There's some kind of near extinct monster sturgeon that spawns in the lake that's protected, if you can believe that crap. I've never seen any fisherman pull anything out of there except crappies—"

Bob relaxed somewhat. "That's true, Sal. The fish are real. Scientists come every year and collect samples, do tests. I've been working with them for years now."

"Then you don't need to get your panties in a bunch, do you? Mr. Mann just wants to drop the water level about ten or twenty feet."

"What's that going to do? You know damn well you're not going to find anything!"

"I do know that, and you know that, but Mann's not going to stop until he gets his way." Sal snorted. "He plans to launch a boat and physically inspect the entire shoreline, ending at the house, then report back to us what he finds. He asked that I go with him. I declined, of course."

"What an idiot," Bob said, shaking his head. "Fine, let him go. But that's on you, not me. If whatever is there is hungry enough to grab a field hand in the shallows, Dakota won't be back to give a report."

"Accidents happen," Sal said with a shrug. "Good to see you too, Bob." He headed over to Dakota, who was in the process of talking on his cell phone.

Bob turned back to the lake. Already the water level had dropped about a foot, revealing some seaweed and algae covered rocks. He gazed at the remains of the house far off in the middle, the second floor just rising above the gently lapping waves hitting its sides.

Later that evening, Bob returned to the shore of the lake. The only noise was the strong wind coming from the north, the whitecaps on the lake barely visible in the deepening gloom. Sunset had passed, leaving everything black except the water, which remained a vivid blue. He'd expected to see unbroken darkness, but far out on Latham's Landing, a light flickered in one of the house's windows.

"Dakota, if that's you, you are in for one hell of a night," he chuckled softly. "And if that's not you...maybe you've already had one." He watched the light for a few minutes, then turned to leave.

"Arrogance," came a sibilant whisper near his left ear.

Bob whipped around, reaching for his gun, and finding only his belt. *Stupid, to come here unarmed. That damned house isn't the only enemy you have.* He swore, looking wildly around, but there was no one there.

"Liar," another voice said, this one to his left.

"I'm no liar," Bob said hotly, sweating bullets as he faced the darkness of the forest edge. It was somehow deeper now, thicker, as if something darker than shadow had come and filled the space. "But I am arrogant, especially in the wake of fools."

Hisses came at him from every direction. Bob shivered but stood his ground.

"Murderer," another louder voice hissed. "Killer."

"I've never murdered anyone, never even shot anyone in the line of duty!"

Part of the darkness seemed to separate from the rest and come towards him. Bob wanted to flee, but on all sides the hissing continued, as if the shadows were alive with snakes.

"Serve and protect," the figure said, enormous yellow eyes opening four feet above Bob's head to peer down at him. "But people died." The yellow eyes stared, slowly moving down close to his face. "I died."

Bob blinked, taking a hitching breath. "Carolyn?"

The figure let out a surprised hiss, the yellow eyes jerking back to tower over him as something cutting struck him, sending him to his knees with a cry of pain, clutching his bloodied cheek.

"Remember," the figure hissed, then turned and moved off into the tree line. There were no other sounds, but the darkness lightened somehow.

Bob staggered to his feet and walked back to his truck, driving himself home with blurred vision. He bandaged himself up in his bathroom, looking at the five parallel cuts across his nose and right cheek.

Barb was right, there is something else out there: Hustermen. And Carolyn's become one of them. He moved to the answering machine, then played back through his messages to the one Barb had recently left him, still demanding her film. He wrote down the number, went back to the bathroom and swallowed two pain pills, then dialed Barb's number.

"Hello?"

"Barb, this is Bob Stahl."

"It's still dark, damn it." There was a noise of something falling. "It's midnight, Bob. Why are you calling me?"

"You want your pictures? Come see me tomorrow, and I'll give them to you, in exchange for some information."

"What information?"

"I want to know everything you know about the Hustermen."

———

Dakota yawned, then stretched inside his sleeping bag. It was a beautiful night. And he had the right to be here enjoying it, after all the bullshit of the last few months.

First, his father had died of a heart attack. Then he'd discovered the missing sheep, that they'd been going missing for a while, and his father had been covering it up. The 'why' hadn't been too hard to figure out after he'd discovered the bank statements which showed the cash payments that had gone into the account, easily double the worth of the lost animals.

Dakota had talked to the other sheep ranchers around the lake, all five of them. They hadn't wanted to admit to any lost animals or payments, but when he showed them his bank statements, they advised him of the process: report the animal missing within twenty-four hours to a telephone number, and the payment was posted by the next morning.

"But don't get greedy and report one that isn't missing," the oldest rancher had warned him. "None of us have, but we were cautioned. I wouldn't ever want to see what was beyond that caution, if you get my meaning, Dakota."

He remembered laughing. "How would they know if a report wasn't real?"

"It's regular," another rancher said. "And spread between us pretty equally, I think. Close to once a month?" The others nodded.

"You don't have to lose any of your own healthy animals," another said. "Just take one down near the shore that you don't use anymore and stake it out there. Hell, I've been going to the stockyard sales and buying up sick animals that would usually go to slaughter and using them. I can get you a couple like I do for the others here, if you want."

"Who set this up?"

"Stahl, after he purchased the rights from us."

"And you went along with it?"

"We used to lose sheep regularly with nothing to show for it, Dakota. We're making money on this, money we need to keep in business. You want to do something else, go ahead, but leave us out of it, okay? We're doing this."

Dakota expelled a breath. He'd agreed not to rock the boat, but he had wanted to know what was taking the sheep because something was, for fuck's sake. So he'd asked Manuel, one of his hands, to take the sickest sheep he owned, stake it on the shore, and watch from a distance. He'd gone down the next day to find the sheep still staked there, lying down, and Manuel missing. There'd been signs of a struggle near the water, and some blood on the shore.

Only in retrospect had Dakota wondered if his first call should have been to the mystery number, to report a person's death. He'd panicked, and reported the death—well, disappearance—to the police. Chief Upner, that ass, had come out to the scene, agreed it was suspicious, and called in the crime lab. They hadn't been clear about what they thought had happened. Hell, they hadn't told him a damn thing.

Now the other ranchers weren't talking to him, and he was jumpy, always looking over his shoulder at his house, waiting for some men to confront him about what had happened. *Stupid really, because if whatever was taking the sheep preferred humans, it was only a matter of time before this situation would have happened. I didn't create a problem; I just brought a flaw in the existing system to light.*

The bushes outside rustled, as if a large animal was walking towards his tent. Dakota's eyes snapped open, and he sat up, taking his shotgun in hand. If there were going to be repercussions from the other ranchers, he was ready.

The tent flap zipped open slowly.

Dakota clicked the safety off, pointing the shotgun. "Say who you are now. Or I'll shoot."

"Me," Manuel said, looking confused, and more than a little worse for wear. His clothes were torn and dirt stained, his expression weary. "You'd better pay me double my salary for this, Mr. Mann."

"Holy Shit," Dakota said, lowering the rifle. "We thought you were dead. We found blood."

"Not my blood," Manuel said with a touch of pride. He stepped into the tent, zipped it up, and pulled his shirt over his head, revealing a rash of bruises and cuts, along with several horrific bites on his arms and shoulders. "Some kind of monster fish. I saw its fin in the water near the shore. I went down to the water, and it attacked me. I had my knife ready and stabbed it, then sliced its belly open. It bit me again, then swam off, bleeding heavily."

"Why didn't you come back to the ranch for help?"

"I was exhausted, and I got onshore, and collapsed. When I woke up, I was on a different shore. Nothing looked familiar. I know that doesn't make sense. I don't know what happened. I'm guessing the tide carried me down the lake a bit. Why are you here looking for me, Boss?"

Dakota levelled the gun at Manuel. "That's the most bullshit story I ever heard. Are you really you? Should I shoot you to find out?"

"Hey! Wait!" Manuel said, trying to get up and instead falling over backward to sprawl on his behind. "I'm telling the truth! I couldn't have been further than a few miles down the shore. But I kept getting turned around. I would walk and walk and not get anywhere, even when I followed the lakeshore. At night, I kept hearing these hisses near me, so I stayed awake all night and hid up in treetops. I know it doesn't make sense." He cast a haunted look at Dakota. "There aren't any trees near the shore I remember seeing on your land, or your neighbors. But there were always a few trees near the shoreline as I walked, when it began to get dark. Always one big enough to climb." His voice fell to a whisper. "Sometimes I felt as if I were climbing the same tree. Last night I carved my initials on a branch because I was
afraid—"

"You're not making sense!" Dakota interrupted. "You've been gone two weeks!"

"That explains why I've been so hungry," Manuel said abruptly, turning and rummaging in Dakota's cooler. "I'm not going to tell you the things I've eaten to stay alive." He began cramming food into his mouth.

Dakota watched him for a while, then put down the gun. "I guess a ghost doesn't need to eat."

Manuel ate all the food in Dakota's cooler, then fell into an exhausted sleep. Keeping an eye on him, Dakota called the police station from his cell phone. "Get the chief out here ASAP. Manuel's been found alive."

———

Carly loaded the last of the lake rocks in the back of her truck and shut the tailgate hard. *Don't want to lose any on the dirt track out of here.* Word was now that the "danger" of Latham's Landing was past, the town of Atlas to the south was planning on expanding. Some millionaire real estate developer had bought up the land just off the south shores of the lake, on either side of the long-derelict, shuttered Captain's bar, and supposedly the land was already being cleared. She'd heard noise earlier that sounded like a bulldozer, and trees going over. *Guess I'll find out in the spring.*

As she went around to get in the driver's seat, she noticed her left rear tire looked a little low. *That's odd. God, it's almost flat. I'd better take it easy getting out of here, I don't want to change a tire in the rain.* She glanced up at the sky. Where had the sun gone? Dark clouds were floating in silently above, covering all the sky across the lake. At least the damn mansion was where it was supposed to be, out there in the water, though it had fallen in some more from when she was out here last.

Carly got back in her car and turned the key. There was a click. She tried again. "What the fuck?" *Battery's dead again.*

Anxiously looking out at the lake, which was beginning to show whitecaps, she reached in the back and pulled out her blue battery charger from the backseat. Turning it to fast charge, she popped the hood, got out hurriedly, and connected it to her truck battery. The first plop of rain on her truck windshield landed as she cranked the key and the engine roared to life.

Leaving the truck running, she disconnected the charger and shoved it in the back, then drove off into the now pouring rain.

It wasn't the first time the battery had been dead after she'd spent a few hours picking rocks. Or the first time she'd used the charger to bring it back to life. Shaking off the chill, she turned off the gravel road onto Atlas Road, breathing a sigh of relief as the tires caught pavement. Accelerating to forty-five mph, she looked uneasily from side to side, as the trees whipped back and forth in the wind, some of them long dead. *Don't fall. Do not fall, please. I just need to get to Town Road.*

As she turned the last corner and emerged from the forest, she jammed on the brake. "What the fuck?" Water was over the end of the road, running steadily out of the ditch. Nearby, land had been cleared, and heavy equipment was parked in several rows. To flatten the land, earth and brush had been pushed in a pile to the side. In the storm, the pile had collapsed a bit into the drainage ditch, blocking it.

Motherfuck. Sure, she could try to drive through the flooded section of road. The truck had four-wheel drive. But if there was a chunk of snapped tree or two hidden in there – and there were for sure – a sharp branch would likely pop her tire. Or she could be swept into the opposite ditch and stranded.

Uneasily, she reversed, and headed back down towards the lake. She wouldn't have to go near the shore, anyway. Atlas Road led down close to Leighton Beach, but it was paved all the way. *It's a longer route to Town Road. but I can't risk my truck.*

She paused as she went past the new development, this time on her driver's side. There was a car in there next to one of the houses. It looked new, too. But there were no lights she could see in the gathering gloom, although it almost seemed like someone was standing out there in front of the house shell in the driving rain, looking at her. *Fucking none of my business, is what that is.* She floored the gas pedal, rocketing past the shadowy human form.

She passed the gravel road leading to the lake, then continued on towards Leighton Beach. There was an old sign leading to it, dirty yet legible. Creepily, there was also a half rotten pumpkin there, its carved triangle eyes and its smiling mouth half gone. *Kids must have been hanging out on the beach again. Weird, the pumpkin face looks eaten.*

She floored the accelerator again, casting a look towards the beach to see if there was any sign of people.

There was a loud bang, and the wheel spun in her hands. She fought it, stepping hard on the brake, the truck fishtailing, then coming to a stop right in the middle of the road.

She straightened the wheel, then pressed the accelerator. The truck moved slowly, a bad grinding squeal coming from the right rear tire.

She opened the door and went out. The back tire was flatter than a pancake, partially lying shredded over the rim. She looked closer at the tire, swearing at the sight of a bunch of nails embedded in the sidewall. *Those weren't there when I left the shoreline.*

Carly looked around, alert, then quickly grabbed a flashlight from the glove compartment, her keys, purse, and her jacket. Zipping it up, she locked the truck, and began walking quickly toward Town Road. *At least the downpour had stopped.*

She alternately walked and jogged when she felt able for the first two miles, her only thought to get as far as possible as fast as possible. When she reached the second mile marker, she stopped, listening. *Nothing.*

Carly resumed walking, allowing herself to reflect on what was happening even as she kept a steady pace. She was sure that the nails had come from a nail gun. Someone had fired them at her truck tires, most likely when she'd passed the new development. As to why...who the hell knew. It could be Chief Stahl defending his turf, or some wacko. God knows the lake seemed to attract enough of them. That guy in the helicopter that had crashed into Cairn Isle two years ago, it was rumored he'd come here to kill women. *Maybe someone else has gotten the same idea...*

Focus! Whomever it was would have expected her to run to the car she'd seen, stay with the truck or maybe call for help. But cell phones didn't work out here, no service. *I'm a local. I know better than to stay put. At the first sign of anything weird, get out and get out fast.*

Carly walked for another two miles, then stopped for a break, stretching her sore legs. There were still no noises, except some birds calling from far off. Dusk was almost full on by now, but she felt better, knowing she was only about another two miles from the main road. *And only three miles from home. Though my ass and everything else is going to be sore when I finally get there.*

She kept walking, getting finally to old Camp Leighton. *Could have been the inspiration for Camp Crystal Lake in the old Friday the 13th movies, if the camp had been a little closer to shore.* There was little more than a gravel drive, now weedy, leading off into a thin forest of dead and dying ash trees. The ramshackle cabins were in a circle just inside some gnarled ancient maple trees. Most of the windows gaped open, their screens long broken.

Fuck me. Carly blinked, staring. Like at the development, there was a bright magenta vehicle there in front of the cabins which looked pretty new. She paused for a moment, then darted closer down the weedy gravel road.

She looked at the Honda's tires. All four were flat. All the doors were locked, the windows shut. There was a spray of what looked like blood across the inside of the driver's side window.

Time to go. Carly backed up, turned, and ran back out to Atlas Road and down it as far as she could until she had to stop to catch her breath. Full dark wasn't far off, and the driving rain was back now, relentless.

I have to get out of here! She continued on, disliking the blackness of the leafless trees as they were slowly meshing with the darkening sky, and the rain that had intensified, like sheets of water pouring down. There was a bite to the air of the winter soon to come. She was wet through by now, even her waterproof shoes leaking near the laces.

You're almost home. Keep going and don't stop.

Carly let out a relieved breath as she neared the last turn. The road should be right there, and with luck, she'd get a ride home.

She panted up the last bit of incline, then took a shuddering breath.

The old sign for Leighton Beach was before her. It was cleaner now, the driving rain washing off the muddy streaks. The rotten pumpkin below it was sliced in half, each end lying neatly on its side in the weeds.

Carly looked around, terrified, then forced herself not to shriek.

Breathe. You've seen things before. Ignore them and just keep going. You know this is the way home.

She ignored the sign and the pumpkin, and kept walking, fortifying herself mentally that she might have to go past the cabins again, and the bloody car. Pushing herself, she walked as fast as she could, breathing hard, forcing away the weariness.

At another turn about a mile later, she saw the sign for Town Road. *Thank you, Jesus.*

She hurried down to the road, breathing sighs of relief as she stepped onto the newer pavement and steady traffic began to pass her. Town Road was the only road Atlas connected to, but many people used it as the only paved road around the lake for miles.

Her leg muscles screaming, she grabbed her mail from the mailbox, then walked up her gravel drive. "Thank God."

She stopped still, her eyes widening at the familiar shadowy figure standing on her front porch, silhouetted in the glow from the light inside. Inside, she could hear her German Shepherd, Inferno, barking his head off along with Jinx and Skinny.

"What do you want?" she called.

The figure didn't answer, just inclined its head, as if it couldn't understand her.

"Who are you?"

The figure moved closer, standing before the front door, right in Carly's path.

Carly put her hand to her neck, taking out her gold cross. "Our Father, who art in Heaven, hallowed be Thy name, Thy kingdom come, Thy will be done on Earth as it is in Heaven..."

The figure seemed to waver, then dissipate into the shadows of the porch. Carley continued with the prayer, holding the cross. By the time she was done, the figure was gone.

She hurried up the stairs and opened the door with the key. Inferno came bounding out, followed by Specter, her black cat. The latter was all fluffed out, sniffing at the doorway with huge eyes. She shooed Specter and Inferno back inside, locked the door, and leaned back into it.

After a few minutes of calming herself down, she went into the kitchen, and gave Inferno, Jinx and Skinny their treats. "Here you go."

The dogs settled down to eat, nonplussed. Specter was also curled sleeping on the couch. *Whatever that was, it's gone now. But I'd better call Pastor Taylor in the morning. She might think I'm bonkers, but she'll come and bless the house, just the same.*

———

Barb sat back in her chair, Cooper dozing at her feet. She put down the novel she'd been reading, then went to her computer, determined yet reluctant. *I've avoided this since I left those messages for Bob Stahl, telling myself that I needed the film from Latham's Landing to pursue my next moves in finding out what happened to Carolyn. I didn't, of course. That was just a way to avoid facing what happened. I have to deal with it.*

Barb sat down at her computer, reading again the scant research information on the Husterman she'd compiled. *All I have is folk stories, really. There are only a few details that even overlap: Evil sprite that lives near water to stay wet and hunts evildoers, mainly used like a Bogeyman for Czechoslovakian parents to make their kids behave.*

She began playing her interview recording again, her pen scratching loud in the stillness. *The hunter Lenny said that the shadow he saw was at least eight feet tall, that the thing was fast, that there was a group of at least five of them.* She pulled up her diagram of disappearances. *My brother Jake was killed by them along with possibly another five people that also disappeared; that makes six to eleven total Hustermen. That means if Carolyn was killed by them also, now there are anywhere from seven to twelve...*She flipped to her notes from Margie, the sister of Sylvia, the old woman aka possible witch who had made the creatures. *Whatever they kill, supposedly they eat the soul, according to Margie. But she also said that Sylvia made them wrong, that sometimes when they kill a new Husterman is created. They have no form, only eyes to see and a mouth to feed. But to kill, they have to have some kind of appendages to hold their prey, right?* "I saw the footprints, Cooper. At least sometimes they are completely solid, when they kill, and then they must have human feet, so it's not a jump to think they are human-shaped. But they're oddly tall for some reason. And why the yellow eyes? Are they reflective, to see in the dark?"

She played the recording again, making more notes. *Margie said that they were only there when it's dark, that they were meting out justice. That Sylvia had had a heart attack and then the Hustermen went wild or something, attacking their granddaughter, the person Sylvia created the first one to protect.*

I have to go talk to Sylvia. She's where all this began. She also had the power to send them away. If she knew how to create them, she must at least have an idea how to stop them.

———

"Hello?" Margie said curiously, as she opened the back screen door for Barb. "Can I help you?"

"Hi, Margie, I came to talk to Sylvia, if she's here?" Barb patted her front shirt pocket. "I need some more information."

"She won't talk to you," Margie said with a trace of apology. "She wouldn't last time if you remember. You really better go."

Time to be blunt. "I'm here to try again. The Hustermen are on the move, as you must be aware. There's more of them than there were, Margie. I think at least twelve."

"Twelve?" Margie squeaked, eyes round in horror. "That can't be."

"It is real. They killed a friend of mine, and she probably became a Husterman herself, too. I have to know how to stop them. They are killing people!"

"Stop scaring her," an old but imperial voice said from behind Barb. She turned to face a very wrinkled yet surprisingly toned woman with thick white hair. "Margie, go back to making the kolochki." She glared over at Barb. "You, come outside."

Barb followed Sylvia outside, surprised when the woman kept walking. "Where are we going?"

"Out of earshot." Sylvia eased down on a weathered wooden bench a little way down the block, near a bus stop. "Sit down and tell me what you want."

Barb sat. "I want to know what you did with the Hustermen to make them leave. I know you did something after your grand-daughter Kelsie was attacked to drive them away."

"Oh, you do, do you?" Sylvia cackled, bright blue eyes flashing.

"Look, they headed north. I tracked them." Barb pushed her map onto Sylvia's lap. "See those dots, those are all people that went miss-ing. One of them was my brother Jake. I found footprints some-times, and most of the time they were...half gone."

"What do you want me to do about it? What's done is done."

"You made them, tell me how to unmake them," Barb said in exasperation.

"You can't unmake them," Sylvia replied darkly. "You talked to Margie. You know the first one...came out wrong. He made more of them. They don't usually seek out humans, you know."

"I don't know anything," Barb said, desperate. "I need to know how to stop them, Sylvia. There are close to thirteen of them now."

"That's bad."

"That's all you've got to say?"

Sylvia glared up at her, indignant. "I did the best I could. All I had were my memories of old stories my grandmother told me. She was from the old country, never learned to speak English, except for a few words. I can't tell you anything that will help you, girl."

"Tell me what you did to make them, and how you did it."

"One. I only made one."

"How?"

Sylvia sighed, then she leaned back. "I captured a local man. He wasn't bad and he wasn't good. Fed him a drugged batch of Zazvorniki I made, his favorite. Then I made him into a vodrik, what you call a Husterman. I'm not going to go into details as it won't help you anyway. But suffice to say I did a ritual that separated the body from the soul and using the flesh as fuel, lets the soul wander free. That's why they are only shadows, because the soul is the energy behind a person, their life force or essence, if you will. They sometimes have enough will or strength of purpose to become completely visible, but it takes a lot of energy to do that. They prefer to be in the shadows because there they can hide not having a body."

Is this all for real, or is she just making things up to tell me? "Why him?

"He was the only person I could be sure to get. I'm an old woman. I don't get around well anymore. Kelsie needed protection."

"How did you make him?"

"My grandmother told an old story to me of a woman making one of her enemies into a Vodrik. I should have remembered the ending, where he turns on her. I should have remembered the Golem of Prague."

"Can it be undone?"

"I told you no, I don't think so. I never heard of a way, at least. I should have made a golem instead."

Barb lapsed into silence.

"Tell me about this place they have gone to."

Barb began with just facts about the murders and history of Latham's Landing, but in the telling the entire story spilled out of her about Helter and Barb, including what she suspected about Carolyn. "I have to help her," she finished.

"You can't help her," Sylvia said, with no real trace of empathy. "But you can help yourself. Don't go near that island. Helter was right. It's marked you, sure as it marked anyone that ever visited. It wants you to return."

Barb shivered. "Can you tell me anything else?"

Sylvia got to her feet tiredly, then began to walk back. "I would ask these questions, Barbara."

"It's Barb."

"Barbara. Why do the Hustermen want to go to Latham's Landing? You say they went directly to it and by what the retired chief said, they are still there."

"Evil draws evil."

"No, it usually doesn't. Evil competes, my dear, almost always. Predators going after the same vulnerable prey. So why would the Hustermen have headed there? What did they have to gain by going there?"

"Largest lake in the area?"

"Why not the Great Lakes? You find out why, and that will give you another weapon. They didn't kill Mr. Stahl so they are not there to hunt humans. I'd say there's something there in the lake in the water. You say that this Sea Room always grows brighter before something happens. Seems to me that it's the heart of whatever's out there. Latham flooded the house right before he died. Maybe he had a reason that wasn't madness? There's some connection to water, or something in the water."

The day was sunny, but Barb shivered, memories of the island flashing before her eyes. Her hand went to her side, resting on the healed knife wound. "Divers have looked for bodies before and usually don't find any."

"You say the island changes. Why not beneath the water like it does on top?"

"I don't understand."

"You said that after the explosion all the new buildings were gone yet the original house wasn't damaged. You say it can't be burned, either. What is special about that original house? Why is it always partly flooded?"

"I don't know," Barb responded, frustrated. "How can I get it to show me what it doesn't want me to see?"

"Trick it. That's the only way I see. But I still advise you to stay away and never go back there." Sylvia walked back to her front door, Barb following as she thought furiously of what to ask in the few seconds left to her.

"How did you send them away?" Barb managed, as Sylvia began to shut the screen door.

A pained expression flitted across the old woman's face. "I didn't. I let the one I'd created try to feed on me, hoping as he was distracted to bind his soul back into his physical remains, and therefore kill him and his progeny. Instead of destroying him, he broke free of me." Sylvia paused. "You might be doing all this for nothing, Barbara. You said the Hustermen went across the ice to the island. Are they still there on the island? You say Latham's Landing seems to be keeping souls there if they die on the island. Could the island have destroyed the Hustermen for you? Could you entice them there and let it destroy them?"

"No," Barb answered. "I'm pretty sure they are on the mainland now." *I didn't think of it before, but all our evidence indicates the Hustermen went to the island and were driven away. Maybe some were killed? I'll have to ask Bob how many he saw.* "I'm here because the retired police chief that bought the island and flooded it completely had a run in with them, and he wouldn't have gone to the island after dark, I'm sure of that. He is trading me my film for whatever I can tell him about the Hustermen." She paused. "Wait, you think killing the original Husterman will kill the ones he made, like a vampire?"

"Maybe," Sylvia shrugged. "I can't say. They are not supposed to make more when they feed."

"What exactly do they feed on?" Barbara countered.

"Evildoer's souls, supposedly. But how are they defining evil? You said your brother was attacked, and your friend. Were they evil?"

Barb pushed down the immediate rush of anger. "Carolyn wasn't evil. My brother wasn't either. You made a monster to protect your granddaughter, not to punish random evil."

Sylvia nodded, considering for a moment. "That might be the key, Barbara. When he broke free of me, he broke with my simple directive to protect my family and regained something of the original Husterman purpose to find and punish evil. Likely they have been drawn to Latham's Landing for that. But for whatever reason, they were repelled, and now they haunt the shore." She paused. "Find whatever is blocking them from the house. I'd guess it's the water."

"They can walk over ice but not water? They are just shadows."

"Shadows that were once men and retain some instincts of men. They walked leaving partial footprints when as shadows they could have flown or drifted on the air, yes? Also, there may be some superstition of running water as a barrier to evil. You wouldn't need them all to believe it, just one. They are acting as a group, not as individuals."

"That can't be, or this would have been solved last winter, Sylvia. The lake was locked in ice all winter!"

"Then something else is keeping them at bay," the old woman insisted. "Your former policeman met them and survived. I'll bet it wasn't his virtue that saved him. Find out what it was, Barbara, and you'll have your answer." She gave a final smile, then shut the door.

CHAPTER FIVE

"I DON'T KNOW WHY WE HAD TO MOVE HERE," FIONA SAID ALOUD, as she kicked a rock near the frame of the half-finished house. "There's no one for me to play with besides you."

Keyserie grimaced, as she put down her ragged paperback horror novel. "I don't like being here with you, either. But you know how it goes. Dad gets a lot of money for overseeing these new housing units. At least he's not around much, he's too busy picking up the pieces after that last foreman bailed."

"He didn't bail on the job. He went crazy and killed people," Fiona corrected. "You think I'm too young to tell me the truth."

"That guy was likely crazy to begin with," Keyserie admonished. "Why don't you go for a walk? Dad says there's a trail in the backyard that leads to a small pond at the edge of our property. A stream feeds into it. I'll bet there's frogs and dragonflies." She flashed an encouraging smile. "I'll get dinner in an hour or so. Just be back by four-thirty, as it'll be getting dark soon after." She turned her attention back to her book.

Fiona made a face, but she also moved off to the backyard. She found the trail without too much trouble, and followed the trail to a pond that was more mud than water, with cattails thickly covering almost all of the remaining water. "Some fun."

She followed a small ditch which fed the pond back to the origin of the water: a stream a couple dozen yards away. The streambed was mostly rocks, but a steady trickle of water was running down the middle. Fiona shaded her eyes against the sun's glare, scanning eagerly for any animals or interesting bugs, but there wasn't much to see except trees, rocks, and water. The trickle of water was too small to wade in.

Irritated, she followed the stream up for a few hundred yards, hoping for a deeper pool with some minnows, crayfish, or frogs. Instead, she came to where the stream emerged from a large drain-pipe. The pipe was connected to a concrete sluiceway that was twice as long as it was high.

Fiona climbed a short flight of stairs to the top. A wide smile broke over her face. "A beach!"

Directly in front of her was some murky deeper water, but there was a walkway around that, a set of concrete stairs leading down to a beach that spread out for at least a mile to her left. In front of her and to her right was a lake which was held back by the sluiceway, with a shoreline of meadow as far as she could see to her right. No one was on the lake or the beach. The meadow was empty except for a herd of sheep far off in the distance.

Excited, Fiona ran down the steps and onto the beach, spending the next hour roaming from one end to the other gathering small shiny rocks, some smoothed glass, and a few snail shells. It was only when she noticed it was getting too dark to see that she thought of home. "Crap!"

Fiona hurried with her treasures back the way she'd come. "Where's the concrete stairs?"

The sluiceway was in front of her, the gurgle of water familiar. But the stairs weren't there. The sun had almost set and the shadows were lengthening, making everything hard to recognize.

Fiona hurried back and forth around the sluiceway, looking all over, wondering if she'd misremembered where the stairs were, her anxiety growing. Without the stairs there was no way to get off the beach. *That water's too deep to wade through. And I can't climb up sheer concrete walls.*

Was there another way home? She turned, biting her lip, then shaded her eyes. There seemed to be someone standing at the other end of the beach now. Maybe someone walking a dog, there were two blurry shapes, both moving toward her slowly. One was running around on all fours, as if it were sniffing the ground.

I don't want to get bitten by a loose dog. Fiona took a step back, turning in the direction of the forest. Maybe she should go around the sluiceway? She'd have to go through the trees, but at least she'd be going in the right direction. Once she found the stream it would be easy to get home.

There was a crackle of a breaking branch as something stepped on it in front of her in the trees. Fiona looked up, scared now. The sun was on the horizon, the sky shades of pink and gold. A light breeze sprang up, blowing her hair around.

Another crackle sounded to her right in the trees.

"Who's there?" She tried to sound brave, but the query came out a croak.

There were more cracks as something came steadily toward her.

A sudden lilting music floated on the wind.

Fiona looked up to see a girl on the lake shore in front of the meadow, playing a flute. The melody was haunting, sad yet beautiful.

The girl motioned emphatically to her to come, not stopping her playing.

Fiona turned to look at the person and their dog. There was now what looked like three dogs excitedly sniffing all over the far end of the beach where she had walked earlier. The figure with them was following them, walking with an odd, lurching limp.

There was a crackle again in the woods at her back, as something resumed moving. Then the abrupt gunshot snapping of branches as whatever it was bolted toward her.

Fiona let out a cry. She dropped her handfuls of treasures and plunged into the water, slogging towards the girl. The water seemed to flow around her, away from her as she pushed through icy chilling waves to her neck. She struggled on, expecting at any minute to be grabbed and dragged backward, or worse, dragged under. For something huge was in the water with her, flashes of iridescent scales and large fins recurring as something repeatedly neared and abruptly retreated.

She emerged gasping on the shore at the girl's feet, dripping wet and shivering.

The girl with the flute stopped playing. "Took you long enough. They nearly had you."

Several splashes sounded behind her, sending small waves over her wet shoes.

Wild-eyed, Fiona looked back at the beach, letting out a whimper. A crowd of shadowy shapes now stood there, swaying slightly as they stood, fixated on her. There were other things on all fours in the water just in front of them, their eyes reflectively shining in the last rays of the setting sun. *Those aren't dogs.*

"Go now," the girl with the flute said. "I'll give you a few minutes. Make use of them and don't return. I will not save you a second time." She put her lips to her instrument and began to play.

"Thank you," Fiona stammered out. She rushed past the girl and ran up the meadow, plunging into the trees past the concrete sluiceway and emerging into the streambed. She ran quickly down the dry edge, stubbing her toes and bruising her arches on rocks. *Where's the trail to the pond? I'm never going to be able to find it in the dark!*

There was a small gleam ahead of her on the ground as the moon came out from behind a cloud. Fiona ran up to the object. It was an old gold coin.

She looked ahead of her, whimpering again in relief to see more gleams, the tiny reflections forming a trail for her to follow. She ran as fast as she could, following them, finding the pond and then the path that led her to the backyard.

The lights of the rented house had never looked so wonderful. She ran to the back porch, only then looking back.

There was nothing shining, the coins had vanished. The forest was a dark hulking shape of unbroken shadow.

"Fiona! Is that you?" Keyserie called. "Where've you been? I've been worried sick!"

"Thank you," Fiona whispered, then hurried inside, locking the door behind her.

———

"Thank you for coming, Chief," Barb said, as she let him in that night. "This is my pastor, Maryanne Taylor."

"Hi, Pastor Taylor," Bob said, casting an odd look at Barbara as he offered his hand to Maryanne. "It's just Bob now, Barb. I'm retired."

"And I'm just Maryanne," the woman said, giving him a serene smile. "Don't mind me, Bob, I just stopped by tonight to see how Barb was doing. And to bring Cooper a few fresh-baked dog biscuits." She patted the dog, who was looking at her hopefully, tail wagging.

"Look, please excuse me, but I don't have time to waste with pleasantries," Bob said curtly. "Barb, I need to know what you know about those spirits or whatever they are." He reached in his pocket and handed her both cameras, plus the film in another bag. "As promised."

Barb took the cameras and film, then put them down on a nearby chair. "Thanks. Now show me the pictures that you got from my film."

Bob scowled at her, but he took them out of his jacket, bringing them to her kitchen table and spreading them out. "I didn't take any stills from your videos. But I saw enough in the few minutes you recorded to believe you when you say you saw wolves. And that you tangled with more than just bad weather and accidents and a serial killer named Mac."

Barb nodded. "You want my whole statement? The one I haven't given to anyone?"

"Um, I do," Maryanne said, her eyes huge as she looked through the pictures. "These are from Latham's Landing, Barb? When you almost died?"

Barb nodded, glancing through the photos. "You can see the silhouette of the belltower in that one photo of the glowing Sea Room."

"You read the papers so you know we didn't find any remains of a belltower," Bob said. "But you also can guess that there was no sign of all these other buildings that your initial shots show when you were landing your boat. The island looks now like it did in my visits years before, except for the wreckage of the helicopter and a snowmobile." He paused. "When I went to the island, I was prevented from going beyond the shore. But you or those with you were there for over a day. Tell me what you saw. What do you think was happening there?"

"Some group was there building onto the old house," Barb said slowly, biting her lip. "We call the house or the island a malevolent force onto itself, but there were ladders, scaffolding, and tools which means a group was there not just some evil force. The belltower went up after dark like magic. I can't explain that. It just formed."

"It formed after the helicopter arrived, though, right?"

"Yes." Barb nodded with understanding. "We saw the helicopter land on what looked like a concrete pad. Where the belltower formed. You think it formed because of Mac?"

"I do," Bob replied. "I think Latham's Landing was helping Mac. There was and is now no clear spot on the island where you could land a helicopter without risking that you'd get blown into the water or smashed into granite by winds when setting down or taking off. I think the island made a spot for him to land to lure him in, gave him cover, and then fed off the fear and violence of his killings."

Barb took a sudden shaky breath, then let it out. "You're right. It was helping him. Just as it acted to keep us stranded there for him to kill. We were attacked multiple times by different manifestations. It was only Carolyn's faith, her blessed bullets, and the herbs that kept the...the manifestations away."

Bob held up the herb twig from his pocket. "I know. I found this on the shore near where you had your large fire. Do you know what it is?"

"I don't understand this," Maryanne interjected. "Bob, you said wolves. I've heard stories about the phantom belltower from parishioners, but nothing about wolves. Are you saying they weren't really there?"

"You can't clearly define what's real and what's not when you're on that island," Barb replied. "The manifestations I witnessed could touch you and harm you as well as just scare you. I can't say that the wolves were real animals, but they were real enough to kill a woman. I saw her die. Two women, if you count Chung Lai."

"No one has mentioned another woman," Maryanne whispered, eyes wide. "Nothing in the papers, no gossip. Who was she?"

"Delilah. Another victim of Mac, someone he brought in the helicopter to hunt and kill on the island." Barb took another deep breath, closing her eyes. "He alluded to that. I'd forgotten. At the last, when he came after me and stabbed me, he said the island had helped him, hid him, in return for him killing people there."

"No other bodies were found?" Maryanne piped in.

"You're not going to believe this, but there's a mermaid there, probably more than one," Bob said reluctantly. "She spoke to me when I was there with the other state cops and feds. She said the reason we never find bodies of those who drown is because they get eaten. She looked like a woman, but she had the needle teeth of a deepwater fish." He cleared his throat. "The way she said it, I think she's been eating them."

Barb bit her lip and nodded once. "I'd call you crazy for saying that, but I've seen demons erupt from stone fountains and attack me, not to mention at least ten separate ghosts. The attacks came in waves until we ran out of the herbs. Then it became an assault from all fronts."

"I'm grateful you escaped, Barb. But how did you manage to escape?" Maryanne put in. "I've lived here long enough to know that people who go there almost never return alive. And who is Helter?"

"Helter was a merc who was there supposedly hired by the owner to destroy the house for the insurance money. He was an expert, which is why I think he succeeded where it was physically possible to do so." Barb turned to Bob. "His explosives did work for the new buildings, as you saw no sign of them when you were there. Even saying that the belltower could appear and disappear at will—making it some kind of manifestation—there was a three-story mansion all framed out with a roof and at least five or six finished outbuildings, not to mention the flight of what had to be fifty or so stone steps you see in these photos. I climbed those steps, and our camp and tents were set up on the landing at the top. I went inside that big building behind the belltower, and it had several floors. Those buildings weren't manifestations. They were real. Destruction of those would leave a lot of wreckage floating in the water, as well as a foundation and piles of blasted wood on the shore. Even if the granite broke apart, there'd be piles of rubble. But no one found anything." She rubbed her eyes. "I'm missing something, something important."

"We already know that the island changes," Bob agreed. "The water can thaw or freeze around it with no warning out of season, storms can come out of nowhere, and time passes differently as soon as you go out on the water. Hell, you had to have heard that Dakota's missing field hand, Manuel, was located after being missing for two weeks. He swears he was only gone two days and stuck to the lakeshore trying to walk out. He didn't die of dehydration, and he wasn't weak from lack of food, just very hungry." He paused. "I think that the mermaid and her kind—if there are more—are responsible for stealing the sheep that go missing from the shore. Yes, it's better than people dying. But Manuel wasn't harmed. He just lost time. How is that possible?"

"There's Carly, too," Maryanne said suddenly. "And a few other locals. People around the lake have been coming to see me, asking me to bless them or their houses, sometimes both. No one has said why, but I'm guessing they've had some near misses." She cleared her throat. "Bob, have there been any disappearances?"

"There was a bad storm about a week back. It caused some flooding of the Town Road when a ditch got blocked by some tree and bush limbs. When crews cleared it out the following morning and got the water diverted, they found two abandoned cars." He paused. "I heard this in private from Chief Upner, so do not mention it to anyone." He let out a breath. "One of the cars had some blood on the front seat. All four tires were flat, sidewalls hit with what looked like four-inch nails from a nail gun. The other car's tires were perfectly fine, but the battery was dead."

"Any bodies?" Barb ventured.

"No. Both were locked, no signs of struggle inside except for the spots of blood. If there were any tracks, the storm washed them away."

"Did you find who the cars belonged to?"

"The one with the dead battery was a couple that was looking to move into the new development. Both are missing. The other car was registered to a contractor that was working on the housing units. He supposedly stayed late to finish up some drywall. He's also missing." He paused. "I'm going to tell you everything I know because I tried my best to stop the deaths and it worked for a while, but it's not working anymore. I'm not sure why flooding the island initially worked. I didn't come up with the idea myself; I was instructed to do it by the group that told me to buy the island and provided me with the money." He paused and took a deep breath. "No, I didn't blow my retirement fund on the purchase, like I let everyone think. I've been well paid to imprison Latham's Landing in solitary confinement. I don't know who the people are who are behind this, or why they suddenly took an interest in Cairn Isle after years of deaths. In any case, the rule that people on the shore were safe seems to be false now. I'm thinking I should drain out the excess water in the lake and hopefully we can make the shoreline safe again. But what I ran into on Carl's Point was something I never saw before. I'm not sure it came from the island, which is why I need to know about these Hustermen." Bob shared his experience with the Hustermen pack at Carl's Point, including his suspicion that Carolyn was one of them now. "These shadows can physically hurt people, so I can believe that they are responsible for the deaths at the development. But Carolyn let me live when I called her by name."

Barb shared everything she knew and had learned about the Hustermen from her visit with Sylvia. "The old witch who made them, Sylvia, said evil competes. That the Hustermen were attracted to Latham's Landing because they had possibly regained their purpose of punishing evil. Given the tracks I saw, they tried to go over to the island on the ice and were repelled."

"Carolyn seems to be their leader now," Bob said heavily. "Possibly she still wants to destroy the island and get her revenge. I don't think I would have gotten away with just a swipe of her talons otherwise."

"Those lacerations on your face were from her? Dear God," Barb whispered. "We have to help her."

"How? You said you didn't learn how to destroy a Husterman."

"Sylvia did say that if we were able to destroy the initial one, that the others might also be destroyed."

"But we don't know how to do that," Maryanne interjected.

"That's what I missed," Barb said, slamming her hand on the table. "The Sea Room. It always illuminates like a miniature sun when something's about to happen. Helter never set charges there, but I think destroying it is the key to ending the evil on the island. Everyone always attacks or visits the island mansion, and the Sea Room is ignored. We need to focus on attacking there instead of the main house. Somehow it is the source of the freezing and thawing, and the bigger ghosts."

"Are you sure it's still there?" Maryanne interjected. "I've heard reports that the house fell down and sank, but I saw it clear as day yesterday when I drove past. The Sea Room is only visible on a calm day, and then only the very top. The rest of it is submerged now."

"Sylvia said water was important. Rumors say that Latham made a pact with a demon. Well, if he did that, did he also have something to do with the murderous mermaid? Did he flood the bottom of the house to give her access?"

"Look, this is all good, but it's not getting us anywhere," Bob interrupted. "We have a lot of suppositions and nothing new to lead us to a solution."

"I do have something new," Barb shot back. "You say you can't burn the original house or destroy it. I agree from what I've seen. But faith and blessings, even white wiccan herbs seem to have a strong effect." She looked pointedly at Maryanne. "We need to align with faith and religion if we're going to beat the island."

"Wait," Maryanne protested. "I'm not qualified for this."

"Yes, you are," Bob quickly assured. "Can faith repel the Huster-men, Barb?"

"They're supposed to feed on evil souls, so it makes sense they'd not attack someone who was good," Barb said with a frown. "But Carolyn wasn't evil. Maybe they are hypersensitive to what most religions calls sin, like lying and thievery?"

"They called me a liar, and a murderer," Bob admitted. "I denied it. They could be attracted instead to strong feelings: hate, guilt, pain, rage."

"That would fit with my brother," Barb said slowly. "He was guilty over a lot of things. If he heard the shadows around him come to life telling him he was guilty, he would have gone along with the Hustermen in condemning himself. Could the killings of the three missing people at the development be explained as the contractor being another killer like Mac? He attacks the couple at the construction site and brings them to the old kid's camp. He kills them and does something with the bodies, maybe puts them in the lake. He then gets caught by the Hustermen and consumed and becomes a Husterman himself."

"Or the Hustermen got all three."

"Or the Hustermen got all three," Bob agreed. "That would make how many?"

"Fourteen or sixteen," Barbara sighed, sitting down at the table. She took out a notebook and a pen. "What do we know really about Cairn Isle? I mean know for a proven fact."

"We know people come to the island and they die. If they die in the water, they get eaten. If they die on the island, we find the bodies, but the souls get stuck on the island as ghosts."

"We don't know that," Barb said drolly, raising her eyebrows. "You'd have to list at least one person that you know died there that you saw the ghost there afterwards."

"You said you saw Mac, the serial killer, after Helter killed him."

"I'm not sure. I thought that Carolyn said that, before I passed out. Yes, I saw people there. I think that they were spirits of people who had died there. But they weren't all evil; one of them tried to help me. Most tried to delay me until Mac could find me, or turn me back towards him, or hurt me themselves."

"Who was this one who tried to help you?"

"A black man, a shaman, I think. He said he'd been brought there to try to cleanse the isle of evil or something to that effect. That he'd failed. There was a black woman there, too, a voodoo priestess, I think. Maybe a witch? She warned him not to help me, that he'd get punished for it. The others I saw, they could have been manifestations of the island, and not ghosts. But I'm sure those two were ghosts of dead human beings. There's also the girl with the flute who warns people at the shoreline. I've had reports mentioning her from other people, and she's been there since the first mass death there a couple decades ago. Something tells me that she's one of the original ghosts. Maybe finding out who she and/or this shaman are will give us a clue?"

"Okay, then we need to hit the library tomorrow and look at headlines, see if a girl with a flute went missing out there," Bob agreed. "I did research for that ad I ran, looking at reported deaths over the years. I'll also look through those files, see if we can find her. The black man and woman may predate my run as sheriff." *Or maybe the run of the paper itself.*

"There may be something important about the original mass death, as you call it," Maryanne mentioned. "I've lived here all my life, and the island was relatively quiet up until that first group of kids rowed over there to party and died. Remember? There were two girls there also at the same time, and one survived. After that it seemed like the deaths were more frequent."

"Was that because the island was more active, or because more thrill-seekers either went to Latham's Landing or went close to the island for a look from the water?" Bob replied. "I know from my time as chief that a lot of the drownings that happened were people that were curious that either hit rocks with watercraft or capsized in sudden storms when they went too close. And since that first mass death as we're calling it, almost every year there's been a group of teens or college kids that have gone to the island for fun that either turned up dead or are still missing."

"I think we need to think outside the box," Barb said, writing furiously. "The house was built at one time by Latham, so it's said. He was a shipbuilder, so he flooded the land and he supposedly flooded it right before he died. Was his body found? I thought his body was missing."

Bob shifted in his chair. "I know that his wife's body wasn't found, but the year that group of college kids doing their thesis on the origin of fear got killed on the island, they also didn't find the bodies, just the vehicles. There was a huge storm that felled a bunch of trees near the shore and flooding, so we didn't find the vehicles for close to a month." He paused. "For a while the island was dormant with a caretaker. Then a group came here to stay over, rented the place, and one of the guys went missing in the kitchen. Supposedly just disappeared when he went looking for some plates. A relative came looking for him I think a year later, and she also went missing on the island. But her friend, Tina, the only person to date besides Barb and Helter that witnessed any ghosts there and lived to get off the island, said that she saw his ghost in the mirror. Tina said she also saw the ghost of the girl with a flute, the ghost of a young boy on the stairs, and the ghost of a teen who had come with another group the same day she'd come with her friend. That there was something in the flooded part of the house that came after her. My police force searched the island and found the body of Tina's friend, the bodies of all the teens and then a very old skeleton of a woman, unidentified. Maybe that was Latham's wife?"

"Does the wife matter?" Maryanne interjected. "No one has ever seen a woman ghost that I heard of in local tales."

"I think its noteworthy that the only ghost that actually attacked Tina was in the flooded part of the house, and that this same flooded section was where the old skeleton and all the bodies of the initial mass killing were found, even though at least a few of the kids were supposedly killed over at the Sea Room," Bob said slowly. "Barb, you're right, this woman's skeleton being dug up and removed plus all the initial deaths may have triggered something. I'll find out more about where that skeleton was taken. I think Sylvia is right. We need to try draining the water away from the island to see if that stops the deaths or lets the Hustermen get to the island to go after the evil forces there. I don't see where any of the other suppositions we've come up with are getting us anywhere. People go there and die, then they get stuck as ghosts, most of them helping to ensnare more victims. Learning who the other ghosts are doesn't help us stop that."

"Look, this evil started somewhere," Barb argued. "Every haunting has an origin story; you just have to go back far enough. Are there any documents from when Latham was first building the house? If something bad happened before that there should be a record of it, like a settlers vs. natives' massacre, or something."

"You think the ground is cursed?" Bob tried for a laugh, but it came out too shrill, adding to the tension. "You've been reading too many horror novels."

"I think that Latham didn't just make a house that suddenly had the power that this island does. I think we need to go back to the beginning, and find out who he bought the land from, how he was able to flood it and make it into a lake. He made the lake, right? We need to find out if workers died here building it. His wife supposedly died here, and he went mad from grief and flooded the place and killed himself. But is any of that true or just old gossip that became local legend?"

"Maybe he killed her."

"I think there's a further mystery," Maryanne added. "Say he killed her, then killed himself. People would've discovered the murder/suicide. They must have had servants, right?"

"Good point," Barb said, still writing furiously. "Servants talk, they might have told their families. Maybe if we can find out the names of the servants they had, we can find a relation who might either have some old papers or know of some firsthand accounts passed down to their children."

"I think we're beyond that," Maryanne said dejectedly. "Latham's time was close to a century ago. We're not going to find anyone living."

"Negative thoughts aren't going to help us. I'm going somewhere with this: why did Latham flood the house, if it wasn't to hide how his wife was killed?"

"No one floods their house purposely, no one else would be able to live there. Maybe in the struggle of killing his wife, he accidentally flooded it. You said that there was a control he used to flood the lake when he first made the house, that he could control the water level. This was so the house wouldn't flood, even in times of high rain. A man with that much forethought suddenly floods his home which he put all these safeguards in place to protect from flooding?"

"Something went wrong all those years ago, something really bad," Barb murmured.

"Possibly Latham intended to flood the house to keep his treasures secret? Maybe he had wealth hidden in the basement, or even some kind of sunken room."

"It's a new thought," Bob admitted. "Okay, let's go back to the paranormal aspect, Barb. The evil entity there is affected by white witchcraft like herbs and Christian-blessed objects like Carolyn's bullets. Helter was also able to destroy the new buildings. But why does the island "reset", for lack of a better word, to the original house?"

"The evil entity is bound to the original house," Barb said finally, pausing in her writing. "When you look at everything we know, that's the only logical conclusion. What I didn't say until now is that there were many cloven hoofprints in the dirt near the new buildings that were too large to be deer. That says demon to me, Bob."

"That says demons plural to me, Barb," he countered grimly.

"Sweet Jesus," Maryanne said, crossing herself.

"Mac was bringing girls there and killing them. He was feeding the island a steady diet of fear and death. Somehow that enabled it to build. Other than the mermaid you say wants to eat human flesh, the house itself lives on fear and death. Again, that smacks of demon."

"That doesn't answer why the new buildings got destroyed when the original house remained," Maryanne interjected.

"Maybe more death and fear were needed before the new part could be as resilient as the original house?" Bob offered. "Or were the newer sections just a façade, like the belltower? I know for a fact that there weren't any deliveries of wood to Cairn Isle. So where did the wood come from? Not to mention all the extra granite for those stairs and foundations. None of the forest around here has been cut. No way did Mac bring it all with his helicopter." He looked at Barb. "Is it possible that the newer sections of house and granite that looked as real as the belltower were just illusion? I mean to say, that they were like the belltower in that they were really there, real enough to sit on, walk on, but not really made of physical materials?"

"That's the best explanation I've heard," Barb admitted.

"Okay, so the new parts were some kind of illusion. How does the original house 'reset'?" Maryanne interjected. "There are pictures of Latham's family at the house. The house is real. It's been there for a hundred years. It follows that it should have been blown up by Helter's explosives."

"Maybe it's only able to be destroyed by water? The original mansion has been slowly collapsing into the water since Bob flooded the lake," Barb commented.

"Um..." Bob shifted his feet. "It...it's been reported to me that the house is not always submerged in the water."

"What? The water recedes?" Maryanne asked.

"No. Um...the house seems to vanish sometimes."

"Decrepit houses don't vanish out of lakes," Barb argued, stopping her writing to stare at him.

"This one does sporadically. There's a rumbling sound that's very loud, a bright glow, and then a crash. One of the locals reported it to me when she saw me in town but asked not to make an official report. I went out there to look, and it was there, just as it always was. I thought she was having fun with me. But a week later, I was making my rounds and I witnessed the whole house just shimmer and vanish. It reappeared with the same breaking noise an hour later, accompanied by the glow and then the low rumble." Bob paused. "A reporter's come to town to investigate. She called me today and left a message. She indicated there were several mass killings in other states where people reported a house where a house either couldn't or shouldn't be. There's always water associated with these "impossible houses", either pools of water partly surrounding them or streams springing up near the foundations. She said she had pictures from some boy's phone of a specific house. She asked that I drop the water level in the lake so she can compare these pictures to the house on Latham's Landing."

"You stopped victims going to it. So, it went out to get victims," Barb mused. "That also explains the lack of deaths here this last year. It's been feeding each time it disappears."

"Houses aren't mobile. They can't move," Bob protested.

"This one can. And apparently does." Barb stared at him angrily. "You knew, didn't you? That it was going out into the world and killing? Before I said anything, or the reporter contacted you."

Bob nodded once reluctantly. "I thought that stopping people going to the house wouldn't work forever. But there wasn't anything else I could think of to do. I had to protect the people here as my first priority—"

"Yeah, you're a real hero."

"Hey, this isn't helping," Maryanne put in. "We need to think about one more thing. Well, two things. One: was there a reason Latham chose to build a house here then create a lake plus the Sea Room and its long bridge? He was rich enough if he loved the ocean to build near the seashore, or to buy up an existing small lake and build on that."

"What do you think is the reason?" Barb asked.

"I'm wondering if he knew there was a dark power here and he tried to bend it to his own purposes," Maryanne said darkly. "And two: assuming that the belltower's only purpose was to give cover to Mac's helicopter when he was on the island, as Bob surmised, what purpose were the other new buildings behind and to other side of the old mansion going to serve?"

"We should be able to find a copy of the deed to the land in the courthouse, so we can figure out when Latham bought the land and from who, even how big the parcel was, if he had to buy a bunch of parcels to make up the entire lake," Bob said slowly. "As far as the new buildings, I think the evil entity wanted more places for Mac or other ghosts to stalk their victims, to increase their fear. If the demonic force or main demon wanted to possess someone, he could've possessed Mac and left the island the first night Mac landed."

Barb nodded. "That fits with my experience. I encountered several ghosts in the new mansion trying to escape Mac. They scared the hell out of me while keeping me running from place to place in panic."

"You're right," Maryanne whispered, her face white. "Whatever is there is extremely cunning. It's got its own plan, which we need to thwart before there are any more deaths. The near misses locally won't stay near misses for long, Bob."

"We need to talk about two more things," Barb amended. "What do we know about the Sea Room? That glow we see when things happen on the island must be the Sea Room lighting up, even submerged."

"As far as I know there haven't been any deaths there," Bob replied. "The bodies are always in the main house. Our police have found signs of violence there before, though: blood and such. Maybe you're right, that the bodies are moved. But who does it, and what would be the purpose to moving the bodies?"

"If we boat over to attack the Sea Room with explosives, then the water that's left in the lake will freeze and the wolves will come. Or something worse," Barb said darkly. "Even if the water level is dropped back to normal or a bit below normal, that's still enough water to drown in, especially if we get inches of rain in a sudden storm."

"Here's a question: what would draining the lake entirely reveal?" Bob said suddenly. "The water level of the lake has always been high with the main house partly flooded in my lifetime. Draining the lake might reveal something in the flooded parts of the house, maybe even in the lakebed between the Sea Room and the house. It's going to take some maneuvering, but I think I can do it."

"It took the evil force there two years to figure out a way to find more victims and reach its tendrils to the mainland, as well as somehow to reconnect with the Sea Room and access its power," Barb murmured, deep in thought. "We need to drain the water as soon as we can."

I was warned to keep the water level high. But maybe I could do it, just for a day. I'd have to get Teeth to help, to make sure that the lake sturgeon flowed out with the water and didn't get stranded. If even one of those protected fish die, I'd have the state officials all over me. "To my knowledge, the area where the lake is hasn't been dry land since before Latham's time. But it must have been dry at one time, just to build the elevated walkway and Sea Room's foundations."

"Yes," Barb mused. "If the water's not there, the island can't trap us. We need to dry up the lake, see what it reveals." She looked at Bob. "Why hasn't anyone ever drained the lake before? Hell, just to see if they could find the remains of the missing people?"

"Because of the protected fish," he said reluctantly. "There's an enormous lake sturgeon that lives in the lake. It's a behemoth that's close to sixty or seventy pounds when it is mature at about twenty years. We really can't drain the entire lake because we'd destroy the ecosystem that support the fish. But the house itself must be on a hill, and a fairly big one at that, because parts of the lake are deep.

We can drop the lake levels to probably about half. It'll be an undertaking, but I think we can do it. The water level will be low enough that we don't have to worry about getting trapped on the island." He stood up and put on his jacket. "I'll have to alert the man who works with the fish. His name's Teeth. He used to run a fishing boat charter business before I closed the lake to people a few years ago."

"If you ruined his business, why would he help you?" Barb asked.

"I know it doesn't make sense, but Teeth prefers the company of fish to people. He never broadcast to me or the public at large that he was working with the sturgeon species recovery. I found out when he showed up at my door, telling me that he would be going out on the lake routinely past my No Trespassing signs to take water and fish samples occasionally to the university."

"You checked that this was legitimate? The university was really working with him?"

Bob nodded. "Of course. He has a recurring grant line that pays him for the work. I don't think he misses the money or the people for his former chartering business, I think he did that mostly so that people boating on his end of the lake wouldn't disturb the fish he was working with. He would take them to spots to catch gamefish fast and divert them away from the sturgeon's main feeding and spawning spots."

"You're telling me that this man routinely goes out boating all around Latham's Landing and hasn't been attacked? He must know about the freezing and thawing. We should talk to him; he might have some information that could help us."

"He won't talk to you, Barb. He doesn't talk to anyone."

"I'm more persistent than most."

"I'm aware of that, but he's more reticent than most. He won't be rude or go ballistic or anything, he'll just excuse himself and leave."

"Have you seen him out on the lake, taking samples?"

"He apparently goes out at night, not in the day. No, I haven't seen him myself, but the lake itself is pretty long and shaped like a jagged tooth. He tends to stay within the end that's narrowest and deepest. The house is roughly in the middle with the beach at the far wide end which is fairly shallow. There are inlets here and there all down the lake where he's got stations set up to check how many fish are feeding there. The adult sturgeon are all tagged. It's surprisingly sophisticated."

"There are no stations right around the island?"

Bob shook his head as he grabbed his coat. "Animals know what the house is, and they stay away. I've never seen any waterbirds wading on the shore there, no seagulls on the docks when they form, or even so much as a frog." *That mermaid or whatever she was, she feeds near the house on the bodies. She'd probably eat the fish, too, if they ventured too close.* "When I raised the level of the lake, the university was supportive because of the sturgeon recovery, as it gave them deeper water to use more of the lake. They're going to fight dropping the water level." Bob got up and went to the door. "I'll also have to call the people who made me the island steward and advise them of what we're going to do. I think they'll agree when I tell them about the local deaths and near misses, as Maryanne called them," Bob answered, as he walked out the door. "They are on our side for whatever reason. Goodnight."

"This all seems so surreal," Maryanne said, as she got her coat on. "I need to go home and pray about this. I'll also do some research about evil spirits." She smiled nervously. "There must be specific prayers that would be useful in this situation. I'll also bless some water and other items, see if I can call a few of my fellow ministers and get their help."

"Will they think you're batty?" Barb asked, hugging her. "Can we count on them to help?"

"I feel in my heart the danger we are facing is real," Maryanne said seriously. "These brothers and sisters in Christ know the lore around my parish, if not the recent developments. It doesn't really matter to me what they think. All that matters is I give us as much protection from God as possible. They can't refuse a request for God's protection, even if they don't believe in the danger themselves. Goodnight."

Barb watched her leave, then shut the door and locked it, pensive. *I'll also go and talk to Carly. Bob and Maryanne are doing all they can. I have to do the same.*

———

Manuel counted as the last of the sheep entered the barn. *Darn it, I'm missing one.* He locked the others in, then warily headed down to the shore, shining his flashlight around as he followed the flocks' tracks in reverse, the rifle slung on his back loaded and ready.

His shoulders slumped when he saw the downed animal a few feet from the lakeshore. Warily, he headed closer to it, looking for wounds. *There's nothing I see. Disease?*

Manual carefully crouched beside the animal and tried to rock it to its feet. Though it wiggled its legs a bit in response and let out a moan, it didn't get up.

"I'm sorry, girl," he murmured. "I'll be back for you." He got up and walked back to the house to his jeep, getting in. *I don't care what the boss and the other sheepmen say, I'm not leaving any living animal near the lake to be food for whatever's in there. I'll try to winch her up, and if that fails, I'll kill her and haul her back on a tarp.* He started the engine, then backed up, swinging the jeep around to face the lake. As he did, he stopped cold, an icy chill in his blood.

The sick sheep was up, standing near the barn. It raised a hoof and pawed at the door.

"Good girl," Manuel praised, getting out and coming over. "You made it up yourself."

The sheep let out what sounded like a cough that became a sort of snort, then almost a rumbling snore, as if it were fighting for breath. It pawed the door again.

There were some terrified baas from the barn, then the flock inside began to scream in panic.

Manuel stopped still, reaching for his gun as the sheep pawed one more time at the door, turning so the huge bloody hole in its side was now visible, the concave wound caked with blood. As he leveled the gun and aimed, the sheep turned to look at him, its dead eyes glazed over, and cocked its head. It let out a snoring sound again that deepened to a threatening growl, its mouth yawning wide.

Manuel fired, the bullet hitting the dead sheep right between the eyes, dropping it in its tracks. But as he watched it flailed again on its side, then awkwardly regained its feet, eerily moving its legs in a disjointed fashion as if it were a spider. It coughed again, then hissed, scuttling toward him.

Manuel fired until his gun was empty, blowing off two of the sheep's legs, the carcass falling over on its side just in front of him. It was still moving, trying to get up with creaking gasps when he doused it with gasoline and burned the carcass. Only then did it stop moving.

CHAPTER SIX

One Month Later

"MY DEFINITION OF JOY IS SITTING HERE ON A COLD NIGHT NEAR A warm woodfire and tucking bits of food into your mouth. That's what you think, right?"

Jinx, the small black and tan German Shepherd mix, wagged her extra-long tail happily, and opened her mouth expectantly again, her eyes going to the last bit of roll lying on Carly's plate. She laughed and gave it to her, then gave a bit of cheese to another German Shepherd-husky mix, Skinny, laying on the floor at her feet, then tossed the last chunk to the enormous black German Shepherd stretched out on the floor. Inferno raised his head and snapped it expertly out of the air, then swallowed and stretched back out with a sigh.

"Well, you may be right," Carly said, leaning back and closing her eyes. *You can't sit here too much longer. There's spring prep coming up fast. And that's besides the normal cleaning up the kitchen and bills and laundry.*

Inferno raised his head suddenly. He let out a threatening growl, looking toward the front door, which lay in shadows two rooms away.

"What is it?" Carly asked.

Inferno leapt to his feet, his hackles up, barking fiercely. Skinny and Jinx ran to his side, standing between Carly and the door, also barking angrily. Carly reached up to her earlobe, fingering her earring. *There can't be anything there, the door is locked plus deadbolted.* She moved past the dogs and reached for the light.

A venomous hiss sounded, as the shadows in front of her *moved*.

"Ahh!" Carly yelled, startled, as she flipped the switch. Light flooded the room, showing it to be empty.

The dogs charged past her, still barking and growling, hackles up as they checked the empty room, then raced to the window, resuming their frantic barking.

Carly moved past them to the door, and switched on the outside light, illuminating most of the fenced backyard. There was a slight motion in the shadows at the end of the yard, then all was still.

Carly got a flashlight, then went out into the yard. She scanned the ground, looking for any sign of anything amiss, but there was nothing.

Something brushed her outer thigh, and she let out a cry, wheeling to see Inferno, his hackles down. "What was it?" she said, scratching him behind the ears.

The dog let out a low growl, still looking beyond the fence.

"C'mon," Carly said, walking back toward the house. "We need to go to bed. And tomorrow I'll ask Pastor Taylor to come back again and bless the inside of the house, too."

———

A half-moon shone down on the water with its perfect reflection mirrored below, together looking as if two glowing eyes watched the shore hungrily. The lake surface roiled in a sudden wind, as whitecaps began rolling fast across its surface, gathering both speed and size. Trees on the shore bent in the howling gale, branches snapping like gunshots, whipping across the sky to slam into the ground or splash into the water.

There was a grinding sound, as if rusty metal gears turned together, then suddenly seized. A light shone beneath the water, the beam erupting up through the surface like a gigantic flashlight. A few miles down the lake the old mansion appeared, at first hazy, then solidified, mists hissing up where the hot dry clapboard was suddenly submerged. Waves rocked against the base of the house, the water churning.

There was a crash of glass breaking, and the front window of the second story shattered, glass tinkling as it arced out in a cloud to shower the porch roof. A man climbed out onto the roof, then immediately jumped off, landing with a splash in the water. He began swimming hard for shore, his dark head bobbing first above then beneath the waves. He was halfway to shore when a dark shadow began tailing him just beneath the water, stalking silently. Soon, two more shadows joined the hunt, and the three began to close in. They darted in as he passed the trespassing prohibited sign on the sunken post.

The man yelled and thrashed in the water, a black stain spreading around him, as another shape darted in for attack. He grabbed hold of the sign, knocking it off the post as he struck at his attacker, and it flashed backward, blood streaming from the knife wound. He swum on, still bleeding, as the two shadows attacked the wounded one, the dark cloudy water engulfing them as he staggered to shore, collapsing on the dry land.

As the moon shone down, the surface of the second story window rippled, the glass reforming into an unbroken sheet with a slight tinkling of glass.

———

"I'm glad you are hosting in your home tonight," Barb said, as she accepted a cup of coffee from Bob. Cooper laid down with a sigh at her feet. "But who is this?" She smiled at the tall, tanned woman with her hair in braids.

"Cheer Daniels," the woman said, offering a hand. "New York Confidential."

"This is the reporter I mentioned," Bob said awkwardly. "I invited her. She's aware of everything, so feel free to talk."

Barb gaped at him. "What?"

"I have seen enough and read enough about Latham's Landing to know there's something bad there," Cheer said, taking back her hand. "I'm here to help if I can. I came here to dig up facts about Mac and his island of terrors. Then I heard about the recent disappearances and contacted Bob to get his statement on what he'd seen during his time as chief. He was kind enough to tell me the truth, trying to save my life. Plus, I've compared descriptions of the house from a couple survivors and blurry or partial photos from a recovered camera and two cell phones of victims." She paused. "They are of the same house. I'm a believer. Moreover, I have spent the day researching Hans Latham on the Internet and looking at some older records that may really help us stop the murders."

"Who's a believer?" Maryanne piped up, as she came in the front door. "It's a cold night out there. You wouldn't think it was spring. It feels more like snow. Thanks for having us, Bob."

"Glad to stay in on a night like this," Bob replied, handing a steaming cup to Maryanne. "Here you go. Does anyone want to start?"

"I was able to contact a few of my friends," Maryanne volunteered. "I am meeting with them tomorrow night. I'll get some holy water, a few cross necklaces and bracelets, even some Christian shirts, candles, and a few other things charged with blessings and prayer. When we're ready to use them, they'll be at my home ready to go."

"I didn't get much with the library records," Barb offered glumly. "I'm sorry also it took so long, but there was delay after delay, as they were changing computer systems. Anyway, there are mentions of the island each year when people die, but I didn't recognize any of the pictures of missing or deceased people I saw in the papers as ghosts I'd seen on the island. There's no mention of any girl with a flute, or any middle-aged black woman or man that were ever killed there, only teens." She paused. "I forgot to mention, I also saw a ship on the lake at night, manned by skeletons. It was a scene right out of the old movie The Fog: full wood pirate ship with three tattered sails appeared out of the mist. The ghosts manning the ship looked at me, but they didn't land on the island, they sailed past."

"Never heard of a ship being seen before," Bob said slowly. "Are you sure you saw it?"

"I didn't want to mention this before, but my guess is it is very likely that all kinds of things have been seen, it's just that the people that saw them died right after," Maryanne said grimly. "I believe you, Barb. What about the true events at the initial death of Latham's wife, or the creation of the island?"

"There was a small article about a coastal shipbuilder Mr. Latham moving here and buying up several farms, then another article ten years later about a tragedy on the island. But it wasn't his wife that died first, it was his youngest son, Hans Jr.. He fell down the main house staircase and broke his neck. That's likely the ghost of the boy on the stairs that we've heard about. There are a few other articles in the next year about mysterious deaths in the county, people going missing. A farmer, a few teens, and a rich young couple who disappeared in their car."

"The mermaid?" Bob asked.

Barb shook her head. "No, because reports of people going missing go on for a couple more years, then Latham suddenly decides to raise the water in his lake and develop the far end. He has the beach put in and that end of the lake widened, and gets funds to change Town Road, so it runs to the lake edge. He arranged for a youth camp to be built near the beach, and then also the Dockhouse where he held private parties, which later became the bed and breakfast then part of the historical society before it closed. He also built or financed several marinas and restaurants on the lake, including the Sea Captain. These changes were put in a very positive light by the paper that Latham wanted to give back to the town and share the land and lake. Every article mentions that he's creating jobs for locals and helping local businesses, as he sold the youth camp and the various marinas and restaurants to locals and employed locals at his Dockhouse. Some of the new owners are named as if every local at the time knew them. Like the owner of the Sea Captain, a literal naval Captain Tiger Garrison."

"We should check out the Dockhouse if he built it and then used it himself exclusively," Bob interjected. "Why would a man who wanted privacy open his own lake to the public? Because something was causing deaths, and he didn't want any of his family to die?"

Barb nodded. "I think you have it exactly, Bob. The first summer with the entire lake being used was a huge success. But that November brought disaster. There's a small article screaming flood as a headline, and it shows pictures of the roiling lake covering the beach and the end of Town Road and encroaching all the way to the youth camp. Apparently thirteen people died in the flood. There's also a picture there of the island, which, guess what? Looks just like it does now, with the one side of the house flooded. Too bad there's no 'before' picture."

"So Latham didn't go crazy and flood the island purposely," Bob mused. "Whatever is in the house now arrived then, and it did its storm trick launching a massive rainfall to flood everything and Latham couldn't let the water out fast enough. Is this when Latham's wife died?"

Barb nodded. "Yes, but it doesn't say how she died, though it's alluded that she likely drowned, and that Latham killed himself shortly after the stock crash of 1929. That's all I have."

"I have a few additions," Cheer spoke up eagerly. "Latham had two sons: Hans Jr. who died in the house and his eldest son Carl who also died by drowning previous to his brother. Similar to Barb's findings, there's no specifics on exactly how he drowned or why. After Latham and his wife died, the house and lake passed to some distant descendants who didn't pay the taxes. Within a few years everything passed to the state, which sold it at auction with almost all its furnishings. It was only after the new owners took possession that people began to disappear, and reading the papers, it's hard to say that it was something in the house or even just the island."

"Because those that went missing weren't on the lake when they went missing?"

Cheer shook her head, her braids moving like shiny snakes. "It seems to be just bad luck. A group of boys went missing at the youth camp, presumed drowned in the lake, though the day was clear. The camp closed because of the bad publicity. There was a murder at the Sea Captain, and a few bad fights, and one of the injured patrons sued. Again, a lot of bad publicity. Captain Garrison had a heart attack from the stress, and his bar closed. The other restaurants went under one by one, until only the two marinas and the Dockhouse was left, the latter in bad shape. The historical society intervened then and bought the mansion and island and the Dockhouse. They arranged tours to the mansion, made the Dockhouse into a bed and breakfast, and put out a request for any artifacts or pictures having to do with Latham, his family, or the island. They must have gotten a plethora, because they made part of the Dockhouse into a small museum dedicated to Latham's Landing. But that went south quickly when there was an accident on one of the tours. A little girl fell in the water, and a man went in after her. He saved her, but he died. Official cause of death was a heart attack. A man named Brad something bought the Sea Captain and renovated it, but again people went missing within a few months, and then Brad went missing himself, so the property ended up at auction again. The museum closed from lack of funds, then the bed and breakfast closed after the first mass killing, and the Dockhouse also ended up at auction. In a span of a couple decades the lake reverted to being used only by fishermen, boat rental shops, and beachgoers, with the rest of the shoreline used as pasture by the local sheep farmers and the former restaurants and bars abandoned. After that, kids began to go to the island or drown around it regularly."

"It sounds to me like there have been missing people and deaths since the house was built, that Latham may have let other people onto the lake, even created it in an effort to keep his own family safe," Barb said slowly. "His plan didn't work, he just bought a few more years. Once he and his were gone and so were all the surrounding businesses, the evil force focused on lakegoers as the last humans it had access to. It follows then that when Bob removed that source, the evil had to find another way to find victims."

"Is there any way to get in the Dockhouse and look at some of the artifacts?" Maryanne asked. "I don't remember anything about a museum."

Barb shook her head. "The museum and bed and breakfast were only around for a few years. The Dockhouse burned down to the foundation after it was abandoned. We can try to check with some of the former employees at the historical society, maybe they saved some souvenirs?" She paused. "Did you get the all-clear to drop the water level, Bob?"

"The behind-the-scenes powers that be weren't keen on the idea. But when I explained about the travelling haunted mansion and mounting deaths, plus the local near misses, I got the go ahead. Teeth was harder to convince. He said he wants to be on hand when we drain the water. I said sure."

"He'll think we're crazy, you know," Barb said, rolling her eyes.

"He might, but that can't be helped. The only way the state would agree was to have him there in case we accidentally strand one of the sturgeons. I did get a diagram of the lake I hadn't seen before of the depth and topology. It indicates the house does sit on a hill, but that it's a pretty short one that's very wide, almost a raised plateau. The Sea Room is also on this same hill. There's a deep valley on one side of the plateau, and a much shallower valley on the other with some odd deep depressions."

"So?" Cheer said.

"So, that's another reason boats crash and there's such large waves in storms – the lake really is shallow around the island, pretty much all the way to the beach. More importantly, this means when we lower the water level, we will end up with deep water at the narrow end where the fish will be, low or no water at the beach end, and the middle of the lake around the house and Sea Room should be pretty dry with only a few pools of water, maybe what looks like a partial moat around both."

"This could really work," Barb said excitedly. "I looked into Carolyn's background, and found out where she lived, then called around to the few wiccan supply stores nearby. I located the one she sourced her herbs from and paid the woman close to six hundred dollars to send me the same things that she gave to Carolyn. They should be here in a week to ten days."

"I'm uncomfortable with this...witchcraft," Maryanne stated, a look of revulsion on her face. She put up her hand, as her two friends and Cheer began to protest. "But I'm choosing to look at it just as herbology, like a vampire with garlic. Barb said the plants worked, and I'm not about to argue. Clearly whatever evil force is there believes the plants to be harmful. That's enough for me."

"And me," Barb continued with a faint smile. "There's no information on any old servants. The old woman's skeleton that was found right after the first mass killing there was going to be cremated, but it was sent instead to the local college for their forensic pathology lab. Bob, any idea why?"

"Mrs. Latham, if this is she, must have died in some unusual way," he said, pursing his lips. "I'll go up there tomorrow and make an inquiry, take pictures and notes." He paused. "Cheer, why don't you come with me? If you say it's for a story, they'll be more inclined to give access."

"Press doesn't always get treated with respect," Cheer said with a grimace. "But I'm glad to help if I can."

Bob's phone rang, and he opened it. Before he could speak, he stopped, his eyes widening. "I'll be right there."

"What's happened?" Maryanne asked.

"There's an unidentified body on the lakeshore," Bob said, as he hung up. "The chief said it looks bitten in places."

———

"Stay back, and don't take pictures," Bob warned, as he left the other three at his car, and headed into the sea of lights. He couldn't help looking out over the dark lake in the direction of the sunken mansion, but there were no lights on the lake. The night was serene and would have been pretty, if not for the overpowering stench of death.

He nodded to the officer on duty, then went to Chief Sal Upner. He was taking a statement from a burly, tanned man that had tattoos of two monster fish running down the inside of both his forearms. *Teeth*. His nickname came not from buckteeth, but because some of his upper front teeth were filed to points, just like a shark's.

Teeth gave a nod to Bob and a slight smile. "Hi."

"So you were out on the lake in your boat, Shark's Smile, and you noticed the body?" Upner asked.

"Smelled him," Teeth said, grimacing. "I followed my nose and used my megawatt flashlight to pinpoint the body. Then I called it in, turned on my hazard emergency lights, and waited for you to get here."

"Were you surprised to find him?" Bob asked pointedly.

Teeth regarded him for a moment before answering. "Honestly, yes, I was. No one's supposed to be out here; you've got it posted to hell and gone. Can't miss those signs. I headed out here to make a circle of the lake as I'm missing a few fish. I thought they might have died and washed up on shore. I noticed one of your signs was off the post as I went past here but didn't think it was anything more than weathering and rotten wood. But the wind was also blowing towards the beach, and I was travelling with it. I smelled the carcass right after I came about to go back down the lake and came right here."

"The body's got to have been here for at least twenty-four hours, probably dead for twice that," the pathologist said, as he took off his gloves. "I'll have more for you tomorrow, Chief." He headed away, his vehicle following the ambulance that headed off toward town, its sirens silent.

"Nothing else was out of place? Nothing else happened?" Upner asked.

Teeth shook his head. "Nothing."

"Alright, go home. I'll contact you tomorrow if we have any more questions."

"Teeth, can you come meet a couple people," Bob said, following as Teeth headed to his boat. "It'll only take a minute."

"Bob, I wanted to talk to you!" Upner shouted after them.

"I'll be right back," Bob yelled back. "One minute!"

Teeth shrugged, then followed Bob back to his truck.

"Teeth, this is Barb. She's the one who was out on the island and survived. You know Maryanne, the pastor? And this is Cheer Daniels, a reporter."

Cheer offered her hand again with a smile. "Glad to meet you."

Teeth made no move to take it. "I have nothing to say." He turned away.

Cooper, who had been standing next to Barb, looked out toward the water, and let out a threatening growl.

"What is it?" Barb said, holding tight to his leash.

Cooper growled again. There was a distant splash, then silence.

"Tell us about the mermaid," Bob said softly. "That's her out there now, isn't it? Checking on what we're talking about, so she can report back to island management. You've seen her, haven't you? She's to blame for this death, isn't she?" He paused. "I've seen her, Teeth. She smiled at me and talked about eating people."

Teeth stopped walking, then glared at Bob, but didn't say anything.

"I starved the house, but it found a way to get what it needed," Bob continued, holding his gaze. "But that left the mermaid and her kin unfed, so they began taking sheep from the shore. But that doesn't explain why Manuel lived when he should have died." He paused. "I think he was returned unharmed because Dakota was going to drop the water level in the lake looking for Manuel's body and for some reason the island can't have that happen."

Teeth was silent, staring at him.

"They're going to ask for a bite sample, Teeth. From you, because of your teeth and because you found the body tonight. I always thought you filed them sharp like a fish for some reason. They are like that because you altered them, right? Or are those your *natural teeth?*"

Teeth held Bob's gaze and said nothing.

"I have the go ahead to drain the water tomorrow back to the level of the historic flooding, to expose the house foundation," Bob stated. "But I'm going to keep draining to expose the entire island surface and most of the lakebed to the beach. I've gotten permission from the University. Can you meet me here at noon?"

"I sleep days, as I work nights," Teeth replied coolly. "It'll have to be tomorrow night. And I work alone."

"Then tomorrow night," Bob agreed. "But be aware that the lake level is already dropping right now. I'll meet you here at dusk, before the sun sets. You can work all night by yourself making sure the fish aren't stranded. In the morning I'll be back to see what's revealed."

"Ayuh," Teeth said coarsely, then grinned at the group baring his filed teeth, the effect like a human shark that made them visibly recoil. He went to his boat, started the engine, then left.

"Are you sure it wasn't him that killed that man?" Cheer whispered. "And ate him?"

"I'm not sure," Bob said, watching the boat motor away over the placid lake. "Not anymore."

————

"What about Manuel?" Cheer asked, as they drove back to Bob's house. "You hadn't told me about him."

Bob filled her in. "It hasn't occurred to me until now, but if the mermaid was killing the sheep, Teeth would have seen something at some point in the last two years. He also would have had to have seen her at least a few times before that with the amount of time he spends on the lake. My guess is that she did drag Manuel in the water, and Teeth somehow got him away from her, saved him."

"What did the chief say about the victim tonight?" Barb asked.

"That the man's femoral artery was bitten through, and that he was attacked in relatively shallow water, like a shark. Also, that there were two other bites on the body, and both were different sizes from the one that killed him. So, there's at least three merfolk, or whatever you want to call them, and they're hunting in a pack."

"If they all bit him, why was there a body to find?" Barb commented.

"I'm guessing he stabbed at least one of them," Bob answered. "There was a hunting knife found on the shore by his hand and an empty scabbard on the man's belt. Upner said he'd have it tested for blood at the police lab."

"But nothing else washed up?"

Bob shook his head. "No. But this is the first time I can remember that a body's washed up on shore. It's like the island doesn't care anymore about covering its tracks and making sure the dead disappear."

"Maybe it's desperation?" Maryanne offered.

A few flakes began to drift down, then more, until they were sticking to the windshield. "Was there supposed to be snow tonight?" Bob said in irritation, turning on the wipers.

"No," Maryanne said hoarsely. "Just rain."

The snow was coming down hard by the time that Bob's car pulled into his driveway. "You're welcome to stay over if you like," he called, as the three women ran to their cars.

"Thanks, but no!" Barb called, as Cooper jumped in the car, and she climbed in after and slammed the door. "We need to get home."

———

"I can't believe this!" Barb raged, as she paced back and forth, looking out her window at the fresh foot of snow blanketing her lawn. Little heads of daffodils that had been ready to open peeked out in clumps from the thick white fluff, while huge clumps swirled down, then blasted against the house as another gust buffeted from the southwest. "What do you mean we're under a travel ban?"

"I mean the lake isn't getting lowered today," Bob said, looking at his own wall of white as the snow began falling faster. "It's supposed to stop by ten a.m., but we've got a good week of cleanup. I have branches down all over my yard, and I wouldn't be talking to you if we didn't have cell phones. My power's out, the internet and cable are out, and the landline is out."

"You still have a landline?" Barb snorted.

"I was the chief for many years, and it's the one number people memorized for me," Bob said tartly. "Go nap or read a book or something. We'll try again next week. Bye."

"Bye," Barb said, hanging up her cell. She looked at Cooper, who wagged his tail. "How about a walk, Cooper? Carly's only about a mile or so, and the roads are cleared."

Cooper barked once, as Barb put her coat on.

———

"I can't believe you came out on a day like today," Carly said, as she let in Barb and Cooper. The four dogs began chasing each other, and Carly pushed past them to open the back door, where all four animals bounded out into the snow. "Here!" Carly said, tossing out three balls.

"Shouldn't you toss one more?" Barb asked.

"You have one dog," Carly joked with a smile. "Only two of my dogs will tussle over a ball, and even then, it's the same ball they want, the others get ignored." She handed Barb a glass of wine. "To what do I owe the pleasure?"

"Don't you think it's a bit early?" Barb said, putting the wine on the counter.

"Maybe for you," Carly said, sipping her wine. "But I need my wits about me once it's dark, hon. I don't often get a day off, and I want to enjoy it. But I'll be stone cold sober before that sky in the west turns colors."

"What have you seen?" Barb asked.

"Nothing," Carly said evasively.

"Tell me," Barb demanded shrilly, making Carly step back. "I swear to you right now that I think we got this snowstorm because something at that lake overheard Bob Stahl last night when he told Teeth that he was going to lower the water in the lake today. It delayed him so it would have time to decide what to do."

Carly was pale now. Her hand shook a bit as she put the glass down on the counter. "It was dumb to threaten that standing right at the lakeshore. Real dumb."

"What's there? What have you seen?"

"The same kinds of things you've seen," Carly shot back, her eyes narrowing. "You almost got killed there. I read the papers. You know what's there: evil."

"Why have you asked Pastor Taylor to bless your house? She said she was here today."

"So much for the privacy of religion," Carly said sarcastically.

"Look, I want to know. I want to stop it, Carly."

"You can't stop it," Carly said anxiously, twisting her hands together. "It followed me home. I had the house blessed and it somehow still got inside. So far, it's not done anything but scare me, but it keeps getting closer." Her eyes bored into Barb's, the edge of panic in her tone. "Closer every time. How long until I wake up at night and something's leaning over me, softly hissing?"

Hisses. Husterman. A wave of fear engulfed Barb, and she shivered, then stood up straight. "I'll stay here with you tonight, if you like."

"Why do you want to involve yourself?" Carly said in surprise. "You're not being targeted."

"Because I have an idea of what's taken an interest in you. And an idea of how to stop it."

———

Carly glanced out at the setting sun, and pulled her curtains across, blocking out the sight. "If Hustermen are souls wandering free, are they draining part of the soul of the victims – or draining life by mistake, leaving a damaged soul that then becomes another Husterman?"

She seems to have taken my explanation seriously. "We don't know," Barb answered. "Carolyn's body wasn't found, and neither was my brother's. If the flesh is the fuel to let the soul wander free as Sylvia said, then it makes sense that if a body isn't found and the Hustermen were known to be in the area at the time, then the missing person became a Husterman, too. Hustermen eat the souls of evildoers, but the two victims I know of weren't evil."

"Maybe that's the problem," Carly said, sitting down heavily in her kitchen chair. "They weren't evil. So they get their soul gnawed on a bit but either the Hustermen can't eat it all because it's not evil, or they don't like the taste or whatever. But a vampire's bite that doesn't kill makes another vampire. So a Husterman that doesn't kill but damages or taints the soul makes another Husterman. A Husterman that does get someone who's really evil ends up killing and leaving a body behind."

"That's the best explanation I've heard," Barb said, her eyes widening. "Damn it, I should have thought of that."

Inferno growled suddenly, then sprang to his feet.

There was movement in the hallway, as the shadows seemed to deepen. The other three dogs began growling too, stepping up to face the threat.

"Get the dogs back behind us," Barb said urgently. She faced the shadows, which were now solid black. "Carolyn, if that's you, please speak to me like you did to Bob Stahl. We want to help."

Carly grabbed Inferno's collar, putting the other two dogs on a dual leash. She led them into the bright kitchen and then came back for Cooper, who whined as she pulled him into the kitchen.

The shadows got blacker, and then a human-like figure made of darkness oozed out of them to stand just inside the doorway.

"Carolyn!" Barb yelled.

"Sister?" the form asked weakly.

Barb wanted to rush forward but held back. *That's not my brother.* "Carolyn, Bob said you were the leader. Please, speak to me."

A much darker form flowed through the doorway, consuming the first. It rose into the air, solidifying. Two bright yellow points of light appeared, focusing on her from seven feet above the floor.

"Husterman," Barb stated, her fingers digging into her palms. "There are no evildoers in this house. Please leave."

"Thief," the shadow whispered, swaying a bit from side to side. Suddenly it looked behind Barb right at Carly, then leaped forward.

Carly shrieked, holding onto her lunging, snarling dogs.

"She's no thief!" Barb shouted, stepping in front of Carly.

"Thief," the shadow repeated, the whisper insistent and hungry.

"They were rocks," Carly gasped. "Just rocks from the shoreline. No one cared I took them."

This isn't Carolyn or my brother. It must be the original Husterman. "Bob Stahl owns the land near the shore. But he wouldn't begrudge her some rocks. Leave this house."

The shadow jerked, then weaved its torso, its eyes steady on Carly. "Trespasser," it hissed. Then it growled and took another step forward.

Does it remember its creation, to attack trespassers? Shit! "Stahl is going to drain the lake. We were going to do it today, but then we had the snowstorm. There are evil souls on the island. You can cross to it and get them. You must get to the island, the evil there is out of control!"

The Husterman blinked its eyes, as if considering her words. "Water," it hissed finally. "Guardian. Protect her from trespassers." The shadows roiled again, the eyes jerking from side to side. "The girl. The old woman. Pain. Suffering."

"Sylvia was sorry she made you wrong. She didn't mean it to happen," Barb said. "But—"

The eyes suddenly focused on her, then dropped with incredible speed to hover right in front of her face. "Liar," it hissed, then growling, moved closer, tensing to spring.

"I'm sorry she made you," Barb shouted, stumbling backwards. "I'm not evil! I almost died on that island when evil things attacked me. You are evil! You killed my brother, and you killed Carolyn by attacking them when they weren't evil. You're a murderer!"

The shadow swayed back and forth, then suddenly it closed its glowing eyes and screeched. The figure dissipated, and the shadows lightened as they became empty of malice once more.

"I did it," Barb said, leaning heavily against the door frame. "My God."

"Wow," Carly said. "Thanks doesn't cover it. But I don't understand what you did that made it leave."

"Somehow, a Husterman can see into your soul, see what's truth, what you've done, maybe what you're guilty about. Makes sense they can see a soul if that's what they're supposed to eat. They could see you took the rocks."

"They did see me take them, maybe," Carly admitted. "I was at the shore a few times getting rocks. That last time was the day of that big storm, when the road flooded and my truck battery died, and I had to walk home. A shadowy figure watched me from near that housing development at the lake where those people got killed. It was waiting for me on my porch when I got home. But I didn't feel guilty then." She shivered. "This is the first time it spoke."

"Before it feeds, it must confront the victim with its crime, like it did just now." Barb suggested. "Even if someone isn't really guilty, they initially feel a flash of guilt when they are accused, like you did with the rocks. That seems to be enough to prompt an attack."

"And another Husterman comes into being because the victim isn't evil." Carly shot her a look of approval. "You've got guts, Barb, to stand up to that thing."

"A Husterman isn't real evil. I've seen enough to know." Barb snorted, her feistiness returning. "What's the worst thing a righteous person can discover about themselves? That they aren't really righteous. It called me a liar and I told it the truth about itself, something it couldn't deny. I don't think you'll have any more problems with Hustermen. But I wouldn't go near the lake for a while, either."

"You don't have to even say it. How can I repay you?"

"Come to my house tomorrow and tell me everything you know about Latham's Landing," Barb said, putting on her coat. "Including your rock picking excursion tale."

"I'll be there, but it's going to be in the daytime tomorrow so I can be home before dark," Carly agreed. "There's more than Hustermen out at night now. Thanks again."

"You're welcome. Come on Cooper."

CHAPTER SEVEN

"I'm not sure what I'm hoping to find, Anita," Maryanne said, as she followed another woman into the storage unit. "I hoped that you'd have some of the documents from the Dockhouse. Any papers I could see about the history of Latham or his family would help. Really anything."

"The fire destroyed most everything," Anita answered in her shrill voice. "We had some of the original furniture from the island, the better pieces. They were hand-carved oak. Some of the paintings of the family, too, but they were pretty deteriorated. It was hard to make out faces or much of anything. As for documents, the only thing we had on display was the deed to the island. That was taken by the state when the island was foreclosed on for taxes. Bob Stahl must have it now."

Maryanne made a note on her pad. "Check. Okay. So, what are you showing me here then?"

"The historical society got a bunch of donations when we announced that we were making the Dockhouse into a museum, and tours of the island were going to start." She paused, as if resigned. "Everybody wanted the tours to be a success. While we were going for a mysterious, maybe even creepy tone, we didn't want to focus on horror or murder. So, we screened the donations. Some of the history we presented was edited."

"Edited how?"

Anita handed Maryanne a half-empty box, then put a few files on the top. "There wasn't much, really. Just the really strange and gruesome events. We didn't want to promote Latham's Landing as a murder house. Now that kind of thing would be popular, but back forty years ago there hadn't been any terrible deaths. Well, that most people knew about, anyway." She grimaced. "Maybe if we'd presented everything we found, we'd have been more of a success."

Or maybe the mass deaths of young adults seeking thrills would just have begun that much sooner. "Can I keep these, or do you want me to make copies?" Maryanne asked.

"I've got to get rid of this storage unit," Anita said with a smile. "It's past time to downsize at my age. You might as well keep them. The other women who worked at the museum with me have either passed on or moved away. Some of what's there is already a copy, if the owner who submitted it wanted to keep the original."

"Thanks for this, Anita. I really appreciate it. Do you want to get a cup of coffee? I'd like to pick your brain if you don't mind."

"Sure," Anita said, following her out and closing the unit door. "Just let me lock up."

———

"I'm sorry for the delay," Professor Godelman said, as he showed Cheer into Latham Hall. "I was out of the country giving some talks on remains of Eastern Europeans during the time of the black plague the last couple weeks."

"That's okay," Cheer assured. "What can you tell me about the skeleton of Latham's wife?"

"Well, first, we aren't sure that this is the skeleton of Latham's wife," Godelman answered. "We only know that this skeleton was dated to be around the correct age as Latham's wife, a woman in her twenties or early thirties. Dating older skeletons is harder with carbon-14 dating. When the skeleton is this young, the process is more accurate."

"So do you think this is Latham's wife?" Cheer asked. "I'm just interested in your personal opinion."

"I don't think it is, no," Godelman said, stopping before a painting of an elegant couple dressed in the high fashion of the 1920's. "Here's a picture of Mr. Latham and his wife. It was gifted to the university back when they donated the money for Latham Hall. This was around the time when Latham was pouring a lot of money into the community, developing tourism around the lake as well as making the beach and summer camp."

Cheer took a couple pictures of the painting. "What exactly did he fund for the University?"

"This Hall, and an endowed chair to study disease. I'm the faculty member that was hired to be the chair." He beamed. "That's why I know a bit of the history. I have Latham to thank for my position here."

"Are there any parameters that the chair has? Specific diseases you must study? You mentioned plague."

"Black plague always fills seats at convention talks," Godelman said with a shrug. "No, there's no stipulation that any specific disease be the chair's specialty."

"Why don't you think this is Latham's wife? She was found in the house foundations."

"Latham was a wealthy man. This woman was poor, or at least, she grew up poor. Her bones show advanced signs of osteoporosis. At her age of death, her bones should have been in prime of life with strong density. These bones are much more brittle than they should be."

"Would being in the water for many years affect that?"

Godelman shook his head. "That shouldn't have had any effect on the bones. Now, I'm not saying that this isn't Latham's wife. She could have had a genetic disorder like Paget's disease, maybe even osteoporosis imperfecta. But I think it more likely that this woman was someone who drowned in the lake many years ago, probably when Latham was first building his house. Possibly she was a maid or a cook. In those days there was usually a graveyard on any big estate and that's where members of the family were buried, along with loyal servants."

"But she was found in the house itself," Cheer remarked pointedly. "Did you find any marks on the bones to indicate how she died?"

Godelman narrowed his eyes, his expression angry. "I don't appreciate what you're implying, Miss. If you knew anything about bodies, which you clearly do not, you'd know that bodies take a long time to decompose, especially if they are wrapped in shrouds that preserve them or interred in rocky ground. Yes, the skeleton was found in the house, but it was a part of the house that has been flooded now for some eighty years at least. Almost every year we have big storms here, and sometimes the lake shore floods. It would have been easy for a body to float to the lake from the shore in the first few years that it was flooded, maybe even in the lake's initial flooding. By the time it arrived, water would have penetrated the wrappings and decay would set in. The body would sink wherever it was as soon as the lungs deflated, with which this particular body wouldn't have been long." He stalked away.

"Why is that? Why wouldn't it have been long?" Cheer chased after him. "Please I need to know."

"This woman had four cracked ribs, with signs that other ribs had broken before and been set so they healed perfectly, which is why I think she had brittle bones. But no, there was no signs of violent death. Now if you'll excuse me." He pushed past her.

"You think she's some anonymous woman who was secretly buried on the lakeshore?"

"You really should do your research," Godelman sneered, turning to face her. "Latham's estate extended all around the lakeshore, which is how he was able to divide it up and sell parcels off to build the businesses and donate land for public works that he funded, like the beach and Camp Leighton. Any undertaking like that is going to cost some people their lives, especially as building his island estate involved hundreds of workers and lasted for several years. Latham funded a park and a cemetery on the few parcels he didn't sell. Both flooded when he flooded the island, and most of the graves were likely washed into the lake." He gave her a final glare. "If you have any more questions go ask someone else." He turned and left.

"A cemetery," Cheer said, hitting rewind on her phone's recording button. Godelman's voice said, "...hundreds of workers and lasted for several years..." She shut it off. "Finally, a real lead."

———

The noise came again from the attic above: a faint clawing, skittering sound of something too big to be a mouse.

Wil awoke in his bed and peeped out beneath his blankets to stare at the ceiling, holding his breath, willing the sound to just be part of his dream. *I do not want to go up there in the dark.*

The sound came again of something digging into wood above him.

"Damn it," Wil swore softly, then got out of bed, slipping into his robe and sneakers. He grabbed his phone and headed to the attic door, picking up a two-foot-long aluminum piece of bicycle frame as he went past his worktable. *Better to have it and not need it than the reverse.*

He put his hand on the door and listened. There was only silence. *I do not want to go up there in the dark.*

The clawing sound came again faintly.

"You're going to regret getting me out of bed," he said aloud, then twisted the door handle and threw open the door. He stomped up the steps and reached for the light switch and flipped it. Nothing happened. *Just great.*

Wil switched on his flashlight on his phone and went up the rest of the steps holding it in front of him with one hand, the piece of aluminum held like a club in the other fist. He stopped at the top of the stairs and panned the flashlight around in a circle. There was nothing to see in the attic except dust and a few old boxes and insulation. He waited a few moments but there was only silence.

Wil sighed and turned, heading toward the stairs. As he did a soft clawing sound came from his left, as if something was burrowing into the wood. With a gasp he swung the light toward the sound, revealing just empty space.

"Damn it," he breathed, then let out a yell as a ragged black shape fluttered down by his ear, dropping the phone. *Just a piece of old tar paper.* As he bent to retrieve it there came a rasp of scrabbling claws, then rapid clicking as whatever it was headed right for him. With a yell he ran down the stairs, a far too large black shape at the top letting out a menacing hiss as he slammed the door and locked it. Breathing hard, he dragged a bookcase in front of the attic door, then also his couch, then stood there listening.

There came a series of clicks and creaks, claws rasping on the stairs as whatever it was descended, then stopped still before the attic door. Wil held his breath, the piece of aluminum held in both hands, ready like a club.

There came another venomous hiss, then the doorknob began to wiggle slightly.

Screw this! Wil turned and ran to his bedroom with his club, locking the door and barricading it behind him.

———

"There were no pics of a girl with a flute that I ever saw," Anita said to Maryanne, shaking her head. "Sorry. I've heard the stories about people seeing her, but I never did. I don't think Latham particularly cared for music." She sipped her coffee. "Next."

Maryanne had made a pile of the articles whose events she was familiar with and those she wasn't. *Most of these are just on various drownings in the lake, dang. Just focus on the others.* "Okay, this brief clipping talks about the Dockhouse when it was first built. It says that Latham made it to house several large boats which he kept under the building, with a dock and stairs leading down to the water made of stone. The upstairs was two stories, with one being a kitchen, dining room and main room for gathering, the second floor being bedrooms, five in total. There's no attic listed. The picture is very grainy, but seems to show the Dockhouse at night with the lights lit and a party going on outside?"

"Yes, I wasn't born then, but that's what it looks like to me. When the historical society converted the Dockhouse in the late 60s, the bedrooms were eventually used as a bed and breakfast, with the main gathering room divided into a small eating area and the space where we displayed the photos and furniture which I mentioned. That didn't work well at all. We only ever had one or two rooms rented at a time, so we couldn't break even, plus someone had to volunteer to stay there overnight with any guests to watch over them and make breakfast in the morning. The boats were long gone even then, and the access door to the boathouse was boarded up. This was after the accident with the man dying on one of the tours to the island. The outside dock was in full use and where we stored the inflatable boats that we rented to people who wanted to see the island."

"You'd just let them go out there all by themselves?" Maryanne asked, incredulous.

"Well, there hadn't been all the deaths back then," Anita replied, taking another sip of coffee. "There was a long disclaimer and a lot of paperwork for anyone who wanted to go. Someone in the party had to be eighteen. We had a number of groups that rented from us that same summer that first group of kids got killed. They all went there and came back okay. People had been going to Latham's Landing to camp out illegally for years while the state had possession." She winked. "It was something of a rite of passage for the young men when I was just married to go there and spend the night. They would bring back a pebble of the red granite as proof."

"No one was ever killed or hurt on the island?"

"No, not then. There were regular drownings on the lake as you see in the clippings, but those were the only deaths." She chuckled. "It's possible that a lot of these island legends were all talk, Maryanne. More than one of those bragging boys probably broke a bit of stone off the Dockhouse for proof and never set foot on the island."

"The Dockhouse was made of the same granite as Latham's Landing?

"It was an odd red granite," Anita mused. "I never saw stone like it anywhere else. It was faded pink in the sun, but if a rock came loose, when it was put back you could see the underside, the part that wasn't weathered. That was deep red, with little sparkles to it. It is the same rock that Latham's mansion's foundation is made of."

"Is the Dockhouse's granite foundation still there?"

Anita nodded. "I think so, though I haven't been out there since the day we closed up the museum the last time before the fire. But there was a lot of that stone: the steps leading to the water, the patio floor, and the foundation the Dockhouse was built on were all made of it. Who would take it?" She looked at her watch. "I'm sorry, but I'm going to have to go in another half hour. I've got to pick up my grandson from school."

"There's a small article about a coastal shipbuilder, Mr. Latham, moving here and buying up several farms. No pictures."

"I won't be able to tell you much about any of the events older than the twenties," Anita said. "I only know what's in those articles."

Maryanne placed a few of the articles back in the box. "Were you ever at the camp or the beach when it was open?"

"Yes, of course. Everyone in town would go to the beach in the summers. It was a great place to swim as a kid. The sand was a light pink those first years, just like the faded granite. There was a concession stand that sold funnel cakes, hot dogs, and ice cream. My son Adam also went to the camp for several years. He learned to swim there."

"And nothing happened?"

"Nothing ever happened at the beach," Anita asserted. "Those were great days, when you could watch the sunset from the beach, see lights all around the lake and hear people laughing, and look out and see the house on the island all lit up, and that great glass house that sits behind it all lit up like a second moon sitting on the water."

"When did things start to go bad? I heard there was a flood that first November."

Anita nodded. "There was a lot of rain from a hurricane that was downgraded to a tropical depression. It stalled and caused the lake to flood, including the beach and the camp and most everything right around the shore, even part of the island house. But the waters receded with no real damage."

"This article says thirteen people died."

"Yes, because two boats were caught out on the lake when the first squalls hit, and they crashed into each other trying to make it back to shore. Two entire families drowned."

"Their names are listed here, the VanMarns and the Herschers. Did you know them?"

"The Herschers weren't locals. I'm not sure, but I think the

VanMarns were visiting Latham at his island. Maybe both families were. Latham often had people boat out to his island. The mansion was huge with seven bedrooms."

"You saw it before it flooded?"

"Only from the shore when I was young. My mom had an older friend Lorelei who worked there as a maid one summer. She said Lorelei told her that there were wild parties, drugs, drinking, orgies, all the things you'd expect of the very rich. But she was paid well to keep her mouth shut and she wouldn't tell my mom more than that, though my mother often begged her for details."

"Is Lorelei still alive?"

Anita shook her head. "She went missing at the end of that summer. You'll see a clipping for her there in that pile."

Maryanne felt a cold shiver, then reached into the pile, bringing out a clipping. "April 10th, 1951. Death of woman remains a cold case. State police continue to investigate the homicide of Lorelei Williams, who went missing September 6th, 1929. She'd spent the summer working as a maid and just picked up her last paycheck, but never cashed it. No one would learn her fate until her remains were found by a group of teens in a wooded area between Acano and Atlas Road." Maryanne looked at Anita. "Isn't that the area the new subdivision is going into?"

"Near it," Anita said, nodding. "It was closer to the shore, where the old cemetery used to be."

"What old cemetery?" Maryanne asked. "I've never heard of one near the lake."

"It hasn't been used in more than fifty years. I only know about it because that's where they put Lorelei after they found her body. Latham paid for an expensive funeral, as Lorelei's mother didn't have two dimes to scrape together. When the lake flooded a few years later and the first floor of the island house got submerged, the cemetery also flooded completely. Several bodies were found out of their graves, including Lorelei's. My mom was very upset. The bodies were quietly reburied in an unmarked section of the town cemetery, and the old cemetery was abandoned. It remains flooded now almost certainly. Even if you drained the water out, you probably couldn't find a single gravestone in all the mud and muck."

"What about the families of the still buried dead? Didn't they move the remaining bodies?"

"The only people in that cemetery were laborers who helped Latham's projects get built, servants whose families had no money for burial, like Lorelei, and possibly some of Latham's family. Latham and his immediate family were all dead by then. There wasn't anyone who complained." Anita looked at her watch. "Down to five minutes, Mary."

Mary hurriedly glanced through the articles. "How did Lorelei die? Did they have any suspects? Regardless of public opinion, who do you think killed her?"

"She was stabbed and strangled, my mom said. There were no suspects. Everyone liked her. I'm not sure who killed her. I never really thought about it before now, but maybe she saw something she shouldn't have seen, and she was killed to make sure she didn't talk about it." Anita shrugged. "She didn't have a boyfriend."

"What about the town centennial celebration? It says there were eight missing persons after the festivities concluded. That seems like a lot."

Anita smiled. "That I know more about. There were three men that drowned in the lake, because they were fishing at night drunk off a dock at the beach. They washed up on the beach a few days later. Two teens eloped; they were located when the girl came back alone a month later, pregnant, her intended having used their savings for a bus ticket to California. Lastly, three kids were on a boat that hit some rocks near the island. Their bodies were never recovered, but their boat was found near the shore with a big hole in the bottom."

"Did you know of the owner of the Sea Captain, a literal naval Captain Tiger Garrison? He supposedly had the bar and then got murdered?"

"He had a heart attack, I think. My father always said it was a very rough place, and I think there were a lot of barfights and brawls. They tried to reopen the place with a new name after Captain Garrison died, but that failed. There was some scandal with the man that bought it. It was rumored that he killed his wife and her daughter and hid the bodies. He disappeared soon after. The place has been closed since."

That man Brad which Barb mentioned. Maryanne spread out her few remaining articles. "Do you know how Latham's wife died, and where she's buried? Or Latham?"

"I heard she died at the house, and that he hung himself in fall 1929, but those are just what I heard. With Lorelei dead my mother didn't have anyone she knew who visited the island after that or knew the Latham family. They kept to themselves, and everyone who visited the island wasn't local. Latham and his wife are supposed to be buried in that same cemetery near the lake, I believe." She smiled. "But how could they be when that cemetery was flooded? I can't say."

Maryanne looked at her. "Speaking to you, I get the feeling that Latham and his family really weren't liked as well as these articles report."

"I think the town soured on him," Anita said, after a pause. "Too many bad things happened after he came. Everyone just wanted to get back to a normal life."

"But you made the island a monument to him and his family," Maryanne persisted.

"I loved history, and wanted to figure out the local mystery, like the others in the Historical Society," Anita replied. "I thought it would be exciting. But all of us who worked at the Dockhouse didn't like staying there overnight, even with guests. Sometimes we'd hear noises like there was a party going on outside, or the rumble of a ship's motor, one far too big for any boat that was still on the lake. There'd be knocking on the door leading to the boathouse under the Dockhouse; I heard it once myself, when I went down there one evening looking for extra canned peaches to serve for breakfast. Scared me half to death."

"Why?"

"Who would be knocking on the other side of a sealed door, one that was never unsealed?" Anita whispered, her eyes boring into Maryanne's. "There was just a stair on the other side that led to the water surface, for a docked boat to drop off passengers. The only way in was underwater."

"Maybe a floating log—"

"It wasn't a log," Anita interrupted. "It called my name. I never stayed there again after that night." She shuddered. "I was glad the Historical Society lost the place soon after for back taxes. And if someone else hadn't burned down the damned place I might have gotten a lighter and gasoline and done it myself. But only in the daytime." She shuddered again and looked at her watch. "I have to go."

"The group of boys who went missing at the camp that were presumed drowned in the lake, did you know anything about them?"

Anita stood up. "That was a horrible event. It was the year after Adam went off to join the Army. I had been so worried about him possibly going off to war, and then was thankful he wasn't home, as he was planning to go teach at the camp that summer if he didn't get accepted to Officer Training School. But if he'd have stayed, maybe he could've prevented the tragedy."

"What happened?"

"One of the new counselors was full of himself and wanting to prove he was brave or something. He took a boatful of boys to the island to spend the night, plus another female counselor who was rumored to be his girlfriend. They say they put the boys to bed and then went to sleep themselves, but when they awoke all the boys had disappeared. All the gear was left there: the tents, food, flashlights, clothes. The parents of the missing boys sued and the camp was forced to close, all because of one idiot's bad judgement. The female counselor committed suicide that fall in the lake, and the male counselor went to trial for reckless endangerment. He never got to tell his side as he was killed by one of the grieving parents on the steps of the court the very first day of the trial." She smiled kindly, but her eyes glittered. "There is some justice."

Gruesome...and maybe the beginning of deaths attributed to the evil on the island. "What about the accident on the boat tour where a little girl fell in the water, and a man went in after her and saved her but died. This clipping says it was a heart attack."

"You'd think that was pretty straightforward, wouldn't you," Anita said, hefting her purse onto her shoulder. "That's the scariest one to me, maybe because it hit close to home. The man who died was my husband, Scoot."

Maryanne gaped at her. "I'm sorry, Anita, I never knew. What happened?"

"He was filling in just for a few hours because Fred the boatman was out at a doctor's appointment. They had finished the island tour and he was herding people onto the boat to bring them back to the Dockhouse. Scoot had been a lifeguard in high school at Leighton Beach, he knew water and boats. The police took statements from the tourists, who said he suddenly yelled "Girl overboard!", tossed a life preserver into the harbor, and then jumped in. When he didn't come up, a couple of the men in the group went in after him. They found his body floating face down."

"I'm sorry, Anita. That doesn't sound like a heart attack."

"It might have been. I think they ruled it a heart attack because he was a good swimmer and there wasn't a mark on him. But what no one could explain is that there was only one child in the group, a little girl. And her father swore she was with him the whole time. She never had been in the water."

Maryanne swallowed hard searching for words.

"Without Scoot, I had a hard time making ends meet. Luckily Adam was grown, and I had just me to take care of." Her eyes narrowed. "Here's a few facts that you won't find on paper: the Sea Room was supposed to be a bedroom, my mother said, and Latham's wife was supposedly going there on the night she died. Or maybe she died there." She pushed in her chair. "I'm telling you this because I want you to stop whatever's out there if you can. You've got God on your side, so you've got a chance anyways."

Maryanne stood. "Anita, I'll try. I've got a group that's going to try. Thank you for your help. Anything else you might remember, no matter how small, please give me a call."

"I owe a debt," Anita said with a sad smile. "We were told not to let anyone else on the island after Scoot died, no exceptions. But when that girl Sandy came asking about the island, looking for her relative that disappeared there, I took her bribe money and slipped her the paperwork, so my ass and the Historical Society were covered. Because the other kids died that same night and they went to the island on their own, Chief Stahl let it slide. But that girl Sandy is dead because of me. I'll help you any way I can."

———

"So, you haven't gone back to your attic?" Brian asked, as he and Wil rode bikes along the park trail. "Not even the next day in the daylight?"

Wil looked at him over the tops of his glasses. "Why would I go up there? I don't have any reason to go up there." He focused again on the road.

"Of course you do! You have to find out what's up there. I'm guessing it's a raccoon. You just moved into the new house, and it was vacant for a year. It makes sense you might have some wildlife that needs to be sent packing."

"Whatever it was, it was too big for a raccoon. If you'd have heard it hiss, you'd have left it alone, too."

"But what if it's trapped up there? You said you fixed some of the siding that was rotten. Maybe you sealed it inside."

"Then it'll die up there," Wil said resolutely, speeding up. "I blocked up the access hatch too. Unless you want to come over and investigate tonight?"

Brian sped up also. "Has it made any more noise?"

"Nothing since that night. That was three days ago. Maybe it's gone."

"I can't believe you don't want to find out what it was."

"Like I said, you're free to come on over and go take a look. I'll unlock the attic door for you."

"No," Brian said, after a pause. "You're probably right. It found its own way out."

———

One week after the snowstorm, the group met at Barb's house.

"I have the herbs," Barb said, holding up a bag. "I didn't realize how much Carolyn had initially purchased; it was literally seven huge boxes full. I sorted out about a tenth to take when we walk in, which will take up two big recyclable bags. They're light to carry but my hands will be full. I'll leave Cooper with Carly. I'm not going to risk his life again."

"I have the blessed crosses, water, and a couple boxes of bullets for you, Bob," Maryanne said, handing them out. "I can also bless each of you and pray before we begin the crossing."

"Teeth is there now, and the water of the lake is dropping fast," Bob said. "We're about seven inches low, as it's been a dry winter, even with that big storm. For what it's worth, the weather is forecast to be mild for the next seventy-two hours. Be aware that Teeth has already spoken to authorities in the sturgeon program, saying that this later level drop is going to stress the fish and make some of them die. He's pushing for the lake to be reflooded. I'm not sure how long we have, so we need to make the most of it."

Cheer related the information she had learned from Godelman. "I think we should check out the section of shore where the cemetery was at first light, that is if we can see any gravestones. The shoreline should be completely drained dry by then."

Maryanne also related the information she had learned from Anita. "Cheer's right, we should visit the cemetery. I called Anita later that day after our talk, and she told me the approximate area of the shore where the graveyard used to be. We should take pictures of any gravestones that are legible to capture names and other information."

"What are we hoping to find?" Cheer asked. "I'm just asking so I know what to look for. I don't want to miss reporting something I may notice that seems unimportant."

"Why do you flood a house that you spent your fortune making sure couldn't be flooded?" Barb said softly. "It's what you do when you have nothing else left to try. We're looking for signs of what Latham tried to cover up. Everything new we learned fits the idea that the house has been associated with death ever since it and the lake were created. Latham tried to mitigate that with good works, but people kept dying. We need to look at the sections of the house that were flooded and see exactly what's there, take pictures. We need to look at the foundations of the bridge that connects the Sea Room to the main island, see if there's anything special about it. We all agree the Sea Room is abnormally far from the house, that Latham did that deliberately for some reason. That walkway and that glass ball had to cost as much as the house itself, even if he manufactured the materials for the latter at cost through his own company. That the Sea Room was a bedroom sounds ludicrous. What if it instead was an altar of some kind? Something water might purify?"

"You're suggesting we flood the Sea Room?" Cheer interjected. "Water hasn't worked to purify the house."

"The Sea Room is built of marine glass. It was possibly built to be submerged," Barb argued. "But in all our research there's no record it was ever submerged until Bob upped the water level in the lake. So why build it at such extravagant expense when he could have used plain glass windows?" She took a breath. "I really don't know what we should look for, Cheer. But if the power on the island is so against losing the water barrier around it, then the water must be covering something."

"Let's meet tomorrow here just before dawn," Bob said, getting up. "We could talk all night about suppositions. We need to go find new facts."

"He's right," Maryanne said, standing up and stretching. "I'll see you tomorrow."

Cheer, Bob, and Maryanne left. Barb watched them go, then went to bed with Cooper snuggled at her feet snoring. It was a long time before she finally fell asleep.

———

The next morning, the foursome set out in Bob's car. They were at the shore at the end of Atlas Road just as the sun was rising. The scent of water was heavy in the air, along with drying seaweed and algae.

"I haven't been here since leaving for the island," Barb said anxiously, as she shut her door. "The air smells the same."

"Look at the difference," Bob said, pointing with his crowbar.

The lake in front of them was missing. Instead, there was an expanse of wet gravel, mud, large rocks, seaweed, algae, broken shells, and intermittent pools of water of varying sizes. A shallow moat of water almost completely surrounded the island for a good fifty feet from its shore, with some deeper pools to the right and left of the island and a few dry paths of lakebed connecting to the island shore. The entire main mansion was a good thirty feet higher than the remaining water and no longer flooded. Long submerged unfaded red granite stairs were visible on one side of the island, shining water on them drying. Many piles of boat wreckage also dotted the exposed lake floor.

"Let's avoid the lakebed for now, and head down the shore to the cemetery," Bob said. "Then let's continue around the side of the island, see if we can get to the house or the Sea Room on those dry paths we see."

"Why wouldn't we be able to use the paths?" Maryanne asked. "There's dry land right there."

"Because when we get closer, they may not be there," Barb said ominously.

In thoughtful silence, they began to walk. The foursome made good time and arrived at the remains of the formerly submerged cemetery an hour later. Large silver maples and willows had grown up around the graves, and most all of the simple square headstones had fallen over. The weathered stones were covered with algae, gleaming wetly in the sunshine. Bob and Barb began prying them up with the crowbar, while Cheer took pictures. There were about thirty stones. "Daniel Dickerson. Aged twenty-one when he passed."

"Erasmus Robin, aged seventeen."

"Here's one that actually has more than a name and death dates. Julius Page, Cary Merrill, Myron Ray, Murdock Dimmock, Jim Bartlett. These brave lads died while excavating rock for the Sea Room," Cheer read, as she took pictures. "That's the last one, though. I don't see any grave for Lorelei."

"Look over there to the East," Maryanne said, pointing. "There's a little mound, and it looks like some fancier graves on it."

The group walked over. There were two obelisks a few feet tall, one large rectangle headstone, and an odd white smooth round stone which was supported by a tripod of red granite. "That's got to be Latham," Barb said.

"Nope, but it is his son, Hans Latham II," Cheer said taking a picture, then another. "He was only eleven when he died."

"The rectangle is for Latham's brother Saul and his wife and child," Maryanne said. "It looks like the mother and child died first, and then the brother a few years later."

Cheer took more pictures. "The right obelisk is for the Van Marns. It looks like the entire family. They were kin to Latham, Mrs. Diane Van Marn was Latham's sister. The left is for the Herschers, they were also kin to Latham, another sister named Jacqueline and her husband and five children."

"If you're on an island with a good sturdy house and a storm was coming, you don't get in a boat with your spouse and all your kids," Maryanne stated. "You stay put on dry land and ride it out. But both families left, and they both drowned. What did they see that they needed to die?"

"Maybe the evil force was systematically killing off Latham's family," Bob offered. "First the siblings, then the kids, then the wife, then Latham."

"Latham and his wife aren't here though," Barb said.

"Neither is Carl, Latham's other son," Bob added.

"Let's look further out?" Cheer offered. "If some of the graves were opened by water in the first historic flood, the graves must be farther away from shore. Even if the bodies floated somewhere else, the headstones have to be near the graves."

"Here!" Maryanne called, near a pile of wreckage a little way away. "It looks like the remains of a sunk wooden boat here. It's on top of what looks like a fallen gravestone."

Barb and Bob pushed while Cheer pulled, and the rotten wood skeleton came free, toppling over on its side, the soft punky wood collapsing. "It is Lorelei," Maryanne said. "She was eighteen."

"And important to Latham, to be here with the family and not with the other laborers," Barb added.

"Maybe the stone landed here when the boat hit it?" Maryanne suggested. "The boat obviously hit the stone when it crashed as we had to pry it free. It probably hit with enough force to slide the stone along the lake bottom."

"Maybe," Barb allowed. "But then why does her stone have all these little flowers inscribed across the top? None of the other laborers have that on theirs. And neither do any of the fancier stones, either."

"She's right," Cheer said, taking a picture. "She was something special to Latham."

"We need to move on," Bob said, looking at his phone. "It's past ten and we haven't gotten to the island."

The group headed out across the empty lake bottom, remarking on the wreckage piles. Swaths of land were mud which their shoes and feet sunk into, while other sections were piles of rocks, some large enough to climb on. There were many rotting piles of wood, and even some of steel metal boats, badly rusted, all with gaping holes in their hulls. "The new ones are all aluminum so they float in, even if in pieces," Bob said, looking at one. "This is The Liberty, one that went missing in my first years of being a cop. Cheer, take pics of any boats we pass with visible names, okay? I'll pass them along to Sal Upner. We can close a few missing persons cases. And please, anyone sees any bones, please call out so we don't disturb them. We'll need to take a picture so Upner can send in a forensics team."

"Sure," Cheer said, snapping a picture of The Liberty.

By eleven, the group was around the side of the island, and in view of the Sea Room, which lay a few miles distant.

"Excellent!" Bob exclaimed. "We can walk up to the house on this side without going into the water. Let's go up and take a look."

"But not the Sea Room," Barb said, pointing. The glass octagon was fully exposed, as well as a solid concrete base which appeared to be at least one story tall. The base was surrounded by water on all sides.

"At least we finally understand how Latham could afford to build the bridge," Bob said. "It's made of single beams and cables for support over most of the expanse, with lakestone only at the house and the Sea Room over a concrete base. The walkway above, which I always thought was all stone, must also be lake rocks over concrete. C'mon, we have to hurry."

The group headed toward the shore.

CHAPTER EIGHT

"You know we're going to get there and they're going to be out of Deep Sea Treasure ice cream," Abby griped to her mom as she stretched her legs out in front of her onto the dashboard. "We've tried two places already."

"Get your feet off the dash," Brienne shot back irritably. *We're just one day into this week road trip of newly retired mother and middle-aged daughter bonding and I'm already thinking it was a mistake. I should have gone on that Viking river cruise with the other newly retired teachers.* "It'll only take a moment to stop. What's The Scoop is supposed to open at five today and it's only another ten miles."

Abby put her feet down with a sigh. "I can't stand coffee-caramel ice cream. Or caramel-nut ice cream. You'd think they'd just sell plain caramel ice cream at the store."

Brienne focused on the road. *Please have the damn ice cream and let the hotel I booked have an in-room bar.*

"That's the harbor," Bob said, pointing to a dry concave area in front of them. There was lakestone all along the shore, and steps cut into the natural rock leading down to the lake floor, the last ten of which were covered with seaweed. The group followed them up and then stood on the small stone landing. "Up above there's a set of granite stairs that leads around back of the house to the beginning of the bridge to the Sea Room." He turned. "This lower stone path that's been submerged looks like it leads along the outside of the house."

"It was pretty," Barb admitted. "Look, the windows along that side are floor to ceiling. Most of them were broken, and it looks like there's also debris piled against the side of the house and inside, maybe pieces of broken dock or boats. But it was beautiful once." She looked at Bob. "Now what?"

"I hoped we could go in a group to the Sea Room after checking out the flooded section of the mansion," Bob said. "This section hasn't ever been dry since it was flooded by Latham, so I hoped we might find something. But it's almost noon now. We could probably clear a path through that wreckage to get inside to look around, but it'll take a few hours."

"No, we can go in there," Cheer said, pointing to a listing, rotted open doorway a few feet away. "I can duck my head in and take a few pictures, anyway. I wouldn't think it's worth going inside the main house, so it shouldn't take long. Then we can walk over, look at the Sea Room, break for lunch, then begin the walk out of here."

"Let's do it," Barb said quickly, glancing nervously at the house. "Maryanne and I'll walk along the outside and take pictures, too." She lit some sage and handed some to Maryanne, and another wrapped bundle to Bob. "Take this and keep it burning the whole time you're in there. Call out regularly."

Cheer carefully navigated the rotten wood, then Bob went after her holding a burning sage stick, its thick smoke wafting in a cloud around them. The listing wooden floor was missing in places, the holes showing the struts and supports below. Light shone through broken glass and intact window tops, but the wreckage at the house base blocked any view of Maryanne and Barb. The floor nearest the house was mostly intact, and showed traces of old varnish, the walls covered with mold and mildew at the top, still saturated and oozing water in rivulets at the bottom. "There's not much here," Cheer said, as she took pictures. "This looks like it was just a long hallway of windows made to view the lakescape from right above water level.

There's a couple remnants of chairs and benches, plus big broken pots that might have held plants."

"I thought Latham flooded it for a reason," Bob mused, as he followed her, wafting the sage around them. "But it may just have been the lowest level of the house, after the basement."

Outside, Barb picked her way down the path of slimy, green-stained paving rocks, Maryanne in tow holding the lit sage. "At least this smells good," Maryanne said, inhaling the smoke deeply. "Where do you think all this wreckage came from?"

"The wood looks like pieces of boats," Barb said after a moment, as she stopped to take a picture. "Possibly they floated inside during the years this porch was flooded. When the water level dropped some of them may have floated out again? The older ones probably sunk years ago in some of the severe storms."

"Do you see any wreckage that looks like pieces of the other buildings you saw the last time you were here?"

"No," Barb said, swallowing. "No new wood shards, no ladder bits, no foundation granite or concrete, no pieces of roof or furniture. No sign at all. The front of the island leading up to the main house looks entirely different. All the stone stairs are gone." *And the belltower is gone, including its foundation and its bell.*

"We're retracing our steps!" Bob shouted from inside. "There's too much wreckage here to go any farther. Meet us back where we started."

The two women turned around, and began picking their way back, Maryanne leading. The foursome regrouped, and Barb breathed a sigh of relief. The group immediately set off for the Sea Room.

———

"Yum," Abby said, as she ate the last bite of cone. "I'm so glad we got some to go, Mom."

"Me, too," Brienne said, as she yawned. "I'm ready for bed."

"It's not even close to seven," Abby said, rolling her eyes. "We could go for a walk. We should get a little exercise; we've been in the car all day."

"Maybe in a little bit," Brienne said, yawning. "I have to go take a shower first." She headed into the bathroom and began to run the water.

She's not going to go for a walk; she's going to fall asleep as soon as she's in her pjs. But I can take a quick one. She's going to be in there for a half hour easy. Abby grabbed the room key, her jacket, and her phone and left quietly, the door locking after her.

She headed down the road. *I'll just go down to the end and be back before she even knows I'm gone.*

Abby walked for a good twenty minutes, enjoying the warm evening and the sounds of the state park forest on her right, and the sounds of children playing on the swings at the playground on her left. The she walked on a bit father, until forest was to either side and the yelling and repetitive metal squeaks had died down to the soft sounds of her footfalls on the dry leaves at her feet.

She stopped finally. *I thought that this road said dead end. But maybe that's not for miles. I'd better be getting back. Mom will freak if she wakes up and I'm gone. Besides I still need to call home and check on the kids.* She turned, heading back the way she'd come.

The return trip was faster, as Abby was hurrying. But the park was empty as she passed it, the swings motionless and silent.

Abby hurried on, then paused as the sound of a child crying came to her. She turned to find a little girl in a pink dress sitting in the parking lot of the park, alone.

She went over. "Do you need help?"

The little girl looked up, nodding. "Can you walk me home?"

Abby produced a phone. "I need to get home myself, but I can call your home and have someone come and get you. What's your phone number?"

The little girl reached out and touched Abby's hand.

———

"I'll kill him," Joe muttered under his breath, as he slammed his car door, walking quickly through the packed parking lot at O'Shaun's. "If he's in there, I'll kill him."

Michelle can't be leaving me for Craig. She just said that because we fought, and she saw me kiss Raquel. "It didn't mean anything. I was just drunk and having fun."

"Women," a man said, stepping out of the shadows. "Always a hassle. But life's not worth living without them." He grinned.

"You said it," Joe replied, forcing a smile as he stepped past and entered the bar. He scanned the room, rage erupting as he saw Michelle sitting on Craig's lap, his arm around her as they shared a beer at the bar. He started for them, swearing.

Michelle caught sight of him coming and bolted off Craig's lap toward the ladies' room. Craig dropped some money on the bar and pushed his way through into the kitchen. Joe ran after him.

Michelle shut the door, leaning on it in case Joe came after her. *I should've left town.*

"You hiding?" a woman asked, coming out of the stall and washing her hands at the sink. She was college age, though her hair was cut in a style easily twenty years out of date.

"Yeah," Michelle said, opening the door to peek out. "My boyfriend's got a temper. I should've never gotten involved with him."

"I can help you get away, if you want?" the woman asked. "I've got a car outside and I was just leaving. You can ride at least to the next town." She offered her hand. "My name's Sandy."

"That'd be great," Michelle said with a grateful smile, shaking her hand. "I'm Michelle."

"Okay, I'll go out first, and you follow me," Sandy instructed. She looked out quick, then hurried off through the crowd. Michelle followed, looking furtively around. She let out a relieved sigh when she was out in the night air.

"C'mon!" Sandy called from the edge of the parking lot. "I'm over here."

Michelle hurried over. "Why'd you park way over here?"

"I always get people dinging my car," Sandy said, her voice oddly muffled. "I hate that. Are you coming or not? I'm going now."

She's weird. Her oversize top and stone-washed jeans are also about thirty years out of fashion. "Wait," Michelle called. "I'm coming." She walked into the shadows, then let out a long scream as she suddenly stepped down into empty space.

———

Joe burst though the employee entrance out into the night. *There's nothing along this side except some swamp, the road to the highway, and the fence separating them. He's not on the road, so he must be trying to get to his truck.* Joe ran around the building, but Craig's truck was empty. "Come out," Joe growled, clenching his hands as he stalked between the silent parked vehicles. "You stole my girl and you're gonna pay."

"Need help?" the same man Joe had seen before stepped from the shadows.

Is he hanging out here trying to sell drugs? "Listen, friend, I don't know you," Joe warned. "I've got a beating to deliver so don't get in the way."

"Just wanted to tell you he headed there," the man said, pointing to a derelict house across an overgrown field. "There's a woman with him."

"Damn them both!" Joe ran straight for the house. The man ran after him, grabbing his arm just as he reached the front stairs.

"What the hell do you want?" Joe yelled, whipping around and balling his fists.

"Just to offer this," the man said, holding out a hunting knife. "He's got a knife of his own."

Joe put his fists down, wary. "Who are you? Do you know me?"

"I'm Mac," the man replied, grinning again. "No, I don't know you. But I had a woman also give me a raw deal. The man she was with hurt me bad because I underestimated him. Just don't want you to make the same mistake."

"I'm grateful," Joe said, taking the knife. "But stay out here. He's mine."

"No problem," Mac replied, stepping back.

Joe ran up the stairs. As he opened the door, he heard a woman's scream. *That's Michelle!* He turned to ask Mac to call 911, but Mac had vanished.

There was another scream from within the house, this one of pain. Joe charged inside, the door slamming shut behind him.

———

Craig walked carefully up the stairs of the old house, his phone flashlight held up in front of him. "Michelle?" *I know that was her screaming. I swore it came from in here.* His foot slipped in something wet, and he caught himself on the railing. *It's wet, too?* With revulsion he looked at his hand, sure he'd see blood. To his surprise it was some kind of seaweed. *What the hell? There's no body of water around here.*

Soft whimpering came from someplace above to the right. "Michelle?" Craig got to the top of the stairs, stopping to listen.

There were footsteps below tinged with sloshing, of someone walking through water.

Craig ducked back flat against the wall, keeping still.

The footsteps came closer, then stopped directly out of sight beneath the staircase.

Craig breathed as silently as he dared, not moving. *What was down there? Ike Fleetman, an ex-Marine, had disappeared several months ago after leaving O'Shauns with two college girls. One of the other patrons had sworn he'd seen Ike heading with the two girls into the woods. In the morning Ike's truck was still in the parking lot. He was still missing.*

The front door of the house burst open as Joe barged in, knife in his hand. He saw Craig immediately. "You bastard! Where's Michelle?"

"Not here," Craig said, holding up his hands. To his shock he saw his right hand held a knife. He dropped it to clatter on the floor. "What the hell?"

Joe launched himself up the stairs with a growl. Craig bent and grabbed the knife as Joe plowed into him, knocking him to the floor.

———

"It took us 'til four to get here," Bob said darkly, as they arrived at the Sea Room. "We have time for about ten minutes to take pictures, and then we have to head back."

Barb cast an apprehensive look at the distant mansion, then at the car on the shore some distance beyond. "Even then, we won't make it back to the car until nearly eight. It will be full dark. We'll have trouble avoiding the pools of water. We have to go out this side of the lake."

"There's stone stairs right here we can take down to the lake bottom," Bob said, pointing. "We won't head back to the car, but instead up to this side of the lake, skirting the Sea Room. Dakota's farm is just over the hill. We can ask him for a ride back to the car."

"And he won't be angry, us just showing up at his door?"

"He'll be surprised, but he'll help," Bob said, taking out his cell phone. "And we won't have to walk to his house. I'll call him now and ask him to pick us up."

Barb watched, expecting that the cell phone wouldn't work. But the call went through, and Dakota agreed to come out in his truck to meet them. "Let's hurry and finish here," Bob said quickly. "Remember to take pictures of everything!"

The group entered the base of the Sea Room through a heavy steel door, for which Bob produced a key. They went through a short hallway with a stairwell leading down on one side, and then up some stairs to another heavy steel door, this one set into a steel frame. "No wonder this place is waterproof," Barb said, as Bob unlocked that door and she entered. "This steel must be several inches thick."

"It's a marine door, the kind you'd have below decks on a ship," Bob said. "Meant to stop water."

"So Latham did mean for this to be submerged," Maryanne breathed. "I have to say, its beautiful."

"More beautiful than I thought," Cheer commented, as she commenced snapping pictures. "It must be something when it's got the water right to the base, or fully submerged on a sunny day."

The Sea Room was made almost entirely of heavy glass in the shape of huge triangles. Despite its known age, the glass was remarkably clear, and the sky could be seen in all directions, as well as the bare lake floor and piles of wreckage and rocks. The clouds parted above them, and the sun came out suddenly, flooding the room with bright light. In between the sections of glass at the top in eight places were crystal prisms which captured the light and threw it back in rainbows about the room. This effect was exacerbated by the floor, which was tiled with mirrors around the edges of the room and silver tiles in the center. Most were unbroken but several on the left side of the room were cracked down the middle. The effect was amazing, as if the sky and the lake floor were all around the four-some, the bright sunlight making the entire Sea Room sparkle like diamonds.

"I never realized it wasn't a perfect sphere, but more oval," Bob said. "But it makes sense, or there wouldn't be much living space."

"Latham got around that too, look." In the center of the Sea Room a set of white metal stairs rose above the floor to a kind of landing. On it were the remains of a bedframe also made of white metal, the mattress missing. Cheer stepped up the first few stairs and snapped a few more pictures. "Can you imagine sleeping here on a moonlit night? Or in a storm? It must have been absolutely crazy beautiful!"

"I'm not sure how he got around the greenhouse effect," Barb said uneasily, fanning herself. "Unless some of these glass triangles open. This is beautiful, yes, but imagine being locked in here. It's spring now and only sixty today, plus mostly cloudy. On a sunny August day, it's got to be cooking in here."

Bob pointed to some hinges near the top of the sphere's glass panels. "I think the panes at the top do open, Barb. There's a metal stair around the outside of the Sea Room at the bottom with a ladder leading to the top. We never saw it before because it's been under water."

"Do we want to open the panes?" Maryanne asked. "To try to purify the place with water? If we can get the levers to work, that is."

"Let's see what's beneath first," Bob replied. "There was a stair-well outside between the two doors. Everyone turn on your flashlights."

"There's another set of stairs leading down there," Barb said. "Over by the left wall. But we shouldn't split up. Damn it all, we should have lit these when we first entered. I forgot." She opened her bag and lit another tied bunch of herbs, passing one to each of the group. "Keep it burning."

Bob led the way down the stairs; Maryanne bringing up the rear. "Looks like this is pretty cleared out, too." The space was a room of concrete resembling a windowless basement. There was a pile of broken furniture, several stained mattresses, and a walk-in closet complete with drawers. "Barb, can you and Maryanne look through the drawers, remove them even to see if anything might have fallen beneath them? Cheer, please take a few more pictures."

"Where are you going?"

"Just out the one door here," Bob said, opening it and propping it open with a piece of rusted metal table, another piece of broken wood in his left hand. "I will stay in sight, promise. I'm pretty sure that this leads to that stairwell we walked past when we entered."

"Stay in sight," Barb warned, as she and Maryanne went into the closet and began pulling out drawers.

Bob walked to the bottom of the stairs, then looked up. There was a stairwell above, but also another watertight door set about halfway up the side in the side of the concrete wall. *That would lead outside. But how would it ever be opened? The entire stairwell would flood. Once it did, you'd have to drop the level of the entire lake to get it drained.* Intrigued, Bob took a step towards the door, then thought better of it. "Cheer?" he called. "Can you come stand in the doorway?"

"Coming," Cheer said, as she took a last picture of Barb and Maryanne searching in the closet. "Barb, can you or Maryanne come stand here, so I can keep Bob in sight? He's found something."

"Sure," Barb said. "All the drawers I checked were empty, and beneath them too."

"I'll be out shortly," Maryanne said. "I've only got three more to check."

"I'll wait then." Bob called.

Maryanne checked beneath the last drawer, revealing a tiny metal ring notepad, the cover an odd flocked brown paper. "Autographs?" She pocketed it, then slid the last drawer back in place. "All set. I found a notepad; not sure how much it'll reveal."

"Are you sure you should open that?" Cheer inquired, as Bob tried to open the door. "There was still water about the base, remember?"

"You girls go up on the landing, and check that the door up there leads out," Bob said, as he put down his herbs and fought with the lock. "This door should lead outside to the lake floor. But I didn't see any door at the base of the Sea Room. Did you?"

"No," Barb said as she hurried up the stairs, Cheer and Maryanne in tow. "There wasn't one. Let's go outside and look."

"I'll stay just inside and watch Bob," Cheer offered.

Barb opened the inner door, which again led into the Sea Room. The view was as breathtaking as before, but the air was noticeably hotter, almost suffocating, the bright light blinding. "Hey, the view is different from here. This is another door," she said, looking at the inside. "One we didn't see before. It's got a pile of junk in front of it, I can only open it a crack. Must be why we didn't notice it."

"Damn lock!" Bob yelled, shaking his right hand, which was now bleeding. "It won't take my keys, any of them."

"But we didn't see any pile of junk when we were in the Sea Room," Maryanne said from behind her. "There was only the white metal bedframe on the dais."

"I don't see the bedframe," Barb whispered back, as she took in the empty mirror tiled floor with its couple piles of junk. "Or the dais." *But that pile in front of this door could be the dais and bedframe...if they'd been crushed into a pile of twisted metal. Maybe to stop us going back in? And we never heard a sound.* She shut the door, and abruptly turned, heading for the outside door. She wrenched it open, letting in a cool breeze, to her abject relief. "Guys, let's get going. The sun is low on the horizon, it must be about five or six. We need to get off the lake by dark and on shore." *Whatever is here knows we are here and it's giving us clear signs to get out...but it's not going to wait much longer.*

"Fine," Bob said, taking his handkerchief out of his pocket and tying it around his hand. "I give up." He and Cheer followed Barb and Maryanne out into the sunlight, then locked the door behind him.

"Is that necessary?" Cheer asked. "Who else would come out here?"

"Probably not, but I don't want The Sea Room to flood until I find out where that mystery door leads," Bob said. "Look at the bottom of the concrete, where we just had to be. There's no door."

"I didn't measure, but the concrete room seemed to me to be smaller than the globe above," Cheer said slowly. "The door you were fighting with was waterproof, yes, but maybe it's not inches thick like the two doors we entered by."

"Yes, but that would mean the door would have to lead to some kind of tunnel under the lake floor," Bob said irritably. "Anything built in the earth would have collapsed long ago with the weight of the water on top of it. But we don't see any sunken sections that would denote a tunnel leading from the base."

"Maybe not," Barb called. She and Maryanne had already gone down the flight of stone steps to the lake bottom and were walking around. "Get down here, Bob. Cheer, you too!"

"Did you find something?"

"Yes! Now get down here."

Bob and Cheer went down the stairs, where Barb was waiting with Maryanne. "I don't see anything."

"Dig a bit with your foot," Barb said. "We're not standing on earth, just a layer of silt. Under it is a huge concrete pad. But it makes sense, right? The Sea Room is big, the concrete and glass and metal that comprise it have to be very heavy. It would need a support under it to make sure it didn't sink or tilt over time, or that the globe didn't fall off the base in a storm. Earth by itself wouldn't have been enough, probably not even rock."

"You think there's a room under the basement of the Sea Room?"

"Yes, and if it's locked and I don't have the key, there's a good chance that whatever Latham stored in there is still there," Bob said. "I have copies of all the keys, which are the same keys I got access to years ago when I was out here for various accidents. So, I'll have to come back with a locksmith."

"Fine, but we need to go," Maryanne insisted. "It's close to dusk."

The group gave the base of the Sea Room a wide berth, though the water there looked to be only a foot or so deep. They headed off toward the shore, which was about a mile away.

"Bob, the door we left the Sea Room by wasn't the same one we entered," Barb said under her breath as they walked. "And when I looked into the room of glass, the view had changed."

"Curious. Do you think we got turned around in the base? If you noticed it was as symmetrical as the globe above."

"No," Barb said darkly. "I think whatever inhabits Latham's Landing is still there, it's just inhibited by the water loss or the herbs or both. If we come back tomorrow, we need to be careful."

When they were a little over halfway, a truck appeared in the deepening gloom, its lights bright as it crested the hill in front of them and parked. Relieved to see Dakota, they walked faster.

"Hey, what's that?" Cheer asked suddenly, pointing down the lake to the right. "Looks like a barn."

The remains of a collapsed roof, long submerged, lay in a little depression. Several piles of fieldstone lay near it, possibly the remnants of a rock foundation. "It's a house and barn," Barb said. "Didn't you say, Cheer, that Latham had bought up several farms to make the lake? This must be one of the farms."

"Stands to reason then that there's another cluster of structures on the other side of the island," Bob said. "We'll have to come back and take pictures of those tomorrow. It's too dark to see tonight."

The group headed for the truck, picking their way around several stagnant pools of water. With relief, one by one they walked onto the shore. "I'm so thankful," Barb said. "I was sure something would happen. I was waiting all day on pins and needles."

"The power of the house revolves around water," Bob said, as they headed toward the truck. "I'll have to find a way to keep the island dry, like it is now. Or possibly just pay a crew to come in and dismantle the house and cart it away. The university can't stop me doing that—"

With a large rumbling two things happened: The Sea Room illuminated like a brilliant sun, and the lights of Dakota's truck abruptly went out.

Barb and Cheer let out shrieks. There was an answering terrified scream from across the lake. A light was on in the mansion's second story, and it wavered as something moved across the window in front of it.

"The house, um, returned with someone inside?" Maryanne managed.

"Like a flytrap," Barb breathed. "That's where the body came from. You were right, Bob."

———

"Earth to Abby. Come in Abby."

Abby blinked her eyes. "Sorry, baby." *That's funny, I must have dreamed I was still on that trip with mom*. She hugged her husband. "I'm feeling not myself. What did you say?"

"Just that I was glad we moved here with Billy and Gina." He kissed her, then got in the car. "I'll be back tomorrow. Keep your doors locked. Love you!"

"You can count on it. Love you." Abby watched him go, then went back inside to finish making breakfast.

After the meal, she took the two kids outside to play. She was just planting some flowers near the driveway when out of the corner of her eye she saw something pull Gina under the porch.

"Gina!" Abby threw down her shovel and ran to the struggling child, pulling the child back.

A stunted man crouched there in the darkness under the porch, his smile eerie. "Do you believe what you are seeing?" he croaked at her.

"Yes," she stammered, terrified.

"Leave now or risk your kids," the dwarf said, then pulled back into the shadows, vanishing.

Petrified, Abby gathered up her kids and put them in the car, instructing them to lock their doors. Then she went in and grabbed her purse and all her cash and drove away to a hotel, calling her husband.

"I'm not going to tell you that you didn't see what you saw," he said when she had finished. "But this sounds like you fell asleep and had a nightmare."

"Gina's terrified to be alone," Abby countered. "I'm not going back to that house, not for anything."

"We'll talk when I get back," he said. "Just stay there."

Abby hung up and called her sister. But her mother answered. "Hi, Mom. What are you doing there?"

"Abby, have you seen Rhonda?"

"No. Why?"

"She went to bring you a housewarming gift. I expected her back hours ago and it's nearly dark. I get no answer at your house."

Damn you Dad for dying and Rhonda for not getting married. And my husband for travelling so much. "Mom, come here to the Comfort Inn on 29 to watch the kids. I'll go check."

"Why are you there instead of at home?"

"Just get here!"

A half hour later, after hugging her kids and her mom, Abby was on her way home. With every mile she felt more and more in danger, every sense in her body telling her to turn around before it was too late.

Suddenly, Abby saw a cat's eyes glow from the side of the road, then a dog ran across in front of her, making her swerve. A block away she caught the silhouette of the stunted man in her lights, the dwarf glaring at her with yellow eyes before he was lost again in shadow, the shock making her cry out.

Her nerves a tattered ruin, she parked her car in the driveway and pocketed the keys, then went up to her front door, turning the knob which opened easily. *I locked this when I left.*

Abby grabbed a crowbar from the toolbox as she passed it, brandishing it as she searched the house, turning on lights as she went.

Finally, she had searched all the rooms but her bedroom. She opened the door silently.

A shape was in her bed, someone lying there.

"Rhonda?"

The figure sat up, cackling with glee, its leathery horned head bobbing as it stepped out of her bed. As it lunged, Abby bolted, running for the front door, but the monster took the back stairs, trying to cut her off. She ran instead into the basement and down the stairs, crouching against the wall. *Why did I run here! I'm in a dead end. There's nothing down here to hide behind or use as a barricade, it's all still outside waiting to be moved in.*

There was a creak of the door above, then the heavy tread as the monstrous demon came down the top stairs.

It knows I'm here. Abby cringed back against the wall, trying to hide. To her surprise, the outline of a door in the wall revealed itself to her. *There's no knob. It's painted to look exactly like the wall.* Using the crowbar, Abby levered open the door, the demon sprinting toward the noise. She slammed the door in its face as it howled in frustration, scrabbling at the other side but unable to find a way to open the door.

Abby turned, the flash of cat eyes in the dark getting her attention. *The cat.* On impulse she ran towards the feline, who abruptly turned and ran from her. She followed it into the open side door of the house next door, shutting and locking the door behind her. The creature led her to the front door of that house. As she emerged onto the porch, a dog barked from behind her.

Startled, Abby turned, just in time to see the canine run inside towards the living room. *The dog.* Again, on impulse she followed the waiting dog into the living room.

Abby gasped, bolting awake, her first breath making her cough and choke. *There must be mold here. I'm allergic and can barely breathe.* Horrified, she looked around her. *This isn't my house, or the hotel I was in with Mom. I'm in the same clothes I was in today eating ice cream. I was on the trip, then I went for a walk, met that lost little girl. Where in the hell am I? How did I get here?*

She was in a dark bedroom illuminated by moonlight. It had once been grand but was now covered in silt, dirt, and mold. There were the remains of huge spiderwebs in the corners, half in shadow. Long dingy white shreds of curtain remnants fluttered at the windows. The wood covering on the walls was an odd tiny fish scale pattern oozing water. The scent of rot and decay permeated the air. The bed she was in was just a mattress covered with a filthy rotting blanket, its once fine wool fibers soaked through and cold against her legs.

Two hands appeared at the base of her bed, then a gnarly unshaven face peered over the edge. "Little girl, are you trying to hide from me?" The man grinned, then began to crawl up the bed toward her.

Where's my crowbar! Abby flailed with her hands, her right seeking out and closing on the familiar metal. She swung hard with all her strength, the metal connecting with the fiend, knocking him sideways with the sharp crack of bone snapping. The man fell off the bed to the floor, unconscious.

Abby dashed for the door and threw it open, desperate to escape. She headed down the corridor. *Is this all a dream? Am I asleep in the hotel room? This house resembles the one in my nightmare, or whatever that was with the dwarf. It looked like my house on the outside, but the layout was wrong, plus there's no hidden wall in my basement.* She ran down the stairs and into the hallway, then cringed back against the door as two men emerged from another bedroom, fighting hard with knives, leaving a trail of blood. *Who the hell are they?*

"What did you do to Michelle?" one yelled. "You should've left her alone, Craig!" He stabbed Craig in the shoulder, the two of them falling sideways through another door as they grappled.

There were the sounds of more struggling interspersed with wet thuds.

Abby saw stealthy movement as a creature slinked up the stairs. She almost stepped forward, remembering the cat who had helped her, then paused, a bad feeling growing within her the more she looked at the thing creeping along. *It resembles a cat, but it's way too big for a cat. Its claws and its neck are too long.*

The thing went into the room where the men had gone. There was a ripping sound of rending meat accompanied by a shriek of terrible pain. A new male voice let out a yell of terror and a low rumble sounded.

That's laughter. It's killing them and laughing. Abby bolted down the stairs and out the front door, the night black as pitch, light from the illuminated windows behind her showing a drained lake and shadowed hulks of rocks. "Help! Please someone help me!" She staggered down to the shore, letting out a scream as she saw the stunted man ahead of her. He was bending over the body of an unconscious woman, both her legs horribly broken. The woman's eyes fluttered.

The dwarf pointed with his hand, baring his long, yellow teeth. "This is no dream, Abby. Get to shore now or die here." His eyes looked past her. "They're coming for you."

With another shriek, Abby dropped her crowbar and took off running, splashing through puddles as she ran through the darkness of the lakebed toward Carl's Point.

————

Faint screams and yells of terror reached the foursome on the mainland as they watched the lights of Latham's Landing go on until the entire house was shining brightly. "We have to help them, whomever they are!" Cheer urged.

"Help!" a voice yelled faintly across the water. "Please someone help me!"

"It's a woman," Barb said. "We can't just let her be killed!"

"We can't go to her," Bob said, as he dialed 911 on his cell. "We'd never get there in time on foot and even if Dakota's truck doesn't have a dead battery, it'd get mired in the mud of the lake bottom. Hello, this is Chief, um, Bob Stahl out at Latham's Landing. Send Sal Upner and an ambulance and whomever else you can reach right now! Someone's at the island and they're in trouble!"

Another terrified scream sounded.

The truck above, the lights still off, suddenly began to roll down the hill toward them, picking up velocity.

"What the hell? Dakota, hit the brakes!" Bob yelled.

The truck barreled toward them. They jumped to the side, evading the vehicle by inches as it plunged past. The truck rolled into the lakebed, where it immediately hit some boat wreckage with a bang of metal.

Another scream sounded on Cairn Isle, then was abruptly cut off. Silence descended, and then the lights in the island mansion all abruptly went out.

"She's dead," Barb whispered.

"Then why's the glass room still bright?" Maryanne whispered.

The Sea Room was brilliant in the gloom against the cloud-packed sky, its light steady and blinding.

"What exactly is illuminating it?" Cheer whispered, shading her eyes with her hand. "There were no lights I saw inside at all."

"Wouldn't matter anyway, electric power is shut off to everything," Bob whispered. "I advise we get to the top of the hill as fast as possible. I don't like that it's so quiet. Something's up." He turned to head up the incline and let out a yell as he fell sideways, tumbling down the hill.

"Bob!" Barb yelled, taking a step.

There was a low growl in front of her, then another to her left. Barb braced herself for an attack, gripping the cross in her pocket. Maryanne began to pray softly aloud, her voice shaking a bit. Shapes rose up from the grass in a circle around the three women, two pairs of yellow orbs glowing. But instead of facing them, the two Hustermen were facing the Sea Room. The shadows let out a hiss, then flowed down the hill following Bob.

"I can't believe this," Cheer managed, then fumbled with her camera, snapping picture after picture.

"Bob!" Barb took a deep breath, then plunged down the hill, moving as fast as she dared. The Hustermen weaved in front of her like two hounds following a trail, darting impossibly fast as they snuffled and growled. Another suddenly joined the two from the left, then two more came slipping past her from behind her. Together, they approached where Bob had fallen. He lay on his back on the grass near the bottom. A white shape was bending over him.

"Stop!" Barb yelled. "He is not evil! He doesn't belong to you."

"He does," a sepulchral voice intoned, as the misty shape rose, becoming a woman in a white filmy gown, bows of white ribbon in her short brown curls.

"Murderess," the Hustermen hissed together. Two lunged at the woman, their shadows enveloping her form. They twined about her tightly, undulating, suffocating her.

The light from the Sea Room brightened, then suddenly dimmed.

There was a howl of pain, and then the woman reappeared as the shadows parted, flitting away from her to regroup with the others. The Hustermen hissed again at her angrily. She let out a tinkle of laughter, then took another step towards Bob.

Barb blocked her way, brandishing holy water in one hand, and the remnants of her burning sage in the other. "Leave."

"You leave," the woman said, advancing. "Or stay and die."

There was the sound of sirens across the lake, as flashing lights came into view.

Barb threw the holy water on the woman ghost. It passed through her with no effect to land on the ground. *This can't be happening!* She let go of the sage as the last ember burned her hand and fumbled in her pockets for other herbs and her matches. *Damn it, I left the herbs behind!*

The Hustermen let out another hiss in unison, as Cheer and Maryanne slid down the hill carrying the herbs.

"Light the herbs now!" Barb yelled. "Quick!"

The ghost straddled Bob where he lay, took his face in her hands, and kissed him on the mouth. His eyes shot open as he awoke, thrashing violently beneath her.

"Stop!" Barb shouted, as she tossed the two flaming smoking bags of herbs at the woman. One landed at her side, the other passing through her, but she flickered wildly, then disappeared, to reappear some distance away, her expression furious.

"Spirit, return to your house," Maryanne intoned, making the sign of the cross. She began reciting the Lord's Prayer.

The woman's eyes narrowed, and she took a step towards Bob, only to stop as if she'd come up against a wall. Cheer and Barb had grabbed the herbs and scattered them about Bob, Maryanne, and themselves, making a messy protective circle.

There was a high-pitched whine, and multiple headlights of ATVs appeared at the far shore, then approached over the lakebed, gaining ground rapidly.

"Here!" Barb shouted, waving her flashlights in the air. "Here!"

The ghost glared at them, then disappeared. The light in the Sea Room went completely dark.

———

"You sure you don't mind us spending the night?" Cheer asked, as she took several quilts and pillows from Barb. Maryanne was making up the couch bed with sheets. Cooper was fast asleep in front of a crackling fire.

"Not at all. You two saved us. I dropped the bags of herbs in the crucial moment when I'd been carrying them all damn day." Barb grimaced. "So stupid."

"We all panicked, even though we went in prepared. None of us want to be alone tonight," Maryanne said. "Though there's not much we can do for Bob."

"He's in good hands at the hospital," Barb said. "He did wake up briefly, before they gave him the sedative." She bit her lip, looking at the two others. "We should go over things, write everything down while its fresh. Are you both awake enough?"

"I don't think I'll sleep tonight until I pass out from exhaustion," Cheer admitted, spreading out the quilt and sitting down. "I'm going to have nightmares for sure."

Maryanne sat down, too. "I can say a blessing over you if you like. How's Bob's heart? Did they say that's what it was?"

Barb nodded. "A mild heart attack. I can imagine that it would have been a major one if the ghost had maintained contact for a few more seconds. She's probably what happened to Anita's husband all those years ago."

"Dakota's still missing?"

Barb nodded. "There was no blood or signs of struggle in his truck. Battery was dead. Do we assume the Hustermen got him?"

"It follows, as they appeared right near where his truck was. What about who screamed from the house?"

"A young woman, unidentified. She was found hysterical some distance from the house with a broken ankle. Upner took her back with him to get a statement and medical treatment, but they had to sedate her for now. I'd say the house brought her here and she was able to escape on foot somehow, maybe because the water was missing. We should talk to her when she's able to talk. Speaking of talking, we need to get down all the details from today. Who wants to go first?"

The three all recounted what they had discovered in the cemetery, on the island, and on the Sea Room, as Barb took notes to document everything. "That's everything. Do we want to put any other possible conclusions or next steps down?"

"We should see if there is anyone still living who knew Lorelei or anything about when she worked for the Lathams," Maryanne said. "I'm guessing she had an affair with Latham, and she witnessed something she was killed for. I'll also go over the notebook I found and see if there's anything in there that's meaningful." She made a face. "Probably not, it's not a diary. It's an autograph book if you can believe it."

"That's odd. The Latham's didn't have movie star guests, from what I read?"

"It looks like it belonged to a young woman for friend auto-graphs," Maryanne said. "Something like a high school yearbook, possibly for those who didn't go past grade school."

"We can hope it's Lorelei's," Barb muttered. "While the holy water seems to work great on the mansion, it had no effect on that woman ghost. She ripped apart the Hustermen like they were tissues. The herbs were the only thing that worked, and I'm not sure she wasn't just caught by surprise. But we do have a new hard fact: there is a woman ghost who's able to kill haunting the Sea Room, one that no one's ever reported before. It's likely she that powers its illumination."

"Do we think that was Latham's wife?" Cheer said. "I did get two shots of her before she disappeared. I'll go tomorrow first thing and develop all the pictures I took. Maybe there's something on them to help." She paused. "But there's something else."

"What?"

"I think whomever the female spirit is, she's got something to do with the woman's skeleton that was found in the house," Cheer said. "If the skeleton is not hers, it's someone who was important to her, either a mother or daughter or some other relative. Removing it made her angry and began all the murders on the island. I think we need to steal the skeleton from the university and rebury it on the island, if we can figure out any possible legal way that could physi-cally be done."

"She's also why the Hustermen were repelled, most likely," Barb agreed, nodding. "The ghosts on the island are too strong for them to vanquish, or at least this new female ghost is. Or maybe the Hustermen are so badly made that they can't feed on anyone who isn't human."

"I'm upset that my faith and the holy water I blessed had no effect," Maryanne said, irritated. "The power of God should work against any evil. That female ghost is evil. She went right after Bob, meaning to kill him. I don't understand why my faith had no effect when burning plants did."

"We don't know your faith had no effect," Barb soothed. "No, the holy water didn't stop her. But I think your prayer did have an effect.

I also got the impression that no one's ever escaped her before...or even fought back."

"There's something there maybe, too," Cheer mused. "Bob was threatening to destroy the island, bulldoze the house or have it taken apart and hauled away. The woman went after him but not us."

"Maybe she just hates men."

"Maybe this has nothing to do with him being a man...or his threat," Maryanne contemplated. "Maybe it has to do with him being the owner of the island. She said he belonged to her. Not that the island belonged to her, but that he did. Why would she say that?"

Barb stifled a yawn. "I've got to go to sleep, it's after midnight. Let's pick this up tomorrow."

———

The night air's too hot for this early in spring, Donna thought to herself as she opened the window in the kitchen wider. *Especially as we just had that foot of snow a week ago.*

"I was going to ask you if you wanted me to put the air conditioner in the window," her husband Allen said from behind her as he hugged her. "It's pretty early, but maybe we are going to have an early summer."

Donna shook her head, looking out into the dark front yard. *What's that big shadow next to the birdfeeder? Must be a deer.* "It's too early. We might get another snowstorm. We've had them before in May."

"I thought the temperature was supposed to drop," her husband said. "That's why you made the prime rib."

"After all the years of living here, you're surprised about weird weather?" Donna teased him, as she checked the meat with a thermometer. "Almost done."

"I'm not surprised so much as confused," Allen said as he got two plates out of the cupboard. "It was supposed to rain a lot, and it hasn't. The temperature was supposed to drop, and instead it's gone up since this afternoon."

"I'm used to storms with a lot of rain coming out of nowhere most anytime of the year, or that strange thaw last winter when all the snow and ice melted."

Her eyes slid over to lock on his, her expression trepidatious as her volume dropped to a whisper. "But I can't remember a time when it was forecast to rain a lot and it didn't. Not ever."

"Maybe it's because no one's out there poking around," Allen said in a hushed tone. "And the lake around it is drained, so even a few inches of water isn't going to be able to have much of an effect—"

There was a clang from outdoors as something metal fell to the ground.

"Damn it," Allen said, putting down the plates on the counter. "It's so warm that the racoons are out already and they're in the bird-seed. I'll be right back." He headed to the door.

"Don't go out there," Donna said sharply, running after him and grasping his arm. "I saw something out the window too big to be a raccoon."

There was another bang from outside.

"I'm not paying another sixty dollars for another birdfeeder from Amazon," Allen griped, pulling away. "It's got to be a bear then. A few shots fired will scare it off." He headed for the hall closet.

"Well, stay on the deck," Donna said, as she headed back to the kitchen. She took out the prime rib and set it on the stove as she heard the front door open, and Allen muttering as he stomped out onto the deck. *I'd better close the windows, maybe it was the smell of the cooking meat that attracted the bear.* She closed the one above the microwave, then headed back into the dining room to close that window and let out a shriek.

The window was open about five inches as she'd left it, a ruin of metal grid on the floor, as if someone had ripped out the screen with their hand and mashed it into a ball.

"Allen! Get in here!" She backed away, then heard a hiss to her left. Slowly she turned, just in time to see a huge shadow looming over her, its yellow orbs bending down to bore into hers.

"Prideful," it hissed softly, then lunged forward as she let out a final shriek.

CHAPTER NINE

THE NEXT NIGHT CHEER, BARB, AND MARYANNE MET AGAIN. "Can I start?" Cheer asked. "I have new information that might make all the difference."

"Sure, good news would be most welcome," Barb affirmed, handing out coffee. "I went to see Bob. He's stable but weak. He will hopefully be out in a couple days. They want to do a lot of tests."

"That's good news," the other two murmured, as they all sipped their drinks.

"Let's hear it," Barb said.

"Okay, let's start with the woman ghost. I got no usable photos of her, the film's just blank, not even a misty form. Like Maryanne said, holy water didn't seem to slow her down."

"Because it wasn't blessed," Maryanne fumed, looking angrier than Barb had ever seen her. "One of my colleagues, I won't name names, decided that he didn't think the water needed an extra blessing as he'd taken it out of the baptismal basin after performing a ceremony. But the water itself hadn't been blessed." She clenched her fist angrily, then relaxed it. "Anyway, I have blessed some new water, and I did three blessings on it instead of one." She handed them each a bottle. "Here you go."

"Thanks," Cheer said as she accepted it. "I think this will work great to ease my mind tonight at bedtime. Something else: the herbs made that female ghost pause her attack, as if she'd never come up against any impediment before. Barb, you said you hadn't seen her. The ghost also didn't recognize you, which makes me think she wasn't aware of what happened with Mac, Helter, Carolyn, and you. Maybe not even know about it. How is that possible?

"Because none of us ever went to the Sea Room," Barb said in sudden realization. "Not even to the bridge entrance on the main island. That ghost was surprised because she must haunt the Sea Room exclusively. There are no documented cases of a woman ghost. But the Sea Room lit up on several occasions right before we witnessed manifestations that attacked us on the main island. I conclude that she's somehow the battery for the demon on Cairn Isle. Let's come back to that. Cheer, were there any ghosts your camera did capture?"

"I had over two hundred pictures," Cheer said tiredly. "Be aware I went as fast as I could looking through these on my computer and then printing some to give to the police department plus blowing several up at the print store, so I might have missed something." She produced a short stack of 3x5s. "Here are shots of all the gravestones, including the rich people." She produced another stack of 3x5s. "Here are pictures of the various boat remains. I put numbers on the back to note how close they were to the island to try to give the police a better means of locating them. Three means closer than halfway to shore, two means farther than halfway from shore and one means right on the line. Then I noticed a pattern."

"What pattern?" Barb asked curiously.

"Bob always said that people that got too close to the island in boats crashed on rocks that seemed to appear magically," Cheer said excitedly. "Yet some of the boat wreckage has rocks near it, and some doesn't. What stood out was that most of the wrecks aren't close to the island. They're instead concentrated over a certain spot of the lake."

"There's likely more we didn't see that are still covered by water," Maryanne protested.

"Even so, look at this shot," Cheer said, passing them a photo.

"Lots of wreckage and rocks," Barb said. "But that's what you've been saying."

"Now look at this one," Cheer said, passing her a second.

"This must be looking down towards the deeper end of the lake. I see mostly unbroken water and almost no wreckage near the large rocks on the exposed lakebed. Why?"

"I don't think that people are chosen to be wrecked by how close they are to the island, unless they are trying to escape after having visited it, like you did. I think it's something else."

"What?"

"Look at this one," Cheer said, handing Barb another photo. "Here's the farmhouse and barn remains we noticed. Just visible beyond is an outcropping of the shore near the old cemetery there's something else. See it?"

"Yes," Maryanne said. "A foundation. Possibly the remains of a church or the Latham family chapel? It makes sense that if there was a graveyard there that there was someplace for holding a funeral close nearby."

"A chapel makes sense, as there was a cemetery right near it. We need to look into when it was flooded. Maybe that is where Latham was buried."

"Great work," Barb praised.

"I'm not finished," Cheer teased, her eyes excited. "Look at these."

She passed out five pictures.

"Holy shit," Barb breathed. "I remember her."

In the first, the dank rotting glass porch of Latham's Landing was shown, broken windows and wreckage to the left, and the interior wall to the right. Near the floor was a broken frame and the remains of a painting. Standing next to it was a little blonde girl in a pink dress, glowering with hate directly into the camera.

"You've seen her?"

"There was a music room in that new addition being built. She hid in the room, chased me, then turned into a horrific monster. It just wears a little girl's shape to get close to victims."

"I'll add something I didn't share before as I wasn't certain it was connected," Cheer said. "I saw video of a little girl in a pink party dress on a surveillance video tape from a convenience store where a person disappeared. She walks out of the range of the camera, then there's a splash of something liquid that lands on the floor."

"Blood?" Barb offered.

Cheer nodded. "I think so. There's also the hand of some other unknown person that enters the edge of the screen that cleans up the blood on the floor before withdrawing."

"Any more of your shots have ghosts in them?" Barb asked.

Cheer passed her the rest of the photos. Another picture showed the long stone bridge from the concrete base of the Sea Room. In the distance a rider in a red coat sat on a bay horse, staring intently. Another was of a group of four teens standing near the edge of the island shore, the front of the house in the background. The last two showed a man watching them angrily from the island shoreline, the back of the house behind him.

"The last two are Mac." Barb's voice cracked. "The house is different than it was, but that's him."

"Are these ghosts or the demon wearing their forms?"

"Could be either," Barb said, putting her face in her hands. "I don't know what to do. We have so many odds and ends."

"I may have some answers, for what it's worth," Maryanne said, producing the little brown notebook. "This autograph book belonged to one of the maids in Latham's household, some girl they call Flip. Most of the notes are just good wishes, but several of the entries thank Flip for working with them at the Oklahoma Laundry. I looked into this, and there was a laundry that operated there back at the turn of the century and for most of this century."

"Nice, but how is this relevant?" Cheer asked.

"Because Lorelei signed this book," Maryanne said, opening it to a marked page and handing it to her. "Read what she wrote."

"Leaves may wither, flowers may die, friends might forget you, but never will I." Barb looked at Maryanne. "Pretty dramatic."

"All the other entries are normal stuff you might find in a yearbook: casual scrawls of good wishes, uneven and messy, with slang and misspellings," Maryanne said. "Lorelei's entry has the poem, and Lorelei's name and Latham's Landing in perfect penmanship beneath it."

TARA FOX HALL

"What do you think it means?"

"That she was educated, something uncommon to most women of that time who weren't aristocracy," Maryanne said. "I don't think she was just a servant. I think she was related to Latham."

"Why would you think that?"

"Because that Oklahoma laundry where she worked belonged to the VanManns and the Hershers, along with a number of other businesses. You know who inherited everything when they died en masse? Latham."

"Wait, hand me those pics of the headstones," Barb asked. She flipped through them. "Look at this. Those two families died a good two months before Lorelei."

Cheer nodded. "I propose whatever her connection to Latham, she either saw something she wasn't supposed to, or she came forward as a relation to claim an inheritance, maybe as an illegitimate child of Latham's brother. She was killed by the demon or Latham, but she was buried with honor because of her station. Latham viewed her as family, which is why she's in the family graveyard. It's a good enough explanation to discard her as our future focus and rule her out as the woman ghost in the Sea Room."

"Wait," Barb said wearily, holding up Cheer's photo of Lorelei's gravestone. "There's one more thing that might mean something. These dates can't make sense unless there's more than one Latham."

"What do you mean?" Cheer asked.

"Lorelei died in September of 1929. The Crash was October 1929. That means Latham died a month after Lorelei... and his wife died before him, so she also died in fall of 1929. So how do we have him doing all these works Anita talks about, like the camp or the businesses? She can't be old enough to remember them."

"It's 1995," Maryanne said gently. "Anita is close to 85 now."

"Which makes her 19 at the time of Latham's death if he died in 1929," Cheer said in puzzlement. "You're right, Barb. I ran across Bob's newspaper spread of death tolls and he begins in 1900 because that was the first year there were drownings. There seems to have been a body of water already here, a much smaller and shallower natural lake. It would have resembled the water level now, actually." She paused. "In regard to Latham's actual death, there's no docu-

140

mented date or resting place. A possible theory is that he faked his death to escape the effects of the 1929 Crash, or to cash in on his life insurance. They didn't fingerprint or do DNA back then so he could have left town and changed his appearance, then come back a few months later to collect the money and take ownership of the island. I don't see any way to know for sure given we have no way to get any more information about him."

"Agreed," Barb said. "So where do we go from here?"

"I think we have to find Latham's grave," Maryanne said. "Or assume that he died on the island and hold a funeral there on the shore to try to put his spirit to rest, along with the other spirits that are haunting the island. People may have died on the lake, but we see no spirits in the water in the pictures, just on the island."

"Would they show up?" Cheer muttered. "Remember that the pictures showed the ghosts or demon on the island, but we didn't see them standing right there with us." She shivered. "The homicidal female ghost we did see but couldn't photograph. We're in over our heads here."

"Yes, true," Maryanne said with a nod. "But the herbs and my prayers worked together to keep us safe enough to go to the island and leave it again without an attack. We must focus on the demon and the woman ghost. We may not be able to do much. But if they are using the island to draw in people to kill, as we surmised the island used Mac, then the demon or evil force want souls. The mermaid, if she really is that and not a ghost or demon manifestation, is another decoy. If she eats the bodies, gross, but her feeding is not the point of the killings, it's just effective cleanup. The goal of Latham's Landing seems to be to trap the souls on the island and draw as much fear from them as possible before death. If we set loose those trapped souls, we weaken the island."

"How does holding a funeral do anything for a haunting?" Cheer asked.

"Why do they call Latham's Landing Cairn Isle? Is it just because of the people who have died there over the years? Many more than that have died in the lake by drowning, right? Most of the deaths are recent, right? So why is the nickname cairn, and not death or murder or haunted isle?"

"Because it sounds cooler?"

"I'm serious," Maryanne argued. "Cairn literally means a tomb, a burial place. Locals called it that starting right after Latham died, from my research. The old story said he flooded the house after his wife died, never says that he died, but it was assumed. So it is her tomb definitely, and it's very likely his tomb also, or at least where he died."

"So?"

"So it's possible no one ever administered any funeral rites for them. We could give them a funeral and put their ghosts to rest."

"What I photographed and saw with my own eyes out there on the island wasn't a simple ghost looking for closure, it was demonic activity," Barb interjected. "Real evil. Sure, it would be nice if laying ghosts to rest would work, but there's no logical reason it would. The demon wouldn't let it."

"Holy water did work against anything manifesting on the main island," Maryanne reminded her. "You said so yourself, Barb." She paused. "All this started when Latham's wife died. That's the catalyst. What if the evil there is able to focus its strength because the island is connected to her death in some way? There has to be some reason that the evil chose to make a home there. Demonic activity usually starts up after some traumatic, violent event takes place. People get murdered every day, and we don't have demonic activity occurring after. If everything at Cairn Isle started by Mrs. Latham's soul not being able to pass on, then giving her rest should allow her to pass on and sever the demon's attachment."

"Yes, fighting the evil with everything we can think of in an attempt to destroy the island seems to result in a draw at best. And that's if we're extremely lucky, prepared, and resourceful," Barb countered. "Maybe you're right, Maryanne, and all that's left is to possibly do some kind of spiritual healing."

"Spiritual healing?" Cheer said, raising her eyebrows. "You're serious?"

"If you don't have anything helpful to add, Cheer, then shut up," Barb snapped angrily. "Who would do this healing, Maryanne? You alone?"

"I could ask a priest I know," Maryanne said reluctantly. "He'd be willing to do a blessing. Father Jacob."

Cheer stood up. "I don't feel like you're taking my ideas seriously here, either of you. We've talked enough. Instead of getting anywhere we keep tossing out more and more theories that we can't prove and are of dubious merit in a best-case scenario. We need to get the skeleton out there and rebury it. I think that's the source of the woman's ghost, and it likely is Latham's wife who he killed out there in the Sea Room and then he brought her back to the main island and flooded the grave to cover it up. It's the simplest explanation that also fits all the evidence."

"If you think you can steal the skeleton, go ahead," Barb said, sitting back and staring at her. "I think you're right for what it's worth, Cheer, I just don't see a way to get the bones without getting arrested. But if you do have a plan, go do it. When you have the bones, call us and we'll go out there and help you bury them."

Cheer glared at her, then abruptly stomped to the door. She left, slamming it behind her.

"I shouldn't have been so nasty," Barb said tiredly, getting to her feet. She headed for the door, but Maryanne stopped her, as the sound of tires squealing out faded in the distance.

"You're being honest. There's no way the university will give up the skeleton legally to us, not for any reason I can think of. And trying to break into the university museum will just get us arrested." Maryanne patted her shoulder. "Earlier you said you'd come back to something about that woman ghost. What was it?"

Barb looked at Maryanne for a moment, then let out a sigh. "You're going to think I'm crazy, even given what you've seen so far. But just hear me out." She took a breath. "I think the woman ghost is the key. We need to communicate with her directly."

Maryanne was incredulous. "That ghost doesn't want to communicate. She wants to kill."

"I have been in contact with a woman who is a kind of psychic. I met her years ago at another haunted house with more than one malevolent spirit that was killing people. I consulted with her a little before I went to Latham's Landing the first time. But I was dumb and didn't take along the holy water like she instructed. She contacted me after she found out what happened to me. I've asked her to come and help us. She should be here tomorrow."

"She's done spiritual healing?"

"She has." *In a manner of speaking.*

"On a house?"

"On a house that was haunted by several ghosts, several of which were powerful and malevolent."

"She cleansed the house?"

"She had help from a few of the ghosts there that were friendly, worked with her against the murderous ones. She can talk to ghosts." Barb took a breath and let it out. "I think she may be able to get this woman ghost to tell us her past. If we know what happened, there's got to be something we can do to appease the ghost."

"This is crazy, but you're right, we are out of options. So, let's go with crazy. What's her name?"

"Jean Bane."

———

Jean walked up a tall escarpment, her legs straining as she went on all fours close to the pinnacle. With a grunt she reached the top, looking out over a sandy beach and small amusement park with only a few rides running. She walked down to the water's edge toward the beach, looking for any written signs to tell her where she was. There were some people on the sand sitting on towels but almost no one in the water, the day overcast and cool. A young pre-teen girl with dark hair was sitting by the bank of the lake, her expression forlorn.

Jean walked up to her. "Is it usually this overcast? Or is there supposed to be rain?"

The girl looked at her then away, shrugging. "Don't know. Don't care."

"I wouldn't go swimming on a day like today," Jean said, shivering as she pulled her jacket tighter around her. *I'm wearing some kind of sundress that's to my knees? But so is she.*

"Not unless you don't want to come back to shore," the girl retorted bleakly.

Something in her tone made Jean shift uncomfortably and forget about her odd clothing. "Don't go in. The water's murky, and it looks like there's some old furniture or pipes or something just under the surface."

"Almost like there was once a town under the lake," the girl said in an icy manner. "Someone forgot about it before they flooded it. Everyone's forgotten about it. Just like everyone's forgotten about me." She frowned. "Or maybe they just don't care."

"I'm sure your family loves you," Jean consoled, even as she began scanning the closest people, looking for someone to ask for help. *This kid needs some counselling. She sounds almost suicidal.* "Why don't we walk over to the concession stand and I'll buy you a drink." She searched her pocket for cash, finding her wallet with relief.

Jean looked up, her eyes rounding in horror to see the girl out in the lake up to her waist, being knocked off balance by waves. A stiff breeze had suddenly come up. "Don't go farther! Come back!" She turned to the beach. "Help! Help! She's going to drown!"

Two lifeguards ran over, charging into the water as Jean kept yelling, telling the girl to return to shore. Oddly enough, before they reached the girl she turned back toward the shore and avoiding them, slugged her way through the water towards the beach, stomping up the sand and heading towards the rides. The lifeguards followed her, with a wave of thanks to Jean.

Jean followed them, losing sight of the girl in the crowd. She went into a small soda shoppe on the small boardwalk and sat down at the counter. A man in a cream and yellow uniform brought her some water. "What'll it be?"

"A root beer float, if you have that? And an order of French fries?"

"Of course," he answered with a nod. "Do you have fifty cents? I don't mean to be presumptuous, but with the war we've had to up our prices."

Jean handed her money to the man, not surprised to see that some of the coin and bill portraits were unfamiliar to her. *I'm in the past. This is either a dream...or a vision.*

A white man with short dark hair in a suit and tie approached her table and sat down. "I'm glad to meet you, Jean. I've been expecting you."

"Who are you?" Jean said bluntly. "What do you want with me?"

The man held his hands up with a disarming smile. "I don't want anything, unless you want to give me something?" He chuckled. "As for who I am, my name is Lunker Leighton."

"That means 'big fish'," Jean said, cocking her head to the side. "A nickname?"

"Just what I'm called," he said, motioning to the waiter, who brought over her fries and float. "But tell me about you. You must be a fisherman to recognize the slang. We don't often get visitors to Leighton Beach, only locals." He grinned. "Lately no visiting fishermen, either."

"This is Leighton Beach?" Jean asked, quickly trying to memorize the name. She sipped some of the float. *Wow, that's real ice cream and real root beer. Delicious!* "Are you the owner?"

Lunker shook his head. "I have the name, that's all. The town owns the beach, the camp and the land all the way to town. Are you staying long?"

Jean studied Lunker as she drained her frosty glass, deciding she liked his manner. "No, I need to get going." She scanned the shore, catching sight of the dark-haired girl getting on a ride close to the water's edge. Oddly, the other rides were all dark now, their lights off. *That's an octopus-style ride, the arms move around as the base spins. It's the kind kids get sick on.* "How late does the beach stay open?"

"Most everyone heads home after dark," Lunker said, standing. "I've got to get going myself. You take care, Jean."

Jean didn't see him leave, her eyes on the girl on the octopus ride. The metal arms were spinning and now the base of the ride was popping up and down. *Jesus, she's taken off her seat belt. She's going to be thrown into the lake!*

Jean ran for the exit, the boardwalk before her empty, the lights around her going dark one after another as she ran under them. She let out a scream as the ride popped up fast, throwing the girl free. Her form hurled out into the turbulent lake, a huge wave closing over her.

"Save her!" she yelled, then sat up in bed, the noise of her shout still echoing in the bedroom. She ran a hand through her sweat-damp hair. "Lunker. Leighton Beach. The girl with dark hair." Then she reached onto her bedside table for a paper and pen.

———

The lake surface stirred slightly, ripples forming as the light wind fled down the length of the water. The house stood quiet and dark on its isle; the black shadows unbroken at its base like a length of black velvet pooled at its feet. The sky was black, the new moon a sliver of light wreathed in clouds high above that gave no lasting brightness.

The herd of sheep grazing on the hill lifted their heads as one as the lighted motorboat chugged softly down from the deep end of the lake to a spot north of the island, it's metal hull laden with equipment. Teeth stopped it a good half mile from Latham's Landing and dropped anchor.

"I know you can hear me," he called out across the water as he set up some depth equipment. "Come to the boat."

There was no answer in the stillness.

Teeth worked along in the darkness, making no sound as he measured the depth of the water, then pulled up anchor and motored in a fan shaped pattern, measuring depth repeatedly. He also dropped a few oxygen diffuser pumps, switching them on as he tossed them overboard. As he pulled up anchor on the next to last stop, there was a splash in the stillness to his left near the shore.

Teeth paused, waiting.

Another splash sounded nearer. Then another.

Teeth sat down in the boat, leaned over the edge, and wiggled his fingers at the surface of the water. "Here, fishy, fishy."

There was a sudden slap of fins against the hull, then the boat rocked hard, spilling Teeth into the bottom of the boat with a curse. He regained his feet, just as another fin slapped the other side of the boat hard, denting the metal and almost flipping the boat.

"Knock it off!" Teeth braced himself for a third hit, but the waters calmed, the rippling surface returning to serenity. He stood, and reached for a pail, then tossed its contents over the side, the chum turning the water inky black. He stored the pail, then turned to motor back the way he had come. "What in the hell?"

There was a faint brightness just visible down the lake. But it was not at Latham's Landing or the Sea Room, where he had seen lights before in his years on the lake. It was past them, making the decrepit mansion cast a long shadow, a shadow that was shifting slightly, indicating the lights behind it were moving.

Has to be headlights. "What idiots thought it was a good idea to come out here in an ATV and ride the lakebed in the middle of the night," Teeth growled, as he started the motor. "Upner's going to hear about this." He roared off north in the direction of his dock, the darkness closing around him as he dialed his phone. Splashes followed him, then subsided.

An hour later, Upner arrived at Carl's Point, Teeth following him. The two cars parked side by side and both men got out. "Why'd you need me to come here?" Teeth growled, slamming his door. "It's nearly dawn, and I've put in a full night already. Just look for tracks. They had to have entered the lakebed at Carl's Point. There's too much wreckage, water, or rocks everywhere else."

"I would have believed you if you'd said there were lights out on Latham's Landing," Upner shot back. "Hell, I wouldn't even have come out here myself for that. But you said you saw at least one ATV out here on the lakebed. We have had six missing people this year, Teeth, if you count the three at the development and old Camp Leighton, plus Donna and Allen, and now Dakota. That's three *locals*. I have been pulling sixteen-hour days and I am still going to get voted out this November. I have two kids; I can't let that happen. I can't have another local go missing. I can't even have one drunk asshole found dead near the lake in an ATV accident."

"That doesn't answer why I'm here," Teeth replied coolly.

"I want to know exactly where the lights were that you saw," Upner retorted coldly. "Because I don't see any lights now."

"Follow me." Teeth navigated a path through some small trees, decaying old wood, and several boulders. "There's a good view of the island from here, but not of the little trench on the far side of it. They're probably in there. There's no way they could have driven out of the lakebed in the time it took us to get back here, and you're right, the entire lakebed's dark now."

"There's no trench on that side," Upner argued as he followed.

"There's a plain all the way to the beach. If they were there, we'd see lights."

"You're wrong. I have measured the lake depth enough years to know," Teeth retorted. "The depression in the lakebed isn't big or wide; thirty feet at its deepest, which is enough to hide in. It starts right off the far side of the island and runs for several miles to where the Dockhouse used to be. Probably why Latham built the Dockhouse where he did, because its deep enough for very large boats to navigate from there to Latham's Landing with no danger of hitting rocks." Teeth paused on the shore and pointed where lights were impossibly emerging from the darkness of the lakebed like a lantern-eyed monster rising up out of blackness. "See I was right. There they are."

"Those headlights are too far apart for an ATV. Is that a car?" Upner said in disbelief. "How in the hell did it get out there without getting stuck?"

The twin headlights began moving again. The lights went out of sight as wreckage blocked them, then reappeared.

"It's following the depression." *That car should be sunk to the top of its tires in water, if not completely submerged.* "How is it driving out there is the better question," Teeth uttered darkly. "And who's driving it?"

"I should radio in for backup. I should've brought an ATV," Upner said, reaching for his radio on his belt. "I am not going to try to walk out there and risk breaking a leg."

"Wait," Teeth cautioned softly, stopping him. "Listen."

"What?"

"Shut up," Teeth hissed. "Look!"

There came an ominous rumble from a long way off. A dog barked. A barely audible murmuring floated on the breeze.

"Whose dog is that? What is that noise?"

"You're hearing conversations carrying on the wind," Teeth said in disbelief. "There's people out there, and someone's got their dog."

"Bullshit!" Upner grabbed for his radio. "I'm calling this in."

As the car climbed slowly towards Latham's mansion on its hill, other lights were coming on along the lakebed in the direction of the beach, one by one. Oddly, some looked to be up in the air at a higher level than the headlights. There were five clusters of lights when a peal of a bell broke through the night air, startling both men so they jumped.

"The belltower must be reforming," Upner murmured. "This can't be happening."

"No," Teeth said, pointing. "Look in front of the car!"

The headlights briefly illuminated a short building: a church built of granite, a bell in its small plain tower ringing hard. The car accelerated, speeding directly up towards the mansion. All the mansion windows illuminated, and a trio of other buildings there also lit up, showing people in evening dress running to get inside.

A sudden roar made both men turn their heads toward the island as a wave of water crested past the mansion on its hill, swirling at its base and slamming into the porch windows on its first floor, smashing them in a tinkling of glass and drowning all in its path. There was a scream, then a chorus of screaming from the valley below. The church bell rang faster, the dire warning too late. The car tried to turn and flee as the incoming wave hit it, sliding it sideways and into a roll that left it resting upside down before black water swallowed it. Water enveloped the church, leaving only the tower visible before it too disappeared, the bell abruptly silenced. More screams sounded as water engulfed the rest of the lakebed, the lights vanishing one by one until there was dead quiet except for lapping water. Then that sound also vanished.

Dawn was breaking to the east, the sky lightening. In the weak light, the lakebed was again a mass of wreckage, pools of water, and piles of rocks. There was no sign of any cars, buildings, or bodies except the decrepit listing mansion on its hill and the Sea Room glittering in the distance like a prism.

"What the hell did we just see?" Upner said as he turned to Teeth, his radio forgotten.

"Latham's legacy," Teeth said ominously. "You need to come back midday with your ATVs and coroner. I'm guessing in that channel you're going to find the remains of a car, the remains of some houses, and more than a few old skeletons."

———

"Jean, this is Bob, Anita, Cheer, and Maryanne," Barb said, as she sat down next to Bob. "Everyone, this is Jean Bane. Jean, thanks for meeting us here."

"Hi," Jean said, sitting down and brushing back a lock of brown hair. "Barb has told me everything new you've discovered about Latham's Landing, plus the local mythology. Is there anything else you all want me to know or specifically keep in mind before I start asking questions?"

"The house was bad enough as a dangerous spot people avoided, back in my youth," Bob said, groaning as he shifted in his easy chair. "But the idea that my flooding it somehow made the entity there able to go off the island to kill random people...well, I can't live with that, that I made it worse. We have to find a way to stop it."

"The legend was that Latham flooded the island after his wife died. But what if he didn't do it because she died?" Jean proposed. "What if he was trying to stop the entity there, to trap it, because it had killed his wife?"

"Flooding the mansion hasn't stopped the entity. We just thought it had for a while."

"Let's look at the history, and stop me if I make any mistakes," Jean said. "The island is abandoned for a lot of years after its flooded, until the tours began, and the first person drowns. Then people go there, and one vanishes, a college-aged male. Tina and her friend Sandy, who is related to the missing male, go there. Sandy dies there, along with a group of four other college kids that went there to party. Their bodies are all found with a much older skeleton, yet not the remains of the original male who went missing. Other groups of college kids go there, they all die, no bodies found, assumed drownings. Barb, you go there with Helter and Carolyn, she vanishes, you and he are seriously injured but don't die, but there are three others that do die with no bodies found – the two cops and the serial killer. Oh, and those two trafficked women. Five deaths. What does this tell us?"

"Not to go there," Bob said.

"Yes," Jean said to his surprise. "So likely no one would have gone to the island for a while even if you hadn't bought the island. Whatever is there waiting is okay to wait for years at a time, so long as people visit eventually, and it can prey on them. But you cut off its future food supply along with its current one. So it reached out for victims."

"We know that," Cheer said irritably.

Jean nodded. "I don't want to rehash all of your findings, so I'll just go to my conclusions. Whatever evil is there at Cairn Isle has been there since the house was built, possibly before that. Latham tried to appease the evil by doing good works. But that revitalizing the shore and hiring locals and investing in the community doesn't point to a demon he was trying to appease that was in his house. They point to your female ghost in the Sea Room, who was somehow Latham's victim and attacks anyone male who comes to the Sea Room."

"Maybe you'll have to rehash some things," Barb interjected. "There's no proof of that."

"Wait," Jean said. "My guess is Sea Room Lady was local, someone with a tie to the community. Latham's efforts didn't work, and she killed his whole family one by one. The Sea Room is directly connected to the storms and flash thaw/freezing tricks: it always lights before these events. So she has to be involved."

"There's a demon or some evil being in a cloak with red eyes on the island," Bob stated.

"Yes," Jean agreed. "The demon likely came because it was attracted to the murders and seems to have appeared either right before or right after the two families died in the first big storm. Latham could have very well summoned it as a last-ditch attempt to fight the female ghost or maybe just to secure his legacy. And that seems to have worked. The woman ghost might like killing but she stays in the Sea Room and so misses out on the souls and life energy of people killed on the island and on the lake: she isn't aggressive, just defensive. Her turf for lack of a better term is the Sea Room. You enter there, she attacks." She paused. "I think we should approach the Sea Room first and ask her to tell us her story. Offer to leave the Sea Room alone and never enter again." She pointedly looked at Bob. "Just us girls. You stay here."

Barb took a sharp intake of breath. "You're saying there's two of them, and they work together, this ghost and the demon."

"I'm not letting you women go without me," Bob began.

"You can come to the island with me when I begin the funeral rites with Cheer," Maryanne assured. "She did get the skeleton after all. We are going to rebury it where it was found."

"How in the hell did you manage that?" Barb gaped at Cheer.

"Our chair? He was having an affair with the president of the University. I got pictures of them which I showed him as proof and threatened to out him to his wife," Cheer said with a grin. "He gave me the bones in trade for the negatives."

"Are you sure it's the right skeleton?"

Cheer nodded. "I checked, and the broken ribs he mentioned were broken, and copies of Bob's notes were enclosed with pictures taken at the time of exhumation."

Bob nodded. "I checked. The dates match, and it's my writing."

"You need to realize that when you flooded the island, you changed the dynamic that had existed for years," Jean said. "The female ghost was appeased and went dormant. But the demon on the main island is resisting going dormant."

"I wanted to stop the killings," Stahl said. "I also was following orders."

"Yes, and we need to speak to those people on a conference call soon," Jean said. "They know a hell of a lot and they showed up out of the blue asking you to do this. Logically they may have hoped for the demon to go dormant as it had before, but they also have to be well aware their plan is not working."

"Believe me, you would not ask to talk to them if you had talked to them before," Bob cautioned.

"You have no idea of the entities I have spoken to, or what I've seen," Jean said with eyes that appeared ancient suddenly. "Threats made by flesh and blood, no matter how bad, just don't compare." She looked at him. "Call them now."

Bob reached for the phone and dialed the number, as if he'd been waiting for this, clicking on the speakerphone.

"Yes?" a male voice answered.

Barb took a sharp breath. "Helter?"

The phone hung up immediately, the dial tone loud in the room.

"So the man who survived with you is behind this?" Jean asked Barb. "Helter?"

"It can't be," Bob said slowly.

"If we call back, will he answer?" Jean asked. "Or is there just a way to get a message to him?"

"There's a way to leave a message," Bob said, nodding.

"Call again and put it on speaker."

Bob dialed. This time the phone rang unanswered for ten times but then there was a click, and then a computer voice indicating to leave a message at the tone.

"This is Jean Bane. I and Barb and Bob and a couple others need to go back to the island to rebury a skeleton and talk to a ghost there. If there is any protection you can offer us, please meet us there tomorrow morning just after dawn on Carl's Point. Thank you."

———

"I don't see anyone," Maryanne said, as she put on her vestments on the shore and picked up her Bible.

"Doesn't mean that there's no one here," Barb said, casting an apprehensive eye towards the island. "It knows we're here."

"It should be happy," Cheer said, as she grabbed a duffel from the back of the truck and handed another to Barb and another to Jean. "Let's rebury the skeleton, then do the funeral."

"Agreed," Maryanne said. They began to pick their way across to the island.

When they were a few feet from the shore, Jean stopped them. "Latham's Landing!" she shouted. "We ask safe passage to return the bones of an unknown woman to you that was dug up some years ago and removed. Please allow us to rebury her with no interference."

There was silence.

"Did you expect a reply?" Cheer whispered.

"Enter," a bass voice boomed, the sound seemingly coming from all around them.

"Come on," Jean said, leading the way. They climbed the same red granite stairs of the harbor, and then headed for the sunken hallway. But instead of the dirt path leading to the expected wooden door, there was a large hole in the ground, raw earth gaping at the edges, the ground at the bottom watery mud.

"This wasn't here before," Cheer whispered fearfully.

"Toss in the bones," Jean ordered, as if this was all expected.

The four women opened their respective bags and emptied in the bones with shaking hands.

"Back away from the hole slowly," Jean said, as she moved back.

"Look in the hole," Maryanne breathed, stopping still, her eyes huge.

The bottom of the hole was now swimming in bones, some of them bleached and white, others grey with mold and green algae.

"Began your funeral rite," Jean said urgently. "Now, Maryanne!"

"Dearly Beloved, we are gathered today to lay the souls of the departed to rest—"

"There is no love here," the same malicious voice intoned harshly. "This is the vale of tears, holy man. A lake of tears. You will drown if you utter one more word, preacher."

"Don't stop," Jean urged. "Keep going!"

Maryanne let out a shriek as a hand reached up out of the ground and grasped her foot. Barb kicked at it, and grabbed hold of her, dragging her back out of reach. More hands burst from the soil, reaching upwards, broken nails dirty and caked with old blood and mold.

"Hear me, souls of the trapped!" Jean yelled, as they hurried to the lakebed. "There is no reason you must stay on the island. He keeps you here imprisoned out of fear! But you are dead...and free! Leave this island! Go now!"

There was a sound that seemed to be the wind rising, but instead there appeared several misty forms. They headed to the edge of the rocky shore, then walked off, disappearing in the sunlight.

"It can't be that easy," Maryanne said.

"It's not going to be," Jean said, as they headed to the Sea Room. "There's definitely a demon or something really bad there, not just a ghost or even ten ghosts. The bad feeling is palpable. What left just now was probably some remnants of ghosts so weak they weren't worth the demon trying to stop them."

"What can we do?" Barb mused.

"Let me have a while to think," Jean said. She went and sat on the shore by herself, staring out at the mansion.

"I'm not sure we made anything better," Cheer said, kicking at stones with her feet.

Water gushed up from the ground suddenly, skeletal hands grasping Cheer's legs. She was pulled down screaming, her eyes pleading as water closed over her head, her arms waving frantically for help.

"Cheer!" Barb screeched, as she went to her knees, Maryanne beside her, rooting in the water, trying to grab Cheer's flailing hands. But other clawed hands reached up eagerly from the water, flesh hanging from them in ribbons, and pulled them both in, water closing over their heads.

"No!" Jean shouted, bolting awake, covered in sweat, her heart pounding so fast she felt nauseous. She took a long shuddering breath, then another, forcing herself to calm down. *A vision or just a bad dream? I can't risk it wasn't a warning.* She got up and went to the phone, dialing Barb's number. "Barb, it's Jean. I need to cancel the planned trip to the island."

"That's okay," Barb said wearily. "We'd have had to cancel anyway. The sheriff's out there now with an archeology team of students from the university."

"Doing what?"

"Excavating a new mass grave."

———

"How did no one know that was there?" Bob said again, as he watched with his binoculars from the shore. "It's ridiculous they won't let me go out there when it's my land. There's got to be thirty college kids there."

"You're in no condition to ride an ATV to get out there, and if you fall off, you're going to end up back in the hospital," Barb reminded him. "Cheer is out there now with Jean taking pictures. Maryanne's out there, too. They'll report back to us tonight, though the pictures will likely be tomorrow."

"So why are you here babysitting me?" Bob asked grumpily.

"Because I heard that there was a dog involved," Barb said softly. "I've seen enough human death. I'm not going to watch a dog skeleton get unearthed."

"You're strange," Bob commented, as he watched what little he could see of the excavation. "A skeleton's a skeleton. Anyone who died out there had to have died almost a hundred years ago."

"Yes, and the ghosts of the dead or something else is still re-enacting those people's horrific last minutes," Barb shot back angrily. "That should tell you that the anger, fear, and pain is still active enough to be dangerous."

"You think that's why Latham flooded the island?" Bob offered. "Because he couldn't get the land while those people, whomever they were, lived?"

Barb didn't answer, looking at the rotting mansion as it sat on its hill, watching them.

———

"We've got five skeletons so far in the first foundation," the grad student reported to Upner and his deputy. "Three adults, a teen, and a baby. Other teams are digging in the other foundation remains. But we have to quit soon, its nearing dusk."

"I just don't understand why we didn't know these were here?" Upner said for the second time.

"I don't think there's anyone alive now that wasn't a very young child at the time that Latham died and the island flooded," the deputy answered. "I asked the librarians about old articles, but there's nothing I remember about people living in the lakebed drowning in the flood."

"For there to be water at the beach, this entire area had to be submerged," another student said. "For the island house to partially flood along its lowest section, the shallowest part of where we are standing now had to be under a good thirty feet of water. The deepest parts where we are digging, more like eighty." She paused for effect. "The remains we found are just bone, so there's no way to tell how they died. Yet they are buried in silt, some with part of the fieldstone foundations of their houses on top of them. That gives me cause to believe that there was either an earthquake, a hurricane, a tornado, or a tidal wave, something powerful enough to knock down the house completely." She paused again. "We are too far north and away from the coast for a hurricane, we haven't ever had a recorded earthquake of magnitude for this kind of damage in this state, and there's no record of any tornado ever hitting this county. That leaves a sudden, massive flood the only explanation left."

"But that doesn't fit the history we do know from our research," Cheer piped up, stepping forward. "Latham created the island and the lake and the beach, and the town and locals prospered for years. The lake didn't flood his mansion until some years after that. And there's no way that the town wouldn't turn against a man who had murdered a bunch of people to build this lake, even if it benefited everyone else and the people killed belonged to a leper colony. At the very least there would be some legend."

"I can only tell you facts," the grad student said. "What you do with them is up to you." She walked back to the nearest digging site.

"What's the plan?" the deputy asked Upner.

"We need to exhume any bodies or bones, and date them," Upner said tiredly, watching as a student used a shovel to scoop out more earth around a skeleton. "Just because we found the bones here doesn't mean they died here in these houses because of some flood."

"But she said—"

"Stones can shift over time, and half of the old graveyard on the shore probably floated out here when the lake flooded a hundred years ago," Upner interrupted. "These could also be bodies of people that drowned in the lake. It would make sense that bodies would get deposited here in the channel if they got stuck in wreckage—"

"But there's no wreckage here in this depression, Sal. Or on the edges of it either."

"—and stones could easily shift with all the storms we have here," Upner said loudly. "People being drowned out here in a boat makes sense and we have records of it happening on file. I've seen it. I never had anyone ever mention they knew anyone besides Latham that died when the island flooded."

"That doesn't mean no one else died," Jean said quietly. She met Upner's anxious gaze, then walked off.

Cheer watched her for a moment, then went back to taking pictures.

Jean walked past Maryanne, who was saying prayers over some of the bones that were being boxed up for transport to the University. She walked on to the base of the island, where Teeth stood by himself. "Do you want to tell me what you and Upner saw last night?"

"I figured it was all over town by now," Teeth said, not turning. "Deputy Dick there's not one for keeping a secret. Neither is Upner."

"You and Upner witnessed a ghostly reenactment of the island flooding. People died, several families at least. There was mention of a car that got upended and a church with a bell."

"Ayuh," Teeth commented.

"Tell me the truth. No more bullshit. I don't want anyone else to die."

Teeth turned to face her. "Then stop poking into this. Flood the island again and open the beach and lake again to boaters and fishermen but barricade the island so nobody goes there. Things will return to the way they were."

"You know this?"

"No," Teeth said, looking away. "But I think it's our best chance."

"Whose side are you on?" Jean asked.

"I'm on the side of the fish," Teeth answered. "They need the water back." He let out a breath. "The lawyers are working on it, and they'll get it back, but not soon enough. I've found five dead sturgeon in the last week. They need the deeper water."

"There's deep water on that entire end of the lake," Jean gestured.

"Not as deep as it was," Teeth retorted. "And not as much space as there was with half the lake dry."

He's not talking about the sturgeon. Jean stared at him. "Tell me about her."

"There's nothing to tell. We just want to be left in peace."

"Who is 'we'?"

"You can either help the fish or not," Teeth said, turning and walking away. "That's all I have to say."

Jean ignored him, carefully going to stand where he had been standing, her feet inside his much bigger prints. *He was looking at something, or for something.* There was the hill in front of her, the mansion at the top of the gentle slope.

The hill was too steep in front of her for a road, especially for a turn of the century car that would have had a higher center of gravity. But a road could have come around the side of the hill and up to the front...which would put the end of it near the mansion's front door.

Jean turned and looked over her shoulder at the students packing up their supplies. Upner and his deputy were still talking. Maryanne was talking to Cheer, gesturing to the place the skeletons had been found.

If the road snaked around the side of the hill, it could come right through where she was standing, and then down through middle of the depression. It would come back up a few miles distant, near opposite Carl's point.

Jean rubbed her eyes. "Please give me some guidance," she said aloud. "I want to help. Please." She stood for a few moments more, then turned to leave.

There was a faint sound of music.

Jean looked to her right, towards the Sea Room. In front of it, about a half mile distance, stood a figure playing a flute near a pool of water.

Jean cast a worried eye at the setting sun, then hurried toward the figure.

CHAPTER TEN

"HI!" JEAN CALLED OUT AS SHE APPROACHED THE FIGURE. "PLEASE, help me."

The girl in the faded shirt stopped playing the silver flute, then turned to face Jean, brushing her long brown hair out of her eyes. "I can't. You should go while you can. It'll be dark soon." Her eyes were full of sorrow and suffering. "You know what'll happen then."

"You heard me ask for help, and you appeared," Jean persisted. "Please tell me what you can. Don't you want to be free?"

The girl's hand clenched around the delicate flute as she looked towards the island. "I can never be free."

"Are you delaying me so I can't get back?" Jean challenged. "Were you just bait to lure me out here?"

The girl swung around to face her as if surprised, then smiled craftily. "I see you know the ways of spirits."

"All too well," Jean said, backing away. "I'm sorry. I need to go. I don't want to be trapped with you here forever."

"I understand," the girl said, then put her flute again to her lips, playing a captivating melancholy melody, two parts craving, one part agony.

All Jean wanted was to stay and listen, but she forced herself to move. *The sun has set.* "Can you offer me any words of wisdom?" Jean called over her shoulder, as she speed-walked back toward the excavation site.

The girl stopped playing, lowering the flute. "I am a warning, the only one you will have. Heed it. Leave and don't return."

"I can't. I understand bad things happened here, that spirits like you are trapped here. But we can't free you if we don't know what happened." Jean took a breath, increasing her volume as she turned to face the ghost. "I came to another place where there were evil ghosts holding good ghosts prisoner. Many bad things happened there. I helped to destroy the evil spirits, and free the good ghosts so that they passed on and found peace."

"I don't want to pass on!" the girl shouted suddenly, her soft voice becoming a banshee howl of wild rage. "This is my home! I will not leave, not ever!" Abruptly the Sea Room illuminated like an enormous snow globe lit with a million-watt LED light.

Jean turned and ran for the lights of the digging students, stumbling in the gloom on rocks and uneven ground. She bent over and rested her hands on her knees when she reached where she had stood with Teeth earlier, gasping and trying to catch her breath. *What's that glittering?* There were thousands of little sparkles shining in the floodlights at her feet.

There came a noise from above her in the direction of the mansion. It sounded like rock music, so far off that she couldn't discern the words, only the faint steady beat.

The house is awake, and it knows we're all down here. She reached down and scooped up a handful of dried mud with sparkles and put it in her pocket, walking quickly back to the others. She went to Upner, his face drawn and haggard. "Any news?"

"Five more bodies, all teens," Upner replied, managing a smile. "All have modern dental work. It's a relief, really. All these years of everyone wondering why some people were never found. We're finally going to be able to close a bunch of cold cases."

"That's a good thing," Jean agreed. "Did Cheer and Maryanne leave already? I don't see them."

"I'm not sure what you mean," Upner said, looking at her oddly. "I didn't see either of them here today."

"No, Cheer was here talking to you," Jean persisted, furrowing her brows. "She said that the legends and research we'd done was at odds with what you supposedly saw."

"All I saw was someone driving out here on the lakebed who then got their car upended in water," Upner said shrilly. "We found the remains of a car, but no bones in it, so they either got out or they washed out of it."

"No footprints? Or was this car from Latham's time?"

Upner looked like he wanted to shout at her, but then he seemed instead to sink into himself. "It's an ancient car. The engine's rusted to shit, the tires are shredded and flat, and it's almost entirely buried in mud. But the headlights look like they're the right distance apart to be what I witnessed. I can't explain it."

"You saw some paranormal activity," Jean reassured. "Just deal with it like you have been. You were shown what you saw to get people to dig out the bodies. But we need to pack up now and get out. Do you hear the music? That's the island. Everyone needs to get out now that the sun has set. The Sea Room is glowing."

Panic electrified the sheriff into immediate action. "Everyone, drop what you're doing and head out!" Upner shouted. "Carrie Ann, account for all your people right now."

The grad student Upner had been talking to shouted to three college kids working in a pile of rocks. They dropped their tools and scrambled toward her. "This is the last of them. Everyone else already left for the day."

"What about Cheer and Maryanne," Jean asked, scanning the gloom. "I don't see them."

"They likely left with the others," Upner said, as he mounted an ATV. "Get on." The other deputy was already on his UTV cranking the engine, the college students sitting in a large wagon he was pulling.

Jean climbed on and rode out with the others. As she looked back, the mansion windows were glowing with multiple lights, the Sea Room behind it blazing.

"Anything happen?" Bob asked as the convoy made it to shore. "We saw the lights go on."

Without responding the college students got into a van, all but the driver scrolling on their phones as the vehicle drove off.

"I saw Cheer and Maryanne out there. Cheer was taking pictures. But no one else remembers seeing them leave. Can you call them?" Jean asked. She turned to Upner. "Are you going out there tomorrow again?"

He nodded. "Every day, until the excavation is finished. But we have to work quickly. We have at most another week before the lakebed is ordered to be flooded again."

"He's right," Bob said reluctantly. "The sturgeon are dying as they need deeper water. I tried to argue for keeping the lake drained, but the judge wouldn't let me explain. He just listened to the University lawyer. We have maybe a week."

"That's not long enough to excavate down very far," Jean remarked meaningfully. "You might miss some bones, Sheriff."

"The only ones who care about excavating old bones is us," Upner said abruptly. "People drown every year, and their bodies are never found. But it's obvious what happened to them."

"Is it?" Jean said softly, looking meaningfully at Barb, who hung up her cell phone.

"I can't get any answer for either Maryanne or Cheer. I left messages to meet at my house in an hour. I have to get home anyway for Cooper."

"Can I ride with you?" Jean asked.

"Sure. Upner, are you giving Bob a ride back to his house?"

Bob gave her a disgruntled look as Upner assented. The men got into Upner's police cruiser while the women left in Barb's vehicle. As the two vehicles pulled away, the faint sound of rock music faded away, the lights in the mansion growing dark. The Sea Room stayed illuminated for several minutes more, then winked out.

———

"I don't know how you did this for years," Upner griped as he drove. "Seeing things and having everyone blame you for the deaths when you were doing all you could to save as many people as possible."

"I knew I was doing the best I could," Bob replied. "But I also drank more back then than I do now to cope with what I had to see on the job. Don't fault yourself. Things have been worse the last few months than they have ever been before."

"Tell me straight. If you were in my shoes, is there anything you'd be doing differently now?"

"I can't think of anything," Bob said, after a moment. "Really, you're doing a good job, Sal. Is there any news on any of the missing or other loose ends, like Manuel or Dakota?"

"I'm not supposed to share case details," Upner grumbled. "But I'm going to be fired anyway so what the hell. Manuel seems to be fine; he's going about his life. He's been taking care of Dakota's flock and farm, probably will buy both before too long."

"Dakota's widow wants to sell?"

"She never was a sheep lover, and they don't have kids. I think she wants shut of this place. Manuel will offer a fair price; he's been into the bank applying for a loan. It's one of the good endings for the survivors. The only thing that's weird is that he's fenced off the shoreline on Dakota's land so the sheep can't access the water at all or get within sight of the lake, not that they drank from the lake before with the streams that run through their pasture—"

"I'm happy for him. Now let's cut the bull. What's bothering you, Sal? You're ready to crack."

"We still don't have any leads for what attacked that bitten body we found. There aren't any sharks in the lake."

But there's that mermaid. "Did you get a bite radius to see how big the mouth had to be?"

"That's another problem. A normal smaller shark's bite diameter is at least 10cm, more like double that. But the bite on the guy who died was only a fraction of that, like a large trout. It's even too small for a sturgeon, which was my next thought. Yet the bite force was over double what it should be for a fish that small." Upner paused. "The coroner remarked that the teeth were weird."

"Weird how?"

"The coroner compared them to all known fish that attack man on this continent. Nothing matches up." Upner pulled to a stop in Bob's driveway. "How can I get behind Teeth's suggestion that we flood the lake again knowing that we've got some kind of monster fish attacking people? This is like that legend from when I was little of that guy who bought the bar on the lake and then went missing with his whole family. My brother always told me it was a monster fish." He coughed. "I didn't know it was a real case until I came to work for you, and you made me review the cold cases for practice."

It's got to be the mermaid, both then and now. I'd forgotten that old case. "Can you get me a copy of that report with the case file? And the older case file, too?"

"Why?" Upner turned quizzically. "You know there's not going to be any answers. That's what's bothering me at the heart of this. I'm a janitor like you were, Bob. I just pick up the pieces afterwards and there's hints of what might have happened, but never any concrete evidence."

"Okay, I'm going to tell you an answer, but you'd better not repeat it," Bob growled. "I saw a mermaid. She talked to me when I was out on the island with those FBI people and admitted she ate the bodies we didn't find. When she smiled her teeth were all pointed like a fish's teeth, but human-sized. I'm betting that's about the right size for your victim."

"Are you screwing with me?" Upner said angrily.

"I'm being straight with you. Maybe if we were all more straight with one another about what we saw, we'd have beat Cairn Isle a long time ago. She's real, Sal. My guess is where there's one, there's others."

"Let's say I believe you. Rationale says there can't be more than a couple as they'd have to be eating something besides just corpses and the occasional sheep. They'd also have to be smart enough to leave the lake fish alone."

"Maybe they used to, when the lake was twice the size and depth it is now," Bob offered. "That's why Teeth wants the lake restored: his fish are getting attacked."

"I will look over the report," Sal said grudgingly. "I will admit this gives another explanation for the bones we found today. Teeth and I were gaslighted."

Bob looked at him keenly. "I'm not following you."

"The bodies didn't wash into that trench and get buried by acci-dent. There's no boat wreckage near the depression at all, but boat remains are all over the rest of the exposed lakebed. Your mermaid used the rocks to weigh the corpses down, so she and her friends could feed on them the way an alligator feeds on prey it stores under the water. That fits the bodies and sheep going missing over the years, the wounds on the few that made it to shore recently, and your mermaid heart-to-heart." Upner paused, then related the flooding of the island Teeth and he had witnessed. "What he and I saw was some kind of illusion, not a true haunting."

"Why show you and Teeth that scene?"

"Us seeing that would guarantee I'd bring people out to dig, and we'd find the bones," Upner said after a moment. *Jean was right.* "The easiest conclusion is that what we saw was a supernatural haunting of a tragic disaster, and because of what we saw much of what we've taken as fact 'til now needs to be rethought because of what we found. Cairn Isle is a master of misdirection." Upner nodded once. "I'll come back in the morning with the files. Can you show me whatever you've been working on with Barb, Cheer, and Maryanne?"

Bob nodded. "Welcome to the resistance."

———

"We have to do something," Sharon said, as she faced the other four parents that had agreed to meet with her after the boy scout troop mass memorial service. "My boy wasn't abducted. He was murdered."

"We don't know that," one of the mother's piped up.

"I do," Dale interjected angrily. "I trust technology. There are videos of my son and most of his troop entering a dilapidated mansion looking for antiques. I can't explain why the house isn't there anymore." He tossed a picture on the floor which landed face up. "That's a blow up from the video of the house where they disappeared." He tossed another picture on top of it. "And this is a picture of Latham's Landing which a reporter sent to me. They look identical, don't they?"

Sharon picked up the pictures, comparing them. "It's the same house, though it looks in better repair in the picture with our kids."

"What are you proposing we do?" the last couple asked.

"I want to know what happened to my son," Dale said. "We need to band together to make a coalition to find out what happened."

One of the couples stood up. "We only agreed to hear you out. But we've heard enough, Dale. This is too crazy. You're saying what? That a house appeared and grabbed our kids, and it "resides" in another state now? Do you have any idea of how crazy you sound? Houses don't move! Likely Greg took a zoom photo of a picture in a book or something and doctored it on his phone as a joke."

"That's time and date stamped for the same hour and day our kids all vanished," Sharon admonished. "This house has something to do with what happened to our kids. We find the house and we may find out what happened to them. I'm for going there and seeing what we can find out. My son was everything to me. I owe it to him to find out what happened."

"I'm with you," Dale said, even as he frowned to see the other couples walking quickly away. "I'm not saying I believe you, but I'm not giving up on my son if there's any chance he's still alive. I'll go, but it's going to take me a couple days to arrange time off."

"Good," Sharon said. "Let's leave the end of this week."

———

"I'm so glad to be home," Barb said, as she let Cooper out into the backyard. "Help yourself if you're hungry, Jean. I'll try Cheer and Maryanne again before bed if they don't call first."

"I'm starving," Jean said, as she brought out cheese, bread, and butter. "I'll make grilled cheese, ok?"

"Anything you make, I'll be glad of," Barb said, pouring a handful of food into Cooper's bowl. He ate quickly, tail thumping happily against her leg. She picked up the bowl and put it in the sink, then made some coffee.

When she and Jean were both sitting on the couch with coffee and their sandwiches, Barb cleared her throat. "You want to tell me what you saw? We saw you run towards the Sea Room, shout a few things, then run back to Upner and the others. But we didn't see anyone near you."

"It was the girl with the flute," Jean said, taking a bite and chewing. "She said she was a warning to stay away. She expressly did not want help."

"I was worried you were going to go towards the island," Barb murmured. "We yelled at you, but you were too far away."

"She said this was her home," Jean remarked, taking another bite. "Very much like what you reported the woman in the Sea Room said. Possibly they are the same lady ghost. This is great cheese, by the way. Thanks."

"But the girl appears with her flute, and the lady attacks people," Barb protested. "Why would you think they are the same spirit?"

"I have known enough ghosts to know they can appear pretty much however they want to," Jean answered. "Or differently to different people. I would argue that the spirit manifests as a girl to warn people to stay away...or to lure people close enough to grab as the woman." She took another bite. "You didn't ask me why I canceled the plan to rebury the skeleton. I had a dream where Cheer got taken, and then you and Maryanne were next. It might have just been a dream, but it might not have. So all of you need to stay on shore from now on and not go back on the island, not even on the lake." She eyed Barb meaningfully. "Sometimes my dreams are premonitions. Believe or don't believe my warning; it's your choice."

"We can't let you go alone, and Bob's still recovering," Barb argued.

"No one should go," Jean stated, then took another bite.

"But...then things will go on like they have been with people going missing or getting hurt."

"No, the island should be flooded again. Bob should put up a floating fence of some kind around the island. But he should open the lake and the shoreline up again to the public or give the entire property up to the University. They can make a fish sanctuary or something."

"Why would you suggest this?"

"I didn't. Teeth said it was our best chance, and I believe him."

Barb stared at her, incredulous. "People will come like I did and go there and be trapped."

"Yes," Jean agreed softly. "But it's only a couple people a year dying. That's better than the close to fifty souls that Cairn Isle has snared this year travelling, if you count the boy scout troop and the others Cheer found." She took another bite. "I think we should focus instead on the Hustermen, which we might be able to actually do something about."

"Like what?" Barb asked cautiously.

"Bob said Carolyn was one of them. We should try to communicate with her and free her. If we can 'unmake' one Husterman, we should be able to free all the others that became Hustermen the same way. That will leave the original, which we then might be able to either lure to the island or also free. That will stop the disappearances on shore. My feeling is that all the locals that have gone missing are because of them, not Latham's Landing."

"Why do you think that?"

"The island's always been careful not to grab too many locals. Even its new 'travelling' is an attempt not to cause death locally. It doesn't want attention; it wants to hide in plain sight. That indicates intelligence." She paused, then reached into her pocket and pulled out the handful of dirt with sparkles, dumping it in a small pile on the table. "This looks to me like granite dust in the earth. Teeth was studying it, so I'm guessing given where I found it that it's the same location where some building used to be."

Barb slid a paper towel under the pile, then brought it under her phone's flashlight. "Yes, its granite dust. Not only that, but there's also a couple small pebbles, enough to show it is red granite. As in the same granite as Latham's mansion and the Dockhouse."

Jean nodded. "I think the island showed Upner what it did as a peace offering. I think it wants things to go back as they were, so it can 'travel' when it needs victims or ensnare the occasional group of thrill-seekers. This is markedly different behavior from the female ghosts that expressly warn us to stay away or be killed and don't care if they are seen or who they attack. There's an indication, in fact, that the island demon is running interference for the female ghosts, *that it has been all along*. The Hustermen are an unwelcome wrench in this strategy because they keep adding to their ranks from the local populace. My feeling is if we act against them, we have a good chance of success as they aren't part of this evil alliance."

"Good points, all of them," Barb said, finishing her sandwich and standing up. "I'm going to try Cheer and Maryanne again." She called both numbers again, again leaving voicemails. "I'm not sure where else to look for them. I suppose they could be at Maryanne's church."

"Unlikely," Jeanne said, checking her watch. "It's close to nine. But if one of them forgot their phone, or the battery's dead, they wouldn't have gotten the message."

"I have to admit, I'm disappointed that Helter's not come forward to help us," Barb said, as she plopped down again on the couch. "He'd be a huge help if he was here."

"Don't blame him," Jean said, finishing her coffee, then getting up and pouring herself more. "I didn't want to help, either. Anyone who really has dealt with this kind of haunting isn't eager to jump into another one. He almost died the first time; he doesn't want to risk his life again."

Barb rolled her eyes. "You're over-understanding."

"Just realistic."

"Speaking of realism, I have a kind of off the wall idea to float you."

"What?"

The phone rang. Barb hurried to answer. "Hello? Maryanne! I'm so glad to hear from you. I was worried." She pushed the speaker-phone button. "Jean is here with me. Did you hear from Cheer?"

"Not since today at the graves," Maryanne said sadly. "I did a lot of praying. I hope if any of those people's spirits contributed to what Upner and Teeth witnessed, God helped them to pass on and find peace."

"Maryanne, I was just telling Jean I had an idea. Remember when you asked me if it was possible that the newer sections of house and granite that looked as real as the belltower were an illusion? I mean real enough to sit on, walk on, but not really made of physical materials? What if that's the reason that the original house and buildings can't be burned is...because they aren't really there?"

"What are you saying? They are there, I've been inside them. Dozens of people have been inside, taken pictures—!"

"Think about it! It fits: the lost time, the reason the house changes, that it can travel distances and appear differently each time, even that it seems to come alive! Because it's a living illusion. When you enter, you enter into the illusion and get lost in it, until it physically causes your death."

"How would something not real cause real death?" Jean asked skeptically.

"You've had real dreams that caused you to feel panic, real physical distress."

"Those were dreams."

"Yes, but to you they felt real. And when they get too awful, your body wakes you up as an escape from the panic, fear, and stress on your body. But you can't wake up in the illusion on the island. You go on and on until you simply die from the exhaustion of being terrified and/or from being attacked/wounded."

Jean chuckled. "A whole new way to think of virtual reality. The Matrix doesn't have you, Latham's Landing does."

"I may be explaining this badly," Barb said, biting her lip. "I'm not saying that the house isn't completely real to anyone experiencing it. I'm saying that it distorts how we think of reality. I got a very real wound from Mac when he was living. I think he would be equally dangerous if not more so now as a ghost on Latham's Landing. I think if his ghost stabbed me there, I'd have a wound from the blade. The illusion is real: it can touch us and everything else in the real world. But it's also mutable to a large extent. That explains why there was no wreckage from the explosion and also possibly the 'travelling' you referred to, Jean. The house isn't really leaving the lake, only the portal to the illusion is. People see different things that get them to enter that portal, and they are transported here where they die or escape. Anyone here sees the house disappear, but what they are seeing is the illusion vanishing, revealing an empty island with no mansion."

"Say we agree," Maryanne said. "Given what you said before, that means that the force on the island was building onto the original facade to make the illusion bigger? Why?"

"They tried to, likely to capture more fear from Mac's victims."

"Who makes the illusion?"

"The demon specifically creates it to entrap people, to make them feel fear and torture them before killing them and taking their souls. The longer the person lasts in the illusion the more it can feed from them."

"Shouldn't we try to exorcise him, then?" Maryanne countered.

"If we get close enough to the island, we are going to get pulled into the illusion and get trapped ourselves," Jean replied. "I think that's what my dream meant. The reason the island is so powerful is that there's more than one influence there and up 'til now they all worked together. We need to separate the demon from the woman in the Sea Room, and both of them from the mermaid. Cheer's got the bones, and she's onto something that the bones must mean something to the island demon, in that the deaths all erupted after the bones were removed." She sipped her coffee. "Tomorrow morning I'll go to the Sea Room and try again to talk to the woman. I'll bring the bones with me as an offering."

"I'll go with you," Barb offered.

"So will I," Maryanne said. "Cheer, too, I'm sure she won't stay behind."

"Good," Jean said.

————

Maryanne hung up the phone, then took a shower. She made herself a mug of cocoa and then sat before her fire wrapped in a blanket. *Am I doing enough? I feel like it's all up to me, even though I know it isn't. I need to be a leader more than I ever have before. But this isn't anything I was trained for. Maybe I should consult with the local district superintendent. But will he even take what I have to say seriously? My colleagues didn't; they sent me out to face real evil with no weapons of faith.*

She sighed, then looked up to the little wooden cross on the mantle with the stuffed beanie of Jesus beside it. "What do you think, Jesus?"

To her surprise and terror, the peaceful, happy-faced doll slowly turned its head and looked at her. "Thou shalt not worship idols," a guttural bass voice intoned. Its little stuffed arm lifted and extended right at her. "Sinner."

Maryanne bolted up, snatched up the fireplace tongs, and knocked the figure and the cross off the mantle with a cry.

The doll landed with a curse, then began to crawl towards her. She grasped it with the tongs as it wriggled and roared, then held it in the fire.

The stuffed thing wriggled as it burned, flame engulfing it. Maryanne held it there with the tongs until it had become a charred lump and stopped moving. Then she cast down the tongs, fell to her knees, and began to pray.

———

Mud-streaked bone glistened slightly in the yellow light from the propane lantern, the eyes of the skull dark as it peered into the cabin through the hole-ridden mesh screen. The man inside was warming his hands next to a propane heater, then he wrapped another blanket around himself with a curse.

The bones creaked as the skeletal fingers tore at the screen, enlarging the holes. Then it drew back suddenly and turned, shambling off into the darkness.

———

Cheer blinked her eyes, the painful throb in her head making it hard for her to see. She made out a bright light far above her in the darkness. *The moon.* Fear coursed through her as she struggled to sit up.

I was taking pictures, and I thought I saw something near a pile of rocks, the farthest one from the island. It looked like a young girl with dark hair. As I got closer, I turned back at a loud noise behind me. It was nothing, just a group of students lifting a piece of boat wreckage out of the way, but I lost sight of the girl in the seconds my attention was diverted. When I got closer to the rock that I'd seen her at, there was no sign of her. Then everything went black.

"You're awake. Good. I want to hear you scream."

Cheer gasped in fear as she looked up at the looming figure. Her expression shifted to incredulity with recognition. "Godelson?"

"Godelman!" His face was a mask of rage. "You can't even get my name right, you sorry excuse for a journalist."

"Better than a sorry excuse for a professor," Cheer said snidely, as she stood. "Untie me. I won't forget this, but I won't press charges, either."

"Oh no." Godelman shook his head. "I'm taking you up to the island. You're so interested in it? You can be its next victim." He shoved her hard, and she fell on her back, knocking the wind out of her. "Where are the bones?"

Faint music carried on the breeze threaded into Cheer's consciousness. With difficulty she turned her face towards the island mansion. *The lights are on.*

"Look, there's someone who wants to see you," Godelman sneered. "Tell me where the bones are."

"Or what?" Cheer challenged, even as she shivered. *Had it grown colder?*

"Or I'll leave you here hobbled," Godelman said. "If people are disappearing from the shore, then whatever's there right now certainly can walk across the lakebed to collect you."

"You get me out of here right now, or you'll never find the skeleton," Cheer growled out. "I promise you that." Her next threat was cut off as she felt cold water soaking into her back and neck.

Godelman moved back a step. "The water's rising. I think it means we won't be alone for long, Cheer. Last chance."

The water rose rapidly as Godelman backed away. "Alright!" Cheer shouted. "Barb has the bones, but she doesn't know it. But you have to rebury them on the island! That's why I took them, to rebury them there! We want to end the deaths!"

"The only death I care about is yours," Godelman said as he turned away. "Goodbye."

Cheer let out a shriek as white hands erupted from the water near her and pulled her beneath the still rising water with a splash.

Godelman whipped around, staring at the place Cheer had been for a moment. A smile was just forming on his face when he was struck in the chest with an aluminum arrow. He sank to his knees, another transfixing his throat before he toppled forward.

A menacing figure with a crossbow came out of the darkness, his grin too white in the shadows. "You're coming back with me, chum. But not before I get little missy alive."

———

"Shh!" a soft voice cautioned. "He'll hear you."

Cheer coughed, then looked up at the dark-haired young girl near her. Then she let out a sharp breath when she saw that the girl's lower half was submerged in water, just a few shiny iridescent scales visible.

"Who are you?" Cheer whispered, trying to stifle her coughing.

"April," the girl said. "You've got to be quiet. Mac won't hurt me, 'cause of my mom and Teeth. But he'll hurt you."

Cheer looked around anxiously, but the night was quiet.

"Can you hold your breath?" April asked. "I can take you to shore, but we've got to go underwater."

"But the lake's dry."

"What's above is dry," April said, pulling Cheer into the water. "The caverns below are still mostly flooded. You're just lucky that there was an opening near you, and my friend helped."

Cheers next words were cut off as she was pulled beneath the water. She was pulled along impossibly fast in cold inky blackness, then pushed upwards to gasp in brief draughts of cool air before being pulled down again. When she was finally pushed up onto the shoreline, she felt sick enough to vomit, her vision blurry.

"Get up," April said, then administered a slap full to Cheer's face, jolting her.

Cheer coughed, then got to all fours, swaying. "Why did you save me? You eat people."

"Because you're going to go get those bones, and bring them to me," April said, baring needle teeth. "Not to the island. Or you won't make it off this lake tonight."

Cheer got to her feet, then nodded. "Okay, I will. But—" An arrow hit her under her right breast, causing her to stagger.

April turned with a hiss, then let out the inhuman high-pitched shriek of a sea monster. She held up her arms, palms out. Another arrow thudded into her chest, spitting her. She clutched at it, then fell backward, laying half in the water and half out, her long shimmering tail spasmodically breaking the surface.

Mac strode up, then kicked her side viciously. "Stupid fish."

"You...you're not allowed..." April gasped, her hands trying to grasp the blood-slick shaft of the arrow.

"You're not allowed to get in my way," Mac said, shoving her with his boot into the deeper water. "I am entitled to my prey. You're not allowed to take anyone on land. You know that."

April coughed, thrashed once more, then her body went slack, floating.

Mac stepped over her, heading towards Cheer who had fallen onto her back. She was struggling to breathe, blood on her lips. He reached for her and went sprawling, letting out a surprised yell. Cheer gurgled out a scream herself, to see a larger mermaid grasping the killer's legs, trying to pull him backwards into the water, her mouth ripping at his thigh, blood running in rivulets around her lips as she thrashed her head from side to side ferociously.

"I'm not dying again, you bitch!" Mac pulled the survival knife at his hip and stabbed the mermaid in the back. She threw herself backward with her tail, ripping free a chunk of thigh which she spat out before vanishing. Mac flailed in the water in a spreading pool of blood, trying to get to his feet.

Cheer pulled out her phone with effort, then pressed the speed dial.

"Who's this?" Bob said sleepily.

"The bones are in Barb's garage, under the wheelbarrow," Cheer said wetly, then coughed. "Don't bury them on the island. One mermaid's dead, the other's fighting Mac. And I'm...I'm.."

"Cheer? Where are you?"

"Bring them to the shore..."

"Cheer!"

"...Teeth..." Cheer went limp, her eyes glazing over as the phone dropped from her hand.

CHAPTER ELEVEN

BOB ARRIVED ON THE SHORE AT CARL'S POINT, THEN UNLOADED the ATV from its trailer. He rode it to the far side of the lake, where Teeth was sitting on a rock, waiting.

Bob struggled to get off the ATV, his face white with pain, then hurried to Cheer's side. He slowed as it became apparent that she was dead. "Did you call this in?"

Teeth nodded. "I got here about ten minutes after you called me. I was on the lake heading home when I heard screams. You called me a few minutes later."

"Did she say anything?"

"She was dead when I got here."

Bob scanned the ground around the body. *The shoreline is dry everywhere except near Cheer. And the nearest pool is a few feet away.* "Were there any other bodies?"

"Just hers."

Bob grabbed hold of Teeth and tried to shake him, but the other man pushed him away as if he were a fly, and he staggered backwards. "You cleaned up this scene."

"I take care of my own, or at least I tried to," Teeth snarled back angrily. "Not that it matters now."

"Where's the mermaids? Cheer told me there were two."

"April's dead. I'm guessing Marissa is also. There was too much blood."

"Why'd you clean it up?"

Teeth ignored him. "They didn't kill this woman, something else did. Take a look at her."

"I know it was Mac. Cheer said he was fighting the mermaids." Bob turned to Teeth. "All these years you were on this lake, why didn't you do something? You had to know what Mac was doing, had to have heard something!"

"Do what?" Teeth shot back. "This is my home. I've lived here all my life. I kept to my own business, and I never had a problem until thrill seekers came here and started dying. Then people trying to blow up the island and people trying to hunt ghosts and mass murderers with helicopters and do-gooders draining the lake. You're all assholes who don't know anything about what you're dealing with, and you just keep making things worse!"

"I know what we are dealing with," a man said, as he walked down from the field above.

"Who the hell are you?" Bob asked.

"Helter Skelter's what I go by." The man smiled grimly. "I'll be waiting for you back at your house, Bob." He looked at Teeth. "Are you with us or against us?"

"I'm on the side of the fish," Teeth said, as he turned to leave. "Good luck."

"HOW CAN YOU NOT WANT TO HELP?" Bob shouted. "After all you've seen?"

"It's because of what I've seen I'm staying out of it," Teeth answered, walking back towards his boat moored in the distance. "You'll do your thing, and the house will do its thing and when the sun comes up the next morning the fish will still need caring for."

There sounded the whine of another ATV approaching.

"Keep the fish in the deep water if you can," Helter warned, as he put up a hood and moved away up the hill towards Manuel's farm, following the new fencing. "Well away from the island and the Sea Room."

"I will." Teeth reached his boat and shoved off, then started the engine. Both he and Helter disappeared from sight. By that time Sal had driven up. "Jesus, Bob what happened?"

"Write it as a hunting accident," Bob said tiredly. "You know what happened, Sal. Can you take it from here?"

"Maybe the best thing for us all is if the lake comes back, Bob," Sal said, as he dialed his cell. "And yes, leave. My report will say I got an anonymous tip. I followed your tracks so return the same way and we're good."

Bob painfully got back on his ATV, started it, and headed back to his vehicle. He loaded the ATV and drove back to his house, where Helter waited on his porch.

"We should call Barb and Maryanne."

"I already did," Bob said. "That's why I left my truck running. Everyone's waiting for us at Barb's house. Chief Upner will meet up with us later if he can."

Helter bristled. "I'm not sharing my information with a cop."

"You will or go back where you came from," Bob bluffed. "You've been content to keep out of the fight so far. Why offer your help now?"

"We're wasting time," Helter said, pushing past him. "I'll drive."

As Bob and Helter pulled up in Bob's truck, Barb opened the front door and Cooper rushed past her, barking happily.

"Hi Coop, glad to see you too," Helter said, crouching to pet the enthusiastic dog.

"Helter!" Barb exclaimed as she ran to embrace him. "I'm glad to see you. But why did you come back now?"

He hugged her. "I got a report there was a woman on the shore dead. I thought it was you."

"Cheer's dead?" Barb asked, her eyes finding Bob, who nodded.

"It was Mac."

"Come in," she said, leading them both inside to where Jean and Maryanne waited. "Did you find anything else?"

"One of the mermaids is dead, maybe more than one. Teeth took their bodies, he said they were family."

"He refused to help," Helter added.

"How did you know she died," Barb said slowly, her expression reproachful, "And yet whomever told you didn't help Cheer themselves?"

"I put a man on nights to watch the mansion with the express instruction not to go past the shoreline under any circumstances. He reported a brief light on the shore closest to the Sea Room which he went to check out, and it was her. There was no ID on the body. He said there was a scream earlier and some splashing."

"It looks like Mac's able to go off the island now, at least into the lakebed," Bob added. "Cheer was killed on shore not far from the edge of Manuel's property line, close to where the lake still has depth. But there's something else: Mac also killed at least one of the mermaids, if not two."

"This is what we wanted to happen, the evil fighting among themselves," Jean said, offering Helter her hand. "Hi, I'm Jean. This is Maryanne."

"Hi. I'm Helter."

"Cheer called me as she died," Bob interjected. "She said that the bones were in your garage, Barb. And expressly not to bury them on the island, but to bring them to the shore. She didn't say why."

"We don't know what Cheer was doing there after dark," Barb said. "She knew it was too dangerous. Crazy as it sounds, the mermaid must have helped her somehow, possibly against Mac. She wouldn't have been there unless she was fleeing something. So, when the mermaid told her not to bring the bones back to rebury, she believed it." She wiped at tears. "She was still trying to help even as she died. We need to deliver the bones."

"Unfortunately, Mac is dead already, so he can't really be removed from play, so to speak," Jean murmured. "Which means he's roaming the lakebed now at night. How long is it until he comes on shore looking for victims? We'll have to go in the daytime."

"I'd advocate for going to the Sea Room right now, Jean, but the police are there," Bob cautioned. "By the time they leave it'll be dark again."

"Cheer is dead. I don't care who sees us," Barb said, standing up. "Let's go right now."

———

"Thank you," Teeth said, taking the large envelope from the lawyer. "This is the first good news I've had in weeks."

"We fully support your work here with the sturgeon," the lawyer said. "What you do is invaluable. The University thanks you for being such a good fish steward, Mr. Teeth. You have done a great job helping to preserve them, and also to harvest eggs for us to use in our other spawning centers."

"You're welcome," Teeth replied, shaking his hand. "I enjoy the work."

"Well, you can get back to it the day after tomorrow," the lawyer said, releasing his hand. "The judge has ordered that the lake be completely restored to its former condition. You'll see documentation that you are to be allowed full access to the lake, the shore, and the island from now on. Everyone else, even the current owner, will need to get approval before he can ever attempt any modifications again." The lawyer smiled. "And approval will not be granted."

"What about those bones that were being excavated in the lakebed? I believed that we'd be delayed if the site proved to be...of historical significance."

"All the bones recovered have turned out to be persons reported missing in the last decade. While we are glad to have found them for their families' sake, there is nothing remarkable about the skeletons. It seems that the storms here mixed with the lakebed topology caused those that drowned to be washed into that trench, where they were caught under some rocks."

Complete bullshit. Keep believing it. "That's good," Teeth commented. "But won't it take more than another day to get the rest of the bones?"

"My understanding is that the university archeological team is there now, and they are using some location devices to check for bones under the ground. Any that remain aren't going to be buried very deeply if they're that recent, so removing them should go quickly."

This could be a big problem. "Glad to hear it. Thank you for coming."

Teeth watched the lawyer drive away, then put the paperwork

inside, went out to his boat and started the engine, heading out into the lake. Partway to the Sea Room, he dropped anchor, and waited.

A head broke the surface a few minutes later, then bobbed toward the boat. Long delicate fingers tipped with iridescent claws reached over the edge of the boat and then grasped the edge, as a ravishingly beautiful woman's face appeared. "What is it, Teeth?"

"The students on the other side of the lake are using a device that can see under the ground. I'm not sure how far they can look under the lakebed. Is anyone over there?"

"I made everyone stay on this side since they drained the lake."

"Not April."

"She never wanted to listen. Neither did her mother. They paid for their mistake."

Teeth didn't reply.

"Are we getting our water back?"

Teeth nodded. "Day after tomorrow, Celine."

"I'm sensing a 'but' here."

"The group you saw go to the island is going to come back and go to the Sea Room before the water returns. We need to pull back in case they try to blow things up again. That guy who was here before and made it off is back."

"Which one?" Celine asked.

"Helter."

Celine was silent, considering.

"Can you help herd the sturgeon away?"

Celine nodded. "We won't lose any more of them." She let go of the boat and pushed off, moving impossibly fast.

"Wait," Teeth called. "There's something else you should know. They have the bones that were dug up from the island. They will be bringing them to the Sea Room."

Celine whipped around, stopping. Her huge iridescent tail broke the surface, then struck the water's surface sharply, causing a giant wave that badly rocked Teeth's boat as he quickly grabbed the sides. "What do they hope to do?"

"They want to put the lady that haunts the Sea Room to rest."

"You could sooner sort all the salt from the sea," Celine mused, looking at the island. She paused as if to say something, then slipped below the surface and was gone.

———

"Are you sure that Manuel won't report us?" Barb asked, as she and the others parked at the top of the hill near the new fencing.

"He won't know we were ever here," Helter assured.

Bob glared at him. "He knows. I asked permission."

The group walked down the hill to the lakebed, giving a wide berth to the cordoned off crime scene where several police photographers were snapping pictures and measuring the ground.

"Are you sure they aren't going to be able to match your footprints?" Maryanne asked.

"There's too much rock there for usable prints," Bob replied. "Besides, it's my land."

There was a splash from the lake. The group turned as one, wary, but it was just a tall wiry woman standing at the edge of an inlet in jeans and a hoodie, skipping stones.

"Hey!" Bob yelled, waving at her. "You can't be here. Didn't you see the No Trespassing signs?"

"I saw them." She skipped another stone.

Bob walked over to her, ready to grasp her shoulder. As he reached for her, she turned impossibly fast, her hand raised with fingers splayed, her menacing grey eyes lustrous as silver beads. "Don't."

Bob stopped in his tracks, the rest of the group behind him, all of them staring at her hand, each finger tipped with rounded claws that also had a pearl luster. *Like the shell of a crab.* "What are you?"

"No one to be trifled with," she said, her grin revealing teeth that resembled long shards of broken glass. "I am here for the bones. Give them to me. I will see they are laid to rest."

"No way," Barb interjected.

"Why are they important to you?" Jean asked. "Who are you?"

"I am Celine. They are not important to me. But I owe a debt, and this will repay it."

"What are you?" Helter asked.

"No more questions," Celine said, shaking her head once. There was a slight musical sound from dozens of tiny shells woven into the ends of her tresses. She produced a book from her pocket. "You want answers. I offer this in trade."

"What is it?" Helter asked.

"A record of sorts," Celine said, offering the book to Barb, who snatched it. "The bones can do you no good. The lady of the glass prison won't care about them, only killing you for trespassing. Once it's known you have them here, those on the island will come in force and take them."

"We can fight them," Barb countered, brandishing her bags of herbs.

"You will be taken. You of all people should know." Celine stared at Barb, her unnatural eyes forcing Barb to drop her gaze. She glanced at Helter. "As should he."

"You know what happened to us? And you didn't come forward to help us when we were trapped there?" Helter accused. "You left us there to be consumed."

"You wouldn't have helped me, either," Celine said with a bitter smile. "I'm not your kind. Give me the bones now. Or I'll take them from you."

"You can't fight us all," Helter said, drawing and cocking a concealed .44 and pointing it at her.

Celine smiled, then began to sing. There were no words, yet the music seemed to reach out and through each of the group, filling them with yearning and the sheer desire to be utterly still, every sense focused on the all-encompassing sounds. Barb went to her knees, her bags of herbs forgotten. Helter lowered his gun, then dropped it at his feet. Bob and Maryanne leaned against one another, then also dropped to their knees. Jean collapsed onto the sand, unconscious.

Continuing to sing, Celine went to each in turn, and removed the bones from their bags and backpacks, assembling them in a small pile. She slid her hoodie over her head, then slid off her jeans, revealing more of iridescent shell and tiny scales, her feet oddly shaped, the toes long and also clawed. She piled the bones in the hoodie and tied them securely with the jeans, then stepped to the water with the parcel, wading in. When she was chest high, she ended the song, disappearing beneath the water, a huge lustrous tail slapping the water once before disappearing.

The sound galvanized the group. Helter cursed and picked up his gun. Barb stood up, as Bob and Maryanne helped each other stand.

"What the hell was that?" Bob said.

"Jean!" Barb said, hurrying to the prone woman.

"She must have hit her head," Maryanne said, crouching beside her and smoothing away Jean's brown hair from the bloody wound. "It's not deep."

"I'm okay," Jean said woozily. "I just fainted."

"Do you faint often?" Helter asked.

"I'm attuned to ghosts, so psychic energy hits me harder than it hits you," Jean said, sitting up with a groan. "That song of hers was laden with extrasensory energy."

"We need to go to the Sea Room," Barb said stubbornly. "We can at least tell the lady about the bones and explain that Celine has them. It's already a little after noon. Daylight's wasting. But Jean, you're hurt. You should head back to my house if you're well enough to make it."

"I am going back," Jean said, getting to her feet. "To my home. Right now."

"You're leaving us?" Barb stammered. "Now?"

"I know ghosts," Jean retorted. "You've got a demon and Hustermen, neither of which is my area of expertise. The ghost I met does not want my help, and neither does the lady in the Sea Room. There's nothing more I can do here to help you." She grabbed Barb's arm. "I warn you again: do not go to the island. I know you've only got today and tomorrow before the lake returns. But I urge you to take time to read what Celine gave you before acting and to think about what she said. Even given her not being human, she had no reason to lie."

"She's part human," Helter protested. "She's a mermaid."

"No," Jean said, looking out to the placid water. "I think she's a siren."

"I'm not sure this was a good idea," Dale said, as he and Sharon got out at Carl's Point, surveying the dried mud lakebed and the house lurking alone out on its hill in the late afternoon sun. "I read you the articles on the recent strange events here. A woman was killed here just last night!"

"We had to come close to dark, or we'd have been noticed by the excavators," Sharon retorted. "Hand me those binoculars. I think I see movement."

Dale handed them to her, as he got out a flashlight. "We're not going to be able to even get over there until after dark. I brought flashlights, but there's more rocks and pools of water than I thought. We should wait for morning and come back at dawn."

"That's the same house from the boy's pictures," Sharon replied, looking over Latham's Landing. "Some of the excavators must have stayed behind. There's a group sitting on the ground outside the house talking and preparing a campfire. We can use their light to guide us."

"I don't see anyone," Dale said, shading his eyes against the setting sun.

"I can't tell if they're adults or older kids," Sharon said, adjusting the binoculars. "It's too blurry."

Dale grabbed them from her and looked. "There's nothing there, Sharon. No one is on the shore."

Sharon grabbed them back and looked again. "Damn it, I just saw them. I must have been focused on another spot on the shore. Give me a sec."

"We don't have time. If they're there, we'll see a fire or meet them on the shore when we get there. C'mon."

The sun was half spent, glowing on the horizon as it slid behind the hills, dappling the small pools of water yellow gold as Dale and Sharon began to walk. As the sun disappeared, shadows began to gather, and Dale and Sharon switched on their flashlights.

A fire sputtered to life on the shore in front of Latham's Landing, a few black silhouettes moving around it.

"Well, you were right," Dale said. "Karl!" he shouted. "Karl!"

"Should you be shouting?" Sharon whispered to him, as they continued to walk.

"I'm not sure they can hear me at this distance," Dale replied. "No one's answering and they're not paying us any attention. Probably have earbuds in listening to videos or music."

"I don't see any screen lights," Sharon murmured. "Only the fire."

Two darker shadows separated from the shadowy porch of Latham's Landing, then headed towards Sharon and Dale.

"Karl!" Dale shouted again. "Karl!"

The two darker shadows picked up the pace, the rising full moon illuminating them enough to reveal two young boys.

"John!" Sharon called, beginning to run herself. "Is that you?"

The two boys began to run flat out. "Mom!" came a faint cry.

Dale and Sharon ran towards the approaching boys, engulfing them in tearful hugs. "John! Karl!"

"Mom!" John cried, trying to burrow under her arms. "Mom!"

"Dad!" Karl ran into his father's arms and hugged him hard, then pushed back. "Get us out of here! They're coming!"

Dale's eyes slid over the campfire, noticing all the silhouettes there were standing at attention. As one, the black shadows erupted into motion, running towards them.

"Run for the car! Go!" Dale pushed Sharon and John. "Go!" Karl was already running hard.

The shadowy figures were halfway to them and gaining fast, eerily silent.

Sharon and John were flailing through deep mud, but they had almost reached the shore. Karl was ten feet from the car when he let out a scream, a horrific shadow with pale yellow orbs rising up in front of him to block his way.

"Envy," the Husterman hissed. "Wrath."

Dale drew the gun at his waist, pointing the 9mm towards the shadow, but he turned instead to shoot a teen bearing down on him with a hunting knife, the boy's eyes murderous. The bullet hit the teen in the chest and he went to his knees with an otherworldly scream, even as the bullet continued out his back to hit the teen behind him in the stomach. Another scream rent the air, the outlines of both teens blurring as mist billowed from their bodies.

The Husterman darted around Karl, even as three other Hustermen emerged from the shadows of the car and trees to attack the two wounded teens. More screams rent the air as both of the wounded were surrounded, the shadows coiling around them and dragging them down.

Dale shot two more of the approaching teens and they fell to their knees, but the others kept coming, the remaining four surrounding Sharon, John, and himself. Soundless, the four approached.

Dale emptied the clip, downing two more as the last two attacked, one stabbing at Sharon with a knife as she tried to protect John, the other going for Dale's head with a club. Dale hit the teen with his gun, knocking him to the ground, then kicking him before turning to help Sharon. She'd been stabbed, but John had hit the teen with a rock, making him stumble. Before the teen could get to his feet a Husterman was on him, rending his throat. Instead of blood, a black-grey mist was leaking out as the teen fell back bonelessly on the ground, his form disappearing. The Husterman gobbled up the black-grey mist eagerly.

Dale pushed Sharon into the car's backseat with John. "Put pressure on it." He turned to get in and a Husterman reared up in front of him, blocking his way. Its yellow orbs gazed into his for a long moment, then it sniffed the air, turning sharply to flow over the top of the car and through his son's open window. Karl let out a shriek as he was enveloped in blackness.

"Stop it! Stop it!" Sharon was also screaming in the backseat, beating at John, another Husterman latched onto him, its mouth over his.

The Hustermen both disengaged, flowing out of the car windows and disappearing into the shadows of the forest.

———

"Did you get anything from that book?" Bob asked, as he sat sipping a beer with Upner. The group was at Barb's house again, Maryanne petting Cooper on the couch, Barb in her easy chair studying Celine's book, Helter cleaning his .44. Jean had packed as fast as possible and departed, saying she would call if she thought of anything helpful.

"I've skimmed it," Barb said finally. "I marked sections that I thought were relevant. Listen and stop me if you think of anything as I read." She cleared her throat and began.

"We came here to live in the small house on the hill when I was five, after Father left us. The valley was all farmland then. We were able to afford the rent as it was cheap, because everyone said the place was haunted, that bad things had happened here and would happen here again." Barb swallowed and continued reading.

"There was an old barn close to the house, a large one for the time and in good condition. When I went inside the first time, I almost felt that I'd been there before. There were no animals in it, just some old hay, and spiders here and there, old clumps of manure almost fossilized they were so old. The front of the barn had a door and a place for tack, and two doors off it, one to the interior of the barn with the loft, and the other to a smaller room where a groom or someone must have slept, as there was a wooden bunk there. But I thought it strange that there were no individual stalls, as the lords who lived here once must have had horses. Otherwise, why have a barn? But when I asked my mother about it, she pointed to a spot of ground near to the barn and said the stable had been there, attached to the barn, but that it had burned down many years before during the massacre."

"The massacre?" Maryanne echoed.

"If this record predates cars, it stands to reason that horses were the only transportation besides walking," Helter supplied. "A fire would kill them or scatter them and whomever lived here first would have no way to get away. Whomever they were, they were massacred, and the house was abandoned until this family came here. Go on, Barb."

"There was also a huge house very near the barn, painted white. It had once been grand, but now the entire porch which ran the length of the house side and faced the direction of town was falling off, listing away from the main house. The house itself was unsafe except for one interior room right inside the front door. That was a place we stored food in winter, as it was not only always cold, but there were never mice there for some reason."

"Evil," Helter muttered. "That's the reason."

"I longed to go onto the porch, but it was unsafe," Barb read on. "At the very corner was a room of windows, with more glass for a roof. Mother said it must have been a greenhouse of some kind, or maybe a sunroom. It was beautiful. But I never went in, as the floor was unsafe, and mother said I'd fall right down into the cellar, and never be seen again."

"That's some mother," Helter said.

"She's just being prudent," Barb commented, flipping through the pages. "It says she liked playing in the barn and running in the fields, helping to farm the land, that in the next years they bought a cow and a horse and put them in the barn. There's nothing about the animals sensing any kind of evil. She even writes of a wild rabbit that's black and brown that she befriended that lived near the barn and became something like a pet. She calls him Petey."

"Sounds like a pet store rabbit that escaped from someone or was set free."

"Okay, finally something's happening. Listen to this: they came in a huge car looking for a spot to have a summer party. It was the biggest car I'd ever seen, bigger than the store's delivery truck in town."

"Maybe a van? A bus?" Maryanne offered.

"A Winnebago?" Helter offered.

"Very funny. 'I told them that the house and barn were not for rent, nor was the land.' She's acting older, almost like the lady of the house. 'The woman with long black hair got out and said the spot was beautiful, that they really wanted to rent it for their party. She loved the house on sight and asked again if she could rent that. I told her no, that no one could live in it, it was unsafe."

"There's that word again, unsafe," Maryanne said. "Don't you think that's an odd choice for a child to use, especially over and over? She doesn't use rotting or falling down."

"Keep going," Bob urged.

"The woman said that the barn was lovely, too, that maybe they could rent that and clean it out. I told her we had one horse and it was his home, and he loved it. I acted as if I owned the place. I wanted her to leave."

"What happened to the cow?" Upner asked.

"Doesn't say. 'Her boy came out of the car then. He was mean to Petey. When Petey nipped him, he went screaming back to the car. His mother was angry, but said he'd be fine. She was persistent, saying again she wanted to rent the barn, was there any way? I said no. Anger filled me and a storm was coming across the fields toward us, darkening the sky.'

'She went back to the car and then her husband came out. He looked a gentleman—suit and short hair and spectacles, a mild smile on his face. But I saw he was used to getting his way, used to the power of what he said coming to pass. He had come to push through the woman's wants to fruition, because that is what he did. He asked if there was running water, a septic tank, or electricity. I said yes for all, but that we only used the three in our own little cottage, and water in the barn. He picked up an old window frame resting against the edge of the barn, then saw it needed repair. He threw it down in disgust and looked at me as if this place was a junk heap. I said nothing. We kept up what little we could, but we had no money to fix things, and no male to help us.'

'Thunder was crackling now, and the sky was a dark purple-blue, the white walls of the old house almost glowing as they stood out against the darkness, the green fields emerald in color. Lightning flashed, illuminating everything, making the old sunroom like a mirror for a split second. The man turned and got back in the car and drove away with his family. I breathed a sigh of relief and went back inside. The storm passed with no rain.'"

"It's almost as if she brought the storm, or her anger did," Bob said. "Does anyone else get that?"

Helter nodded.

Upner also nodded. "I also find the description of the house similar to what the mansion now looks like, with the row of windows facing south. Is it a coincidence that the modern version and that the original house have the same section damaged?"

"I got that, too," Bob agreed. "I also want to add that this same section of the house in present day is also always where we found any bodies of people killed on the island. Even the staged scene of Mac and Chung Lai were on this same side, in the water. Read on, Barb."

"'The next day our landlord came. Our home was just a little house, a trailer-cottage on a concrete pad with a small concrete patio. It was cold in winter, but it was the most beautiful place in summer because of the fields spreading out below us and the many wildflowers.'"

"'I saw the landlord through the front window curtains, chuckling and beaming as he talked to the man and woman with the long dark hair, and the boy pulled the heads off of all my mother's roses. When they were gone, my mother and I went out to talk to the landlord. He was giddy. He hadn't been able to get anyone interested in the white house for years as no one wanted to come out here so far from town with no real roads and the stories of the bad things that happened here long ago. But now these rich people had come and needed a place for their party. Better yet, he hadn't rented to them. He had sold them the land, sold them everything: the house, the barn, all the land, and even our little trailer on its pad. We were to be evicted, though he'd gotten assurances from the rich people that we could remain until the end of spring. I was too horrified to speak, and he left, still smiling about his windfall of profit.'"

"I'm guessing something really bad is coming," Helter murmured.

"'Days passed, and people came in big trucks. They cleaned the barn out, and the horse, who wasn't really ours either, was sold to a family across town, too far for me to walk to see him. But at least he was safe. Petey was run over by one of the big trucks. I saw him die. I took his body later and buried it near the base of our hill, near the church. The white house was in the process of being torn down and rebuilt, and the barn was being gutted, so there was no safe place to bury him where his grave would lie undisturbed.'"

"This is in line with the church at the base of the hill, the one whose bell was ringing in Teeth and Upner's ghostly reenactment they witnessed," Bob added. "This rich couple must be Latham and his wife and son. Go on, Barb."

"'My mother found a spot for us to live close to town. She would get a better job there, she said. That this was all for the best. I saw she was lying, trying to make us believe that leaving our home wouldn't kill us.'"

"The party took place the night before we were supposed to leave. On the big night, the house and its rebuilt glass room, which I would never enter, was shining with candlelight. A large stable now stood behind the refurbished barn, filled with a dozen horses and a full-time groom. Cars began arriving up the long new road, and the once peaceful night was loud with boisterous talk and the instruments of a large band. I went out with my rage to watch, wishing with all I had that another storm would come and scare them away. As I stood there, a dark man appeared. I never saw where he came from. He said I could help if I gave him all my hate and rage, that there was power in emotion. I told him he could have it all if he'd make them go away, wash them off the top of the hill to drown."

"He took me there on the field, a storm building in the sky above us, lightning zigzagging across the sky, the rain falling in sheets. I passed out and awoke lying in running water, my dress soaked through, and my thighs smeared with my blood, my skin torn by his long sharp fingernails. I struggled home, slogging through the rising water up to my waist, to finally climb to dry land near my house. The water had washed the blood away, and I took refuge with my family, as we huddled indoors, wondering if the rain would ever stop."

"In the morning, our hill had become an island, and the big new house was deserted. Even the groom and the horses were all gone. We found out later that some had made it back to town, their cars just making it out of the rising water, others having to abandon their cars and swim. But many others, like the new owners, had not. Their car had washed away off the road as they tried to flee and was partly sunken at the base of the hill.'"

"What Teeth and Upner saw was real," Maryanne mused, and crossed herself.

"'I was filled with glee for what I had done. I relished our new isolation, even as my mother and my sister worried that the water would never go down and we'd starve. For our nearest neighbors had fled or drowned, their homes completely submerged along with the church, its familiar bell stilled and silent.'"

"This is the beginning of the flooding and drowning deaths," Bob mused. "The place was cursed from way back. It wasn't Latham who summoned the demon. He's been here all along."

"It was in league with this girl, whomever she is," Maryanne added. "Sorry, go on, Barb."

"'But the water receded, and in time the family of the new owners, the man's brother, arrived to take possession. The man, the hated man with spectacles, is with him! His wife and child died in the flood, but he is alive!'" She paused. "We are down to the last entries, but it's also the last pages of the diary. There's something weird here too, in that the diary has no dates at all, just spaces in between entries. And the end looks like it has a gap of years within the same pages, which makes no sense."

"Go on."

"'He is still going to make us leave!'" She paused. "I think this girl's family did leave as the next lines are that Latham's rebuilding the mansion, making it look exactly as it did before, except this time he adds a long bridge and a whole house of glass." She glanced sorrowfully at Maryanne. "She also reports that Latham has bought up all the farms that flooded in the valley, as well as the church. The priest who stayed to ring the bell and warn everyone of the flood saved a handful of people, but he drowned himself and the church was shunned after that, as was the valley. Latham left the houses to be reflooded as they were likely ruined anyway, but the church he raided for its stone: red granite, a local specialty that was mined further on down the valley."

"He must have bought the quarry and taken all the red granite that was there as well as the entire church," Bob mused. "It explains how he could make the entire foundations of the mansion and Dock-house of granite without spending a fortune. Also, why the sand on the beach was pink: because that was probably all that was left of the granite deposit. Possibly also why the lakebed has those deeper pockets in strange places: they are the mining tunnels from excavation."

Barb nodded. "This girl becomes obsessed with the Sea Room. She sneaks back in the late afternoons to avoid Latham's security, at least until he finishes everything and floods his new lake. Then she watches from the beach. She writes 'I hate that crystal ball even as I love to watch the way it glitters in the light like a beautiful prism.' The second to last entry reads 'At night the ball glows like a moon on the water, shimmering. Every night Latham rides to it on his horse, and I wish he would break his stupid neck.'" Barb paused. "Something must happen to infuriate this girl. Her last entry says "'I will go out tonight to the field and find the dark man, I will offer him anything, my life, my soul, my living heart, to make them leave. This is my home, and I will never leave it! And anyone who comes to take it from me will die!'"

"So, this girl made a lasting pact with the demon," Bob mused. "She is the force behind the water, its rising and falling. She is the one who is the power making the Sea Room glow, a structure that must be based on the sunroom she was never allowed in."

"She sounds more to me like the girl with the flute," Barb countered. "Given what she said to Jean and how she appears. The woman in the Sea Room is more likely Latham's wife who drowned in the flood."

"Two female ghosts who both think they are defending their land?" Maryanne said in confusion. "The same land?"

"Possibly. Flute girl thinks the island is hers. Sea Room lady is angered whenever people encroach on her territory," Barb added. "Which is why many times people go missing or have encounters on the island, the Sea Room isn't glowing. But what about when people try to leave the house? Why would Sea Room lady try to stop them leaving?"

"Possibly they are the same spirit appearing as two different people?" Helter offered.

"That would mean that this girl who hated Latham somehow became his wife," Maryanne argued. "Latham built the Sea Room for his wife, remember. She was headed there when she died." She paused. "Actually, his second wife. Latham had to have remarried, as he had Hans Jr. At least this explains when and how his other older son Carl died. Possibly also why Latham named that outcropping Carl's Point. Likely that's where he and the first Mrs. Latham were buried."

"Maybe the ghost of this girl possessed Latham's second wife?" Barb offered. "Or maybe the girl became a demon herself with all that hate and rage and possessed the wife. Either way, I don't see how this helps us. Besides, we are only thinking about her. If the demon right now doesn't have her rage to feed on because the island is isolated from the Sea Room, what's he doing for power?"

"He's manifesting the house other places, and absorbing souls there. But it's just the house, never the Sea Room. Something about the location must amplify his power," Maryanne said. "Bad things happening here again and again for centuries. It's all tied together."

"Tied in intractable knots," Bob muttered. "Those people who saw a shadowy figure over the years thought they saw Latham's ghost, but maybe that was the demon in its true form. We are dealing with up to four entities or groups: Celine, Teeth and the "fish", the demon and its manifestations and its legion of damned souls, Sea Room Lady, and Flute Girl. They seem to feed off one another; they together are what fuels the island's power. Teeth has said he and Celine will stay away, so they are out of the fight. We need to turn the other three against one another to truly destroy the house."

"How can we do that?" Maryanne asked.

"We need to figure out what happened with Latham, that he lost control of the demon," Barb said. "He must have somehow appeased the demon and severed it from the girl because he lived on the island successfully for a while, long enough to get remarried, get a new heir and do a few years of good deeds before everything went to hell."

"The girl doesn't want anyone coming to the island," Helter mused. "We need to appease the girl and/or the Sea Room lady and try to make her spirit at rest so it can move on. If we can remove the power from the Sea Room, we can sever the house from its power to regenerate or alter weather. Then we can destroy the house and get away alive." He paused. "I met the demon when I was setting charges on the island. He tried to get me to be like Mac, to bring him souls. I refused and he laid me out. When I came to, I was missing my gear and he'd destroyed all the charges I'd set which hadn't been protected by holy symbols. Celine is nothing compared to him. We can't reason with him. So, we have to turn the other ghosts to our side."

"A good plan, if, and it's a big if, our conclusions are mostly correct. Is our priest willing to make a try to placate the spirit?" Bob looked hopefully at Maryanne.

"Yes. I can design a funeral of sorts to put her to rest."

"Good. We should also get holy water and some defensive herbs to protect ourselves. The demon isn't going to just let us go to the Sea Room and perform the ritual unimpeded."

"You have to be fast and prepared," Upner cautioned. "I can run interference for you with my deputies and keep anyone from accessing Carl's Point while you execute your plan. But that also means that I won't be able to actually come with you for the real work."

"You need to be close by ready to call in reinforcements," Barb said solemnly. "Doing this is declaring open war. I've seen what that means. But if a group of police on official business descended at any point, the demon will go right into hiding, giving us time to escape." She hit Upner lightly on his shoulder. "You're our failsafe."

"I agree," Bob added. "But we do have to act at dawn before the lake is refilled so thawing or freezing can't affect us getting there or getting away if we have to abort. That means a solid plan with a schedule. Let's get to work."

———

"How did you get those ghosts or whatever they were to stop using only regular bullets?" Sharon asked wearily, as she waited in the ER to be seen, her hand pressed to her bloody side, the thick combine pad staunching the steady bleeding. "If that's what they were. They disappeared so I'm guessing they weren't human."

"You'd better just hold your side," Dale cautioned, as he hugged Karl who was asleep on his lap, the boy looking much younger than his age. John was curled up asleep beside him, his head on Dale's leg, covered with Dale's large coat. "It's your bad luck there was a car accident a half hour before we came in and only one surgeon on staff."

"They called another, and I'll be on the table shortly. Besides, they don't think any organs got hit. The teen had a paring knife. Answer me."

"If I'm going to believe that a ghost house took my son, I don't think it's a far stretch to reason that blessed bullets might be needed to get him back. I was a scout myself. It pays to always be prepared." He took a bottle out of his pocket of clear water, then dabbed his finger in it and spread it on each boy's forehead. Neither boy awakened. Dale let out a heavy sigh of relief.

"Did you expect there to be demons in our kids?" Sharon murmured.

"I think each boy was carrying something. They got infected by whatever evil is on Latham's Landing. Those things that attacked us in the car took care of whatever it was," Dale whispered. "Just like they devoured those teens that came after our kids. You and I don't share a common faith, but both of us raised our boys to believe in God. I think they lasted so long because they had prayer to cling to. Their faith saved them." He paused, then muttered darkly. "And the sheer luck that the entire troop was taken all at once."

"What are you saying?" Sharon asked in horror.

"The boys have been on that island these last two weeks, getting picked off one by one. Karl and John stuck together: they pooled their food and took turns keeping watch while the other slept, sneaking down to the water at night these last couple nights to drink. The others are all dead, Sharon. Karl and John told me all this while you were getting examined."

"Dear God," she said, crossing herself.

"John and Karl were going to make a break for it tonight as they were starving and starting to feel sick from drinking the stagnant lake water. They made a pact that if one of them was caught they'd sacrifice themselves so the other could get away. We were just in time."

CHAPTER TWELVE

CARLY LAY IN BED, THINKING, AS HER DOGS SNOOZED AROUND HER bed. *Maybe I should've gone to help Barb. I know she's working with some others to try to make things better. But if I go do that and get killed, who'll take care of my dogs? They'd end up in a shelter.*

Her cell phone rang in the other room.

Who can it be this late? I should've turned it off. I forgot again. Carly stifled a yarn, got up, and answered it. "Hello?"

"Thank Jesus you answered!" Kim whispered frantically. "Can you please come over here? Luke's drunk again and he swears he's going to find out who's behind the lights we've been seeing down in the old camp. He left and I'm all alone."

Carly looked out the window, where a light rain was pattering on the windows. *Why me?* "Why don't you come over here?"

"He took the car, Carly. We only have one. And the puppy's been howling out there like he's terrified. Luke hasn't housetrained it so he said I can't bring it inside. But every time I go out there to check on it, I feel like there's someone out there watching me."

That asshole had to get a puppy. "I'll be over shortly, Kim. But only if you bring the dog inside now. Go get the puppy right now. Understand?"

"Ok. Thanks."

Carly looked in confusion at the dial tone, then hung up the phone. She pulled on some clothes. As she went towards the door, she heard padding behind her. She looked over her shoulder to see Inferno, his expression expectant.

"Are you sure?" she asked. "I think you should guard the house. But I'd be glad of your company."

Inferno went past her to the door and stood before it, waiting.

"Okay."

The night was very windy, but Carly was relieved to see the rain was just a light drizzle. She made it to Kim's in about ten minutes, pulling into the driveway. The house was completely lit up, the front door ajar. *Not a good sign.*

She opened the car door, listening for barking. There was none.

Cue backup. Carly got out her cell phone and dialed 911.

"911. Please describe your emergency."

"It's Carly Copernick. I'm at 72 Lakeside Lane, Kim and Luke's house. Please have Sal Upner meet me here. Luke is missing. Kim called me for help, and now she's missing, too."

"Please remain on the line."

Two things happened. There was a shriek of a frightened dog from the house, and the phone abruptly went dead.

Inferno whined, then growled, his hackles rising.

I can't sit out here and wait for the cops, not with a puppy in there. "You stay next to me," Carly said, as she got out of the car and Inferno jumped out also. "I say wait, you wait. I say run, you run."

Inferno trotted to the front door, then slipped inside, Carly following him. They checked the first floor, where there was no sign of any struggle. There was fresh coffee perking on the stove, and two empty cups waiting on the counter. Carly moved past them and looked out the window to the backyard.

Lightning flashed silently, the bolt illuminating a doghouse and stake in the ground with a chain, but no dog.

The sharp crack of nearby thunder shook the house. There was a noise from upstairs of an animal jumping, then sliding, claws scrabbling. Inferno's ears went up, then he bolted for the stairs.

"Damn it!" Carly went after him, getting to the top stair just as all the house lights went out. Heart pounding in fear, she resisted turning on her phone. *I need my night vision. Inferno can see fine. My best weapon is faith. Sal will be here soon.*

Carly walked carefully down the hallway. Kim's two-story was an old farmhouse with many bedrooms on either side of the main hall. All the doors were open. Moonlight shone through the windows of each room out onto the hallway floor. Between the patches of light were inky spaces that looked bottomless. When she got to the last bedroom, she caught sight of two lights shining far off through trees. *Those are the lights Kim must have meant.* Carly shivered. *Lakeside Lane's the closest road to Leighton Beach. Someone or something is out there.*

Thunder boomed again, shaking the house.

There was a scratch of claws on wood behind her. She turned with a gasp.

Inferno ran out of a room with his ears back, whining. Another much smaller mongrel puppy followed him, tail wagging hopefully even as it keened plaintively.

"Inferno!" Carly darted after the dogs, running down the stairs.

Inferno cleared the stairs in two leaps and headed for the open front door. He ran outside as the puppy veered suddenly to the right, and continued down another flight of stairs, still whining.

Carly stopped at the base of the stairs, then turned and looked down into the basement, as the puppy disappeared into the inky blackness. "What are you doing? Get up here! Come on!"

From above her a booming demonic voice intoned "No!"

The command chilled Carly. *It's no human making that sound.* She ran after Inferno.

"No!" the voice repeated, then divulged into a mournful howl as the front door slammed shut by itself.

Carly grasped the handle and pulled. The door wouldn't budge. *Oh shit, I'm locked in, I'm locked in!*

There was another shriek from the puppy in the basement, then terrified howling. The emotional sound broke Carly's paralysis, rage filling her to overflowing, clearing her head to a single-minded purpose. She let go of the door and turned to face the evil force, furious. "How dare you?!"

Carly headed for the basement, clicking on her phone's flashlight and descending the stairs. *There's an exit door on the landing. Hurry!*

The puppy was cowering on a small dirty bed inside a much too-big crate. Carly grabbed it in her arms, and ran for the stairs, fumbling with the handle, then the locked screen door.

"You can't escape," the demonic voice said from the darkness behind her. The stairs behind her let out a creak, then another.

"We are leaving!" Carly yelled, throwing the weight of her shoulder against the screen door, the cheap lock giving way with a rasp of metal. She ran out and around the house to her car. Inferno was waiting there, whining. She let him in the back and put the puppy in the front seat, then got in herself, locking the doors in relief.

She cranked the car to life, then looked up at the house. A shadowy figure watched from the backyard, another on the porch. Then the one in the backyard headed toward her. The car engine coughed, threatening to stall out. Carly reversed immediately and gunned the car even as a police car approached and passed her heading to the house, sirens wailing.

———

"Stupid women," Vinnie said aloud, as he watched Carly drive off. "They worry constantly about the supernatural when there's other things that are a lot more deadly." He let the curtain fall back into place as more lightning split the sky. "Come on out, Kim!"

"Why did you do that voice trick?" Kim said, as she emerged from a closet to another crack of thunder. "And go out on the porch? I thought we agreed we were just luring her here to get the dog. You were supposed to be quiet and stay hidden."

Bitch is hearing things. I didn't say anything or go outside. "She's scared of shadows. But that's good, she can report another scary story. When Luke's found with the shotgun against his temple out in the cabins, it'll be blamed on the lake house, and we can take the insurance money and get out of here. And you're the one that wanted to be rid of the puppy."

Kim shrugged. "He wets on the rug. She's a dog lover so she'll take good care of him. Are you sure that the insurance will pay if it's ruled a suicide?"

Vinnie nodded, as he slipped his arm around her. "My father committed suicide to save our farm. It allowed my brother to not only keep the farm but expand to new markets. Too bad he kept it all because of my dad's will." He kissed her ear. "Damn it, there's a police car pulling up!"

"Shit, she called Upner," Kim cursed. "Get out of here, Vinnie. I'm going to have to do some explaining."

"No, we've both got to go," Vinnie said, grabbing her hand and pulling her to the basement. "We'll wait in the woods, then you can make up some story tomorrow and call the police, so they can find Luke. Quick, out the cellar door."

The couple slipped out, as Chief Upner entered the front door, gun drawn. "Hello? Kim?" He searched the downstairs first, finding the breaker in the basement thrown. He turned it back on, then searched the rest of the now-illuminated house.

His radio crackled. "Chief Upner?"

"Yes?"

"Carly called to say she's back at her house. She said something had chased her out of the house. She passed you coming in."

"Who chased her?"

"She said it was something. Not someone."

"Nice," Upner muttered. "Tell her to come in tomorrow for questioning. There's no one here, but someone threw that breaker, not something. But their car is also gone, which means they likely went somewhere."

"She maintains Kim called her, that Luke went to the cabins to check on lights they saw, and that Kim thought someone was watching the house. Chief, she said she also saw two lights on through the trees down near Leighton Beach."

"Hmm." *Luke would never have driven to the cabins, not when it's ten minutes' walk through the forest. We both went to Camp Leighton the year before it closed; he knows his way around in the dark well enough. So, he either went there for some other reason by car...or he didn't go there at all and he only told Kim he did. And where is Kim?* "I'll drive down to the cabins and look for his car. Ask my two deputies to meet me there."

"Roger."

Rain began to pour down as Upner trudged to his car, the roar of the wind increasing. "Great, that's makes the night just perfect."

———

"I need a vacation," Sal remarked aloud as he drove. The night was now a full force gale, the trees thrashing around like they were being tortured. "At least it's warm."

As he pulled into the entrance to the camp, he carefully avoided the fallen sign, then felt a sinking feeling as he saw Luke's parked car, its lights all off. *I don't see anyone sitting inside. But that doesn't mean his body isn't in there.* Sal sat in his car for a moment, considering his options. *Cell and radios only worked sporadically out here. If Luke's in the car, then he's dead. Same if he's here in the woods. I know better than to go off looking by myself here in the dark.* He picked up his radio. "Dispatch?"

———

"Why is he just sitting there?" Vinnie murmured, watching from some nearby bushes in his raingear. He'd left Kim secreted in the cabin where he'd been staying this past week, after telling her to extinguish the propane lanterns hanging in the windows that he'd used to make the mysterious lights. "Go investigate and find Luke already. I'm getting soaked here."

Rasping on gravel of another car approaching made his head whip around. "Dammit, it's Orwell. We've got to go now." He backed away and headed for his cabin as the headlights passed over where he'd been.

———

Vinnie should have been back by now. What's keeping him? I hate being here alone in the dark. Kim wanted to pace the room, but she wasn't familiar with the layout, and Vinnie's sleeping bag, porn magazines, hot plate, and other supplies were lying all over the floor. *Pig.* She turned again hopefully towards the window.

A grinning fleshless skull stared back at her. It tore through the old metal screen with cold bony fingers, grasping her roughly, sliding its dry finger bones into her open mouth to stifle her cry as the other arm wrapped like a steel band around her chest and pulled her out the ruined window.

Kim fought it, gagging at the taste of dirt and mold, and bit down hard. One of her teeth cracked as the fingerbones separated from the hand. She spit them out and gasped for breath, the exposed nerve in her tooth a white-hot agony.

The skeleton didn't seem to notice the loss of its digits. It dragged her towards the lake as she began to scream.

———

"Kim?" Vinnie knocked at the door. "Let me in. You should head toward the sheriff's car. He's here with his deputy. Make up some story about getting chased out of your house by a shadow."

There was no answer. Car doors slammed in the distance.

Stupid woman. "Kim, are you there? Open the door. I have to get my stuff and get out of here. They'll have a forensics team out here tomorrow morning at first light. They can't find any sign of me here or I'll be a suspect."

There were flashlights in the distance, some talking.

Vinnie swore, then pushed at the door. It opened up. He grabbed the flashlight he'd left near the door and turned it on, carefully shielding. *Where did she go? Maybe she already heard the cops and left. I'd better hurry.* Vinnie grabbed his gear, packing it in his backpack and duffel as fast as he could. Leaving the garbage, empty cans, and magazines, he hurried out the door, taking off in the direction of the highway.

———

"Looks like he committed suicide," Deputy Rich said, looking over the gruesome sight of Luke sitting with his shotgun in a mess of blood and brains. "I'd never have guessed it."

"I don't believe it," Sal admitted. *But maybe he killed himself rather than be murdered out here. That I believe.* "Call it in. We'll come back at first light, after the team's taken a look."

Deputy Rich nodded, lifting his radio.

"Help! Help!" came a cry from far off.

Rich and Sal looked at one another, then drew their guns and ran after the sound, straight towards the lake.

———

"Help!"

That's Kim. She must have gone back to the house and be calling for the deputies to give me time to get away. Vinnie nodded in approval. "Good girl." He headed away from the sound, towards the lake.

He walked along an old gravel path, picking his way past raised tree roots and fallen limbs. Once this path had been wide enough to drive a camp vehicle on to bring the boats in after lessons, but the forest had narrowed it to a small deer path in the decades since. *This should lead me to the camp road. I can walk on that to the highway. I'll just have to watch out for cars.*

There was a crack of branches breaking underfoot. Vinnie paused and waited, puzzled at an odd, snuffling sound. *An opossum?*

Another crack sounded, then another, as something came toward him.

He turned, his eyes seeking in the gloom and finding a whitish creature a hundred yards away. Cloaked in a shroud of pale grey murkiness, it swayed slightly from side to side as it came, its lumpy head twisting and turning, nodding as if its neck was broken. *Holy shit, is it looking for my scent?* He took an involuntary step backward, a branch snapping under his weight.

The creature stiffened, its head jerking up, its face moving slightly then stopping still, pinpoint red eyes staring directly at him. Then it launched itself with a shriek, its flailing sticklike limbs reaching eagerly toward him as it struggled over the thick underbrush.

Vinnie yelped and ran for the beach, his sense of direction keen as he found the old camp path, overgrown but much easier than the forest. He sprinted toward the clearing ahead, as the raggedy creature ran after him, its excited triumphant wail swelling as it reached the path and began to gain on him.

———

Kim struggled with the skeleton, beating against it with her hands, her writhing ineffectually as it dragged her closer to the beach. "Help! Help!"

A soft haunting melody trickled through the air faintly. The skeleton stopped and stood still as if listening, its grip on Kim loosening. She pulled free and ran, falling several times and bloodying her arms and face, sobbing and sure that bony arms would soon close about her neck. But the skeleton had lost all interest in her. It shambled toward the unseen source of the music, towards the water's edge.

Kim ran crying right into the arms of Deputy Rich, who lost his hold on his gun and dropped it as she slammed into him, knocking them both to the ground. She screeched louder, flailing against him. "Help! No, let go of me! No!"

"Kim!" Sal said, reaching out and yanking her to her feet, away from Rich who now was holding a bloody nose. He shook her. "There's no one here but us! Who were you running from?"

"Dead bones," she gasped, blinking. "It dragged me toward the water."

Another scream stabbed the night, making the two policemen jump. Rich grabbed his gun, pointing it into the darkness alongside Sal. Kim let out a shriek and ran away into the woods, her path taking her back the way the two men had come.

Rich and Sal looked at one another, then holstered their guns and followed her at a run.

———

The grey shrouded figure carried the limp body of Vinnie, his broken neck lolling, into the muddy lakebed. It dropped him in a large puddle of water near the beginning of the trench, watching the body float for a few seconds before greenish white hands pulled it down into the water. Then the figure fluffed its tattered shroud, the coverings billowing suddenly despite the lack of wind before collapsing into a pile of grey-black shadow, the flowing surface solidifying, a sheen forming along with ridges, until the mass resembled a large rock, not unlike several others at the end of the trench.

The skeleton watched from the lakeshore, its neckbones cracking slightly as it turned its empty eye sockets that did see toward the three fleeing people. Then it shambled back into the forest, disappearing into darkness.

————

"I've given her a sedative," the First Responder said, as his coworker helped settle Kim in the ambulance. "Does either of you want to tell me what happened?"

"What did she say happened?"

"That a skeleton dragged her out of her house and towards the camp, then toward the beach. She says she bit its fingers off." He shrugged. "She did bite something hard as one of her back teeth is cracked all the way through. I gave her some morphine and called the local all-night dentist. He's going to meet us at the hospital."

"We didn't see a skeleton," Deputy Rich said. "Her husband shot himself. I think the shock of seeing the body was enough to have her jumping at shadows."

"Strange then that she didn't mention her husband at all," the First Responder said sarcastically. "I've got to go." He got in, and the ambulance drove off, sirens flashing.

"Do we go back to the camp?" Rich asked, turning to Sal. "You know there was someone else there in trouble."

"Not tonight," Sal said. "Go home and get some sleep and we'll investigate tomorrow."

"How can you say that?" Rich said, incredulously. "We can't just leave someone out there. What if Kim was telling the truth?"

"If she was, then whomever screamed is dead," Sal pronounced bluntly. "Do you think your gun's going to stop a walking skeleton?"

"No," Rich muttered, looking toward the dark forest. "But I took an oath to protect and serve."

"They are going to flood the lake again tomorrow or the next day," Sal said wearily. "We have to hold on until then. Things will get better after that."

"What if they don't?" Rich looked at him accusingly. "You remember Hal who we went to school with? He went to Leighton Beach walking with his girlfriend, Chloe. She went missing. The police thought he'd tried something, and she'd run away from him and he'd caught up with her. When they found her the next afternoon walking on the highway, she was mute, with choke marks on her throat and a broken arm. Her family packed her up and they left town. Hal protested he hadn't touched her, that they hadn't gone anywhere near the water when she disappeared. He went to relieve himself and she was just gone. He said he looked all over, called for her, and stayed out there all night and never found her."

"I know, Rich. I was there! Hal said they weren't anywhere near the water, that there was something else out there in woods, and it had gotten Chloe." Sal took a breath. "But then how did she get away? I don't think Kim would be breathing now if she hadn't run into us."

"Maybe someone else distracted whatever it was, and it got them instead?" Rich offered. "Why do you think that the monsters will stop when the water's back?"

"Because I've been here before looking for missing people," Sal said tiredly. "The beach is where it always was. But there was a lagoon near the cabins in the beginning where beginner swimming and boating was taught to the youngest campers. I saw it in pictures my grandmother showed me, when my dad went here in summers when he was little."

"So?"

"So, near the cabins there used to be a clear shot to the lake. A kid did drown there the last season the lake was open. He was practicing his diving at night for the competition at the end of the summer. Supposedly he got a cramp and drowned. But maybe something pulled him under and kept him there instead."

"And you know this how? You were a toddler."

"My grandmother told me the story and warned me if I ever went near the lagoon that she'd paddle my bottom. I never did, and neither did any of the other kids from town, especially after they closed the camp. But you and I saw that cabin where someone's been staying for at least a couple weeks. Those are the lights Luke saw. Them living there, maybe even just the lights at night, lured something out of the lake."

"Why didn't it get them before now?"

"I don't have the answers to your questions," Sal snapped, as he got into his car. "And I can't afford to lose a deputy, Rich. Please, go home."

CHAPTER THIRTEEN

"ARE WE READY?" BOB ASKED, LOOKING OUT OVER THE GROUP IN the early dawn as they stood assembled on Barb's porch. "Does everyone know the plan and what parts they need to play?"

"I have the herbs and blessed water," Barb said. "I'm going with Maryanne to the Sea Room to help lay the female ghost to rest."

"I'm going with Bob to the main isle to distract the demon," Helter said. He patted his two large duffle bags. "I have enough surprises here to get the job done."

"Does everyone have holy water?" Maryanne asked, proffering six water bottles. "I blessed and brought extra."

Everyone took an extra, including Helter.

"I wanted to add before we started," Barb began uncomfortably. "We aren't taking Jean's advice. She said to focus on stopping the Hustermen and to leave the island alone."

"Why are you saying this now?" Helter snapped at her. "Sorry, but I want to get started. We all agreed talking this through last night that this was the best plan. We don't know what will hurt the Hustermen or even if they can be hurt at all. We know what will hurt the demon and laying the spirits to rest is a solid plan."

"I'm not saying we shouldn't go," Barb retorted. "Hear me out. I just skimmed the diary the night we got it because we were pressed for time. I spent yesterday reading it from cover to cover hoping to discover something we could use. I need to tell you what I found." She took out a piece of paper. "First, the diary's author was Laura Munson. Her name was written in the margins on a page with remarks about how she likes her first name but hates her last name. Her older sister was Jenny."

"This is worth knowing," Maryanne said, jotting notes in her notebook. "I can add the names into the ritual. Go on but go slow so I can write."

"Laura had a few odd experiences in the years she lived here, which she mentions. She thinks she sees a young woman in the old white house on that glass porch she loves. She initially thinks it's Jenny, but it's not, as her sister is outside at the time. She asks whomever it is to let her inside, but instead it motions to her to come in. The porch door that always had a locked padlock opens right up, but Jenny stops her in time. The inference I'm drawing is that Laura saw the demon manifesting and would have fallen into the basement to her death. After that her mother and sister don't let her go to the old house anymore to retrieve food, and they all begin to avoid it." Barb paused. "Laura also thinks she sees a little girl outside the old house, trying to get in. It's always in winter, during a full moon. There are only a few lines devoted to it, 'she's trying again, like last year, peering in the windows, trying the door. But she can't get in. Mother said she's just a restless spirit that's harmless, to ignore her.'"

"What the hell?" Bob exclaimed. "A ghost?"

"Just wait," Barb enticed. "Laura also has recurring dreams of a mansion that sound like nightmares. It's the only time in the diary that she sounds scared. Listen to this: 'I never saw the outside, only the house's center, its heart, where there were fireplaces in a strange pattern, not back to back, but facing in one direction where the innermost four rooms came together; each fireplace on the wall to the right, the wall to the left bare, but then the room nearest it had that same pattern. That would mean that the chimneys would all need to go up all four walls inside to join into one big chimney above. When I told my mother she laughed and said it didn't make sense because it was just a dream.'"

"Here's another mention from a few weeks later. 'Last night I dreamed again that I'm a lady in a grand house. I have dreamed of it each night this week. There's a cat toy on a shelf with other knick-knacks but no other stuffed toys. In the first dream it was poorly made and obviously fake. But in the second and third dreams of this place, the toy became more real, with a wind up on its back so it will purr. Tonight, in the dream the cat was in an open drawer purring by itself, as if the cat had jumped there. When I petted it, the fur wasn't plush material anymore, but felt like an odd mix of fake fur and real fur, tabby-striped. I think it can move on its own. Mom told me again that it was just a dream. But I think The House is becoming real just like that cat.' She writes it from then on like that, in capitals."

"This sounds like the demon entering her dreams, since it can't get to her in the physical world," Bob mused. "Sorry, Barb, go on."

"Can you condense some of it?" Helter asked, looking at his watch. "We're losing the dawn today."

Barb nodded. "She has several more dreams the next week where she's back in the house, and the house looks damaged like a fire, but the damage is illogical, like those chimneys she mentioned previously. She spends several pages trying to work out what that might mean with no conclusions. She also refers here to feeling trapped in the house for days in a single dream."

"Why is that important?" Upner asked as he walked up to them. "Sorry I'm late. My men are in position, with cars at the end of Town Road and Atlas Road. I'll be here myself. I can have everyone stay in position until dusk."

"What if we aren't back by then?" Maryanne ventured. "Last time it took us hours just to walk to the island."

"I can't lose any deputies," Upner stated defensively. "They are in place to keep people from recording or bringing in anyone who might stop you. But I can't ask them to fight what's here after dark knowing they can't win. I will keep watch until dark. If you aren't back by sunset, I'll call the state police."

"We should be done much sooner than before," Barb assured Maryanne. "I'll hurry." She turned back to her notes. "'Why do I keep dreaming of The House?' Laura asks this several times through the rest of the diary without recounting dreams, so there are more that she's not writing down. And this other eerie remark, 'The cat is scary now. Big as a dog and he watches us with a tiger's eyes. They shine in the moonlight dreadfully like his long claws. He has free rein of The House. No matter where we run, he always finds us, and we wake up screaming.'"

Maryanne crossed herself.

"This is the last nightmare she writes of, and they have become nightmares by now: 'I dreamed I was at The House with Jennifer. She is distraught, a widow dressed in black, but I am in white. My shawl has blood on the fringe. We went from room to room, trying to find a way out, but there were no doors leading outside. Some of the rooms were still burned black, others furnished. There was a man in the mirror looking back at me. He tried to strangle Jenny! Footsteps followed us sometimes. We always find the tiger waiting for us. His claws are long and terrible. He slashed Jenny's dress, and her scream woke me up. I could not wake her, so our mother threw some cold water on her face.'"

"Jesus Christ," Helter said, then looked apologetically at Maryanne. "Sorry, but that's scary as hell, especially for a little girl. When was this in relation to Latham, Barb?"

"This entry is right before Latham's family shows up," Barb said, folding the paper and putting it in her pocket. "My take is that the demon, having reached them through dreams, is using their nightmares to feed him fear, much as he uses Cairn Isle today. Instead of random dreams though, he created some kind of dream mansion where he can control what they experience. Then he spends time honing everything to make the dream as terrifying as possible to them, including how to manipulate time to harvest the greatest amount of fear."

"Latham's appearance saved them," Bob mused. "Why settle for the dreams of a family of three when you can have real life widespread murder and disaster?"

"Yes," Barb agreed. "This location must have always been a place where the demon frequented. When he sees Latham, he sees an opportunity to move out of dreams and build a lasting feeding ground for fear in reality."

"This also explains why Laura's mother is eager to pack up and go," Helter added.

"But why isn't Laura, if she's having all these nightmares?" Maryanne asked.

"She's either in the first stages of possession, or she's just angry enough at Latham's intrusion that it pushes away everything else, including her fear," Barb replied, running her hand through her hair. "I guess it doesn't matter. We're wasting time."

The group drove to Carl's Point in two vehicles, Sal following in his patrol car. He left them at the dirt road to Carl's Point, pulling across the road and parking to block it.

"What we are is stymied again," Bob growled as he got out of the SUV, gesturing emphatically. "It's not there."

Helter groaned and Barb swore, looking toward the hill where the mansion of Latham's Landing should have stood. The island was empty except for the old garage and the granite docks and stairs.

"Let's all go to the Sea Room," Maryanne stated quietly. "It's there. I admit I'd feel a lot better knowing you two men were outside while we women go inside."

"You go ahead," Helter said, shouldering his bag. "I'm going to lay a few surprises, but I'll catch up." He headed toward the empty hill.

"C'mon," Barb said. Bob, Maryanne, and she headed via the lake floor towards the Sea Room.

———

"We need to do this," Richelle insisted, as she shook the can of spray paint. "If you don't care enough about our friends that died, then go home."

"Which of the popular kids that got killed was your friend?" James asked sarcastically. "They all told you to go back to the afford-able housing apartments where you came from. You're just doing this because you wanted to make that mural and get your picture in the paper. You don't give a damn about the kids that got shot." He grabbed for the can.

"Okay, fine!" Richelle snapped, pulling away from him. "You're right. I don't care about them. But I do want to raise awareness. Those kids might have been assholes, but they shouldn't have been killed eating lunch, either. The guidance counselor was wrong not to approve a mural with the names of the kids that died."

"Well, they didn't."

"What's it going to hurt?" Richelle cajoled, as she began painting on the side of the school. "They're not going to let us come back here for another few weeks, until they clean up the damage. By then I'll be done, and they'll leave the mural alone, because the newspaper will have published a photo and some sappy piece about how I used art to heal the wounds of our school."

James shook his head and walked off.

"Where are you going?"

"I'm going to look at the damage, see what's to see. I was sick that day like you, so I missed it." He ambled in through a door hanging half off its hinges, ducking under a Police Scene Do Not Cross taped barrier and entered the gym.

James looked around, surprised at the level of mess and destruction. "That guy was messed up. But then you'd have to be to make an explosive to blow up a school, then blow yourself up by mistake before you even speak to one person."

The gym was filled with fallen down roofing tiles and debris, but there were neither signs of any wildlife, nor any bloodstains. The explosion had killed the would-be terrorist when it caved in part of the roof. He'd been standing near the inner wall of the gym, the cafeteria and its students on the other side of his ultimate goal. Though the bomber hadn't gotten that far, the detonation of his bombs all at once had blown out the shared wall, taking out the nearest table of students which happened to be the cheerleaders, their captain, and the male and female stars of the basketball teams. *Twenty kids were all blown to ragged chunks. There's got to be some huge bloodstains in there.*

As James neared the ruined shared wall of the gym and cafeteria, he felt a sense of foreboding. Just visible in the gloom were the twisted metal and warped plastic of the lunch tables in a semicircle where they'd been thrown by the blast, edges scorched and discolored. There were dark irregular stains on the open floor just visible in the fading light from the row of windows to the west, giving the room an eerie glow. There was an emptiness of life that was palpable in the wreckage, but something else was there filling the copious shadows. Almost like it was waiting with hushed breath for him to come within reach...

"James? James!"

Glad he could flee and not lose face with his sister, James turned around and ran back the way he'd come. Richelle motioned to him as he ducked under the hanging door, and he ran towards her, narrowly avoiding the headlights of a car pulling in beside the building.

"Damn it," Richelle swore. "Now I'll have to come back on the weekend."

"Why?" James asked. "That was just someone turning around."

There was a crack of thunder above them. "Because of that," she answered angrily. "I bought water base paint to make the initial sketch with. It'll just wash right off. C'mon."

As they went around the back of the building, they stopped in surprise. "Who would have known there was a lake here? I thought the reservoir didn't come this close to the school."

"I don't know, I never came around this side of the school. I didn't know there was anything back here." James didn't like the look of the water. It seemed to snake on out to the left out of sight meshing with the horizon, the visible end dark and still. *Why can't I see the Bryne Dairy gas station sign from here? Or the Home Depot?*

"Look," Richelle pointed. "About three feet below the level of that rear terrace, there's a spot to dock a small boat. Almost like they left a space for one."

"They might have," James agreed, as they walked along the water's edge. "We had a lot of flooding these last couple years. I guess it's not surprising that there's a lot of water in the reservoir, especially as the dam was put in place to ensure this city had enough drinking water. This school used to be a combination town hall, courthouse, and seat of government years ago when the town of Torrance formed."

"Aren't you the scholar," Richelle teased.

"We can't all be famous artists," James replied, grinning. "Some of us have to actually work to get into college. We've come this far. Let's climb to the top and see what's on the other side of that wall.

It's sprinkling but I don't hear any more thunder. I think the storm's going to miss us."

A few minutes later, the twosome looked down from the top of the terrace. Fog and gloom obscured most of the lake which lay about twenty feet below. But around the last outcropping of the shore a few miles up, there were large indistinct shapes out on the water. "Hey, Rich, those might be islands. That bigger one there in the middle looks like it has a house on it. Must have been built by trappers or something a long time ago. It looks like it's about to fall down."

"I thought you hadn't been back here before?" Richelle gave him a sidelong glance. "Maybe with Sadine?"

James gave his sister an aloof look. "Not a chance." His phone chimed. "Time to go. Mom wants us home."

"Hey!" a voice called from behind them. "Can I use your phone?"

Richelle and James turned as a twenty-something man came up to them, his expression sheepish. "Who are you?"

"My name's Daryl. I was hiking with some friends around the lake and my girlfriend Nikki twisted her ankle. My phone is dead, and the others left theirs at home."

"Where's your friends?" Richelle asked, handing him her cell phone.

"Down there, near that house," Daryl said, pointing. He began dialing. "It seemed like it would be fun to check the place out, so we took a boat we found on the shore there and rowed over. But everything went right to hell." He listened for a moment, then shook his head and handed it back. "I'm not getting through. I'm not sure what's the matter. If you can call the police when you get home, please just direct them to come help us. We're helping her limp back, but it's slow going." He flashed them a smile. "Thanks again." He ran off down the lakeshore in the direction of the house.

"If we were good, we'd go with him and help him rescue his girl-friend," James mused, as Richelle dialed her phone.

"That's bizarre," she said, hanging up. "I'm not getting any signal at all now, nothing. Check yours, James."

James took out his phone, frowning. "No, mine's also not

showing any signal. We better go back towards the school and call the police before we take off, then Mom. It's going to be dark soon."

The twosome walked back over the terrace, and then beyond that along the reservoir shore. The daylight waned as the light drizzle that had been falling intensified into a steady downpour.

"Shouldn't we be there by now?" Richelle asked in irritation. "We didn't walk that far."

"I don't know if it's the dark or the rain, but I can't see the school," James said, as he picked up the pace. "But I know we came this way. Hurry up, Mom's going to worry."

The duo walked for another five minutes, then Richelle stopped suddenly. "James, I know we didn't come this far."

"We came this way," James said stubbornly. "Come on. There's a shape ahead. It's got to be the school."

The duo pushed on, then stopped again in surprise, looking up at the dark looming building in front of them. "That's not the school. It's the house we saw in the distance."

"It can't be."

"It is," Richelle insisted. "C'mon!" She ran past the house and kept running, James running after her. She reached the terrace with James at her heels and stopped to catch her breath. Ahead of her were Daryl and three other college-age youths standing in the rain, blocking their way.

"What do you want?" Richelle challenged. "Move aside."

"You're not very kind," Daryl intoned, as he moved aside. "But go ahead." The other three behind him also parted their ranks.

Richelle and James ran past him and his friends without a word, giving them as wide a berth as possible. The twosome reached the top of the terrace and let out relieved sighs to see the lights of the school shining in the distance. A police car waited there while someone outside it walked around with a flashlight.

"I've never been so glad to see a cop," James said with a laugh. "You think—?" He was cut short as he was yanked backwards by his shirt, two of the college kids grabbing him and pulling him over the edge of the terrace. James let out a yell, then there was a splash.

"James!" Richelle screamed, scrambling to the terrace edge. Down below there was only water, a ripple in a widening circle. She took breath to scream again and felt herself propelled forwards, flailing as she fell, her scream tearing loose.

Daryl looked in the distance at the police car as it grew blurry, then disappeared. He turned and dove off the terrace. A faint splash was heard as the terrace and water also shimmered, then disappeared as the sky lightened, the outline of large neon lights in the distance visible once again.

———

Helter was setting up the last few charges in the old garage when he heard a loud cracking sound. *That's got to be the house returning.* He finished quickly, then ran out the garage door and onto the old stone bridge, moving as fast as possible towards the still dark Sea Room.

Latham's Landing appeared, its misty outline solidifying. Bubbles rose in the deep water near the north shore of the island, then two heads appeared, swimming hard. Richelle and James reached the rocky island shore and collapsed, panting, and coughing up water.

"What the hell just happened?" James managed.

"I don't know," Richelle answered, then coughed again. She stood. "But we need to get away from this house now. Avoid the water, there was something else in there with us." She wiggled her left foot, the heel of her shoe ripped off. "Something tried to taste me before chowing down or I'd have lost my foot."

"Let's go," James said, as he got up unassisted. "We should be able to walk out if we walk down the shoreline. The terrace should be in that direction with the school behind it."

"How did you figure that?" Richelle questioned, looking at him strangely. "We weren't ever on this island."

"The island had a rocky point where it got close to the shore," James said with a smirk. "I was paying attention as always." The smile left his face. "Be careful and go slow. The rain let up for now, but this fog is terrible. I can't see any lights at all." James turned on the flashlight on his phone and the twosome began to walk along the shoreline.

———

"Chief?" Upner's radio crackled.

Deputy Rich. "Yes?"

"We've got a problem."

I should have known this would happen. "What do you see?"

"Nothing so far," Rich answered nervously, casting his eyes out over the empty lakebed. *Why did I agree to this?* "But so you know, I can't reach Jake. You told him to block off Town Road at the main highway. I left him only ten minutes ago in place. Now I'm not getting any answer—"

"Leave Atlas Road now and fall back to his location," Upner instructed. "Keep talking to me until you get there.

Rich started the SUV and moved off. *It's good I'm going. I didn't sleep at all last night. I'm so tired I'm seeing rocks appear out of nowhere. But I'd swear those weren't there when I parked.* He drove around the two large boulders at the side of the road, then continued on, still talking to Upner.

"Do you see anything out of the ordinary?" Upner said.

"Looks like a sheet caught in a bush down near the camp turnoff," Rich replied, as he drove past. "Something white anyway. Wind must have come up, its moving in the breeze."

Upner rolled down his window and put his hand out. *There's no wind at all.*

"Jake's in position," Rich said disgustedly. "He's not answering his radio because he's chatting up some girl. Sorry, two girls. They're close to jailbait. I don't see any car."

"Go tell him to keep his mind on his work," Upner rebuked. Then a crawling sensation made him shudder. *No car.* He added quickly. "Rich, leave the radio on when you talk to him. I want to know what he says back."

"Got it." A car door slammed. "Jake, what's this?"

"This is Nikki and Marie," Jake answered. "Girls, this is my fellow officer, Deputy Rich."

"Hello," two female voices flirted. "We're so glad you're here. We've been trying to get Officer Jake to give us an escort back to our car. It stopped down near the project." She tittered. "We went to look for ghosts. But we were supposed to be back hours ago and we've got to get home."

"I kept telling them I couldn't leave," Jake said sheepishly. "But now you're here—"

"Shouldn't we call a tow truck?" Rich interrupted.

"We ran out of gas," one of the girls said. "See, that's why we have this gas can. But it's going to be heavy hauling it all the way back to the car. Can you please give us a ride?"

"Sorry, girls, but we have to call it in and get a tow truck out here," Rich replied cordially. "Because of the current situation, I'll have to get two state troopers to accompany the tow truck. You're welcome to wait with us if you want."

"No, we'll start walking," one of the girls said angrily. "So much for public service."

"Why did you do that?" Jake hissed to Rich after a few moments. "They need help. And we were told to keep everyone away from the lake!"

"I just drove past the development," Rich whispered, watching the two figures walk quickly out of sight. "There's no car there, Jake." He returned to the radio. "You hear all that, Chief?"

"Yes," Upner said, his voice cracking in fear. "You see anything else you call me immediately. You don't get me answering in five seconds, call in the state police. I'll do the same. Understood?"

"Agreed."

———

"Are we ready?" Barb asked, as she lit another batch of herbs and completed the circle of protection around herself and Maryanne. They were at the outside door of the Sea Room on the stone and concrete bridge support.

Maryanne nodded, then began to recite a funeral mass. "Spirits of this place, please hear my words and be comforted. In life you knew pain and sadness, and most of you met untimely ends. I come here today in friendship to ask for your forgiveness for what happened to you. We cannot change the past. But we can alter the future, your future. Do not cling to the horrors you endured in life. Free yourself from your mortal pain and suffering and cast aside the shackles of this world. A loving God waits for you in Heaven, and those that loved you in life wait beside Him to welcome you to Paradise. I have not come to exorcize you or force you to leave. I come in peace to give you peace if you will accept your death—"

There was a huge rumbling noise, as if something was breaking. "The house returned," Barb whispered aloud.

"—and embrace everlasting life with God." Maryanne made the sign of the cross, then cast a cup of holy water on the door of the Sea Room. The liquid boiled up instantly, turning to steam.

Lights came on throughout the mansion, shining like a beacon. There was a canine howl far off in the direction of the beach. Shapes came into view, running hard. An answering howl sounded, more shapes running out from the shoreline near Carl's Point.

"Bob, get up here now!" Barb called, as the female ghost materialized inside the Sea Room, looking at them through the heavy marine glass hatefully.

"Please come out and speak to me," Maryanne implored the female ghost. "I have the power to give you peace through the love and mercy of God."

"You are going to die," the woman said, as she walked through the glass wall to stand before the circle of herbs. "You were a fool to return."

Bob hurried and stepped into the circle of herbs, his gun drawn in one hand, a crucifix in the other.

The ghost took a step forward.

"Please!" Maryanne said urgently. "This is not about me. It's about you. No matter what you did in life, you don't deserve this, to exist here all alone being used by a demon as a power source until you run dry and become nothingness. Don't you want to rest?"

The ghost considered her words, the woman's expression surprised. "I...must do this. It's my penance."

"Tell me your sin, and I will absolve you," Maryanne promised, holding up her cross in blessing. "God doesn't want your suffering. The demon of the isle wants it to keep himself strong. Free yourself and be at peace."

There was another howl, much closer. The running shapes were a mile out, coming fast. Barb lit another pile of herbs and put her own rifle to her shoulder, taking aim.

"I cannot free myself. I cannot leave this place."

Barb shot one wolf, then another, then another, the blessed hollow point bullets tearing into their bodies and exploding. As each wolf fell, the creature uttered a tortured scream, then its body collapsed into a wisp of smoke that disappeared in the gathering wind.

"You do not have to stay here!" Maryanne shouted, as a crack of thunder sounded, and light rain began to fall. "You are a human spirit, not evil. You cannot be kept from Heaven! Confess your sins and be free!"

"I thank you, but I cannot leave," the woman said, bowing her head as she executed a perfect curtsey. "But I implore you to leave. My husband is coming. He won't just kill you. He'll play a little first."

"Don't shoot!" Helter yelled, as he ran up breathing hard. "There are two kids on the island. They came back with the house."

"Get in the circle!" Barb yelled, as she and Bob tried to shelter the burning herbs that were guttering and hissing in the gathering storm.

A man in a riding habit on a bay horse trotted into view as Helter leapt into the protective circle with the others. The rider stopped just outside the circle, looking at them. "You can't win this. You know that."

"We might not," Maryanne answered, making the sign of the cross. "But I have faith and hope."

"Hope is the faithful's sword in the darkness," the man said as he dismounted, his appearance altering to a cloaked figure as the horse vanished. "But there's a mirror to those words: that hope, long held and reluctant, is that much more devastating when broken into shards. Done repeatedly, it's enough to destroy anyone. Even you."

Barb uncapped a bottle of holy water and threw it at him. The being let out a hateful anguished screech and disappeared, thick black smoke billowing up.

"We can't keep the circle intact; the herbs are getting too wet!" Bob yelled. He turned to the female ghost. "Please, may we come inside the Sea Room and try to lay you to rest? What do you have to lose?"

The female ghost smiled. "Yes, I can always kill you." She laughed. "And it would be easier there." She gestured. "Go in."

"Thank you," Maryanne said, making the sign of the cross over the ghost as she passed. The lady winced and closed her eyes as Bob and Barb hurried after her, Helter bringing up the rear bearing armfuls of the sodden smoking herbs from the circle.

The group went to the interior of the glass structure, the female ghost appearing again before them. "Where did you die?" Maryanne asked. "I would like to pray over that spot, please."

The lady ghost shook her head once, oddly confused. "I didn't die in here. I was never allowed here. This was my husband's playroom, his exclusive domain, him and his whore, his sea wife." Her hands clenched into fists at her sides. "I drowned running here, when the house and bridge flooded." Her expression became lost, pained. "Hans promised me that we'd be safe, that our home would never flood. I thought if there was one place safe it would be in here. But a wave of water struck me and pushed me into the lake."

"I'm sorry," Maryanne said, again making the sign of the cross over the woman. "What happened was not your fault. Let go of your hate and pain. You do not deserve to endure here like this. Let go and pass on."

"No!" the female ghost drew herself up, her eyes flashing. "I vowed with my dying breath that he would never set foot here again! I have kept him out!"

"Yes, but at what cost?" Barb interjected, as she finished laying out another protective circle of herbs, Helter and Bob lighting it. "You're guarding an empty box. What is here for Latham to want now, old broken junk? Whatever mistress he might have kept here is long dead, not even her ghost is here. They're all free but you. Let it go and pass on...Laura."

The female ghost recoiled, as Helter suddenly doused her with holy water. She convulsed, black smoke again rising up in a cloud as the outline of the woman wavered, her sexy deep green dress turning light blue, frills and ruffles appearing, the short curly brown hair lengthening to long dark tresses. The female figure collapsed, the black smoke solidifying to another female figure, this one with short hair and red eyes. Baring fangs, it launched itself at Helter. His gun came up as he sidestepped, firing his automatic, the bullets hitting the monster several times in the chest. It staggered and kept coming.

"Go!" Helter yelled, pushing Barb in front of him as Bob stepped in front of Maryanne, his gun drawn. Barb ran out of the Sea Room with Helter right after her, the staggering monster at their heels.

Bob turned to Maryanne. "We've got to do what we can while they're distracting the demon. I'll keep the circle burning. Hurry!"

"Light the candles," Maryanne said, as she opened her bible and began to read. "Our Father, who art in Heaven, hallowed be Thy name..."

————

"Barb?" Helter said, stopping suddenly. Instead of the lake and the stone bridge, he was on the back porch of a house on a quiet suburb street, faint lamplight showing an empty lawn. "Hello?"

"Get in here," a voice called gruffly from inside. "The game's about to begin."

Helter reloaded and holstered his gun, then went inside. *This is my brother's house in Chesterfield. What am I doing here? And why do I have my gun?* "Ed?"

Ed sat in his recliner in the living room, his son on his lap half asleep, his daughter sitting at the coffee table eating crackers. "Tell Lon to bring me a beer, would ya?"

Lon, Helter's older brother, came into the room with two beers and handed one to Ed. "Quit your griping, I'm coming. Pizza and wings are here."

The pizza delivery guy appeared behind Lon, setting bags on the coffee table. "You mind if we stay and watch too?"

Lon nodded and returned to the kitchen with him, as Helter uneasily watched another man come from behind the pizza guy and sit in the last living room chair. *He's got a gun. But I can't do anything, or I might shoot the kid.* Helter took his niece's hand and walked to the kitchen with her, stopping cold as he saw the body of Lon crumpled against the wall, his chest a red ruin. He pulled his niece to the door, grabbing her coat from the hook as he shoved the door open. There was a shout from inside and shots. Helter picked the girl up in his arms and ran as fast as he could to the front of the house, then across the street and the next, hiding behind a fence. He felt at his hip for his gun, but his holster was empty. *What the hell? There's no way I lost my gun.* Realization dawned with a chill up his spine and the sudden aching of the ragged scars on his chest. *Shit, I'm trapped in Latham's Landing illusion. I have to figure out how to break free.* He helped the girl put on her coat, then sat huddled with her against the fence, listening.

"Why are we here?" the girl whispered. "I'm cold."

If those guys have a brain, they'll follow me because they're going to be worried that I am going to find cops or tell somebody. I don't dare try to go all the way over to Main Street to stores because there's not enough cover. "We're playing hide and seek. Be very quiet."

Stealthy movements approached.

I have to get out of here. Helter headed with the girl down toward the old factory and the railroad tracks, taking cover in back of an abandoned big tenement at the end of a short dead end. *Shit, I'm boxed in.* At the back of the tenement was a drop off of a good two or three stories where land had been excavated for a parking garage. The only way down was a fallen rusty chain-link fence which had once blocked the concrete cliff. *It extends down all the way. Will it support me and her? I don't have a choice, they're coming!* "Hold onto my neck and don't let go."

Helter climbed down the groaning fence, his heart beating faster with every tortured metal creak. He let go at the bottom and taking her hand again, hurried with his niece to the next street over. He stopped, looking on all sides for some safe haven and finding only dark houses.

Sounds of swearing and the creak of metal under stress spurred him on. Again, Helter lifted his niece and ran with her across another four streets, taking shelter under a large tree as he tried to recover his breath. *I'm about to collapse from exhaustion. We have to hide. I need a church.*

Helter blinked in surprise, the lighted sign a block down with its cross fueling his tired body with adrenaline. He hurried to the door and knocked. "Please let us in. Please!"

The door opened, a reverend looking at him quizzically. "It's the middle of the night. Can you come back at eight?"

Helter barged past with an apologetic smile. "I'm sorry, but I need Jesus right now. Please, say a prayer over me and my niece, I beg you."

"Very well," the reverend said with a yawn, taking the little girl's hand. "Follow me." Helter locked the door of the church and braced it with a chair, then followed them.

———

"Why aren't we seeing any lights?" Richelle asked, as she followed James down the shore. "We should be seeing either illumination in the night sky above the school, or the tall signs of the fast-food places and gas stations in the other direction."

"I don't know for the second time," James said irritably. "The island's not that big and we already walked most of the way down this side. My phone's already down to fifty percent."

"Mine's good," Richelle assured. "I'll turn it on once we find the outcropping you saw, so you can conserve—"

There was a sharp skittering of rocks behind them.

Richelle and James stopped still, and looked behind them in the gloom, waiting for the noise to repeat. There was only silence.

"Who's there?" Richelle called.

"Why did you do that?" James hissed. "If there's someone there it's not a friend."

"C'mon," Richelle said, grabbing his arm as she hurried on. "We need to keep moving."

The siblings stumbled on until they reached a large sheer rock outcropping a few minutes later. "We can't climb over that," Richelle said, placing her hands on the smooth cold stone.

"At least the rain stopped," James said, as he looked inland. "I think there's another building up there, Richelle. At least there are stairs here."

There was a splash in the water to their left, resulting ripples hitting the shore.

Pebbles skittered again on the shore behind them as something moved unseen in the darkness.

Richelle let out a scream as the stone beneath her hands moved, the surface becoming fluid as the rock bulged up, unfolding as a knob of a head raised out of the crevice, two reflective eyes shining in the light of James's phone. It clicked softly, then reached for her with stubby arms tipped with crab pincers.

Richelle let out a shriek as it grabbed her. James punched the monster in the back of the head, pulling Richelle away and giving her a push. "Run!"

Richelle ran up the stairs. James followed after delivering a kick to the monster's head.

At the top, Richelle was faced with a road to her left leading away on the bridge, a badly listing garage missing its doors to her right and another granite staircase in front of her leading down into shadows. She turned to look for James, but he wasn't there. "James!" she screamed, the rising wind stealing her voice. *I'll go into the garage. I can wait for him there out of the wind. He's got to come up. He's probably just making sure that thing is dead.* She passed through the doorway into the dark interior.

"Richelle!" James called, as he walked around the base of the garage. He stopped still, looking at the back of the mansion, the door off its hinges. *She wouldn't have gone in there. But what if something grabbed her and took her inside?* Uneasily he stole quickly to the door and peered in, then stepped inside. "Richelle?"

James turned on his phone's flashlight again. *Damn it, I'm down to forty percent.*

A sudden lightness out a nearby window hit him in the eyes. He squinted, then stepped to the window, widening his eyes. A view of the suburbs lay before him. *Where the hell am I?*

James turned to the door he'd just stepped through in confusion, then went outside. Ahead was a street of dark and quiet houses, just off a busy street with a highway running above, its faint noise just audible. *River Creek Road, our old house.* Horrified, James looked behind him, the creek across the end of the street dried up. *The drought summer we left. When I found out our homeowner association landscaper was burying mementos in his yard. And he found me.*

"Hey boy," a big man walked out of the shadows of the doorway behind him. "I'm glad I found you before you could squeal." He crooked a finger. "C'mere."

James bolted past the man with a yell, the man grabbing but missing his shoulder by inches.

That was James! "James?" Richelle said, as she exited the old garage. She moved in the direction of the noise, finally coming to the back of the mansion, its door standing open. Anxiously, she stepped inside.

"Richelle," Maime said pleasantly as she set down a plate of sandwiches on a laden table. "Where have you been? I've been holding off dinner for you."

"That's great, I'm starved," Richelle said, as she sat down. "Hi Max. I'm grateful to see your wife cooked too much as always."

Max nodded, his mouth busy.

"Have you seen James?" Richelle mentioned, reaching for a sandwich. "I was looking for him for something. I can't remember what though." She gave an embarrassed smile. "Thanks for dinner."

"He's meeting us tonight in Joplin," Maime reminded Richelle as she sat down. "We're supposed to leave right after dinner, remember? We've had such a great time visiting your cousins. I wanted our last meal together here at our cabin to be memorable."

Richelle shook her head. *No, something's not right.* "He and I were just together. It can't be a dream; it's been hours since I slept." *I don't remember driving up to the family cabin, either. I was someplace else...*

"Eat and then we'll go," Maime encouraged. "I went to all this trouble." She picked up her fork.

Her stomach rumbling, Richelle scarfed down the sandwich. Then Maime cleared the table and packed the remaining food in the cooler. "Everyone go to the john; we've got to get on the road."

Why am I so uneasy? Something's wrong, I can feel it. "I don't need to go," Richelle said, moving to stand near the door. "Do you need me to carry anything?"

Maime shook her head, grabbing her purse. "Let's go wait in the car. Max can carry out the cooler after he's done."

The two women headed out to the car, Maime getting behind the wheel. "I'll start it when he comes out," she said, checking her phone.

Richelle looked at her own phone. "I'm getting no service. Are you?"

"I'm okay," Maime said, not looking up. "But you're right that I should leave it alone and save the battery."

Ten minutes went by, then fifteen. "I'm going in to see if he fell in," Maime said, annoyed. She got out and walked back into the house.

Richelle waited a few minutes, then ten, then twenty. Anxious, she got out of the car, and headed back to the house.

Maime was in the living room, on her knees in front of her husband, who was sitting in the easy chair, looking straight ahead. "Please, Max, we've got to go now."

"Can't," he said softly. "I have work to do."

"You have work to get back to," Maime corrected, standing up and trying to pull him to his feet. "Come on now."

"No." Max began getting some paperclips and erasers and nails out of the junk drawer. He began arranging them on the nearby table.

"Is there something wrong?" Richelle asked tactfully.

"He gets like this sometimes," Maime said, uncomfortable. "Early dementia. Give it an hour or so. If I try to force him, he usually begins yelling. We should be able to make it home on time even with the delay."

Richelle looked at Max uneasily. *My mom should have warned me. But I shouldn't be rude.* "Okay."

An hour passed, then two, then three. Max seemed to get worse instead of better, building little piles of things in front of the TV, calling them his "offerings." He also took some sheets of note paper and began writing up "reports" with an official-looking format with his name, date, and time, but the words in the text were just jumbles of letters and numbers with no meaning interspersed with regular words.

Richelle, her nerves in shreds, finally could stand it no longer. "I should get going, I have school tomorrow. I can drive and send help if you'll tell me who to send?"

Maime looked at her reproachfully. "You load the cooler and I'll bring him out. You're right. It's time."

Richelle grabbed the cooler and lugged it to the car. Again, she waited, but this time only a few minutes. Stomping back to the house to demand the keys, she was flabbergasted to find Maime in a maid's uniform, cleaning the house. "What the hell are you doing?"

"Picking up the place," Maime replied grumpily. "People always leave it a mess when they go."

Richelle looked around, uneasy again. *I swear some creature just darted under the couch.* "Where's Max?"

"Not sure," she said breezily, tucking a few phones into her apron from beneath a chair, then a letter and a pen from the top of the TV.

Whose cell phones are those? None of us were writing any letters. Richelle opened her mouth to speak, her words dying in her throat as she saw out the window that dusk was here, and night was falling. "I'm leaving and not coming back this time. Please come with me."

"Sorry. My place is here," Maime said, not looking up from her tidying.

"Give me the car keys."

"No," she said, turning to close the window curtains. There was a sudden rustling from under the couch.

Richelle picked up a small end table and hit Maime, knocking her down. *She's too heavy to try to drag to the car.* Quickly she rummaged in the fallen woman's pockets, finding the keys.

A hiss sounded from under the couch, then a clawing sound.

Richelle stood up suddenly, looking in confusion down at her arms. *I'm dressed in my nightshirt for bed, slippers on my feet.* She looked around, fear replacing confusion. *My cousins got rid of this furniture years ago, when they first retired. None of this should be here.* Her legs weakened and she clutched the back of the easy chair. *None of us should be here because Max died of his dementia years ago...and Maime followed him a year later.*

A cat slinked out from under the couch, then wound its way around Richelle's legs. "Cable," she said affectionately, petting its head in relief.

Another hiss sounded from beneath the couch.

Richelle gathered up Cable and ran for the car, not bothering to shut the door. But the driveway stood empty. *The car's gone.*

The trees above Richelle creaked. *Weird, when there's no wind.*

The neighbor's solar motion lights suddenly illuminated. *Something is up there in the trees above me.*

A louder noise of something moving inside the cabin behind her made Richelle's head turn, even as Cable was docile in her arms. *That's not Maime.*

Richelle carried the cat past the garage quickly and down the short driveway to the street, looking for a place to hide. A small derelict house sat in front of her with a light on in the basement. A shadow passed in front of the light. *Something is down there.*

Richelle hurriedly kept walking. The road seemed to close in, the trees above her dark. On both sides of her, shapes moved to the sounds of a soft, eager hissing. *They sound like cats but all I see are huge shadows.* They swiped at her, and she jerked away, weaving a rickrack pattern as she walked. To her sides, the shadows darted back and forth, narrowly missing her with talons, but in front of her a brightly-lit highway grew steadily nearer. *Keep walking!*

Richelle finally made it to the highway, Cable suddenly gone from her arms. Something shone in the bright light at her feet. *A knife?*

Richelle picked up the stiletto knife with a wavy handle, a name delicately carved into the blade. She dropped it as soon as her hand closed around the handle, letting out a cry. *Just the feel of it is evil!*

Richelle staggered back, blinking. She was in an old house, the floor thick with dust, the wallpaper peeling, covered in black mold, water in pools on the floor.

There was a purring in front of her, loud in the stillness.

Richelle looked up horrified to see a cat with glowing red eyes laying on the seat of a what could only be described as a chair used for torture, sharp points on its armrests and back. The cat stretched, unsheathing its claws which were unnaturally long, then looked her in the eye.

Richelle took a step back.

A deep voice intoned. "You should not have found your way out."

Richelle turned and ran.

The cat let out a roar, then lunged at her, becoming larger with every jump. Richelle reached the door and slammed it in time, incredible force hitting the door. It cracked in the middle but held.

Richelle turned with a gasp, bumping into a couple. "I'm sorry, I didn't see you."

"That's okay," James said, giving her a hug. "You look great, sis. You were the cutest bridesmaid of the lot."

"You look great, too," Richelle lied, concerned. *He looks pale as death.* "Do you want to head home? I've enjoyed as much of Maime and Max's wedding reception as is good for me."

"Soon," James said vaguely, beaming at his date, a woman in a green dress Richelle didn't recognize. "How about we meet at the door in a half-hour?"

Richelle nodded, relieved. *He wants to get a little snuggling in.* "Sure." She walked carefully back to the wedding reception. *Everything is oddly subdued. That's right, there's no band. They cancelled at the last minute. Well, I have time for a last drink.*

Richelle talked to her father, then to a couple of the other brides-maids. Guests began to leave. Close to a half-hour later, she finished her drink and walked to the door looking for James. *He's not here. I'll grab a cookie to go.*

Richelle walked to the dessert table to find that the food was all packed up, the cake gone, the table bare, even the caterers vanished. Suddenly, wary, she looked around, noticing that almost all of the guests had gone. *I've got to find James or I'm going to get left behind.*

Grabbing a last abandoned wedding favor of a sachet, Richelle ran to the coatroom and got her coat, then stepped outside in pouring rain, to her horror realizing she was in her stockings that soaked through instantly. *I kicked my shoes off when I was dancing earlier. Damn it!*

Richelle reentered the reception hall, and headed to the door, stunned to find when she tried the handle that it was locked. *Every-one's left!*

The light clicked off above her, leaving her in darkness. *Oh God, I'm alone.* She took a deep breath, shivering as she stepped back to the doorway. *Why is it so cold in here? And the air is stale, like it's been closed up for years.* The air grew heavy suddenly with an ominous feeling of something there, as if the darkness was gathering itself to pounce.

Richelle turned and ran through the doorway out into the rain.

———

James stopped still, uneasily watching as the police car drew near. It stopped across the street from him, and the driver's side window rolled down. "Do you live on this street?"

James looked around in confusion, relief etching his face. "Yes, right there with my mom and sister."

"Well, get inside," the cop barked at him. "We're under curfew. There's a missing kid. You don't need to go missing, too."

James hurried inside, bolting the door behind him in relief. "Richelle, you home?"

There was no answer.

James went into the kitchen, his stomach rumbling. His eyes caught sight of his mother's note. *That's right. She's got that client she's meeting to rehearse his testimony.* He fixed himself a sandwich and ate it, then headed into the living room to watch TV. He called Richelle on her cell, but there was no answer.

There was a knock at the door. James answered it expecting Richelle, but instead his best friend Vern was there. "Hi. What's up?"

Vern strolled in without saying anything, heading toward the living room. He went right to an object on the floor which James hadn't seen, a lighted cell phone. "Whose is this?"

"I don't know. Is it unlocked?"

"Yeah," Vern said in surprise. "And it's logged in to a police website." He opened the email. "An officer named Hawk Lease."

"Toss it out the window," James said, worried. "I need to find my sister."

"I'm happy to take it off your hands," Vern said, pocketing it. "Later."

After Vern left, James locked the door, then went to check the back door. As he turned a strange guy was suddenly there, blocking him.

"What do you want?" James said, grabbing a kitchen knife.

The man flashed a badge. "I'm detective Hawk Lease. Your neighbor filed a report. He wants to press charges against you for trespassing. Will you please come with me?"

"No way in hell," James challenged, brandishing the knife. "He's a pedophile and a liar. I testified against him and he was sent to prison years ago. Now tell me who you really are."

The room seemed to grow darker. The man's shape blurred, even as he stepped forward menacingly.

James turned and fled, running into the garage, dropping the knife, and slamming the door in the cop's face.

James turned suddenly and staggered, trying to make sense of his surroundings. He was in a strange apartment, small but cozy. There were sounds of traffic outside, and a lot of lights.

"James, thank you for visiting," his grandmother said, coming into the room and giving him a hug.

"Grandma," James said, hugging his grandmother with relief. "I'm glad to see you."

"I was glad to see you, too, but you'd better be getting back to campus," his grandmother said. "You said you had a big test tomorrow."

James let her go reluctantly. "You're right. But I'll be back soon." He said his goodbyes as she walked him to the door, then hurried out into the darkening streets, just making it back to campus as night fell. *It's good I was able to find them that smaller apartment. They're closer to everything including the hospital here. I can check in with them like I promised Mom every couple days.* James headed for his dorm, then caught sight of Vern heading into the engineering building. *Damn it, that's right. I was supposed to meet him fifteen minutes ago in the library. He must be late, too, or he wouldn't be taking the shortcut through there.* James followed Vern, catching up to him just inside the building. "Vern!"

"Hey," his friend said, turning with a smile. "Glad to see you're late, too."

"Had to see my grandparents. Is anyone else meeting us in the library?"

"Daryl cancelled, and Nikki is sick. Sam and Marie are already on spring break, so it's just us."

The names made James shiver, even as he was able to picture each of them. *I'm glad they aren't here.* "Good."

Vern tried the door ahead of him, but it wouldn't open. "Damn it to hell, the lock's engaged. It never occurred to me that they would lock this connection up."

"Screw it. We'll have to go around." James and Vern backtracked, only to find the lobby where they had entered the building was also dark, the doors all locked.

"Hey, there's another way into the library," Vern said. "We can go to the cellar level. There're no doors on it past the basement door of this building."

"Are you sure?" James said, looking in vain out the door for anyone to walk by he could signal to for help. "I never heard of that."

"That's because you're a freshman here and I'm a sophomore," Vern chuckled. "Follow me." He headed back into the darkness, using his phone as a flashlight.

James went to follow him, then stopped still. *Vern's behind me a year in school, not ahead of me. No way he's ahead of me in college.* He turned in desperation to the lighted empty walkways outside, then picked up a huge plant. With a mighty shove, he tossed it against the base of the locked outer door, shattering it. He crawled through, letting out a yell when he felt the skin of his thigh press against the broken glass and part in a warm rush of blood.

James awoke in a pool of water and blood, his body half out of the mansion's large broken first floor window, rain pelting down and drenching him. With shaking fingers, he reached down and tried to staunch the bleeding. *I've cut my artery. I've got to get a tourniquet.*

White hands grasped his legs, and he let out a scream as he was pulled back inside into darkness. The scream cut off with a gurgle, swallowed by the pounding rain.

Richelle hid behind the machinery in the knock-off factory cellar, looking out quickly as she fumbled in her pocket. *I need to get high. Only damn reason I work here in this sweatshop hellhole.* She pulled out the needle, and then inexpertly tried to jab herself and missed.

What the hell am I doing? "I'm not a drug addict," Richelle said aloud, lowering the needle, then dropping it and grinding it beneath her shoe. "I was never a drug addict. Dad was, but I never saw him do it. This isn't real." She turned, just in time for a hand to close over her mouth.

"Shouldn't have seen what you saw," a voice hissed in her ear. "But at least you won't tell anyone about it."

Richelle's vision went dark. She awoke to find herself lying on some canvas, James lying near her. She was still in the cellar, a grimy window shining down sunlight a few feet away.

"Richelle?" James said weakly, as he stirred. "Thank God I found you."

"Shh!" Richelle urged. She rolled over to get up, just as two men entered the room, one of them brandishing a needle.

"Hold her." The henchman grabbed hold of Richelle, even as the man with the needle pulled up James's shirt. He struggled to rise, fighting the man with the needle.

Richelle struggled, letting out a shriek as she saw the fake doctor stick James and depress the plunger. James's eyes rolled up as he went slack, sagging down to the concrete.

The doctor filled the needle again, then approached Richelle. She struggled, breaking free as the doctor stabbed down. Richelle let out another shriek as she felt the needle invade her body, the poison burning in her arm. She kicked, breaking free of both men, and running for the exit, a last look at James confirming he was dead.

She ran up the stairs, the two men cutting her off and blocking her, one again brandishing the needle full of poison, the other a gun. She darted around them, scurrying up the stairs. With a yell, Richelle pulled down a few loose boards standing against the wall and threw them down the stairs, knocking both men to the concrete floor, the needle shattering, the gun falling useless from the unconscious man's fingers. Richelle threw down another two boards for good measure, then sank to her knees, suddenly weak and dizzy. *I can't get out. I'm dying. I'm dying. I'm—*

Within the mansion, Richelle collapsed to the dusty floor, unconscious. Her chest heaved once more, then stilled.

A large creature eagerly slunk down the stairs towards the body, its throaty growl of pleasure breaking the silence. Crouching beside her, the hulking figure began to feed.

———

Barb put her head up, looking around in surprise. She was at her grandmother's house, the lawn pristine and the house well-tended. Before she could speak, she heard her mother calling to her. "Barb, get the cat, he needs to come in! It'll be dinner time soon."

Barb headed toward the road, where the white cat was stalking something lying on the ground. As she got closer and scooped him up in her arms, she saw it was an albino weasel or ferret, its jaws open in a smile of death. Shuddering, she ran back to the house. Her mother met her at the door. "The doctor is coming," her mother intoned as Barb entered the house.

Abruptly, Barb stopped still. She was in her house, Cooper oddly absent. *Why is the TV on?* She headed towards the living room bracing herself to find a stranger, but no one was there. On the television was one of her favorite movie stars in a film she'd never seen, the action riveting. *When did this get made?* She went to sit on the couch just as the actor took the heroine in his arms for a passionate kiss. *I hope no one bothers me for the next hour.*

The hero was embracing his heroine. *This is pretty racy. I can't believe I missed seeing this.*

There was a knock at the door, and before Barb could get up, her mother walked in. "You really should go."

"I just need to finish this movie—" Barb protested, but her mother grabbed hold of her and propelled her towards the bedroom door. "Hey!"

Barb stumbled through the door, then looked about in confusion.

She was not in her house, but on a street in some city, the yards small squares and the houses in neat rows. No people were present.

A small black dog the size of a lab puppy sat in front of her on the opposite side of the street, wagging its tail leisurely. It panted, looking at her expectantly.

Barb crossed the street to it, and it began walking. Intrigued, she followed it to a nearby park to a water fountain where it sat down. Barb turned on the fountain, filling a small bowl and placing it near the dog, which lapped greedily. The dog began walking back the way it came, Barb again following. As she crossed the street out of the park, the dog suddenly ran off, tail between its legs. The sun went behind a cloud, the light fading.

Anxious, Barb hurried back the way she'd come, hoping to find the place she'd first seen the black dog. But every step was suddenly causing her pain. She was floundering by the next block and grabbed onto a tree for support.

There was suddenly intense pressure on the middle of her upper back, right where the pain was worst. Barb snapped upright with a yelp, then fell sideways. Strong arms caught her, and she turned, her face breaking into a wide smile of relief. "Neyhera!"

The tall, lanky man with black hair, dark eyes, and deeply tanned skin grinned at her, then let her go. Joy suffused Barb, and she hugged him again. *My oldest friend.* "Thank you!"

Neyhera hugged her back hard, then let her go. "I'll help you. But you must go, they are looking for you." He gestured to the door of what looked like a curio shop. "Quickly!"

Barb stepped through the door, Neyhera right behind her. They were outside, the day balmy, the city streets around her lined with stones, no trees visible at all, only buildings. She felt him push something into her hand and turned to face him, offering up the handful of plant blossoms. "What's this?"

"The doctor will try to poison you," he warned urgently, then pressed another handful of dried plant leaves into her hands. "Do not let him touch you. You'll feel him coming like always. Keep moving and look for a door."

"What's this?" Barb asked again, offering up the dried leaves.

"Antidote," he said, handing her a key. "And to keep your mind clear. Hurry!"

Barb put the flower blossoms in her right hand with the key, and the dried leaves in her left, and began forcing her way through the crowds. She'd only gone a half block when she felt like she was being watched. A quick look to her left showed the doctor and his henchman pushing their way toward her. She evaded them, moving as fast as possible. But as she moved on, the streets began to cross other streets, and she had no idea if she was heading for the edge of the city or doubling back, as the streets curved back and forth.

She let out a gasp and drew back as the doctor suddenly appeared in front of her, reaching for her, the swipe of his hand missing her to fall on another woman's shoulder. Barb turned and ran, but that street led to a dead end. They had her cornered.

She slipped past the henchman and then also the doctor, using a foursome as a shield, then a couple. But as she ran past, the doctor held his hand to his lips and blew.

Barb began wheezing, her lungs struggling to expand, her heart speeding up, her thoughts a jumble. She staggered on, as the doctor and his henchman stalked after her. She stuck the key in her pocket and lifted her hands to her lips, looking at the plants. *Which is the antidote and which is to clear my thoughts?* In desperation, Barb crammed a few of each type of plant into her mouth and chewed. Instead of the expected bitter taste, the taste was light and faintly sweet. Her head cleared and her breathing eased. Finishing the rest of both plants, she stepped finally to a door in the wall and hurried through it.

Barb stepped to the railing, looking over it to a vast ocean. *Now a cruise ship?* Other people milled all over the deck, some sitting on chairs, others near the railing, kids playing. Worried about another attack, Barb hurried to the far end of the ship and joined what looked like a spa session of some kind, wrapping herself in a robe, a towel around her hair, and lay down on a table. A tech began to apply some kind of cream mask to her face and put some wet cloth pads over her eyes.

There's a gamble that I won't be able to see my enemy coming but I also can't just run from scenario to scenario. Whatever Neyhera gave me to clear my thoughts, it worked above and beyond. I'm Barb and I came here to destroy Latham's Landing and help Helter while Maryanne lays the Sea Room ghost to rest. My theory of there being an illusion here that pulls people in was right. I was wrong though in thinking it could just pull people on the island in. Now I'm stuck in the illusion. I have to not only escape the doctor— who must be the demon—I need to get out of the trap before I die from a fear-induced heart attack.

There was a sudden scream and Barb sat up, the pads falling from her eyes. The henchman was muscling his way towards her as the women in the spa group scattered, a grin on his face, a survival knife in his hand. *Mac! It doesn't look like him, but I remember that knife!*

Barb rolled off the table as Mac slashed open the belly of one of the women and then swung the knife in an arc to stab her. Barb shoved a chair in his way, then ran towards the ship's center. *Doors are portals. I need a door.* She hurried through several doorways with Mac in pursuit, then saw the ship kitchen. She threw herself through it just as Mac caught up to her.

CHAPTER FOURTEEN

"Should we pray again?" Bob asked, as Maryanne rose from her kneeling position beside the motionless female figure, who was still in a crumpled heap where she'd fallen. "Or lay her to rest?"

"Yes, I just need more holy water," Maryanne said, as she fetched two more bottles.

"Those are the last ones," Bob said uneasily. "Are we going to talk about what happened?"

"Maybe after we get out of this," Maryanne said dryly, as she splashed some of the holy water on the female figure. There was no effect.

"We made a critical error," Bob persisted. "The dark man or evil force, it also possessed Latham. They weren't just allies. Somehow it was also using this ghost or spirit at the same time. It's hopped from person to person, using them for all they were worth then discarding them."

"That's what evil does," Maryanne said.

"It was aware what we were planning."

"Yes, but it didn't expect what happened which means it is not completely in control here. Please, get on your knees and pray."

As Maryanne and Bob knelt at the side of the fallen female and began to pray, rain began to fall in sheets on the top of the Sea Room, the sky outside black as night.

There was a skittering at the glass, breaking the twosome's concentration.

"What are those?" Maryanne whispered.

Creatures resembling large toads were outside the glass howling and hopping up on the glass, their toes clawed.

"Nothing good," Bob said, closing his eyes. "Pray!"

———

Barb stopped, then gaped. She was in a nightclub, the lighting dim, the crowds around her smoking, drinking, and talking, a few couples dancing. A window to her immediate right showed a window through which streetlights shone in darkness. Her outfit had also changed to slinky pants, a tank top and full makeup according to the mirrored wall in front of her. *How can this be?*

Barb felt eyes on her and looked up. Two men were approaching intently from the catwalk, one in white with thick glasses and a white box hat, the other in black sans knife. *The doctor and another of his henchman.* She hurried off towards another room to her left. *They're hunting me. Where can I hide?*

A hand grasped hers, and she started, until she saw it was Neyhera, his clothing changed to reflect the club atmosphere. "Come." He pulled her into his embrace, then through the door she'd been heading toward.

Here there was no music and less people, but a movie was being filmed. "You," the director said, gesturing to Neyhera. "You're on. Get in there."

"Play along," Neyhera whispered. "Lay down on your stomach."

Barb lay down, her arms ready at her sides to push up for a quick escape. Neyhera lay down on her, then embraced her with his arms. *The weight of him feels so good.*

"Okay, action!"

Neyhera began to murmur inaudible endearments as he nuzzled her hair and pushed his body against hers. From the corner of her eye, she saw both the doctor and his henchman searching for her, but they didn't see her under Neyhera. They left the room.

"Cut!"

Neyhera got to his feet. "Get up."

Barb got up reluctantly. "Do we have to? I like this."

"We must go," he insisted.

Neyhera drew Barb after him through a few doors, then she pulled back on his hand, stopping him. He turned to her. "We can't stop here—"

"I know you're helping me," Barb said fervently. "Moreover, I know you. Thank you." She squeezed his hand, overcome with sudden powerful emotion. "I love you."

Neyhera's expression was utter surprise coupled with complete shock, as he looked at her speechless. *He's very uncomfortable. He must not love me.*

"You don't feel that," he said finally, then tried to lead her on again.

Barb stopped him. "I do feel it, completely. Thank you again for what you've done for me. I know this, all of this, isn't real, though it can kill me. I also know you are real. I wanted you to know I knew. There's no time to stop what's happening and tell you, but there's never going to be time. So I'm telling you now, here."

Neyhera's surprise deepened if that were possible. He smiled at her, then hugged her close, holding her longer than he had before. "Come," he said, releasing her. He led her to another door. "Go! He's coming!"

Barb ran for the door and passed through, taking stock of the Italian restaurant she was now in. She ran through the dining room, then hid behind a full booth. Unlike before, this time the doctor was right behind her, stalking through the restaurant, the survival knife in his hand. Barb got up to flee and the henchman was before her, blocking her way. He indicated an empty table nearby. "Sit."

Barb sat down, scanning the restaurant for Neyhera, but he wasn't there. The doctor—the demon—came to the table and sat down, the knife gone. "You led us on a chase," he chided. "We aren't evil, Barbara. You—"

Another woman joined them, sitting on Barb's side of the table.

"Hi, do you know if the food's good here?" She turned to Barb. "I like pasta."

"You are not important." The doctor took some powder from his hand and blew it onto the woman in response. She began to choke, her face purpling as her hands slapped the table and she tried to get up and fell back, unable to breathe. Barb bolted, slipping past the woman to run past the doctor and his henchman as they grabbed for her and missed. She ran to the front door of the restaurant, then pushed through.

Barb appeared on the shore of Latham's Landing, the house in front of her. The lights were on, but it was full daylight, the rain light. She hurried to the house, but the windows were shut along the sides. She tried the door, but it was also padlocked. As she hammered the lock open with a piece of firewood from the porch, she threw open the door, revealing another door within it, this one also locked.

"He's coming," a moaning voice warned on the wind. Barb tugged at the door, terrified to see the doctor striding up the pathway to the house, the steel of the survival knife in his hand shining in the sun, fresh blood spattered on his clothes.

The key! Barb dug in her pocket, brought out the key and tried it in the padlock. The door opened smoothly, and she shut it in the doctor's face, his inhuman roar of rage rocking the house.

———

"Where am I?" the female ghost asked, as she sat up.

"The Sea Room," Maryanne said, making the sign of the cross over her.

"Tell us your name, and we'll lay you to rest, Mrs. Latham," Bob urged, his eyes on the creatures that massed all around fighting the glass walls to get to them.

"Jennifer Latham," the female said, as she got to her feet. "Please free me. Let me leave this hated place."

Maryanne made the sign of the cross over her again. "Eternal rest grant unto Jennifer Latham, O Lord, and let perpetual light shine upon her. May her soul and the souls of all her faithful departed kin, through the mercy of God, rest in peace. Amen. Like the seed buried in the ground, you have produced the harvest of eternal life for us; make us always dead to sin and alive to God. Take Jennifer into your safekeeping, let her dwell with you and be at peace, O Lord. Give her rest after her long strife. In Jesus name we pray. Amen."

Jennifer closed her eyes and smiled beatifically, as her form began to shimmer and sparkle. The creatures outside let out a screech of rage as one, renewing their efforts at the glass. But as Jennifer vanished, her glow fading, the screech became one of loss and terror, the creatures collapsing into mist that blew away, the rain tapering off as the sun came out, turning the Sea Room again into a prism of color and light.

"We did it," Maryanne said wearily.

"We did," Bob said, gathering up the few remains of the herbs. "Now we have to go help Barb and Helter." Holding onto one another, they grabbed their other remaining supplies and headed for the door.

———

"Helter!" Barb called, as she stood just inside the door.

There were footsteps from upstairs but no answer. They came toward her in a measured gait, unhurried.

Barb cast a look outside to the sunny day. *That's not Helter up there. Helter, wherever you are, get here now!*

"Barb!" Helter exclaimed, as he walked through the door beneath the central staircase. "Where were you?"

"Forget that. We have to get out of here," Barb said, grabbing his hand. She opened the front door and pulled him through, slamming it and locking it with her key.

"Where did you get a key to the house?" Helter asked in confusion.

"Later," Barb said, hurrying to the shoreline. "We've got to hurry."

"What's the rush?"

"That," she said, pointing to the horizon. A mass of roiling black clouds spread across the whole north, the space beneath them dark and blurry with pounding rain. "We get a fast inch or three of rain and we won't be walking out of here. Which means we'll still be here to drown tomorrow when the lake refloods, if something else doesn't kill us by then."

"What do you want to do?" Helter said. "I don't know where my charges are or my guns."

"Your knapsack is on your back and your gun is in your hand," Barb responded, looking at him oddly. She drew and raised her own gun. "Are you really you?"

Helter put his gun in his holster and put his hands up. "Yes, I'm me."

Barb pulled out her bottle and squirted some holy water on him, with no effect. Then she put some on herself.

"But how do I know that's real holy water?" Helter asked skeptically. "Or that you are you?"

Barb hurriedly recited the Lord's prayer. "Satisfied?"

Helter nodded and put his hands down as thunder echoed distantly. "More than satisfied. Your holy water or your praying cleared my head. I was trapped in the illusion. Your theory was right."

Barb nodded. "I was trapped, too. Did you see the two kids that came back with the house? Are they still alive?"

Helter shook his head. "No idea. Even if we find them, we don't know if they're compromised."

There was a far-off shout. Two figures were coming off the stone bridge from the direction of the Sea Room. "That's Maryanne and Bob. Go, try to help them to shore," Helter urged. "I'll be right behind you. I'm going to blow the charges."

"You tried that once before," Barb called back, as she hurried towards Bob and Maryanne. "It's not going to work. Just come on."

Helter shook his head once, as he dug in his backpack, bringing out a radio controller. "I owe a debt. If Bob and Maryanne are coming, they did what we set out to do, which means the house can't leech power from the Sea Room anymore to rebuild. I didn't lay charges to blow up the house from inside. I put mining charges in the earth around the entire foundation to turn this whole damn island into a crater." He tapped in a sequence, then destroyed the controller by smashing it with a rock. "You've got ten minutes, Barb. Go!"

Helter turned to come face to face with a man in a suit. He raised his gun, but the man was quicker, punching him in the face and knocking him flat.

"Helter!" Barb screamed.

The man in the suit looked at her, his eyes flashing red briefly. Then he ran toward her.

Barb took off running towards Bob and Maryanne. As she reached them the man in the suit caught up with her, his hand digging into her shoulder. Bob's bullet hit him in the temple, and he fell back, the wound leaking black smoke.

Maryanne was suddenly there, a dagger with a cross-shaped handle in her hand. She plunged it down into the demon. Its face split into a mass of teeth-filled maw and reptilian eyes, an inhuman bellow of pain earsplitting. The monster reached up and grasped Maryanne's arm, bending it back and breaking the bone with a sharp crack. She screamed and fell back, holding her bloody arm. Bob emptied his gun into the creature, the wounds giant holes as the blessed hollow points exploded and the thing went to its knees. Barb shot the creature in the back and head, more holes opening up with a fresh scream of anguish. A glistening scabrous tentacle ripped out of the bloody ruin, ripping the gun away from Barb and breaking two of her fingers as it ripped her fingernails from their roots. It darted toward her chest like a spear to skewer her, stopped at the last second by a fresh barrage from Bob's reloaded gun. But as he emptied the gun the woman in the green dress appeared again beside him, grabbing him in her arms and covering his lips with hers.

"Bob!"

Bob convulsed twice, then slid down, his eyes already glazing over. As the woman turned, reaching for Barb, Helter shot her from the ground where he lay, emptying his gun. She shook, her body becoming misty as black smoke filled the air.

Helter ran toward Barb, grabbing her and Maryanne. "Run! I'll hold her off!"

Barb began to help Maryanne towards the far shore of Carl's Point. The rain was pelting down now, the lightning lighting up the dark sky in regular jagged lines. Rivers of rainwater were already running down the surrounding hills into the lake, the many scattered small pools rising and coming together across the lakebed.

Helter stood on the lakebed with his reloaded gun raised, facing both the woman in the green dress and the man in the suit on the island shore, other figures approaching from behind them, the island house's windows fully lit in colors of red and orange. "Mrs. and Mr. Latham," he shouted. "Go to Hell!"

"You first," the woman hissed, opening her arms as she advanced on him.

Helter emptied his gun again into her as the woman advanced, each shot making her hiss in pain but still she kept coming. She grabbed hold of him, knocking his gun out of his hands. As she moved to cover his lips with hers, a shadow darted in from the side, its lamp-like yellow eyes glowing in the gloom as it bit into her.

The woman dropped Helter, laughing as she batted it aside with a clawed hand, the dark misty form shrieking in pain as it retreated.

Several more Hustermen came out of the darkness and swirled around her, hissing as they formed a barrier between the evil woman and the prone Helter.

"Murderess."

"Liar."

"Prideful."

More joined them, the forms surrounding the female demon in a swirling unbroken circle of shadow as they hissed in unison. "Anger. Vengeful. Envious."

One last Husterman flowed in out of the darkness as the others parted before it, separating into a wall of Hustermen surrounding the demonic woman, their glowing eyes swaying back and forth. "Evil," a feminine voice hissed loudly, as the last shadow reared up over the evil female specter like a ravening snake. "We judge you, demon spawn."

"Carolyn?" Helter said.

The Husterman looked over at Helter with its lamp-like eyes, then faced the malevolent female again. "Evil," it repeated.

"Takes one to know one," the woman in green said, baring needle teeth.

"Evil!" the Hustermen roared together, then launched themselves at the woman en masse. She laughed as she ripped several of the shades apart, but her laugher turned to screams as the rest covered her in a mass of writhing shadows. The screech rose into a bursting wail, black smoke erupting from the shadows in several directions as it tried to escape. The Hustermen followed it, gulping down the black smoke, the wail ending in ragged crunching as the evil spirit was consumed utterly.

"Die!" Helter yelled in satisfaction. He let out another yell of pain as an arrow hit him square in the chest, and he fell back to the ground, the deluge pounding down and mixing with his seeping blood.

Several Hustermen flowed over and surrounded him, hissing outwards at the approaching figures of Mac and an old woman in a brightly colored turban carrying a basket. Behind them came others, including a dwarfish hopping figure and a little girl in a ruffled dress skipping along.

"Give us our prey," Mac demanded, raising a knife that glittered silver in the deepening gloom.

"I want his eyes," the old woman said as she drew closer, taking out a skinning knife.

"I claim his heart," the little girl said in sing-song, raising her hands tipped with talons.

The Hustermen hissed, the shadows again assembling en masse, their yellow eyes shining. "Evil!" they hissed as one.

The dwarf darted in, grabbing Helter's leg, his maw opening to reveal sharp teeth ready to bite. A Husterman swirled around him, knocking him back as it fought with him. The rest of the Hustermen attacked as the army of evil spirits rushed in and tried to finish Helter.

Mac alone got through and brought the shining knife down, a Husterman diverting his aim at the last second, the knife missing Helter's throat and instead driving through his hand and into the wreck of a boat beneath.

Helter opened his eyes at the sharp pain of being stabbed, kicking out with the last of his strength at Mac who was straddling him. *I can't breathe to scream.*

Mac tugged at the handle, desperately trying to get the knife out for another try, his other hand grasping the Husterman as it tried to bite into him. Mac wrenched the knife free with a cry of triumph, then stabbed the Husterman between the eyes. A rip appeared in the solid shadow and the Husterman screamed.

I'm dying. Helter looked down at the arrow in his chest, blood steadily seeping up in time to his heartbeat. His eyes darted to the left and right. *Where's my gun?*

The Hustermen had devoured most of the ghosts or they had fled. Yet the evil spirits had destroyed many of the Hustermen. The Husterman attacking Mac wavered as the killer stabbed the shadow form again, opening another fissure. Its lamp-like eyes dimmed, and the Husterman broke free of him, its tattered shadow retreating with a hiss.

Mac grinned. "I'll be right with you." He turned back to stab Helter, bringing the knife up as Helter's fingers touched the smooth grip of his gun.

Die! Helter thought, grasping the gun loosely and pulling the trigger. The bullet slammed through Mac's head. He let out a screech and dropped the knife, black smoke leaking out of the bullet hole in his temple.

The wounded Husterman pushed Mac aside, engulfing Helter's body. Helter let out a gasp.

"Damn you," Mac said as he got to his feet, the bullet hole in his head healing. "You're going to pay for that." He picked up the knife, and then launched himself at the tattered Husterman feeding off Helter, meaning to stab them both. But he hit the ground as the now whole Husterman evaded him, another Husterman appearing beside it.

Mac opened his mouth to yell, his knife coming up to stab. Both Hustermen attacked him together, ripping the evil spirit in two and devouring him.

There was a resounding BOOM as Helter's charges went off, the old mansion collapsing as the ground under it was obliterated, the granite of the dock breaking into shards, the garage and the end of the stone bridge breaking apart and falling into the rising water. Smoke billowed up, but was quickly dissipated by the raging storm, buckets of water pounding down, the lakebed disappearing feet at a time under the rising lake.

Maryanne and Barb staggered onto the shore of Carl's Point, both of them collapsing onto the dry land in relief.

"We made it," Maryanne said, and passed out.

Barb's smile faded as she beheld strange shadowy shapes sniffing on the shore near the old cemetery, casting to and fro across the dry sections of lakebed like animals hunting. *Those things aren't dogs.* "Maryanne, wake up."

Excited, the shapes moved faster as they crossed the path that Barb and Maryanne had walked to shore. An eager inhuman howl sounded.

"Maryanne," Barb yelled in terror, shaking the pastor. "Wake up! Where's your car keys?"

More human shapes were coming from down near the beach, following the leaping creatures that were running directly toward them.

"Maryanne! Wake up!"

The things would be on them soon. Barb got to her feet, pulling out her last defense, a gold cross. She brandished it like a shield.

A haunting music filled the air. Near her on the shore stood a girl with a flute, playing an irresistible tune.

The sniffing shapes paused. Then they came straight for the girl, the shambling figures following them.

"What are you doing?" Barb yelled.

"Saving you," the girl said, and resumed playing.

As the shapes ran toward the girl, several surviving Hustermen emerged from the shoreline and surrounded them, devouring the figures one by one until none were left.

The girl continued to play for a few seconds, then ended her song.

The Hustermen looked at Barb and the unconscious Maryanne for a moment, their eyes glowing. They then turned and flowed down the shore, merging with the night.

"Thank you," Barb said to the girl, cradling Maryanne in her arms.

"Thank you," the girl replied. "I and my sister can rest now." She lay the flute on the ground and walked off down the shoreline, her form fading to mist.

Barb dialed 911 and gave them the information, then called Upner. "It's over. Bob's gone." She sat on the shore and waited, watching where the island had been, just in case.

EPILOGUE

MARYANNE TOOK OFF HER MANTLE WITH A PLEASED SIGH. "I HOPE you liked the message."

"I did," Barb said. "Congratulations, I think every available pew was full."

"It's been crowded for the last few weeks." Maryanne beamed. "Come in."

"Everyone knows locally what we did, even as they are keeping quiet to all the outsiders asking questions," Barb said, as she entered Maryanne's office. "Fighting evil does matter to people."

"I'm glad to have made a difference. But I feel guilty too. I haven't been able to pay for my lunch in the local diner for the last week."

"People are grateful."

"God just worked through me." Maryanne sat down and motioned to Barb to sit. "So, it's really gone then? Have you been out there?"

"The island house is destroyed along with the docks and porch and granite base. There's a blasted hole in the earth. I saw it flood. The island itself isn't there anymore. The Sea Room is still intact, as is about half the stone bridge that leads to it."

"But what about the demon, or Latham, whatever you want to call him?"

"No sign of him. But it's early yet. Teeth's keeping an eye out."

"He's back to his work with the sturgeon?"

Barb nodded. "The lake's back to its highest level. Teeth's fish are back to normal, or so he says. He said there have been no more lights in the Sea Room. With the remains of the island truly flooded, that's the only place left for ghosts to haunt."

"No sign of any ghosts? Not even the girl with the flute that saved us?"

"No, nothing. Laura's gone, along with her sister Jennifer. But we'll have to go through several years of nobody dying or going missing before I believe the island is dormant."

"I agree." Maryanne smiled. "I say a prayer every dawn, giving thanks."

"Bob's gone," Barb said heavily. "They found his body."

"I know," Maryanne said gently. "I'm doing his funeral this week-end. He asked to be cremated."

"Do you think his soul...got out in time?"

"I think so," Maryanne assured. "But I think he would be okay if it didn't. Bob cared about justice and taking a stand against evil, or he wouldn't have been a policeman. If his ghost somehow is part of Latham's Landing now, then he can only be a force for good."

"I can't help but feel guilty," Barb whispered. "You and I stayed outside when us four went to the island. Cheer and Bob went into that flooded section. Is it really just chance that they are both dead while we survived?"

"There's so much we can never know," Maryanne said after a moment. "Somehow Laura's sister Jennifer married Latham, maybe in an effort to allow the family to stay and not have to leave after her sister died. Both of them died there, with Laura likely killed by Latham. The original evil spirit on the island stayed around because the tortured souls of Jennifer and Laura were an easy feeding source, as was the island mansion and lake because of bad things that happened there. The repeated murder, fear, and suffering attracted evil people over the years and additional evil spirits, some worse than others. Whatever that female entity was, it was almost as bad as Latham's demon."

"And he's still there," Barb murmured uneasily. "The Hustermen consumed her, but not him." She took a shuddering breath. "Helter's body wasn't found. He's a Husterman now, too."

"We went out against overwhelming odds and lived," Maryanne said, holding up her arm in its cast. "We got off lightly with some minor broken bones. Helter and Bob gave their lives, as did Cheer. Our sacrifices ended the horror, Barb. We did what we set out to do, more even, really. There's been no deaths, disappearances, sightings, or anything odd this last week. We have to cling to that."

Except they never found those last two kids the house brought back, either. "You're right. We broke the power of the island," Barb agreed. "Water cleanses, too. We'll know in time if it's enough." She paused. "But I didn't come here to ask about that. Did you find out anything?"

Maryanne shook her head. "I don't have any answers. There's no relevant information in any of the texts I checked. Are you sure you didn't just hear the name in a movie?"

"'Neyhera' isn't a common name," Barb replied. "It gives back no search results online. None, Maryanne! Can you think of anything you ever tried to look up that gave no results?"

"Well, no, but are you sure of the spelling? You heard this only while in the illusion."

"I shouted out his name like I had known it all my life and I felt like I knew him like my oldest friend," Barb said in agitation, getting up to pace. "I trusted him utterly. But I never knew anyone like him or anyone with that name in my life. So, who was he?"

"Could Neyhera just be an aspect of yourself that manifested to show you the way out?"

"I can't believe you're the pastor and I'm having to convince you that an angel of some kind saved my life."

"I'm not sure an angel would have laid on top of you and faked sexual motions," Maryanne said uncomfortably. "If you're adamant that this Neyhera was a force for good, I believe you. But I think he was a good spirit like the others that you say helped you before on the island, not an angel."

Barb shook her head. "I trusted him completely. I felt like I had known him all my life. But more than that Maryanne: I loved him. I mean loved him utterly, completely. The feeling was so strong I stopped him from leading me to safety to blurt it out. He was uncomfortable hearing it and pushed me to keep going." She paused. "I've had time to examine my feelings, and I believe he was an angel because he gave me the means to overcome the illusion of Latham's Landing and because I loved him. I'd have died there if not for him and Helter wouldn't have made it to blow up his charges if I hadn't gotten out and helped him out." She paused again. "I think Neyhera misunderstood me at first and thought he'd gone too far trying to protect me, that I was confessing romantic love because of his intervention. I misunderstood myself what I was feeling. What I felt was pure love, not desire. I have never felt love so strongly in my life without desire, Maryanne."

"I'm not sure what you want me to say, Barb."

"I want to know why he saved me and he didn't save Bob or Helter," Barb whispered, tears in her eyes. "Or the others that died. There were so many."

"I can't answer that," Maryanne said, hugging her, and drawing back. "But the reason I asked you about the spelling is that the word Nehera or similar spellings does have a meaning. It means "light.""

———

Barb was sitting with Cooper that night watching TV when there was a knock at her door. She answered it with her gun, putting it in plain view of the man standing there. "Yes?"

"Put down the cannon," the gruff voice said. "I'm not here to make a fuss."

"What do you want?"

The man lay an envelope on the porch floor. "For you to take over for Bob, now he's gone. Enclosed is a copy of Bob's will. His family—a sister in another state—gets his house and stuff. You get Latham's Landing and the surrounding property."

"I don't want it, so you can pick that envelope up and give it to someone else."

"Do you really want another idiot messing about out there?" The figure walked down the stairs. "Think it over." A car started up, and then drove off into the night.

Barb left the envelope there, locked her door and went to bed.

The next morning at dawn another knock sounded on her door. Barb staggered to the door, to find Cooper growling at it. Again, she got her gun and opened it.

"You're the last person I expected."

"Everyone's got to be somewhere," Celine said smoothly, the shells in her hair tinkling faintly. "Will you please come outside? Your dog seems to hate me."

"He's usually right about people," Barb said, but she came out with her gun, keeping a distance between herself and Celine. "What do you want?"

"You're the new owner of the island and lake," Celine said, gesturing to the envelope. "I want to buy it from you." She held out a heavy ring of gold. "I can pay whatever price you ask."

"You can have it and keep the ring," Barb said. "I want answers instead. Sit." She gestured with the gun.

"I'd rather pay in gold," Celine said with a frown, but she sat.

"That diary you gave me," Barb said, as she sat down. "I went to look it over again while I was waiting for Maryanne to pull through surgery. But it wasn't where I left it. All that was there was a wad of nasty-smelling lakeweed."

Celine smiled. "Sorry about that."

"Was anything in the diary real?"

Celine nodded, her expression solemn. "Everything, to the best of my memory. I only knew Laura briefly. I never saw her family."

"Why not?"

"Haven't you put everything together?" Celine asked dryly. "You saw my true nature. Do you think I belong here in a lake? That I was born here?"

Barb looked at her blankly, then realization suddenly dawned. "The Sea Room. It was never meant to keep water out. It was made of marine glass to keep water in."

Celine nodded. "My prison for more than a few years. Until Laura came here to try to destroy the house one night. She came to the Sea

Room first, intending to use the bridge to get to the mansion. Instead, she found me."

"Was it called the Sea Room then?"

Celine nodded. "A fishbowl complete with a fish. I warned her of the evil force, but she knew more of it than I did. She told me everything she had endured from Latham and promised to free me. A short time later she finally did."

"How did she flood the island?"

"I surmise she sabotaged Latham's mechanism at the north end of the lake and opened the floodgate. Latham killed her, but not before she also opened the door at the side of the base of the Sea Room and the lock on the glass prison."

"The door Bob saw when we were there?"

Celine nodded. "The water flooded up and I was able to get out into the lake. Latham's wife came to stop me. She was always jealous."

"Was he...did he...?"

"No. I would have killed him if he ever dared to come within reach," Celine said, her jagged teeth bared. "I was just a possession to him, though he called me his sea wife." She dropped her eyes. "I caused Jennifer's death, created the wave that washed her off the bridge and into the lake to drown. I never meant for her ghost to be trapped there."

"I'm asking because of the other, um, merfolk," Barb said delicately.

"Only April and her mother, Marissa, and they weren't like me," Celine said with a trace of regret. "I helped them to hide in the lake as a favor to Teeth years ago." She cocked her head to one side, offering a charming smile Barb found disquieting. "There won't be any more sheep that go missing."

"What do you know about the evil forces on the island and the Sea Room?"

Celine shook her head. "The demon was here when I got here, and Latham was already its vassal. Some years ago, the female evil force arrived here. Together they dragged in more evil humans and more victims."

"What part did you play in everything that happened on the

lake?"

"I did what I could to protect myself and the others that call the lake home," Celine said cagily, after a pause. "I never worked with the evil forces if that's what you're asking. Some others, like Marissa, did because it offered her an easier path." Her silver eyes shone eerily. "But evil has a way of corrupting everything it touches in time."

"Why did you stay after you were freed?"

"Laura was trapped here. I saw her ghost and heard her playing the flute. She died saving me. I didn't know how to free her because I also didn't dare go onto the island. I had no path to get her bones back once they were removed. Once you brought them back, I reburied her away from the island. That freed her spirit. She was never evil; she was taken in by an evil spirit who bent her to its will in life and then held her a prisoner in death." She shrugged. "Besides, where would I go? I'm likely the last of my kind."

"What's beneath the lake? Teeth said there were caverns."

"I'd advise you not to try to investigate," Celine said, smiling nastily. "I'm not the only living trophy Latham brought back from his travels."

"I don't want there to be more deaths on the lake."

"Teeth will make sure that everyone behaves," Celine said, standing. "Nothing there will seek out the living, only clean up the dead. I think that the remaining Hustermen will also help to keep anything clinging to the remains of the island from reaching the mainland. Once I have control, I'll also open the beach again and resume the development near the old camp, maybe open that up, too. Happiness and joy of the living is the best cure for this lake. Laura cleared out all of the truly remaining nasties with a little help from the Hustermen. You saw her do it."

"What were those...things?"

"The pieces left of victims and killers," Celine said after a moment. "They felt only hunger. When the boundaries of the island began to shift, they were able to get off the island and infest the lakeshore. When the lake was drained, some of the more dangerous things were able to reach the shore and go hunting. The female evil force added to their ranks by creating constructs to actively locate and bring back prey. Now they are all gone. The shore is safe again."

"What about the Hustermen? They attack people."

"I think they stayed around because the house was such a bastion of evil, with a plethora of evil spirits. They hunted down more than a few of the evil creatures who made it to shore. With the evil gone they will likely move on or perhaps dissipate in time. I had heard of their kind but never seen one—"

"What about Latham?"

"I killed him long ago," Celine admitted with satisfaction. "His spirit was fodder for the evil on the island. He's long since consumed, body and spirit. What wore his shape is greatly weakened, and he is the only true evil left on this lake. There's no island now for a hunting ground. He'll have to move on and pick a new spot."

"There was a maid named Lorelai who worked for Latham years ago. Do you know what happened to her?"

"Yes. She heard me singing and was trying to unlock the Sea Room inner door. She had been secretly sleeping within the base of the Sea Room to get away from one of Latham's relatives. He'd threatened her after she revealed she was an illegitimate relation. From what I heard, I believe the demon killed her while masquerading as this man." Celine shook her head. "He put the Sea Room so far from the house so that I couldn't call for help or be discovered accidentally, not thinking that anyone who saw it would want a closer look."

"Why didn't boaters and fishermen see you swimming around in there when the lake was first opened to people?"

"Latham enforced a perimeter with the demon's help. Initially all the people who met with accidents were people that got too close to the Sea Room, or Latham's other secrets. Also, Latham never filled the room with water deeper than ten to fifteen feet. He didn't want me to be able to access the top windows."

"Why did he have them? To let out heat?"

Celine shook her head. "That's how he would watch me. I liked the heat, as I come from a tropical climate. I was used to hours in the sun. I had never seen snow. Coming here to this place almost killed me. But I adapted to cold freshwater in time. Another reason I can't go home."

"All right," Barb said, nodding. "Let me call my lawyer in the morning. I'll get him to arrange a deed transfer."

"Thank you," Celine said, as she went to leave.

"Wait!" Barb called. "How do you know that Laura's spirit was really good? You said you didn't really know her. Why did she help you?"

"I promised her I'd kill Latham if she freed me," Celine answered. She turned and winked. "I wouldn't have gifted just anyone my flute." She drove away.

———

Later that same night, the phone rang.

"Barb!"

"Upner? What is it?"

"Did you hear the news? You need to call your lawyer. They're going to sue you to get the deed to the island."

"'They who'? What are you talking about? I have papers that say right here I'm the legal heir. I just talked to my lawyers this morning to set up a day to finalize everything."

"You remember that movie studio, Pandora, that was trying to make that movie about Latham's Landing? Bob refused to let them film on the island! Well, they did some DNA test on the skeleton at the university last year and sent it into one of those companies that find relatives! Well, they found one of Latham's descendants! He's suing to get the island back!"

"You can't be serious."

"The movie studio quietly bought the old Dockhouse two years ago. They've been pissed off ever since Bob denied them access to the island. I don't think they expected to find any living heirs, but they did."

"There's no proof that the skeleton found in the house all those years ago belonged to Mrs. Latham." *It's technically Mrs. Latham's sister.*

"The skeleton was found on the island inside the house. It's the right age per decomposition to have died in the 1920's according to the University. The woman was the right age to be Latham's wife according to her bone growth."

But was it? Cheer reported that Godelman said the skeleton had some odd bone fragility. Maybe that can be used to argue for it not being his wife? Something to check on. "Why did it take so long to find Latham's long-lost heir?"

"He apparently just joined for fun with a bunch of his college friends, total fluke. When he did, the match notified him, and Pandora jumped on him. This guy says he's going to rebuild the island mansion and then lease it to the studio to film a new movie, plus sell off all the lots around the lake to developers to make mansions."

"Over my dead body," Barb said. She hung up, then dialed another number. "Hello? I've got a situation here. A living heir of Latham's has been discovered that is suing to get the island."

"We know," a deadly cold voice said in measured tones. "Here's what we're going to do."

Barb listened to all she was told, then hung up. Carefully, she went to her bookshelf and took down the ancient silver flute. "His plan may or may not work. But I know mine will."

Outside her window, two pairs of glowing orbs looked from Barb to each other. One let out a hiss, then the black shapes retreated into the shadows of the backyard and disappeared.

TO BE CONTINUED
IN
YEAR OF THE SIREN

THANK YOU FOR READING

Did you enjoy this book?

We invite you to leave a review at the website of your choice, such as Goodreads, Amazon, Barnes & Noble, etc.

DID YOU KNOW THAT LEAVING A REVIEW...

- Helps other readers find books they may enjoy.
- Gives you a chance to let your voice be heard.
- Gives authors recognition for their hard work.
- Doesn't have to be long. A sentence or two about why you liked the book will do.

ABOUT TARA FOX HALL

Tara Fox Hall's writing credits include nonfiction, horror, suspense, action-adventure, erotica, and contemporary and historical paranormal romance. She is the author of the paranormal action-adventure *Lash* series and the vampire romantic suspense *Promise Me* series.

Tara divides her free time unequally between writing novels and short stories, chainsawing firewood, caring for stray animals, sewing cat and dog beds for donation to animal shelters, and target practice.

www.tarafoxhall.com

ALSO BY TARA FOX HALL

with Melange Books and Satin Romance

Latham's Landing

Latham's Landing, An Anthology

Latham's Landing II: Return to Cairn Isle

Unhallowed Love Series

A Good Year

Year of the Demon

Promise Me Series

Promise Me

Broken Promise

Taken in the Night

Taken For His Own

Immortal Confessions

Promise Me Anthology

Her Secret

Point of No Return

Lost Paradise

Dark Solace

Eye of the Storm

Tempest of Vengeance

Sundown & Serena

Hope's Return

Fate's Prison

Web of Memory

Forever

Freedom: Elle's Story

Immortal Reckoning

Novellas

Return To Me

Surrender to Me

The Oath

Night Music

Anthologies

Her Frozen Heart in Frozen

One Perfect Moment in Propose To Me

A Love For Michelle in Second Chance for Love

Make Me Behave by Tara Fox Hall & Nancy Pirri

Make Me Behave 2

www.ingramcontent.com/pod-product-compliance
Lightning Source LLC
Chambersburg PA
CBHW020613260626
47157CB00003B/986